George Manvi

Patience Wins

George Manville Fenn

Patience Wins

1st Edition | ISBN: 978-3-75231-414-4

Place of Publication: Frankfurt am Main, Germany

Year of Publication: 2020

Outlook Verlag GmbH, Germany.

George Manville Fenn

"Patience Wins"

Chapter One.

A Family Council.

"I say, Uncle Dick, do tell me what sort of a place it is."

"Oh, you'll see when you get there!"

"Uncle Jack, you tell me then; what's it like?"

"Like! What, Arrowfield? Ask Uncle Bob."

"There, Uncle Bob, I'm to ask you. Do tell me what sort of a place it is?"

"Get out, you young nuisance!"

"What a shame!" I said. "Here are you three great clever men, who know all about it; you've been down half a dozen times, and yet you won't answer a civil question when you are asked."

I looked in an ill-used way at my three uncles, as they sat at the table covered with papers; and except that one would be a little darker than the other, I could not help thinking how very much they were alike, and at the same time like my father, only that he had some grey coming at the sides of his head. They were all big fine-looking men between thirty and forty, stern enough when they were busy, but wonderfully good-tempered and full of fun when business was over; and I'm afraid they spoiled me.

When, as I say, business was over, they were ready for anything with me, and though I had a great feeling of reverence, almost dread, for my father, my three big uncles always seemed to me like companions, and they treated me as if I were their equal.

Cricket! Ah! Many's the game we've had together. They'd take me fishing, and give me the best pitch, and see that I caught fish if they did not.

Tops, marbles, kite-flying, football; insect and egg collecting; geology, botany, chemistry; they were at home with all, and I shared in the game or pursuit as eagerly as they.

I've known the time when they'd charge into the room at Canonbury, where I was busy with the private tutor—for I did not go to school—with "Mr Headley, Mr Russell would like to speak to you;" and as soon as he had left the room, seize hold of me, and drag me out of my chair with, "Come along, Cob: work's closed for the day. *Country!*"

Then away we'd go for a delicious day's collecting, or something of the kind.

They used to call it slackening their bands, and mine.

Time had glided on very happily till I was sixteen, and there was some talk of my being sent to a great engineer's establishment for five or six years to learn all I could before being taken on at our own place in Bermondsey, where Russell and Company carried on business, and knocked copper and brass and tin about, and made bronze, and gun-metal, and did a great deal for other firms with furnaces, and forges, and steam-engines, wheels, and lathes.

My father was "Russell"—Alexander—and Uncle Dick, Uncle Jack, and Uncle Bob were "Company." The business, as I say, was in Bermondsey, but we lived together and didn't live together at Canonbury.

That sounds curious, but I'll explain:—We had two houses next door to each other. Captain's quarters, and the barracks.

My father's house was the Captain's quarters, where I lived with my mother and sister. The next door, where my uncles were, they called the barracks, where they had their bedrooms and sitting-room; but they took all their meals at our table.

As I said before things had gone on very happily till I was sixteen—a big sturdy ugly boy.

Uncle Dick said I was the ugliest boy he knew.

Uncle Jack said I was the most stupid.

Uncle Bob said I was the most ignorant.

But we were the best of friends all the same.

And now after a great deal of discussion with my father, and several visits, my three uncles were seated at the table, and I had asked them about Arrowfield, and you have read their answers.

I attacked them again.

"Oh, I say," I cried, "don't talk to a fellow as if he were a little boy!

3

Come, Uncle Dick, what sort of a place is Arrowfield?"

"Land of fire."

"Oh!" I cried. "Is it, Uncle Jack?"

"Land of smoke."

"Land of fire and smoke!" I cried excitedly. "Uncle Bob, are they making fun of me?"

"Land of noise, and gloom, and fog," said Uncle Bob. "A horrible place in a hole."

"And are we going there?"

"Don't know," said Uncle Bob. "Wait and see."

They went on with their drawings and calculations, and I sat by the fire in the barrack room, that is, in their sitting-room, trying to read, but with my head in a whirl of excitement about Arrowfield, when my father came in, laid his hand on my head, and turned to my uncles.

"Well, boys," he said, "how do you bring it in? What's to be done?"

"Sit down, and let's settle it, Alick," said Uncle Dick, leaning back and spreading his big beard all over his chest.

"Ah, do!" cried Uncle Jack, rubbing his curly head.

"Once and for all," said Uncle Bob, drawing his chair forward, stooping down, taking up his left leg and holding it across his right knee.

My father drew forward an easy-chair, looking very serious, and resting his hand on the back before sitting down, he said without looking at me:

"Go to your mother and sister, Jacob."

I rose quickly, but with my forehead wrinkling all over, and I turned a pitiful look on my three uncles.

"What are you going to send him away for?" said Uncle Dick.

"Because this is not boys' business."

"Oh, nonsense!" said Uncle Jack. "He'll be as interested in it as we are."

"Yes, let him stop and hear," said Uncle Bob.

"Very good. I'm agreeable," said my father. "Sit down, Jacob."

I darted a grateful look at my uncles, spreading it round so that they all

4

had a glance, and dropped back into my seat.

"Well," said my father, "am I to speak?"

"Yes."

This was in chorus; and my father sat thinking for a few minutes, during which I exchanged looks and nods with my uncles, all of which was very satisfactory.

"Well," said my father at last, "to put it in short, plain English, we four have each our little capital embarked in our works."

Here there were three nods.

"We've all tried everything we knew to make the place a success, but year after year goes by and we find ourselves worse off. In three more bad years we shall be ruined."

"And Jacob will have to set to work and keep us all," said Uncle Dick.

My father looked round at me and nodded, smiling sadly, and I could see that he was in great trouble.

"Here is our position, then, boys: Grandison and Company are waiting for our answer in Bermondsey. They'll buy everything as it stands at a fair valuation; that's one half. The other is: the agents at Arrowfield are waiting also for our answer about the works to let there."

Here he paused for a few moments and then went on:

"We must look the matter full in the face. If we stay as we are the trade is so depreciating that we shall be ruined. If we go to Arrowfield we shall have to begin entirely afresh; to fight against a great many difficulties; the workmen there are ready to strike, to turn upon you and destroy."

Uncle Dick made believe to spit in his hands.

"To commit outrages."

Uncle Jack tucked up his sleeves.

"And ratten and blow up."

Uncle Bob half took off his coat.

"In short, boys, we shall have a terribly hard fight; but there is ten times the opening there, and we may make a great success. That is our position, in short," said my father. "What do you say?"

My three uncles looked hard at him and then at one another, seemed to read each other's eyes, and turned back to him.

"You're oldest, Alick, and head of the firm," said Uncle Dick; "settle it."

"No," said my father, "it shall be settled by you three."

"I know what I think," said Uncle Jack; "but I'd rather you'd say."

"My mind's made up," said Uncle Bob, "but I don't want to be speaker. You settle it, Alick."

"No," said my father; "I have laid the case before you three, who have equal stakes in the risk, and you shall settle the matter."

There was a dead silence in the room, which was so still that the sputtering noise made by the big lamp and the tinkle of a few cinders that fell from the fire sounded painfully loud. They looked at each other, but no one spoke, till Uncle Dick had fidgeted about in his chair for some time, and then, giving his big beard a twitch, he bent forward.

I heard my other uncles sigh as if they were relieved, and they sat back farther in their seats listening for what Uncle Dick, who was the eldest, might wish to say.

"Look here," he cried at last.

Everybody did look there, but saw nothing but Uncle Dick, who kept tugging at one lock of his beard, as if that was the string that would let loose a whole shower-bath of words.

"Well!" he said, and there was another pause.

"Here," he cried, as if seized by a sudden fit of inspiration, "let's hear what Cob has to say."

"Bravo! Hear, hear, hear!" cried my two uncles in chorus, and Uncle Dick smiled and nodded and looked as if he felt highly satisfied with himself; while I, with a face that seemed to be all on fire, jumped up excitedly and cried:

"Let's all go and begin again."

"That's it—that settles it," cried Uncle Bob.

"Yes, yes," said Uncle Dick and Uncle Jack. "He's quite right. We'll go."

Then all three beat upon the table with book and pencil and compasses, and cried, "Hear, hear, hear!" while I shrank back into my chair, and felt half ashamed of myself as I glanced at my father and wondered whether he was angry on account of what I had proposed.

"That is settled then," he said quietly. "Jacob has been your spokesman; and now let me add my opinion that you have taken the right course. What I propose is this, that one of us stays and carries on the business here till the others have got the Arrowfield affair in full swing. Who will stay?"

There was no answer.

"Shall I?" said my father.

"Yes, if you will," they chorused.

"Very good," said my father. "I am glad to do so, for that will give me plenty of time to make arrangements for Jacob here."

"But he must go with us," said Uncle Dick.

"Yes, of course," said Uncle Jack.

"Couldn't go without him."

"But his education as an engineer?"

"Now, look here, Alick," said Uncle Dick, "don't you think he'll learn as much with us down at the new works as in any London place?"

My father sat silent and thoughtful, while I watched the play of his countenance and trembled as I saw how he was on the balance. For it would have been terrible to me to have gone away now just as a new life of excitement and adventure was opening out.

"Do you really feel that you would like Jacob to go with you?" said my father at last.

There was a unanimous "Yes!" at this, and my heart gave a jump.

"Well, then," said my father, "he shall go."

That settled the business, except a general shaking of hands, for we were all delighted, little thinking, in our innocence, of the troubles, the perils, and the dangers through which we should have to go.

Chapter Two.

A Fiery Place.

No time was lost. The agreements were signed, and Uncle Dick packed up his traps, as he called them, that is to say, his books, clothes, and models and contrivances, so as to go down at once, take possession of the works, and get apartments for us.

I should have liked to go with him, but I had to stay for another week, and then, after a hearty farewell, we others started, my father, mother, and sister seeing us off by rail; and until I saw the trees, hedges, and houses seeming to fly by me I could hardly believe that we were really on our way.

Of course I felt a little low-spirited at leaving home, and I was a little angry with myself for seeming to be so glad to get away from those who had been so patient and kind, but I soon found myself arguing that it would have been just the same if I had left home only to go to some business place in London. Still I was looking very gloomy when Uncle Jack clapped me on the shoulder, and asked me if I didn't feel like beginning to be a man.

"No," I said sadly, as I looked out of the window at the flying landscape, so that he should not see my face. "I feel more as if I was beginning to be a great girl."

"Nonsense!" said Uncle Bob; "you're going to be a man now, and help us."

"Am I?" said I sadly.

"To be sure you are. There, put that gloomy face in your pocket and learn geography."

They both chatted to me, and I felt a little better, but anything but cheerful, for it was my first time of leaving home. I looked at the landscape, and the towns and churches we passed, but nothing seemed to interest me till, well on in my journey, I saw a sort of wooden tower close to the line, with a wheel standing half out of the top. There was an engine-house close by—there was no doubt about it, for I could see the puffs of white steam at the top, and a chimney. There was a great mound of black slate and rubbish by the end; but even though the railway had a siding close up to it, and a number of trucks were standing waiting, I did not realise what the place was till Uncle Jack said:

"First time you've seen a coal-pit, eh?"

"Is that a coal-pit?" I said, looking at the place more eagerly.

"Those are the works. Of course you can't see the shaft, because that's only like a big square well."

"But I thought it would be a much more interesting place," I said.

"Interesting enough down below; but of course there is nothing to see at the top but the engine, cage, and mouth of the shaft."

That brightened me up at once. There was something to think about in connection with a coal-mine—the great deep shaft, the cage going up and down, the miners with their safety-lamps and picks. I saw it all in imagination as we dashed by another and another mine. Then I began to think about the accidents of which I had read; when men unfastened their wire-gauze lamps, so that they might do that which was forbidden in a mine, smoke their pipes. The match struck or the opened lamp set fire to the gas, when there was an awful explosion, and after that the terrible dangers of the after-damp, that fearful foul air which no man could breathe for long and live.

There were hundreds of thoughts like this to take my attention as we raced on by the fast train till, to my surprise, I found that it was getting dark, and the day had passed.

"Here we are close to it," said Uncle Jack; "look, my lad."

I gazed out of the window on our right as the train glided on, to see the glare as of a city on fire: the glow of a dull red flickered and danced upon the dense clouds that overhung the place. Tall chimneys stood up like black stakes or posts set up in the reflection of open furnace doors. Here a keen bright light went straight up through the smoke with the edges exactly defined—here it was a sharp glare, there a dull red glow, and everywhere there seemed to be fire and reflection, and red or golden smoke mingled with a dull throbbing booming sound, which, faintly heard at first, grew louder and louder as the train slackened speed, and the pant and pulsation of the engine ceased.

"Isn't something dreadful the matter?" I said, as I gazed excitedly from the window.

"Matter!" said Uncle Jack laughing.

"Yes, isn't the place on fire? Look! Look! There there!"

I pointed to a fierce glare that seemed to reach up into the sky, cutting the dense cloud like millions of golden arrows shot from some mighty engine all at once.

"Yes, I see, old fellow," said Uncle Jack. "They have just tapped a furnace, and the molten metal is running into the moulds, that's all."

"But the whole town looks as if it were in a blaze," I said nervously.

"So did our works sometimes, didn't they? Well, here we are in a town where there are hundreds upon hundreds of works ten times as big as ours. Nearly everybody is either forging, or casting, or grinding. The place is full of steam-engines, while the quantity of coal that is burnt here every day must be prodigious. Aha! Here's Uncle Dick."

He had caught sight of us before we saw him, and threw open the carriage-door ready to half haul us out, as he shook hands as if we had not met for months.

"That's right," he cried. "I *am* glad you've come. I've a cab waiting. Here, porter, lay hold of this baggage. Well, Cob, what do you think of Arrowfield?"

"Looks horrible," I said in the disappointed tones of one who is tired and hungry.

"Yes, outside," said Uncle Dick; "but wait till you see the inside."

Uncle Dick was soon standing in what he called the inside of Arrowfield—that is to say the inside of the comfortable furnished lodgings he had taken right up a hill, where, over a cosy tea-table with hot country cakes and the juiciest of hot mutton chops, I soon forgot the wearisome nature of our journey, and the dismal look of the town.

"Eat away, my boys," cried Uncle Dick. "Yeat, as they call it here. The place is all right; everything ready for work, and we'll set to with stout hearts, and make up for lost time."

"When do we begin, uncle—to-morrow?"

"No, no: not till next Monday morning. To-morrow we'll have a look over the works, and then we'll idle a bit—have a few runs into the country round, and see what it's like."

"Black dismal place," I said dolefully.

"Says he's tired out and wants to go to bed," said Uncle Jack, giving his eye a peculiar cock at his brothers.

"I didn't," I cried.

"Not in words, my fine fellow, but you looked it."

"Then I won't look so again," I cried. "I say, don't talk to me as if I were a little boy to be sent to bed."

"Well, you're not a man yet, Cob. Is he, boys?"

Uncle Dick was in high spirits, and he took up a candle and held it close to my cheek.

"What's the matter?" I said. "Is it black? I shouldn't wonder."

"Not a bit, Cob," he said seriously. "You can't even see a bit of the finest down growing."

"Oh, I say," I cried, "it's too bad! I don't pretend to be a man at sixteen; but now I've come down here to help you in the new works, you oughtn't to treat me as if I were a little boy."

"Avast joking!" said Uncle Dick quietly, for the comely landlady came in to clear away the tea-things, and she had just finished when there was a double knock at the front door.

We heard it opened, and a deep voice speaking, and directly after the landlady came in with a card.

"Mr Tomplin, gentlemen," she said. "He's at the door, and I was to say that if it was inconvenient for you to see him to-night, perhaps you would call at his office when you were down the town."

"Oh, ask him in, Mrs Stephenson," cried Uncle Dick; and as she left the room—"it's the solicitor to whom I brought the letter of introduction from the bank."

It was a short dark man in black coat and waistcoat and pepper-and-salt trousers who was shown in. He had little sharp eyes that seemed to glitter. So did his hair, which was of light-grey, and stood up all over his head as if it was on white fire. He had not a particle of hair on his face, which looked as if he was a very good customer to the barber.

He shook hands very heartily with all of us, nodding pleasantly the while; and when he sat down he took out a brown-and-yellow silk handkerchief and blew his nose like a horn.

"Welcome to Yorkshire, gentlemen!" he said. "My old friends at the bank send me a very warm letter of recommendation about you, and I'm at your service. Professional consultations at the usual fee, six and eight or thirteen and four, according to length. Friendly consultations— Thank you, I'm much obliged. This is a friendly consultation. Now what can I do for you?"

He looked round at us all, and I felt favourably impressed. So did my uncles, as Uncle Dick answered for all.

"Nothing at present, sir. By and by we shall be glad to come to you for legal and friendly advice too."

"That's right," said Mr Tomplin. "You've taken the Rivulet Works, I hear."

"Yes, down there by the stream."

"What are you going to do?—carry on the old forging and grinding?"

"Oh, dear, no!" said Uncle Dick. "We are going in for odds and ends, sir. To introduce, I hope, a good many improvements in several branches of the trades carried on here, principally in forging."

Mr Tomplin drew in his lips and filled his face with wrinkles.

"Going to introduce new inventions, eh?" he said.

"Yes, sir, but only one at a time," said Uncle Jack.

"And have you brought a regiment of soldiers with you, gentlemen?"

"Brought a what?" said Uncle Bob, laughing.

"Regiment of soldiers, sir, and a company of artillerymen with a couple of guns."

"Ha! Ha! Ha!" laughed Uncle Dick, showing his white teeth. "Mr Tomplin means to besiege Arrowfield."

"No, I don't, my dear sir. I mean to turn your works into a fort to defend yourselves against your enemies."

"My dear sir," said Uncle Jack, "we haven't an enemy in the world."

"Not at the present moment, sir, I'll be bound," said Mr Tomplin, taking snuff, and then blowing his nose so violently that I wondered he did not have an accident with it and split the sides. "Not at the present moment, gentlemen; but as soon as it is known that you are going to introduce new kinds of machinery, our enlightened townsmen will declare you are going to take the bread out of their mouths and destroy everything you make."

"Take the bread out of their mouths, my dear Mr Tomplin!" said Uncle Jack. "Why, what we do will put bread in their mouths by making more work."

"Of course it will, my dear sirs."

"Then why should they interfere?"

"Because of their ignorance, gentlemen. They won't see it. Take my advice: there's plenty to be done by clever business men. Start some steady manufacture to employ hands as the work suggests. Only use present-day machinery if you wish to be at peace."

"We do wish to be at peace, Mr Tomplin," said Uncle Bob; "but we do not mean to let a set of ignorant workmen frighten us out of our projects."

"Hear, hear!" said Uncle Dick and Uncle Jack; and I put in a small "hear" at the end.

"Well, gentlemen, I felt it to be my duty to tell you," said Mr Tomplin, taking more snuff and making more noise. "You will have attacks made upon you to such an extent that you had better be in the bush in Queensland among the blacks."

"But not serious attacks?" said Uncle Jack. "Attempts to frighten us?"

"Attempts to frighten you! Well, you may call them that," said Mr Tomplin; "but there have been two men nearly beaten to death with sticks, one factory set on fire, and two gunpowder explosions during the past year. Take my advice, gentlemen, and don't put yourself in opposition to the workmen if you are going to settle down here."

He rose, shook hands, and went away, leaving us looking at each other across the table.

"Cheerful place Arrowfield seems to be," said Uncle Dick.

"Promises to be lively," said Uncle Jack.

"What do you say, Cob?" cried Uncle Bob. "Shall we give up, be frightened, and run away like dogs with our tails between our legs?"

"No!" I cried, thumping the table with my fist. "I wouldn't be frightened out of anything I felt to be right."

"Bravo! Bravo! Bravo!" cried my uncles.

"At least I don't think I would," I said. "Perhaps I really am a coward after all."

"Well," said Uncle Dick, "I don't feel like giving up for such a thing as this. I'd sooner buy pistols and guns and fight. It can't be so bad as the old gentleman says. He's only scaring us. There, it's ten o'clock; you fellows are tired, and we want to breakfast early and go and see the works, so let's get to bed."

We were far enough out of the smoke for our bedrooms to be beautifully white and sweet, and I was delighted with mine, as I saw what a snug little place it was. I said "Good-night!" and had shut my door, when, going to my window, I drew aside the blind, and found that I was looking right down upon the town.

"Oh!" I ejaculated, and I ran out to the next room, which was Uncle

Dick's. "Look!" I cried. "Now you'll believe me. The town is on fire."

He drew up the blind, and threw up his window, when we both looked down at what seemed to be the dying out of a tremendous conflagration—dying out, save in one place, where there was a furious rush of light right up into the air, with sparks flying and flickering tongues of flame darting up and sinking down again, while the red and tawny-yellow smoke rolled away.

"On fire, Cob!" he said quietly. "Yes, the town's on fire, but in the proper way. Arrowfield is a fiery place—all furnaces. There's nothing the matter, lad."

"But there! There!" I cried, "where the sparks are roaring and rushing out with all that flame."

"There! Oh! That's nothing, my boy. The town is always like this."

"But you don't see where I mean," I cried, still doubting, and pointing down to our right.

"Oh, yes! I do, my dear boy. That is where they are making the Bessemer steel."

Chapter Three.

A Bad Beginning.

I thought when I lay down, after putting out my candle, that I should never get a wink of sleep. There was a dull glow upon my window-blind, and I could hear a distant clangour and a curious faint roar; but all at once, so it seemed to me, I opened my eyes, and the dull glow had given place to bright sunshine on my window-blind, and jumping out of bed I found that I had slept heartily till nearly breakfast time, for the chinking of cups in saucers fell upon my ear.

I looked out of the window, and there lay the town with the smoke hanging over it in a dense cloud, but the banging of a wash-jug against a basin warned me that Uncle Dick was on the move, and the next moment *tap, tap, tap,* came three blows on my wall, which I knew as well as could be were given with the edge of a hair-brush, and I replied in the same way.

"Ha, ha!" cried Uncle Bob, "if they are going to give us fried ham like that for breakfast—"

"And such eggs!" cried Uncle Jack.

"And such bread!" said Uncle Dick, hewing off a great slice.

"And such coffee and milk!" I said, taking up the idea that I was sure was coming, "we won't go back to London."

"Right!" said Uncle Dick. "Bah! Just as if we were going to be frightened away by a set of old women's tales. They've got police here, and laws."

The matter was discussed until breakfast was over, and by that time my three giants of uncles had decided that they would not stir for an army of discontented workmen, but would do their duty to themselves and their partner in London.

"But look here, boys," said Uncle Dick; "if we are going to war, we don't want women in the way."

"No," said Uncle Jack.

"So you had better write and tell Alick to keep on the old place till the company must have it, and by that time we shall know what we are about."

This was done directly after breakfast, and as soon as the letter had been despatched we went off to see the works.

"I shall never like this place," I said, as we went down towards the town. "London was smoky enough, but this is terrible."

"Oh, wait a bit!" said Uncle Dick, and as we strode on with me trying to take long steps to keep up with my companions, I could not help seeing how the people kept staring at them. And though there were plenty of big fine men in the town, I soon saw that my uncles stood out amongst them as being remarkable for their size and frank handsome looks. This was the more plainly to be seen, since the majority of the work-people we passed were pale, thin, and degenerate looking little men, with big muscular arms, and a general appearance of everything else having been sacrificed to make those limbs strong.

The farther we went the more unsatisfactory the town looked. We were leaving the great works to the right, and our way lay through streets and streets of dingy-looking houses all alike, and with the open channels in front foul with soapy water and the refuse which the people threw out.

I looked up with disgust painted on my face so strongly that Uncle Bob laughed.

15

"Here, let's get this fellow a bower somewhere by a beautiful stream," he cried, laughing. Then more seriously, "Never mind the dirt, Cob," he cried. "Dirty work brings clean money."

"Oh, I don't mind," I said. "Which way now?"

"Down here," said Uncle Dick; and he led us down a nasty dirty street, worse than any we had yet passed, and so on and on, for about half an hour, till we were once more where wheels whirred, and we could hear the harsh churring noise of blades being held upon rapidly revolving stones. Now and then, too, I caught sight of water on our right, down through lanes where houses and works were crowded together.

"Do you notice one thing, Cob?" said Uncle Dick.

"One thing!" I said; "there's so much to notice that I don't know what to look at first."

"I'll tell you what I mean," he said. "You can hear the rush and rumble of machinery, can't you?"

"Yes," I said, "like wheels whizzing and stones rolling, as if giant tinkers were grinding enormous scissors."

"Exactly," he said; "but you very seldom hear the hiss of steam out here."

"No. Have they a different kind of engines?"

"Yes, a very different kind. Your steam-engine goes because the water is made hot: these machines go with the water kept cold."

"Oh, I see! By hydraulic presses."

"No, not by hydraulic presses, Cob; by hydraulic power. Look here."

We were getting quite in the outskirts now, and on rising ground, and, drawing me on one side, he showed me that the works we were by were dependent on water-power alone.

"Why, it's like one of those old flour-mills up the country rivers," I exclaimed, "with their mill-dam, and water-wheel."

"And without the willows and lilies and silver buttercups, Cob," said Uncle Jack.

"And the great jack and chub and tench we used to fish out," said Uncle Bob.

"Yes," I said; "I suppose one would catch old saucepans, dead cats, and old shoes in a dirty pool like this."

"Yes," said Uncle Dick, "and our wheel-bands when the trades'-union people attack us."

"Why should they throw them in here?" I said, as I looked at the great deep-looking piece of water held up by a strong stone-built dam, and fed by a stream at the farther end.

"Because it would be the handiest place. These are our works."

I looked at the stone-built prison-like place in disgust. It was wonderfully strongly-built, and with small windows protected by iron bars, but such a desolate unornamental spot. It stood low down by the broad shallow stream that ran on toward the town in what must once have been the bed of the river; but the steep banks had been utilised by the builders on each side, and everywhere one saw similar-looking places so arranged that their foundation walls caught and held up the water that came down, and was directed into the dam, and trickled out at the lower end after it had turned a great slimy water-wheel. "This is our place, boys; come and have a look at it." He led us down a narrow passage half-way to the stream, and then rang at a gate in a stone wall; and while we waited low down there I looked at the high rough stone wall and the two-storied factory with its rows of strong iron-barred windows, and thought of what Mr Templin had said the night before, coming to the conclusion that it was a pretty strong fortress in its way. For here was a stout high wall; down along by the stream there was a high blank wall right from the stones over which the water trickled to the double row of little windows; while from the top corner by the water-wheel, which was fixed at the far end of the works, there was the dam of deep water, which acted the part of a moat, running off almost to a point where the stream came in, so that the place was about the shape of the annexed triangle: the works occupying the whole of the base, the rest being the deep stone-walled dam.

"I think we could keep out the enemy if he came," I said to Uncle Bob; and just then a short-haired, palefaced man, with bent shoulders, bare arms, and an ugly squint, opened the gate and scowled at us.

"Is your master in?" said Uncle Dick.

"No-ah," said the man sourly; "and he wean't be here to-day."

"That's a bad job," said Uncle Dick. "Well, never mind; we want to go round the works."

"Nay, yow wean't come in here."

He was in the act of banging the gate, but Uncle Dick placed one of his great brown hands against it and thrust it open, driving the man back, but only for a moment, for he flew at my uncle, caught him by the arm and waist, thrust forward a leg, and tried to throw him out by a clever wrestling trick.

But Uncle Dick was too quick for him. Wrenching himself on one side he threw his left arm over the fellow's neck, as he bent down, the right arm under his leg, and whirled him up perfectly helpless, but kicking with all his might.

"Come inside and shut that gate," said Uncle Dick, panting with his exertion. "Now look here, my fine fellow, it would serve you right if I dropped you into that dam to cool you down. But there, get on your legs," he cried contemptuously, "and learn to be civil to strangers when they come."

The scuffle and noise brought about a dozen workmen out of the place, each in wooden clogs, with a rough wet apron about him, and his sleeves rolled up nearly to the shoulder.

They came forward, looking very fierce and as if they were going to attack us, headed by the fellow with the squint, who was no sooner at liberty than he snatched up a rough piece of iron bar and rolled up his right sleeve ready for a fresh attack.

"Give me that stick, Cob," said Uncle Dick quickly; and I handed him the light Malacca cane I carried.

He had just seized it when the man raised the iron bar, and I felt sick as I saw the blow that was aimed at my uncle's head.

I need not have felt troubled though, for, big as he was, he jumped aside, avoided the bar with the greatest ease, and almost at the same moment there was a whizz and a cut like lightning delivered by Uncle Dick with my light cane.

It struck the assailant on the tendons of the leg beneath the knee, and he uttered a yell and went down as if killed.

"Coom on, lads!" cried one of the others; and they rushed towards us, headed by a heavy thick-set fellow; but no one flinched, and they hesitated as they came close up.

"Take that fellow away," said Uncle Jack sternly; "and look here, while you stay, if any gentleman comes to the gate don't send a surly dog like that."

"Who are yow? What d'ye want? Happen yow'll get some'at if yo' stay."

"I want to go round the place. I am one of the proprietors who have taken it."

"Eh, you be—be you? Here, lads, this is one o' chaps as is turning us out. We've got the wheels ti' Saturday, and we wean't hev no one here."

"No, no," rose in chorus. "Open gate, lads, and hev 'em out."

"Keep back!" said Uncle Dick, stepping forward; "keep back, unless you want to be hurt. No one is going to interfere with your rights, which end on Saturday night."

"Eh! But if it hedn't been for yow we could ha kep' on."

"Well, you'll have to get some other place," said Uncle Dick; "we want this."

He turned his back on them and spoke to his brothers, who both, knowing their great strength, which they cultivated by muscular exercise, had stood quite calm and patient, but watchful, and ready to go to their brother's aid in an instant should he need assistance.

"Come on and look round," said Uncle Dick coolly; and he did not even glance at the squinting man, who had tried to get up, but sank down again and sat grinning with pain and holding his injured leg.

The calm indifference with which my three uncles towered above the undersized, pallid-looking fellows, and walked by them to the entrance to the stone building had more effect than a score of blows, and the men stopped clustered round their companion, and talked to him in a low voice. But I was not six feet two like Uncle Bob, nor six feet one like Uncle Jack, nor six feet three like Uncle Dick. I was only an ordinary lad of sixteen, and much easier prey for their hate, and this they saw and showed.

For as I followed last, and was about to enter the door, a shower of stones and pieces of iron came whizzing about me, and falling with a rattle and clangour upon the cobble stones with which the place was paved.

Unfortunately, one piece, stone or iron, struck me on the shoulder, a heavy blow that made me feel sick, and I needed all the fortitude I could call up to hide my pain, for I was afraid to say or do anything that would cause fresh trouble.

So I followed my uncles into the spacious ground-floor of the works, all wet and dripping with the water from the grindstones which had just been left by the men, and were still whizzing round waiting to be used.

"Plenty of room here," said Uncle Dick, "and plenty of power, you see," he continued, pointing to the shaft and wheels above our heads. "Ugly-looking place this," he went on, pointing to a trap-door at the end, which he lifted; and I looked down with a shudder to see a great shaft turning slowly round; and there was a slimy set of rotten wooden steps going right down into the blackness, where the water was falling with a curiously hollow echoing sound.

As I turned from looking down I saw that the men had followed us, and the fellow with the squint seemed to have one of his unpleasant eyes fixed upon me, and he gave me a peculiar look and grin that I had good reason to remember.

"This is the way to the big wheel," said Uncle Dick, throwing open a door at the end. "They go out here to oil and repair it when it's out of gear. Nasty spot too, but there's a wonderful supply of cheap power."

With the men growling and muttering behind us we looked through into a great half-lit stone chamber that inclosed the great wheel on one side, leaving a portion visible as we had seen it from the outside; and here again I shuddered and felt uncomfortable, it seemed such a horrible place to fall into and from which there would be no escape, unless one could swim in the surging water below, and then clamber into the wheel, and climb through it like a squirrel.

The walls were dripping and green, and they echoed and seemed to whisper back to the great wheel as it turned and splashed and swung down its long arms, each doubling itself on the wall by making a moving shadow.

The place had such a fascination for me that I stood with one hand upon the door and a foot inside looking down at the faintly seen black water, listening to the echoes, and then watching the wheel as it turned, one pale spot on the rim catching my eye especially. As I watched it I saw it go down into the darkness with a tremendous sweep, with a great deal of splashing and falling of water; then after being out of sight for a few moments it came into view again, was whirled round, and dashed down.

I don't know how it was, but I felt myself thinking that suppose anyone fell into the horrible pit below me, he would swim round by the slimy walls trying to find a place to cling to, and finding none he would be swept round to the wheel, to which in his despair he would cling. Then he would be dragged out of the water, swung round, and—

"Do you hear, Cob?" cried Uncle Jack. "What is there to attract you, my lad? Come along."

I seemed to be roused out of a dream, and starting back, the door was closed, and I followed the others as they went to the far end of the great ground-floor to a door opening upon a stone staircase.

We had to pass the men, who were standing about close to their grindstones, beside which were little piles of the articles they were grinding—common knives, sickles, and scythe blades, ugly weapons if the men rose against us as they seemed disposed to do.

They muttered and talked to themselves, but they did not seem inclined to make any farther attack; while as we reached the stairs I heard the harsh shrieking of blades that were being held upon the stones, and I knew that some men must have begun work.

The upper floor was of the same size as the lower, but divided into four rooms by partitions, and here too were shafts and wheels turning from their connection with the great water-wheel. Over that a small room had been built supported by an arch stretching from the works to a stone wall, and as we looked out of the narrow iron-barred window down upon the deep dam, Uncle Bob said laughingly:

"What a place for you, Cob! You could drop a line out of the window, and catch fish like fun."

I laughed, and we all had a good look round before examining the side buildings, where there were forges and furnaces, and a tall chimney-shaft ran up quite a hundred feet.

"Plenty of room to do any amount of work," cried Uncle Jack. "I think the place a bargain."

"Yes," said Uncle Bob, "where we can carry out our inventions; and if anybody is disagreeable, we can shut ourselves up like knights in a castle and laugh at all attacks."

"Yes," said Uncle Dick thoughtfully; "but I wish we had not begun by quarrelling with those men."

"Let's try and make friends as we go out," said Uncle Jack.

It was a good proposal; and, under the impression that a gallon or two of beer would heal the sore place, we went into the big workshop or mill, where all the men had now resumed their tasks, and were grinding away as if to make up for lost time.

One man was seated alone on a stone bench, and as we entered he half turned, and I saw that it was Uncle Dick's opponent.

He looked at us for a moment and then turned scowling away.

My uncles whispered together, and then Uncle Dick stepped forward and said:

"I'm sorry we had this little upset, my lads. It all arose out of a mistake. We have taken these works, and of course wanted to look round them, but we do not wish to put you to any inconvenience. Will you—"

He stopped short, for as soon as he began to speak the men seemed to press down their blades that they were grinding harder and harder, making them send forth such a deafening churring screech that he paused quite in despair of making himself heard.

"My lads!" he said, trying again.

Not a man turned his head, and it was plain enough that they would not hear.

"Let me speak to him," said Uncle Bob, catching his brother by the arm, for Uncle Dick was going to address the man on the stone.

Uncle Dick nodded, for he felt that it would be better for someone else to speak; but the man got up, scowled at Uncle Bob, and when he held out a couple of half-crowns to him to buy beer to drink our healths the fellow made a derisive gesture, walked to his stone, and sat down.

"Just as they like," said Uncle Dick. "We apologised and behaved like gentlemen. If they choose to behave like blackguards, let them. Come along."

We turned to the door, my fate, as usual, being to come last; and as we passed through not a head was turned, every man pressing down some steel implement upon his whirling stone, and making it shriek, and, in spite of the water in which the wheel revolved, send forth a shower of sparks.

The noise was deafening, but as we passed into the yard on the way to the lane the grinding suddenly ceased, and when we had the gate well open the men had gathered at the door of the works, and gave vent to a savage hooting and yelling which continued after we had passed through, and as we went along by the side of the dam we were saluted by a shower of stones and pieces of iron thrown from the yard.

"Well," said Uncle Bob, "this is learning something with a vengeance. I didn't think we had such savages in Christian England."

By this time we were out of the reach of the men, and going on towards the top of the dam, when Uncle Dick, who had been looking very serious and thoughtful, said:

"I'm sorry, very sorry this has happened. It has set these men against us."

"No," said Uncle Jack quietly; "the mischief was done before we came. This place has been to let for a long time."

"Yes," said Uncle Bob, "that's why we got it so cheaply."

"And," continued Uncle Jack, "these fellows have had the run of the works to do their grinding for almost nothing. They were wild with us for taking the place and turning them out."

"Yes," said Uncle Dick, "that's the case, no doubt; but I'm very sorry I began by hurting that fellow all the same."

"I'm not, Uncle Dick," I said, as I compressed my lips with pain. "They are great cowards or they would not have thrown a piece of iron at me;" and I laid my hand upon my shoulder, to draw it back wet with blood.

Chapter Four.

Our Engine.

"Bravo, Spartan!" cried Uncle Bob, as he stood looking on, when, after walking some distance, Uncle Dick insisted upon my taking off my jacket in a lane and having the place bathed.

"Oh, it's nothing," I said, "only it was tiresome for it to bleed."

"Nothing like being prepared for emergencies," said Uncle Jack, taking out his pocket-book, and from one of the pockets a piece of sticking-plaster and a pair of scissors. "I'm always cutting or pinching my fingers. Wonder whether we could have stuck Cob's head on again if it had been cut off?"

I opined not as I submitted to the rough surgery that went on, and then refusing absolutely to be treated as a sick person, and go back, I tramped on by them, mile after mile, to see something of the fine open country out to the west of the town before we settled down to work.

We were astonished, for as we got away from the smoky pit in which Arrowfield lay, we found, in following the bank of the rivulet that supplied our works, that the country was lovely and romantic too. Hill, dale, and ravine were all about us, rippling stream, hanging wood, grove and garden, with a thousand pretty views in every direction, as we climbed on to the higher ground, till at last cultivation seemed to have been left behind, and we were where the hills towered up with ragged stony tops, and their slopes all purple heather, heath, and moss.

"Look, look!" I cried, as I saw a covey of birds skim by; "partridges!"

"No," said Uncle Bob, watching where they dropped; "not partridges, my lad—grouse."

"What, here!" I said; "and so near the town."

"Near! Why we are seven or eight miles away."

"But I thought grouse were Scotch birds."

"They are birds of the moors," said Uncle Bob; "and here you have them stretching for miles all over the hills. This is about as wild a bit of country as you could see. Why, the country people here call those hills mountains."

"But are they mountains?" I said; "they don't look very high."

"Higher than you think, my lad, with precipice and ravine. Why, look— you can see the top of that one is among the clouds."

"I should have thought it was a mist resting upon it."

"Well, what is the difference?" said Uncle Bob, smiling.

Just then we reached a spot where a stream crossed the road, and the sight of the rippling water, clear as crystal, took our attention from the hills and vales that spread around. My first idea was to run down to the edge of the stream, which was so dotted with great stones that I was soon quite in the middle, looking after the shadowy shapes that I had seen dart away.

My uncles followed me, and we forgot all about the work and troubles with the rough grinders, as we searched for the trout and crept up to where we could see some good-sized, broad-tailed fellow sunning himself till he caught sight of the intruders, and darted away like a flash of light.

But Uncle Dick put a stop to our idling there, leading us back to the road and insisting upon our continuing along it for another mile.

"I want to show you our engine," he said.

"Our engine out here!" I cried. "It's some trick."

"You wait and see," he replied.

We went on through the beautiful breezy country for some distance farther, till on one side we were looking down into a valley and on the other side into a lake, and I soon found that the lake had been formed just as we schoolboys used to make a dam across a ditch or stream when we were going to bale it out and get the fish.

"Why," I cried, as we walked out on to the great embankment, "this has all been made."

"To be sure," said Uncle Dick. "Just the same as our little dam is at the works. That was formed by building a strong stone wall across a hollow streamlet; this was made by raising this great embankment right across the valley here and stopping the stream that ran through it. That's the way some of the lakes have been made in Switzerland."

"What, by men?"

"No, by nature. A great landslip takes place from the mountains, rushes down, and fills up a valley, and the water is stopped from running away."

We walked right out along what seemed like a vast railway embankment, on one side sloping right away down into the valley, where the remains of the stream that had been cut off trickled on towards Arrowfield. On the other side the slope went down into the lake of water, which stretched away toward the moorlands for quite a mile.

"This needs to be tremendously strong," said Uncle Jack thoughtfully, as we walked on till we were right in the middle and first stood looking down the valley, winding in and out, with its scattered houses, farms, and mills, and then turned to look upward towards the moorland and along the dammed-up lake.

"Why, this embankment must be a quarter of a mile long," said Uncle Jack thoughtfully.

"What a pond for fishing!" I cried, as I imagined it to be peopled by large jack and shoals of smaller fish. "How deep is it, I wonder?"

Did you ever know a boy yet who did not want to know how deep a piece of water was, when he saw it?

"Deep!" said Uncle Dick; "that's easily seen. Deep as it is from here to the bottom of the valley on the other side: eighty or ninety feet. I should say this embankment is over a hundred in perpendicular height."

"Look here," said Uncle Jack suddenly; "if I know anything about engineering, this great dam is not safe."

"Not safe!" I said nervously. "Let's get off it at once."

"I daresay it will hold to-day," said Uncle Dick dryly, "but you can run off if you like, Cob."

"Are you coming?"

"Not just at present," he said, smiling grimly.

I put my hands in my pockets and stood looking at the great embankment, which formed a level road or path of about twelve feet wide where we stood, and then sloped down, as I have said, like a railway embankment far down into the valley on our left, and to the water on our right.

"I don't care," said Uncle Jack, knitting his brows as he scanned the place well, "I say it is not safe. Here is about a quarter of a mile of earthen wall that has no natural strength for holding together like a wall of bonded stone or brick."

"But look at its weight," said Uncle Bob.

"Yes, that is its only strength—its weight; but look at the weight of the water, about a mile of water seventy or eighty feet deep just here. Perhaps only sixty. The pressure of this water against it must be tremendous."

"Of course," said Uncle Dick thoughtfully; "but you forget the shape of the wall, Jack. It is like an elongated pyramid: broad at the base and coming up nearly to a point."

"No," said Uncle Jack, "I've not forgotten all that. Of course it is all the stronger for it, the wider the base is made. But I'm not satisfied, and if I had made this dam I should have made this wall twice as thick or three times as thick; and I don't know that I should have felt satisfied with its stability then."

"Well done, old conscientious!" cried Uncle Bob, laughing. "Let's get on."

"Stop a moment," I cried. "Uncle Dick said he would show us our engine."

"Well, there it is," said Uncle Dick, pointing to the dammed-up lake. "Isn't it powerful enough for you. This reservoir was made by a water company to supply all our little dams, and keep all our mills going. It gathers the water off the moorlands, saves it up, and lets us have it in a regular supply. What would be the consequences of a burst, Jack?" he said, turning to his brother.

"Don't talk about it man," said Uncle Jack frowning. "Why, this body of water broken loose would sweep down that valley and scour everything away with it—houses, mills, rocks, all would go like corks."

"Why, it would carry away our works, then," I cried. "The place is right down by the water side."

"I hope not," said Uncle Jack. "No I should say the force would be exhausted before it got so far as that, eight or nine miles away."

"Well, it does look dangerous," said Uncle Bob. "The weight must be tremendous. How would it go if it did burst?"

"I say, uncle, I'm only a coward, please. Hadn't we better go off here?"

They all laughed, and we went on across the dam.

"How would it go!" said Uncle Jack thoughtfully. "It is impossible to say. Probably the water would eat a little hole through the top somewhere and that would rapidly grow bigger, the water pouring through in a stream, and cutting its way down till the solidity of the wall being destroyed by the continuity being broken great masses would crumble away all at once, and the pent-up waters would rush through."

"And if they came down and washed away our works just as we were making our fortunes, you would say I was to blame for taking such a dangerous place."

"There, come along," cried Uncle Bob, "don't let's meet troubles half-way. I want a ramble over those hills. There, Cob, now we're safe," he said, as we left the great dam behind. "Now, then, who's for some lunch, eh?"

This last question was suggested by the sight of a snug little village inn, where we had a hearty meal and a rest, and then tramped off to meet with an unexpected adventure among the hills.

As soon as one gets into a hilly country the feeling that comes over one is that he ought to get up higher, and I had that sensation strongly.

But what a glorious walk it was! We left the road as soon as we could and struck right away as the crow flies for one of several tremendous hills that we saw in the distance. Under our feet was the purple heath with great patches of whortleberry, that tiny shrub that bears the little purply grey fruit. Then there was short elastic wiry grass and orange-yellow bird's-foot trefoil. Anon we came to great patches of furze of a dwarf kind with small prickles, and of an elegant growth, the purple and yellow making the place look like some vast wild garden.

"We always seem to be climbing up," said Uncle Dick.

"When we are not sliding down," said Uncle Jack, laughing.

"I've been looking for a bit of level ground for a race," said Uncle Bob. "My word! What a wild place it is!"

"But how beautiful!" I cried, as we sat down on some rough blocks of stone, with the pure thyme-scented air blowing on our cheeks, larks singing above our heads, and all around the hum of insects or bees hurrying from blossom to blossom; while we saw the grasshoppers slowly climbing up to the top of some strand of grass, take a look round, and then set their spring legs in motion and take a good leap.

"What a difference in the hills!" said Uncle Jack, looking thoughtfully from some that were smooth of outline to others that were all rugged and looked as if great jagged masses of stone had been piled upon their tops.

"Yes," said Uncle Dick. "Two formations. Mountain limestone yonder; this we are on, with all these rough pieces on the surface and sticking out everywhere, is millstone-grit."

"Which is millstone-grit?" I cried.

"This," he said, taking out a little hammer and chipping one of the stones by us to show me that it was a sandstone full of hard fragments of silica. "You might open a quarry anywhere here and cut millstones, but of course some of the stone is better for the purpose than others."

"Yes," said Uncle Jack thoughtfully. "Arrowfield is famously situated for its purpose—plenty of coal for forging, plenty of water to work mills, plenty of quarries to get millstones for grinding."

"Come along," cried Uncle Bob, starting up; and before we had gone far the grouse flew, skimming away before us, and soon after we came to a lovely mountain stream that sparkled and danced as it dashed down in hundreds of little cataracts and falls.

Leaving this, though the sight of the little trout darting about was temptation enough to make me stay, we tramped on over the rugged ground, in and out among stones or piled-up rocks, now skirting or leaping boggy places dotted with cotton-rush, where the bog-roots were here green and soft, there of a delicate pinky white, where the water had been dried away.

To a London boy, accustomed to country runs among inclosed fields and hedges, or at times into a park or upon a common, this vast stretch of hilly, wild uncultivated land was glorious, and I was ready to see any wonder without surprise.

It seemed to me, as we tramped on examining the bits of stone, the herbs and flowers, that at any moment we might come upon the lair of some wild beast; and so we did over and over again, but it was not the den of wolf or bear, but of a rabbit burrowed into the sandy side of some great bank. Farther on we started a hare, which went off in its curious hopping fashion to be out of sight in a few moments.

Almost directly after, as we were clambering over a steep slope, Uncle Bob stopped short, and stood there sniffing.

"What is it?" I cried.

"Fox," he said, looking round.

"Nonsense!" cried Uncle Dick.

"You wouldn't find, eh? What a nasty, dank, sour odour!" cried Uncle Jack, in his quiet, thoughtful way.

"A fox has gone by here during the last few minutes, I'm sure," cried Uncle Bob, looking round searchingly. "I'll be bound to say he is up among those tufts of ling and has just taken refuge there. Spread out and hunt."

The tufts he pointed to were right on a ridge of the hill we were climbing, and separating we hurried up there just in time to see a little reddish animal, with long, drooping, bushy tail, run in amongst the heath fifty yards down the slope away to our left.

"That's the consequence of having a good nose," said Uncle Bob triumphantly; and now, as we were on a high eminence, we took a good look round so as to make our plans.

"Hadn't we better turn back now?" said Uncle Jack. "We shall have several hours' walk before we get to Arrowfield, and shall have done as much as Cob can manage."

"Oh, I'm not a bit tired!" I cried.

"Well," said Uncle Dick, "I think we had better go forward. I'm not very learned over the topography of the district, but if I'm not much mistaken that round hill or mountain before us is Dome Tor."

"Well?" said Uncle Jack.

"Well, I propose that we make straight for it, go over it, and then ask our way to the nearest town or village where there is a railway-station, and ride back."

"Capital!" I cried.

"Whom will you ask to direct us?" said Uncle Jack dryly.

"Ah! To be sure," said Uncle Bob. "I've seen nothing but a sheep or two for hours, and they look so horribly stupid I don't think it is of any use to ask them."

"Oh! We must meet some one if we keep on," said Uncle Dick. "What do you say? Seems a pity not to climb that hill now we are so near."

"Yes, as we are out for a holiday," said Uncle Bob. "After to-day we must put our necks in the collar and work. I vote for Dick."

"So do I," said Uncle Jack.

"Come along then, boys," cried Uncle Dick; and now we set ourselves steadily to get over the ground, taking as straight a line as we could, but having to deviate a good deal on account of streams and bogs and rough patches of stone. But it was a glorious walk, during which there was always something to examine; and at last we felt that we were steadily going up the great rounded mass known as Dome Tor.

We had not been plodding far before I found that it was entirely different to the hills we had climbed that day, for, in place of great masses of rugged, weatherworn rock, the stone we found here and there was slaty and splintery, the narrow tracks up which we walked being full of slippery fragments, making it tiresome travelling.

These tracks were evidently made by the sheep, of which we saw a few here and there, but no shepherd, no houses, nothing to break the utter solitude of the scene, and as we paused for a rest about half-way up Uncle Dick looked round at the glorious prospect, bathed in the warm glow of the setting sun.

"Ah!" he said, "this is beautiful nature. Over yonder, at Arrowfield, we shall have nature to deal with that is not beautiful. But come, boys, I want a big meat tea, and we've miles to go yet before we can get it."

We all jumped up and tramped on, with a curious sensation coming into my legs, as if the joints wanted oiling. But I said nothing, only trudged away, on and on, till at last we reached the rounded top, hot, out of breath, and glad to inhale the fresh breeze that was blowing.

The view was splendid, but the sun had set, and there were clouds beginning to gather, while, on looking round, though we could see a house here and a house there in the distance, it did not seem very clear to either of us which way we were to go.

"We are clever ones," said Uncle Dick, "starting out on a trip like this without a pocket guide and a map: never mind, our way must be west, and sooner or later we shall come to a road, and then to a village."

"But we shall never be able to reach a railway-station to-night," said Uncle Bob.

"Not unless we try," said Uncle Jack in his dry way.

"Then let's try," said Uncle Dick, "and—well, that is strange."

As we reached the top the wind had been blowing sharply in our faces, but this had ceased while we had been lying about admiring the prospect, and in place a few soft moist puffs had come from quite another quarter; and as we looked there seemed to be a cloud of white smoke starting up out of a valley below us. As we watched it we suddenly became aware of another rolling along the short rough turf and over the shaley paths. Then a patch seemed to form here, another there, and these patches appeared to be stretching out their hands to each other all round the mountain till they formed a grey bank of mist, over the top of which we could see the distant country.

"We must be moving," said Uncle Dick, "or we shall be lost in the fog. North-west must be our way, but let's push down here where the slope's easy, and get beyond the mist, and then we can see what we had better do."

He led the way, and before we could realise it the dense white steamy fog was all around us, and we could hardly see each other.

"All right!" said Uncle Dick; "keep together."

"Can you see where you are going, Dick?" said Uncle Jack.

"No, I'm as if I was blindfolded with a white crape handkerchief."

"No precipices here, are there?" I cried nervously, for it seemed so strange to be walking through this dense mist.

"No, I hope not," cried Uncle Dick out of the mist ahead. "You keep talking, and follow me, I'll answer you, or else we shall be separated, and that won't do now. All right!"

"All right!" we chorused back.

"All right!" cried Uncle Dick; "nice easy slope here, but slippery."

"All right!" we chorused.

"All ri— Take—"

We stopped short in horror wondering what had happened, for Uncle Dick's words seemed cut in two, there was a rustling scrambling sound, and then all was white fog and silence, broken only by our panting breath.

"Dick! Where are you?" cried Uncle Jack taking a step forward.

"Mind!" cried Uncle Bob, catching him by the arm.

It was well he did, for that was the rustling scrambling noise again falling on my ears, with a panting struggle, and two voices in the dense fog seeming to utter ejaculations of horror and dread.

Chapter Five.

A Night of Anxiety.

I looked in the direction from which the sounds came, but there was nothing visible, save the thick white fog, and in my excitement and horror, thinking I was looking in the wrong direction, I turned sharply round.

White fog.

I looked in another direction.

White fog.

Then I seemed to lose my head altogether, and hurried here and there with my hands extended, completely astray.

It only took moments, swift moments, for all this to take place, and then I heard voices that I knew, but sounding muffled and as if a long way off.

"Cob! Where are you, Cob?"

"Here," I shouted. "I'll try and come."

"No, no!"—it was Uncle Jack who spoke—"don't stir for your life."

"But," I shouted, with my voice sounding as if I was covered with a blanket, "I want to come to you."

"Stop where you are," he cried. "I command you."

I stayed where I was, and the next moment a fresh voice cried to me, as if pitying my condition:

"Cob, lad."

"Yes," I cried.

"There is a horrible precipice. Don't stir."

It was Uncle Bob who said this to comfort me, and make me safe from running risks, but he made me turn all of a cold perspiration, and I stood there shivering, listening to the murmur of voices that came to me in a stifled way.

At last I could bear it no longer. It seemed so strange. Only a minute or two ago we were all together on the top of a great hill admiring the prospect. Now we were separated. Then all seemed open and clear, and we were looking away for miles: now I seemed shut-in by this pale white gloom that stopped my sight, and almost my hearing, while it numbed and confused my faculties in a way that I could not have felt possible.

"Uncle Jack!" I cried, as a sudden recollection came back of a cry I had heard.

"He is not here," cried Uncle Bob. "He is trying to find a way down."

"Where is Uncle Dick?"

"Hush, boy! Don't ask."

"But, uncle, I may come to you, may I not?" I cried, trembling with the dread of what had happened, for in spite of my confused state I realised now that Uncle Dick must have fallen.

"My boy," he shouted back, "I daren't say yes. The place ends here in a terrible way. We two nearly went over, and I dare not stir, for I cannot see a yard from my feet. I am on a very steep slope too."

"But where has Uncle Jack gone then?"

"Ahoy!" came from somewhere behind me, and apparently below.

"Ahoy! Uncle Jack," I yelled.

"Ahoy, boy! I want to come to you. Keep shouting *here—here—here*."

I did as he bade me, and he kept answering me, and for a minute or two he seemed to be coming nearer. Then his voice sounded more distant, and more distant still; then ceased.

"Cob, I can't hear him," came from near me out of the dense gloom. "Can you?"

"No!" I said with a shiver.

"Ahoy, Jack!" roared Uncle Bob.

"Ahoy-oy!" came from a distance in a curiously stifled way.

"Give it up till the fog clears off. Stand still."

There was no reply, and once more the terrible silence seemed to cling round me. The gloom increased, and I sank on my knees, not daring to stand now, but listening, if I may say so, with all my might.

What had happened? What was going to happen? Were we to stay there all night in the darkness, shivering with cold and damp? Only a little while ago I had been tired and hot; now I did not feel the fatigue, but was shivering with cold, and my hands and face were wet.

I wanted to call out to Uncle Bob again, but the sensation came over me—the strange, wild fancy that something had happened to him, and I dared not speak for fear of finding that it was true.

All at once as I knelt there, listening intently for the slightest sound, I fancied I heard some one breathing. Then the sound stopped. Then it came nearer, and the dense mist parted, and a figure was upon me, crawling close by me without seeing me; and crying "Uncle Bob!" I started forward and caught at him as I thought. My hands seized moist wool for a moment, and then it was jerked out of my hands, as, with a frightened *Baa!* Its wearer bounded away.

"What's that?" came from my left and below me, in the same old suffocated tone.

"A sheep," I cried, trembling with the start the creature had given me.

"Did you see which way it went?"

"Yes—beyond me."

"Then it must be safe your way, Cob. I'll try and crawl to you, lad, but I'm so unnerved I can hardly make up my mind to stir."

"Let me come to you," I cried.

"No, no! I'll try and get to you. Where are you?"

"Here," I cried.

"All right!" came back in answer; but matters did not seem all right, for Uncle Bob's voice suddenly seemed to grow more distant, and when I shouted to him my cry came back as if I had put my face against a wall and spoken within an inch or two thereof.

"I think we'd better give it up, Cob," he shouted now from somewhere quite different. "It is not safe to stir."

I did not think so, and determined to make an attempt to get to him.

For, now that I had grown a little used to the fog, it did not seem so appalling, though it had grown thicker and darker till I seemed quite shut-in.

"I'll stop where I am, Cob," came now as if from above me; "and I daresay in a short time the wind will rise."

I answered, but I felt as if I could not keep still. I had been scared by the sudden separation from my companions, but the startled feeling having passed away I did not realise the extent of our danger. In fact it seemed absurd for three strong men and a lad like me to be upset in this way by a mist.

Uncle Dick had had a fall, but I would not believe it had been serious. Perhaps he had only slipped down some long slope.

I crouched there in the darkness, straining my eyes to try and pierce the mist, and at last, unable to restrain my impatience, I began to crawl slowly on hands and knees in the direction whence my uncle's voice seemed to come.

I crept a yard at a time very carefully, feeling round with my hands before I ventured to move, and satisfying myself that the ground was solid all around.

It seemed so easy, and it was so impossible that I could come to any harm this way, that I grew more confident, and passing my hand over the rough shale chips that were spread around amongst the short grass, I began to wonder how my uncles could have been so timid, and not have made a brave effort to escape from our difficulty.

I kept on, growing more and more confident each moment in spite of the thick darkness that surrounded me, for it seemed so much easier than crouching there doing nothing for myself. But I went very cautiously, for I found I was on a steep slope, and that very little would have been required to send me sliding down.

Creep, creep, creep, a yard in two or three minutes, but still I was progressing somewhere, and even at this rate I thought that I could join either of my companions when I chose.

I had made up my mind to go a few yards further and then speak, feeling sure that I should be close to Uncle Bob, and that then we could go on together and find Uncle Jack.

I had just come to this conclusion, and was thrusting out my right hand again, when, as I tried to set it down, there was nothing there.

I drew it in sharply and set it down close to the other as I knelt, and then passed it slowly from me over the loose scraps of slaty stone to find it touch the edge of a bank that seemed to have been cut off perpendicularly, and on passing my hand over, it touched first soft turf and earth and then scrappy loose fragments of shale.

This did not startle me, for it appeared to be only a little depression in the ground, but thrusting out one foot I found that go over too, so that I knew I must be parallel with the edge of the trench or crack in the earth.

I picked up a piece of shale and threw it from me, listening for its fall, but no sound came, so I sat down with one leg over the depression and kicked with my heel to loosen a bit of the soil.

I was a couple of feet back, and as I kicked I felt the ground I sat upon quiver; then there was a loud rushing sound, and I threw myself down clinging with my hands, for a great piece of the edge right up to where I sat had given way and gone down, leaving me with my legs hanging over the edge, and but for my sudden effort I should have fallen.

"What was that?" cried a voice some distance above me.

"It is I, Uncle Bob," I panted. "Come and help me."

I heard a fierce drawing in of the breath, and then a low crawling sound, and little bits of stone seemed to be moved close by me.

"Where are you, boy?" came again.

"Here."

"Can you crawl to me? I'm close by your head."

"No," I gasped. "If I move I'm afraid I shall fall."

There was the same fierce drawing in of the breath, the crawling sound again, and a hand touched my face, passed round it, and took a tight hold of my collar.

"Lie quite still, Cob," was whispered; "I'm going to draw you up. Now!"

I felt myself dragged up suddenly, and at the same moment the earth and stones upon which I had been lying dropped from under me with a loud hissing rushing sound, and then I was lying quite still, clinging to Uncle Bob's hand, which was very wet and cold.

"How did you come there?" he said at length.

"Crawled there, trying to get to you," I said.

"And nearly went down that fearful precipice, you foolish fellow. But there: you are safe."

"I did not know it was so dangerous," I faltered.

"Dangerous!" he cried. "It is awful in this horrible darkness. The mountain seems to have been cut in half somewhere about here, and this fog confuses so that it is impossible to stir. We must wait till it blows off I think we are safe now, but I dare not try to find a better place. Dare you?"

"Not after what I have just escaped from," I said dolefully.

"Are you cold?"

"Ye–es," I said with a shiver. "It is so damp."

"Creep close to me, then," he said. "We shall keep each other warm."

We sat like that for hours, and still the fog kept as dense as ever, only that overhead there was a faint light, which grew stronger and then died out over and over again. The stillness was awful, but I had a companion, and that made my position less painful. He would not talk, though as a rule he was very bright and chatty; now he would only say, "Wait and see;" and we waited.

The change came, after those long terrible hours of anxiety, like magic. One moment it was thick darkness; the next I felt, as it were, a feather brush across my cheek.

"Did you feel that?" I said quickly.

"Feel what, Cob?"

"Something breathing against us?" "No—

yes!" he cried joyfully. "It was the wind."

The same touch came again, but stronger. There was light above our heads. I could dimly see my companion, and then a cloud that looked white and strange in the moonlight was gliding slowly away from us over what seemed to be a vast black chasm whose edge was only a few yards away.

It was wonderful how quickly that mist departed and went skimming away into the distance, as if a great curtain were being drawn, leaving the sky sparkling with stars and the moon shining bright and clear.

"You see now the danger from which you escaped?" said Uncle Bob with a shudder.

"Yes," I said; "but did—do you think—"

He looked at me without answering, and just then there came from behind us a loud "Ahoy!"

"Ahoy!" shouted back Uncle Bob; and as we turned in the direction of the cry we could see Uncle Jack waving his white handkerchief to us, and we were soon after by his side.

They gripped hands without a word as they met, and then after a short silence Uncle Jack said:

"We had better get on and descend on the other, side."

"But Uncle Dick!" I cried impetuously; "are you not going to search for Uncle Dick?"

The brothers turned upon me quite fiercely, but neither of them spoke; and for the next hour we went stumbling on down the steep slope of the great hill, trying to keep to the sheep-tracks, which showed pretty plainly in the moonlight, but every now and then we went astray.

My uncles were wonderfully quiet, but they kept steadily on; and I did not like to break their communings, and so trudged behind them, noting that they kept as near as seemed practicable to the place where the mountain ended in a precipice; and now after some walking I could look back and see that the moon was shining full upon the face of the hill, which looked grey and as if one end had been dug right away.

On we went silently and with a settled determined aim, about which no one spoke, but perhaps thought all the more.

I know that I thought so much about the end of our quest that I kept shuddering as I trudged on, with sore feet, feeling that in a short time we should be turning sharp round to our left so as to get to the foot of the great precipice, where the hill had been gnawed away by time, and where the loose earth still kept shivering down.

It was as I expected; we turned sharp off to the left and were soon walking with our faces towards the grey-looking face, that at first looked high, but, as we went on, towered up more and more till the height seemed terrific.

It was a weary heart-rending walk before we reached the hill-like slope where the loose shaley rock and earth was ever falling to add to the *débris* up which we climbed.

"There's no telling exactly where he must have come over," said Uncle Jack, after we had searched about some time, expecting moment by moment to come upon the insensible form of our companion. "We must spread out more."

For we neither of us would own to the possibility of Uncle Dick being killed. For my part I imagined that he would have a broken leg, perhaps, or a sprained ankle. If he had fallen head-first he might have put out his shoulder or broken his collar-bone. I would not imagine anything worse.

The moon was not so clear now, for fleecy clouds began to sail across it and made the search more difficult, as we clambered on over the shale, which in the steepest parts gave way under our feet. But I determinedly climbed on, sure that if I got very high up I should be able to look down and see where Uncle Dick was lying.

To this end I toiled higher and higher, till I could fairly consider that I was touching the face of the mountain where the slope of *débris* began; and I now found that the precipice sloped too, being anything but perpendicular.

"Can you see him, Cob?" cried Uncle Jack from below.

"No," I said despondently.

"Stay where you are," he cried again, "quite still."

That was impossible, for where I stood the shale was so small and loose that I was sliding down slowly; but I made very little noise, and just then Uncle Jack uttered a tremendous—

"Dick, ahoy!"

There was a pause and he shouted again:

"Dick, ahoy!"

"Ahoy!" came back faintly from somewhere a long way off.

"There he is!" I cried.

"No—an echo," said Uncle Jack. "Ahoy!"

"Ahoy!" came back.

"There, you see—an echo."

"Ahoy!" came again.

"That's no echo," cried Uncle Bob joyfully. "Dick!"

He shouted as loudly as he could.

"Ahoy!"

"There! It was no echo. He's all right; and after falling down here he has worked his way out and round the other side, where we went up first, while we came down the other way and missed him."

"Dick, ahoy!" he shouted again; "where away?"

"Ahoy!" came back, and we had to consult.

"If we go up one way to meet him he will come down the other," said Uncle Bob. "There's nothing for it but to wait till morning or divide, and one of us go up one side while the other two go up the other."

Uncle Jack snapped his watch-case down after examining the face by the pale light of the moon.

"Two o'clock," he said, throwing himself on the loose shale. "Ten minutes ago, when we were in doubt, I felt as if I could go on for hours with the search. Now I know that poor old Dick is alive I can't walk another yard."

I had slipped and scrambled down to him now, and Uncle Bob turned to me.

"How are you, Cob?" he said.

"The skin is off one of my heels, and I have a blister on my big toe."

"And I'm dead beat," said Uncle Bob, sinking down. "You're right, Jack, we must have a rest. Let's wait till it's light. It will be broad day by four o'clock, and we can signal to him which way to come."

I nestled down close to him, relieved in mind and body, and I was just thinking that though scraps of slaty stone and brashy earth were not good things for stuffing a feather-bed, they were, all the same, very comfortable for a weary person to lie upon, when I felt a hand laid upon my shoulder, and opening my eyes found the sun shining brightly and Uncle Dick looking down in my face.

"Have I been asleep?" I said confusedly.

"Four hours, Cob," said Uncle Jack. "You lay down at two. It is now six."

"But I dreamed something about you, Uncle Dick," I said confusedly. "I thought you were lost."

"Well, not exactly lost, Cob," he said; "but I slipped over that tremendous slope up yonder, and came down with a rush, stunning myself and making a lot of bruises that are very sore. I must have come down a terrible distance, and I lay, I suppose, for a couple of hours before I could get up and try to make my way back."

"But you are not—not broken," I cried, now thoroughly awake and holding his hand.

"No, Cob," he said smiling; "not broken, but starving and very faint."

A three miles' walk took us to where we obtained a very hearty breakfast, and here the farmer willingly drove us to the nearest station, from whence by a roundabout way we journeyed back to Arrowfield, and found the landlady in conference with Mr Tomplin, who had come to our place on receiving a message from Mrs Stephenson that we had gone down to the works and not returned, her impression being that the men had drowned us all in the dam.

Chapter Six.

"Do let me come."

The rest of the week soon slipped by, and my uncles took possession of the works, but not peaceably.

The agent who had had the letting went down to meet my uncles and give them formal possession.

When he got there he was attacked by the work-people, with words first, and then with stones and pails of water.

The consequence was that he went home with a cut head and his clothes soaked.

"But what's to be done?" said Uncle Dick to him. "We want the place according to the agreement."

The agent looked up, holding one hand to his head, and looking white and scared.

"Call themselves men!" he said, "I call them wild beasts."

"Call them what you like," said Uncle Dick; "wild beasts if you will, but get them out."

"But I can't," groaned the man dismally. "See what a state I'm in! They've spoiled my second best suit."

"Very tiresome," said Uncle Dick, who was growing impatient; "but are you going to get these people out? We've two truck-loads of machinery waiting to be delivered."

"Don't I tell you I can't," said the agent angrily. "Take possession yourself. There, I give you leave."

"Very well," said Uncle Dick. "You assure me that these men have no legal right to be there."

"Not the slightest. They were only allowed to be there till the place was let."

"That's right; then we take possession at once, sir."

"And good luck to you!" said the agent as we went out.

"What are you going to do?" asked Uncle Bob.

"Take possession."

"When?"

"To-night. Will you come?"

"Will I come?" said Uncle Bob with a half laugh. "You might as well ask Jack."

"It may mean trouble to-morrow."

"There's nothing done without trouble," said Uncle Bob coolly. "I like ease better, but I'll take my share."

I was wildly excited, and began thinking that we should all be armed with swords and guns, so that I was terribly disappointed when that evening I found Uncle Dick enter the room with a brown-paper parcel in his hand that looked like a book, and followed by Uncle Jack looking as peaceable as could be.

"Where's Uncle Bob?" I said.

"Waiting for us outside."

"Why doesn't he come in?"

"He's busy."

I wondered what Uncle Bob was busy about; but I noticed that my uncles were preparing for the expedition, putting some tools and a small lantern in a travelling-bag. After this Uncle Jack took it open downstairs ready for starting.

"Look here, Cob," said Uncle Dick; "we are going down to the works."

"What! To-night?"

"Yes, my lad, to-night."

"But you can't get in. The men have the key."

"I have the agent's keys. There are two sets, and I am going down now. Look here; take a book and amuse yourself, and go to bed in good time. Perhaps we shall be late."

"Why, you are going to stop all night," I cried, "so as to be there before the men?"

"I confess," he said, laughing in my excited face.

"And I sha'n't see any of the fun," I cried.

"There will not be any fun, Cob."

"Oh, yes, there will, uncle," I said. "I say, do let me come."

He shook his head, and as I could make no impression on him I gave up, and slipped down to Uncle Jack, who was watching Mrs Stephenson cut some huge sandwiches for provender during the night.

"I say, uncle," I whispered, "I know what you are going to do. Take me."

"No, no," he said. "It will be no work for boys."

He was so quiet and stern that I felt it was of no use to press him, so I left the kitchen and went to the front door to try Uncle Bob for my last resource.

I opened the door gently, and started back, for there was a savage growl, and I just made out the dark form of a big-headed dog tugging at a string.

"Down, Piter!" said Uncle Bob. "Who is it? You, Cob? Here, Piter, make friends with him. Come out."

I went out rather slowly, for the dog was growling ominously; but at a word from Uncle Bob he ceased, and began to smell me all round the legs, stopping longest about my calves, as if he thought that would be the best place for a bite.

"Pat him, Cob, and pull his ears."

I stooped down rather unwillingly, and began patting the ugliest head I ever saw in my life. For Piter—otherwise Jupiter—was a brindled bull-dog with an enormous head, protruding lower jaw, pinched-in nose, and grinning teeth. The sides of his head seemed swollen, and his chest broad, his body lank and lean, ending in a shabby little thin tail.

"Why, he has no ears," I said.

"They are cut pretty short, poor fellow. But isn't he a beauty, Cob?"

"Beauty!" I said, laughing. "But where did you get him?"

"Mr Tomplin has lent him to us."

"But what for?"

"Garrison for the fort," my boy. "I think we can trust him."

I commenced my attack then.

"I should so like to go!" I said. "It isn't as if I was a nuisance. I wasn't so bad when we were out all night by Dome Tor."

"Well, there, I'll talk them over," he said. "Here, you stop and hold the dog, while I go in."

"What, hold him?"

"Yes, to be sure. I won't be long."

"But, uncle," I said, "he looks such a brute, as if he'd eat a fellow."

"My dear Cob, I sha'n't be above a quarter of an hour. He couldn't get through more than one leg by that time."

"Now you're laughing at me," I said.

"Hold the dog, then, you young coward!"

"I'm not," I said in an injured tone; and I caught at the leather thong, for if it had been a lion I should have held on then.

I wanted to say, "Don't be long," but I was ashamed, and I looked rather wistfully over my shoulder as he went in, leaving me with the dog.

Piter uttered a low whine as the door closed, and then growled angrily and gave a short deep-toned bark.

This done, he growled at me, smelled me all round, making my legs seem to curdle as his blunt nose touched them, and then after winding the thong round me twice he stood up on his hind-legs, placing his paws against my chest and his ugly muzzle between them.

My heart was beating fast, but the act was so friendly that I patted the great head; and the end of it was, that I sat down on the door-step, and when Uncle Bob came out again Piter and I had fraternised, and he had been showing me as hard as he could that he was my born slave, that he was ready for a bit of fun at any time, and also to defend me against any enemy who should attack.

Piter's ways were simple. To show the first he licked my hand. For the second, he turned over on his back, patted at me with his paws, and mumbled my legs, took a hold of my trousers and dragged at them, and butted at me with his bullet head. For the last, he suddenly sprang to his feet as a step was heard, crouched by me ready for a spring, and made some thunder inside him somewhere.

This done, he tried to show me what fun it was to tie himself up in a knot with the leathern thong, and strangle himself till his eyes stood out of his head.

"Why, you have made friends," said Uncle Bob, coming out. "Good dog, then."

"May I go?" I said eagerly.

"Yes. They've given in. I had a hard fight, sir, so you must do me credit."

Half an hour after, we four were on our way to our own works, just as if we were stealing through the dark to commit a burglary, and I noticed that though there were no swords and guns, each of my uncles carried a very stout heavy stick, that seemed to me like a yard of bad headache, cut very thick.

The streets looked very miserable as we advanced, leaving behind us the noise and roar and glow of the panting machinery which every now and then whistled and screamed as if rejoicing over the metal it was cutting and forming and working into endless shapes. There behind us was the red cloud against which the light from a thousand furnaces was glowing, while every now and then came a deafening roar as if some explosion had taken place.

I glanced down at Piter expecting to see him startled, but he was Arrowfield born, and paid not the slightest heed to noise, passing through a bright flash of light that shot from an open door as if it were the usual thing, and he did not even twitch his tail as we walked on by a wall that seemed to quiver and shake as some great piece of machinery worked away, throbbing and thudding inside.

"Here we are at last," said Uncle Dick, as we reached the corner of our place, where a lamp shed a ghastly kind of glow upon the dark triangular shaped dam.

The big stone building looked silent and ghostly in the gloom, while the great chimney stood up like a giant sentry watching over it, and placed there by the men whom it was our misfortune to have to dislodge.

We had a perfect right to be there, but one and all spoke in whispers as we looked round at the buildings about, to see in one of a row of houses that there were lights, and in a big stone building similar to ours the faint glow of a fire left to smoulder till the morning. But look which way we would, there was not a soul about, and all was still.

As we drew closer I could hear the dripping of the water as it ran in by the wheel where it was not securely stopped; and every now and then there was an echoing plash from the great shut-in cave, but no light in any of the windows.

"Come and hold the bag, Jack," whispered Uncle Dick; and then laughingly as we grouped about the gate with the dog sniffing at the bottom: "If you see a policeman coming, give me fair warning. I hope that dog will not bark. I feel just like a burglar."

Piter uttered a low growl, but remained silent, while Uncle Dick opened the gate and we entered.

As soon as we were inside the yard the bag was put under requisition again, a great screw-driver taken out, the lantern lit, and with all the skill and expedition of one accustomed to the use of tools, Uncle Dick unscrewed and took off the lock, laid it aside, and fitted on, very ingeniously, so that the old key-hole should do again, one of the new patent locks he had brought with him in the brown-paper parcel I had seen.

This took some little time, but it was effected at last, and Uncle Dick said:

"That is something towards making the place our own. Their key will not be worth much now."

Securing the gate by turning the key of the new lock, we went next to the door leading into the works, which was also locked, but the key the agent had supplied opened it directly, and this time Uncle Dick held box and lantern while Uncle Jack took off the old and fitted on the second new lock that we had brought.

It was a curious scene in the darkness of that great stone-floored echoing place, where an observer who watched would have seen a round glass eye shedding a bright light on a particular part of the big dirty door, and in the golden ring the bull's-eye made, a pair of large white hands busy at work fixing, turning a gimlet, putting in and fastening screws, while only now and then could a face be seen in the ring of light.

"There," said Uncle Jack at last, as he turned the well-oiled key and made the bolt of the lock play in and out of its socket, "now I think we can call the place our own."

"I say, Uncle Bob," I whispered—I don't know why, unless it was the darkness that made me speak low—"I should like to see those fellows' faces when they come to the gate to-morrow morning."

"Especially Old Squintum's," said Uncle Bob laughing. "Pleasant countenance that man has, Cob. If ever he is modelled I should like to have a copy. Now, boys, what next?"

"Next!" said Uncle Dick; "we'll just have a look round this place and see what there is belonging to the men, and we'll put all together so as to be able to give it up when they come."

"The small grindstones are theirs, are they not?" said Uncle Bob.

"No; the agent says that everything belongs to the works and will be found in the inventory. All we have to turn out will be the blades they are grinding."

Uncle Dick went forward from grindstone to grindstone, but only in one place was anything waiting to be ground, and that was a bundle of black-looking, newly-forged scythe blades, neatly tied up with bands of wire.

He went on from end to end, making the light play on grindstone, trough, and the rusty sand that lay about; but nothing else was to be seen, and after reaching the door leading into the great chamber where the water-wheel revolved, he turned back the light, looking like some dancing will-o'-the-wisp as he directed it here and there, greatly to the puzzlement of Piter, to whom it was something new.

He tugged at the stout leathern thong once or twice, but I held on and he ceased, contenting himself with a low uneasy whine now and then, and looking up to me with his great protruding eyes, as if for an explanation.

"Now let's have a look round upwards," said Uncle Dick. "I'm glad the men have left so few of their traps here. Cob, my lad, you need not hold that dog. Take the swivel off his collar and let him go. He can't get away."

"Besides," said Uncle Bob, "this is to be his home."

I stooped down and unhooked the spring swivel, to Piter's great delight, which he displayed by scuffling about our feet, trying to get himself trodden upon by all in turn, and ending by making a rush at the bull's-eye lantern, and knocking his head against the round glass.

"Pretty little creature!" said Uncle Bob. "Well, I should have given him credit for more sense than a moth."

Piter growled as if he were dissatisfied with the result, and then his hideous little crinkled black nose was seen as he smelt the lantern all round, and, apparently gratified by the odour of the oil, he licked his black lips.

"Now then, upstairs," said Uncle Dick, leading the way with the lantern. But as soon as the light fell upon the flight of stone stairs Piter went to the front with a rush, his claws pattered on the stones, and he was up at the top waiting for us, after giving a scratch at a rough door, his ugly countenance looking down curiously out of the darkness.

"Good dog!" said Uncle Dick as he reached the landing and unlatched the door.

Piter squeezed himself through almost before the door was six inches open, and the next moment he burst into a furious deep-mouthed bay.

"Someone there!" cried Uncle Dick, and he rushed in, lantern in hand, to make the light play round, while my uncles changed the hold of their stout sticks, holding them cudgel fashion ready for action.

The light rested directly on the face and chest of a man sitting up between a couple of rusty lathes, where a quantity of straw had been thrown down, and at the first glimpse it was evident that the dog had just aroused him from a heavy sleep.

His eyes were half-closed, bits of oat straw were sticking in his short dark hair, and glistened like fragments of pale gold in the light cast by the bull's-eye, while two blackened and roughened hands were applied to his eyes as if he were trying to rub them bright.

Piter's was an ugly face; but the countenance of an ugly animal is pleasanter to look upon than that of an ugly degraded human being, and as I saw the rough stubbly jaws open, displaying some yellow and blackened teeth that glistened in the light as their owner yawned widely, I began to think our dog handsome by comparison.

The man growled as if not yet awake, and rubbed away at his eyes with his big fists, as if they, too, required a great deal of polishing to make them bright enough to see.

At last he dropped his fists and stared straight before him—no, that's a mistake, he stared with the range of his eyes crossing, and then seemed to have some confused idea that there was a light before him, and a dog making a noise, for he growled out:

"Lie down!"

Then, bending forward, he swept an arm round, as if in search of something, which he caught hold of at last, and we understood why he was so confused. For it was a large stone bottle he had taken up. From this he removed the cork with a dull *Fop!* Raised the bottle with both hands, took a long draught, and corked the bottle again with a sigh, set it down beside him, and after yawning loudly shouted once more at the dog, "Get out! Lie down!"

Then he settled himself as if about to do what he had bidden the dog, but a gleam of intelligence appeared to have come now into his brain.

There was no mistaking the man: it was the squinting ruffian who had attacked us when we came first, and there was no doubt that he had been staying there to keep watch and hold the place against us, for a candle was stuck in a ginger-beer bottle on the frame of the lathe beyond him, and this candle had guttered down and gone out.

We none of us spoke, but stood in the black shadow invisible to the man, who could only see the bright light of the bull's-eye staring him full in the face.

"Lie down, will yer!" he growled savagely. "Makin' shut a row! Lie down or—"

He shouted this last in such a fierce tone of menace that it would have scared some dogs.

It had a different effect on Piter, who growled angrily.

"Don't, then," shouted the man; "howl and bark—make a row, but if yer touch me I'll take yer down and drownd yer in the wheel-pit. D'yer hear? In the wheel-pit!"

This was said in a low drowsy tone and as if the fellow were nearly asleep, and as the light played upon his half-closed dreamy eyes he muttered and stared at it as if completely overcome by sleep.

It was perfectly ridiculous, and yet horrible, to see that rough head and hideous face nodding and blinking at the light as the fellow supported himself on both his hands in an ape-like attitude that was more animal than human.

All this was a matter of a minute or so, and then the ugly cross eyes closed, opened sharply, and were brought to bear upon the light one after the other by movements of the head, just as a magpie looks at a young bird before he kills it with a stroke of his bill.

Then a glimpse of intelligence seemed to shoot from them, and the man sat up sharply.

"What's that light?" he said roughly. "Police! What do you want?"

"What are you doing here?" said Uncle Jack in his deep voice.

"Doing, p'liceman! Keeping wetch. Set o' Lonnoners trying to get howd o' wucks, and me and my mates wean't hev 'em. Just keeping wetch. Good-night!"

He sat up, staring harder at the light, and then tried to see behind it.

"Well," he cried, "why don't you go, mate? Shut door efter you."

"Hold the dog, Cob," said Uncle Jack. "Bob, you take the lantern and open the door and the gate. Lay hold of one side, Dick, I'll take the other, and we'll put him out."

But the man was wide-awake now; and as I darted at Piter and got my hands in his collar and held him back, the fellow made a dash at something lying on the lathe, and as the lantern was changed from hand to hand I caught sight of the barrel of an old horse-pistol.

"Take care!" I shouted, as I dragged Piter back. "Pistol."

"Yes, pistol, do yer hear?" roared the fellow starting up. "Pistol! And I'll shute the first as comes anigh me."

There was a click here, and all was in darkness, for Uncle Bob turned the shade of the lantern and hid it within his coat.

"Put that pistol down, my man, and no harm shall come to you; but you must get out of this place directly."

"What! Get out! Yes, out you go, whoever you are," roared the fellow. "I can see you, and I'll bring down the first as stirs. This here's a good owd pistol, and she hits hard. Now then open that light and let's see you go down. This here's my place and my mates', and we don't want none else here. Now then."

I was struggling in the dark with Piter, and only held him back, there was such strength in his small body, by lifting him by his collar and holding him against me standing on his hind-legs.

But, engaged as I was, I had an excited ear for what was going on, and I trembled, as I expected to see the flash of the pistol and feel its bullet strike me or the dog.

As the man uttered his threats I heard a sharp whispering and a quick movement or two in the dark, and then all at once I saw the light open, and after a flash here and there shine full upon the fellow, who immediately turned the pistol on the holder of the lantern.

"Now then," he cried, "yer give in, don't yer? Yes or no 'fore I fires. Yah!"

He turned sharply round in my direction as I struggled with Piter, whom the sight of the black-looking ruffian had made furious.

But the man had not turned upon me.

He had caught sight of Uncle Jack springing at him, the light showing him as he advanced.

There was a flash, a loud report, and almost preceding it, if not quite, the sound of a sharp rap given with a stick upon flesh and bone.

The next instant there was a hoarse yell and the noise made by the pistol falling upon the floor.

"Hurt, Jack?" cried Uncle Dick, as my heart seemed to stand still.

"Scratched, that's all," was the reply. "Here, come and tie this wild beast's hands. I think I can hold him now."

It almost sounded like a rash assertion, as the light played upon the desperate struggle that was going on. I could see Uncle Jack and the man, now down, now up, and at last, after wrestling here and there, the man, in spite of Uncle Jack's great strength, seeming to have the mastery. There was a loud panting and a crushing fall, both going down, and Uncle Jack rising up to kneel upon his adversary's chest.

"Like fighting a bull," panted Uncle Jack. "What arms the fellow has! Got the rope?"

"Yes," said Uncle Dick, rattling the things in the bag. "Can you turn him over?"

No sooner said than done. The man heard the order, and prepared to resist being turned on one side. Uncle Jack noted this and attacked the other side so quickly that the man was over upon his face before he could change his tactics.

"Keep that dog back, Cob, or he'll eat him," said Uncle Bob, making the lantern play on the prostrate man, whose arms were dexterously dragged behind him and tightly tied.

"There," said Uncle Jack. "Now you can get up and go. Ah, would you, coward!"

This was in answer to a furious kick the fellow tried to deliver as soon as he had regained his feet.

"If he attempts to kick again, loose the dog at him, Cob," cried Uncle Dick sharply.

Then in an undertone to me:

"No: don't! But let him think you will."

"You'll hev it for this," cried the man furiously.

"Right," said Uncle Jack. "Now, then, have you anything here belonging to you? No! Down you come then."

He collared his prisoner, who turned to kick at him; but a savage snarl from Piter, as I half let him go, checked the fellow, and he suffered himself to be marched to the door, where he stopped.

"Ma beer," he growled, looking back at the stone bottle.

"Beer! No, you've had enough of that," said Uncle Dick. "Go on down."

The man walked quietly down the stairs; but when he found that he was to be thrust out into the lane he began to struggle again, and shout, but a fierce hand at his throat stopped that and he was led down to the gate in the wall, where it became my task now to hold the lantern while Uncles Dick and Bob grasped our prisoner's arms and left Uncle Jack free to untie the cord.

"Be ready to unlock the gate, Cob," whispered Uncle Jack, as he held his prisoner by one twist of the rope round his arms like a leash. "Now, then, ready! Back, dog, back!"

Piter shrank away, and then at a concerted moment the gate was thrown open, the three brothers loosed their hold of the prisoner at the same moment, and just as he was turning to try and re-enter, a sharp thrust of the foot sent him flying forward, the gate was banged to, and locked, and we were congratulating ourselves upon having ridded ourselves of an ugly customer, when the gate shook from the effect of a tremendous blow that sounded as if it had been dealt with a paving-stone.

Chapter Seven.

A useful Ally.

"Take no notice," said Uncle Dick.

We listened, and I laughed as I heard the rattling noise made by a key as if our friend was trying to get in, after which he seemed to realise what had been done, and went away grumbling fiercely.

"Now for a quiet look round upstairs," said Uncle Dick; and all being quiet and we in possession we turned in at the dark door to inspect our fort.

There was something creepy and yet thoroughly attractive in the business. The place looked dark and romantic in the gloom; there was a spice of danger in the work, and the excitement made my blood seem to dance in my veins.

"Hallo!" I cried, as we were entering the door; "there's something wrong," for I heard a rustling noise and a dull thud as if someone had jumped down from a little height.

At the same moment we found out how useful Piter was going to be, for he started off with a furious rush, barking tremendously, and as we followed him to the end of the yard we were in time for a scuffle, a savage burst of expressions, and then my heart, which had been throbbing furiously, seemed to stand still, for there was a howl, a tremendous splash, then silence.

"Quick, boys!" cried Uncle Jack. "Here, join hands. I'll go in and fetch him out. Take the light, Cob."

I gladly seized the lantern and made the light play on the surface of the water where it was disturbed, and as I did so Piter came up from the edge whining softly and twitching his little stump of a tail.

Then a head and shoulders appeared, and the surface of the dam was beaten tremendously, but so close to the edge that by standing on the stonework and holding by Uncle Bob's hand Uncle Jack was able to stretch out his stick to the struggling man, to have it clutched directly, and the fellow was drawn ashore.

He gave himself a shake like a dog as soon as he was on dry land, and stood for a moment or two growling and using ugly language that seemed to agree with his mouth.

Then he turned upon us.

"Aw right!" he said, "I'll pay thee for this. Set the dawg on me, you did, and then pitched me into the watter. Aw reight! I'll pay thee for this."

"Open the gate, Bob," said Uncle Jack, who now took the fellow by the collar and thrust him forward while I held the light as the man went on threatening and telling us what he meant to do.

But the cold water had pretty well quenched his fierce anger, and though he threatened a great deal he did not attempt to do anything till he was by the gate, where a buzz of voices outside seemed to inspirit him.

"Hey, lads!" he cried, "in wi' you when gate's opened."

"Take care," whispered Uncle Dick. "Be ready to bang the gate. We must have him out. Here, Piter."

The dog answered with a bark, and then our invader being held ready the gate was opened by me, and the three brothers thrust the prisoner they were going to set at liberty half-way out.

Only half-way, for he was driven back by a rush of his companions, who had been aroused by his shouting.

The stronger outside party would have prevailed no doubt had not our four-footed companion made a savage charge among the rough legs, with such effect that there was a series of yells from the front men, who became at once on our side to the extent of driving their friends back; and before they could recover from the surprise consequent upon the dog's assault, the gate was banged to and locked.

"Show the light, and see where that fellow came over the wall, Cob," whispered Uncle Dick; and I made the light play along the top, expecting to see a head every moment. But instead of a head a pair of hands appeared over the coping-stones—a pair of great black hands, whose nails showed thick and stubby in the lantern light.

"There, take that," said Uncle Dick, giving the hands a quick tap with his stick. "I don't want to hurt you, though I could."

By that he meant do serious injury, for he certainly hurt the owner of the hands to the extent of giving pain, for there was a savage yell and the hands disappeared.

Then there was a loud scuffling noise and a fresh pair of hands appeared, but they shared the fate of the others and went out of sight.

"Nice place this," said Uncle Bob suddenly. "Didn't take return tickets, did you?"

"Return tickets! No," said Uncle Jack in a low angry voice. "What! Are you tired of it already?"

"Tired! Well, I don't know, but certainly this is more lively than Canonbury. There's something cheerful about the place. Put up your umbrellas, it hails."

I was nervous and excited, but I could not help laughing at this, for Uncle Bob's ideas of hailstones were peculiar. The first that fell was a paving-stone as big as a half-quartern loaf, and it was followed by quite a shower of the round cobbles or pebbles nearly the size of a fist that are used so much in some country places for paths.

Fortunately no one was hit, while this bombardment was succeeded by another assault or attempt to carry the place by what soldiers call a *coup de main.*

But this failed, for the hands that were to deal the *coup* received such ugly taps from sticks as they appeared on the top of the wall that their owners dropped back and began throwing over stones and angry words again.

Only one of our assailants seemed to have the courage to persevere, and this proved to be our old friend. For as I directed the light along the top of the wall a pair of hands appeared accompanied by the usual scuffing.

Uncle Dick only tapped them, but possibly not hard enough, for the arms followed the hands, then appeared the head and fierce eyes of the man we had found asleep.

"Coom on, lads; we've got un now," he shouted, and in another minute he would have been over; but Uncle Dick felt it was time for stronger measures than tapping hands, and he let his stick come down with such a sharp rap on the great coarse head that it disappeared directly, and a yelling chorus was succeeded by another shower of stones.

We went into shelter in the doorway, with Piter playing the part of sentry in front, the dog walking up and down looking at the top of the wall growling as he went, and now and then opening and shutting his teeth with a loud snap like a trap.

On the other side of the wall we could hear the talking of the men, quite a little crowd having apparently assembled, and being harangued by one of their party.

"So it makes you think of Canonbury, does it, Bob?" said Uncle Jack.

"Well, yes," said my uncle.

"It makes me feel angry," said Uncle Jack, "and as if the more these scoundrels are obstinate and interfere with me, the more determined I shall grow."

"We must call in the help of the police," said Uncle Dick.

"And they will be watched away," said Uncle Jack. "No, we must depend upon ourselves, and I dare say we can win. What's that?"

I listened, and said that I did not hear anything.

"I did," said Uncle Jack. "It was the tap made by a ladder that has been reared against a house."

I made the light play against the top of the wall and along it from end to end.

Then Uncle Jack took it and examined the top, but nothing was visible and saying it was fancy he handed the lantern to me, when all at once there was a double thud as of two people leaping down from the wall; and as I turned the light in the direction from which the sounds came there was our squinting enemy, and directly behind him a great rough fellow, both armed with sticks and charging down upon us where we stood.

I heard my uncles draw a long breath as if preparing for the fight. Then they let their sticks fall to their sides, and a simultaneous roar of laughter burst forth.

It did not take a minute, and the various little changes followed each other so quickly that I was confused and puzzled.

One moment I felt a curious shrinking as I saw the faces of two savage men rushing at us to drive us out of the place; the next I was looking at their backs as they ran along the yard.

For no sooner did Piter see them than he made a dash at their legs, growling like some fierce wild beast, and showing his teeth to such good effect that the men ran from him blindly yelling one to the other; and the next thing I heard was a couple of splashes in the dam.

"Why, they're trying to swim across," cried Uncle Dick; and we at once ran to the end of the yard to where it was bounded by the stone-bordered dam.

"Show the light, Cob," cried Uncle Jack; and as I made it play upon the water there was one man swimming steadily for the other side, with Piter standing at the edge baying him furiously, but the other man was not visible.

Then the surface of the water was disturbed and a hand appeared, then another, to begin beating and splashing.

"Why, the fellow can't swim," cried Uncle Jack; and catching his brother's hand he reached out, holding his stick ready for the man to grasp.

It was an exciting scene in the darkness, with the ring of light cast by the lantern playing upon the dark surface of the water, which seemed to be black rippled with gold; and there in the midst was the distorted face of the workman, as he yelled for help and seemed in imminent danger of drowning.

He made two or three snatches at the stick, but missed it, and his struggles took him farther from the edge into the deep water close by, where the wall that supported the great wheel was at right angles to where we stood.

It was a terribly dangerous and slippery place, but Uncle Jack did not hesitate. Walking along a slippery ledge that was lapped by the water, he managed to reach the drowning man, holding to him his stick; and then as the fellow clutched it tightly he managed to guide him towards the edge, where Uncle Dick knelt down, and at last caught him by the collar and drew him out, dripping and half insensible.

"Down, dog!" cried Uncle Dick as Piter made a dash at his enemy, who now lay perfectly motionless.

Piter growled a remonstrance and drew back slowly, but as he reached the man's feet he made a sudden dart down and gave one of his ankles a pinch with his trap-like jaws.

The effect was instantaneous. The man jumped up and shook his fist in our faces.

"Yow'll get it for this here," he roared. "Yow threw me in dam and then set your dawg at me. Yow'll hev it for this. Yow'll see. Yow'll—"

"Look here," said Uncle Bob, mimicking the fellow's broad rough speech, "hadn't yow better go home and take off your wet things?"

"Yow pitched me in dam and set dawg at me," cried the fellow again.

"Go home and get off your wet things and go to bed," said Uncle Jack, "and don't come worrying us again—do you hear?"

"Yow pitched me in dam and set dawg at me," cried the man again; and from the other side of the pool the man who had swum across and been joined by some companions yelled out:

"Gi'e it to un, Chawny—gi'e it to un."

"Yow pitched me in dam and set dawg—"

"Look here," roared Uncle Bob, "if you're not out of this place in half a minute I will pitch you in the dam, and set the dog at you as well. Here, Piter."

"Give's leg over the wall," growled the man.

"No. Go out of the gate," said Uncle Jack; and standing ready to avoid a rush we opened the gate in the wall and let the fellow go free.

We got him out and escaped a rush, for the little crowd were all up by the side of the dam, whence they could see into the yard; but as we sent Chawny, as he was called, out through the gate, and he turned to stand there, dripping, and ready to shake his fist in our faces, they came charging down.

Uncle Bob banged the door to, though, as our enemy repeated his angry charge:

"Yow pitched me in dam and set dawg at me."

Then the door was closed and we prepared for the next attack from the murmuring crowd outside.

But none came, and the voices gradually grew fainter and died away, while, taking it in turns, we watched till morning began to break without any farther demonstration on the part of the enemy.

"We're safe for this time, boys," said Uncle Dick.

"Now go and have a few hours' rest. I'll call you when the men come."

We were only too glad, and ten minutes later we were all asleep on some shavings and straw in the upper workshop, while Uncle Dick and Piter kept guard.

Chapter Eight.

On Guard.

It seemed as if it had all been a dream when I awoke and found Uncle Bob was shaking me.

"Come, young fellow," he cried; "breakfast's ready."

I did not feel ready for my breakfast if it was, especially a breakfast of bread and meat with no chair, no table, no cloth, no tea, coffee, or bread and butter.

Such a good example was shown me, though, that I took the thick sandwich offered to me, and I was soon forgetting my drowsiness and eating heartily.

We were not interrupted, and when we had ended our meal, went round the place to see what was to be done.

The first thing was placing the property that could be claimed by the men close by the gate ready for them, and when this was done Piter and I walked up and down the yard listening to the steps outside, and waiting to give a signal if any of the men should come.

No men came, however, and there was not a single call till afternoon, when a sharp rapping at the gate was answered by two of my uncles, and the dog, who seemed puzzled as to the best pair of legs to peer between, deciding at last in favour of Uncle Bob's.

To our surprise, when the gate was opened, there were no men waiting, but half a dozen women, one of whom announced that they had came for their masters' "traps," and the said "traps" being handed to them, they went off without a word, not even condescending to say "Thank you."

"Come," said Uncle Bob, after the various things had been carried off, and Piter had stood looking on twitching his ears and blinking at them, as if he did not war with women, "Come, we've won the game."

"Don't be too sure, my boy," said Uncle Dick.

"But they have, given up."

"Given up expecting to use the works. But what are they going to do in revenge?"

"Revenge!"

"Yes. You may depend upon it we are marked men, and that we shall have to fight hard to hold our own."

60

As the day went on—a day busily spent in making plans for the future of our factory, we had one or two applications from men who were seeking work, and if we had any doubt before of how our coming was to be received, we realised it in the yells and hootings that greeted the men who came in a friendly spirit.

Uncle Dick went off directly after breakfast to see about the machinery waiting at the railway being delivered, and it was late in the afternoon before he returned.

"One of us will have to stay always on the premises for the present," he said, "so I have ordered some furniture and a carpenter to come and board up and make that corner office comfortable. We must make shift."

The matter was discussed, and finally it was settled that two of our party were to be always on the premises, and until we were satisfied that there was no more fear of interference, one was to keep watch half the night with the dog, and then be relieved by the other.

"We shall have to make a man of you, Cob," said Uncle Jack. "You must take your turn with us."

"I'm ready," I replied; and very proud I felt of being trusted.

Of course I felt nervous, but at the same time rather disappointed, for everything went on in the most business like way. Carpenters and fitters were set to work, and, helped by the indomitable perseverance and energy of my uncles, a great deal of fresh machinery was soon in position. New shafts and bands, a new furnace for preparing our own steel after a fashion invented by Uncle Dick. New grindstones and polishing-wheels, new forges with tilt-hammers, and anvils.

By degrees I found what was going to be our chief business, and that was the production of cutlery of a peculiar temper especially for surgical instruments and swords, Uncle Dick having an idea that he could produce blades equal to Damascus or the finest Spanish steel.

The days glided by with the works growing more complete, and each night half our party on guard at Fort Industry, as Uncle Bob christened the place. And though the couple who had slept at the lodgings went down to the place every morning feeling nervous, and wondering whether anything had happened in the night, it was always to find that all was going on perfectly smoothly, and that there was nothing to mind.

Piter had a kennel just inside the entry, and as each new hand was engaged he was introduced to the dog, who inspected him, and never afterwards so much as growled.

Uncle Dick took the lead, and under his orders the change rapidly took place.

There was one hindrance, though, and that occurred in connection with the furnaces, for the chimney-shaft needed some repair at the top. This, however, proved to be an easy task, scaffolding not being necessary, projecting bars answering the purpose of the rounds of a ladder having been built in when the shaft was erected, with this end in view.

At last everything was, as Uncle Dick called it, complete for the present. There was a good supply of water, and one morning the furnace was lit, so were the forges, and step by step we progressed till there was quite a busy scene, the floors and rafters in the forge and furnace building glowing and seeming turned to gold; while from out of the chimney there rose every morning a great volume of smoke that rolled out and bent over, and formed itself into vast feathery plumes.

I could hardly believe it true when it was announced that we had been down in Arrowfield a month: but so it was.

But little had been done beyond getting the machinery at the works ready for work to come; now, however, some of the projects were to be put in action.

"For," said Uncle Dick, "if we should go on forging and grinding as other manufacturers do, we only enter into competition with them, and I dare say we should be beaten. We must do something different and better, and that's why we have come. To-morrow I begin to make my new tempered steel."

Uncle Dick kept his word, and the next morning men were at work arranging fire-bricks for a little furnace which was duly made, and then so much blistered steel was laid in a peculiar way with so much iron, and a certain heat was got up and increased and lowered several times till Uncle Dick was satisfied. He told me that the colour assumed by the metal was the test by which he judged whether it was progressing satisfactorily, and this knowledge could only come by experience.

Everything was progressing most favourably. The men who had been engaged worked well; we had seen no more of those who had had to vacate the works, and all was as it should be. In fact our affairs were so prosperous that to me it seemed great folly for watch to be kept in the works night after night.

I thought it the greatest nonsense possible one night when I had been very busy all day, and it had come to my turn, and I told Uncle Jack so.

"Those fellows were a bit cross at having to turn out," I said. "Of course they were, and they made a fuss. You don't suppose they will come again?"

"I don't know, Cob," said Uncle Jack quietly.

"But is it likely?" I said pettishly.

"I can't say, my boy—who can? Strange things have been done down in Arrowfield by foolish workmen before now."

"Oh, yes!" I said; "but that's in the past. It isn't likely that they will come and annoy us. Besides, there's Piter. He'd soon startle any one away."

"You think then that there is no occasion for us to watch, Cob?"

"Yes," I cried eagerly, "that's just what I think. We can go to bed and leave Piter to keep guard. He would soon give the alarm."

"Then you had better go to bed, Cob," said Uncle Jack quietly.

"And of course you won't get up when it comes to your turn."

"No," he said; "certainly not."

"That's right," I cried triumphantly. "I am glad we have got over this scare."

"Are you?" he said dryly.

"Am I, Uncle Jack! Why, of course I am. All is locked up. I'll go and unchain Piter, and then we'll go and get a good night's rest."

"Yes," he said; "you may as well unchain Piter."

I ran and set the dog at liberty, and he started off to make the circuit of the place, while I went back to Uncle Jack, who was lighting the bull's-eye lantern that we always used when on guard.

"Why, uncle," I said wonderingly; "we sha'n't want that to-night."

"I shall," he said. "Good-night!"

"No, no," I cried. "We arranged to go to bed."

"You arranged to go to bed, Cob, but I did not. You don't suppose I could behave so unfairly to my brothers as to neglect the task they placed in my hands."

He did not say any more. It was quite sufficient. I felt the rebuff, and was thoroughly awake now and ashamed of what I had proposed.

Without a word I took the lantern and held out my hand.

"Good-night, Uncle Jack!" I said.

He had seemed cold and stern just before. Now he was his quiet old self again, and he took my hand, nodded, and said:

"Two o'clock, Cob. Good-night!"

I saw him go along the great workshop, enter the office and close the door, and then I started on my rounds.

It was anything but a cheerful task, that keeping watch over the works during the night, and I liked the first watch from ten to two less than the second watch from two to six, for in the latter you had the day breaking about four o'clock, and then it was light until six.

For, however much one might tell oneself that there was no danger—no likelihood of anything happening, the darkness in places, the faint glow from partly extinct fires, and the curious shadows cast on the whitewashed walls were all disposed to be startling; and, well as I knew the place, I often found myself shrinking as I came suddenly upon some piece of machinery that assumed in the darkness the aspect of some horrible monster about to seize me as I went my rounds.

Upon the other hand, there was a pleasant feeling of importance in going about that great dark place of a night, with a lantern at my belt, a stout stick in my hand, and a bull-dog at my heels, and this sensation helped to make the work more bearable.

On this particular night I had paced silently all about the place several times, thinking a good deal about my little encounter with Uncle Jack, and about the last letters I had had from my father. Then, as all seemed perfectly right, I had seated myself by the big furnace, which emitted a dull red glow, not sufficient to light the place, but enough to make it pleasantly warm, and to show that if a blast were directed in the coals, a fierce fire would soon be kindled.

I did not feel at all sleepy now; in fact, in spite of the warmth this furnace-house would not have been a pleasant place to sleep in, for the windows on either side were open, having no glass, only iron bars, and those on one side looked over the dam, while the others were in the wall that abutted on the lane leading down to the little river.

Piter had been with me all through my walk round, but, seeing me settle down, he had leaped on to the hot ashes and proceeded to curl himself up in a nice warm place, where the probabilities were that he would soon begin to cook.

Piter had been corrected for this half a dozen times over, but he had to be bullied again, and leaping off the hot ashes he had lowered his tail and trotted back to his kennel, where he curled himself up.

All was very still as I sat there, except that the boom and throb of the busy town where the furnaces and steam-engines were at work kept going and coming in waves of sound; and as I sat, I found myself thinking about the beauty of the steel that my uncles had set themselves to produce; and how, when a piece was snapped across, breaking like a bit of glass, the fracture looked all of a silvery bluish-grey.

Then I began thinking about our tall chimney, and what an unpleasant place mine would be to sit in if there were a furious storm, and the shaft were blown down; and then, with all the intention to be watchful, I began to grow drowsy, and jumping up, walked up and down the furnace-house and round the smouldering fire, whose chimney was a great inverted funnel depending from the open roof.

I grew tired of walking about and sat down again, to begin thinking once more.

How far is it from thinking to sleeping and dreaming? Who can answer that question?

To me it seemed that I was sitting thinking, and that as I thought there in the darkness, where I could see the fire throwing up its feeble glow on to the dim-looking open windows on either side, some great animal came softly in through the window on my left, and then disappeared for a few moments, to appear again on my right where the wall overlooked the lane.

That window seemed to be darkened for a minute or two, and then became light again, while once more that on my left grew dark, and I saw the figure glide out.

I seemed, as I say, to have been thinking, and as I thought it all appeared to be a dream, for it would have been impossible for any one to have crept in at one window, passing the furnace and back again without disturbing me.

Yes; I told myself it was all fancy, and as I thought I told myself that I started awake, and looked sharply at first one window, and then at the other, half expecting to see someone there.

"I was asleep and dreaming," I said to myself; and, starting up impatiently, I walked right out of the furnace-house across the strip of yard, and in at the door, making Piter give his stumpy tail a sharp rapping noise upon the floor of his kennel.

I went on all through the grinding workshop, and listened at the end of the place to the water trickling and dripping down in the great water-floored cellar.

That place had an attraction for me, and I stood listening for some minutes before walking back, thoroughly awake now.

I was so used to the place that I had no need to open the lantern, but threaded my way here and there without touching a thing, and I was able to pass right through to the upper floor in the same way.

Everything was correct, and Uncle Jack sleeping soundly, as I hoped to be after another hour or so's watching.

I would not disturb him, but stole out again, and along the workshop to the head of the stairs, where I descended and stooped to pat Piter again before looking about the yard, and then walking slowly into the warm furnace-house.

Then, after a glance at the windows where I had fancied I had seen someone creep in, I sat down in my old place enjoying the warmth, and once more the drowsy sensation crept over me.

How long it was before I dropped asleep I can't tell, but, bad watchman that I was, I did drop asleep, and began dreaming about the great dam miles away up the valley; and there it seemed to me I was fishing with a long line for some of the great pike that lurked far down in the depths.

As I fished my line seemed to pass over a window-sill and scraped against it, and made a noise which set me wondering how large the fish must be that was running away with it.

And then I was awake, with the perspiration upon my forehead and my hands damp, listening.

It was no fishing-line. I was not by the great dam up the river, but there in our own furnace-house, and something was making a strange rustling noise.

66

For some few moments I could not tell where the noise was. There was the rustling, and it seemed straight before me. Then I knew it was there, for immediately in front on the open fire something was moving and causing a series of little nickers and sparkles in the glowing ashes.

What could it be? What did it mean?

I was so startled that I was ready to leap up and run out of the place, and it was some time before I could summon up courage enough to stretch out a hand, and try to touch whatever it was that moved the glowing ashes.

Wire!

Yes; there was no doubt of it—wire. A long thin wire stretched pretty tightly reached right across me, and evidently passed from the window overlooking the lane across the furnace and out of the window by the side of the dam.

What did it mean—what was going to happen?

I asked myself these questions as I bent towards the furnace, touching the wire which glided on through my hand towards the window by the dam.

It was all a matter of moments, and I could feel that someone must be drawing the wire out there by the dam, though how I could not tell, for it seemed to me that there was nothing but deep water there.

"Some one must have floated down the dam in a boat," I thought in a flash; but no explanation came to the next part of my question, what was it for?

As I bent forward there wondering what it could mean, I began to understand that there must be some one out in the lane at the other end of the wire, and in proof of this surmise I heard a low scraping noise at the window on my right, and then a hiss as if someone had drawn his breath in between his lips.

What could it mean?

I was one moment for shouting, "Who's there?" the next for turning on my bull's-eye; and again the next for running and rousing up Uncle Jack.

Then I thought that I would shout and call to Piter; but I felt that if I did either of these things I should lose the clue that was gliding through my hands.

What could it mean?

The wire, invisible to me, kept softly stirring the glowing ashes, and seemed to be visible there. Elsewhere it was lost in the black darkness about me, but I felt it plainly enough, and in my intense excitement, hundreds of yards seemed to have passed through my hand before I felt a check and in a flash knew what was intended.

For, all at once, as the wire glided on, something struck against my hand gently, and raising the other it came in contact with a large canister wrapped round and round with stout soft cord.

What for?

I knew in an instant; I had read of such outrages, and it was to guard against them that we watched, and kept that dog.

I had hold of a large canister of gunpowder, and the soft cord wrapped around it was prepared fuse.

I comprehended too the horrible ingenuity of the scheme, which was to draw, by means of the wire, the canister of gunpowder on to the furnace, so that the fuse might catch fire, and that would give the miscreants who were engaged time to escape before the powder was fired and brought the chimney-shaft toppling down.

For a moment I trembled and felt ready to drop the canister, and run for my life.

Then I felt strong, for I knew that if I kept the canister in my hands the fuse could not touch the smouldering ashes and the plan would fail.

But how to do this without being heard by the men who must be on either side of the furnace-house.

It was easy enough; I had but to hold the canister high up above the fire, and pass it over till it was beyond the burning ashes and then let it continue its course to the other window.

It was a great risk, not of explosion, but of being heard; but with a curious feeling of reckless excitement upon me I held up the canister, stepping softly over the ash floor, and guiding the terrible machine on till the danger was passed.

Then stealing after it I climbed gently on to the broad bench beneath the clean window, and with my head just beneath it touched the wire, and waited till the canister touched my hand again.

I had made no plans, but, urged on by the spirit of the moment, I seized the canister with both hands, gave it a tremendous jerk, and with my face at the window roared out:

"Now, fire! Fire! Shoot 'em down!"

I stood on the work-bench then, astounded at the effect of my cry.

Behind me there was a jerk at the wire, which snapped, and I heard the rush of feet in the lane, while before me out from the window there came a yell, a tremendous splash, and then the sound of water being beaten, and cries for help.

At the same moment Piter came rushing into the furnace house, barking furiously, and directly after there was the noise of feet on the stairs, and Uncle Jack came in.

"What is it, Cob? Where's your light?" he cried.

I had forgotten the lantern, but I turned it on now as I tucked the canister beneath my arm.

"There's a man or two men drowning out here in the dam," I panted hoarsely; and Uncle Jack leaped on to the bench by my side.

"Give me the lantern," he cried; and, taking it from my wet hands, he turned it on, held it to the open window, and made it play upon the surface of the dam.

"There are two men there, swimming to the side," he cried. "Stop, you scoundrels!" he roared; but the beating noise in the water increased. One seemed to get his footing and held out his hand to his companion in distress. The next minute I saw that they had gained the stone wall at the side, over which they clambered, and from there we heard them drop down on to the gravel stones.

"They're gone, Cob," said my uncle.

"Shall we run after them?" I said.

"It would be madness," he replied. "Down, Piter! Quiet, good dog!"

"Now what's the meaning of it all?" he said after turning the light round the place. "What did you hear? Were they getting in?"

"No," I said; "they were trying to draw this canister on to the fire with the wire; but I heard them and got hold of it."

Uncle Jack turned the light of the bull's-eye on to the canister I held, and then turned it off again, as if there were danger of its doing some harm with the light alone, even after it had passed through glass.

"Why, Cob," he said huskily, "did you get hold of that?"

"Yes, I stopped it," I said, trembling now that the excitement had passed.

"But was the fuse alight?"

"No," I said; "they were going to draw it over the fire there, only I found it out in time."

"Why, Cob," he whispered, "there's a dozen pounds of powder here wrapped round with all this fuse. Come with me to put it in a place of safety: why, it would have half-wrecked our works."

"Would it?" I said.

"Would it, boy! It would have been destruction, perhaps death. Cob," he whispered huskily, "ought we to go on watching?"

"Oh, Uncle Jack," I said, "I suppose I am foolish because I am so young!"

"Cob, my boy," he said softly; "if you had been ten times as old you could not have done better than you have done to-night. Here, let's place this dreadful canister in the water chamber: it will be safer there."

"But the men; will they come again?"

"Not to-night, my lad. I think we are safe for a few hours to come. But what of the future, if these blind savages will do such things as this?"

Chapter Nine.

Drowning an Enemy.

I did not sleep that morning, but kept watch with Uncle Jack, and as soon as the men came to work I hurried off to Mrs Stephenson's to tell the others of the night's adventures.

Half an hour later they were with me at the works, where a quiet examination was made, everything being done so as not to take the attention of the work-people, who were now busy.

We had first of all a good look round outside, and found that beneath the window of the furnace-house there were some half dozen great nails or spikes carefully driven into the wall, between the stones, so as to make quite a flight of steps for an active man, and across the window lay a tangled-together length of thin wire.

We did not stop to draw out the nails for fear of exciting attention, but strolled back at once into the works.

And now once for all, when I say *we*, please to understand that it is not out of conceit, for my share in our adventures was always very small, but to avoid uncling you all too much, and making so many repetitions of the names of Uncle Dick, Uncle Jack, and Uncle Bob.

I saw several of the men look up from their work as we went through the grinding-shop, but they went on again with their task, making the blades they ground shriek as they pressed them against the swiftly revolving stones.

"They must know all about it, Uncle Bob," I whispered, and he gave me a meaning look.

"Yes," he said softly; "that's the worst of it, my lad. Master and man ought to shake hands and determine to fight one for the other; but, as you see, they take opposite sides, and it is war."

We went next into the wheel-pit and had a look round, after which Uncle Jack spoke aloud to the man who acted as general engineer, and said he thought that the great axle wanted seeing to and fresh cleaning.

The man nodded, and said gruffly that he would see to it, and then, as he turned away, I saw him wink at one of the men grinding at a stone and thrust his tongue into his cheek.

Just then he caught my eye, his countenance changed, and he looked as foolish as a boy found out in some peccadillo, but the next instant he scowled at me, and his fierce dark eyes said as plainly as if they spoke:

"Say a word about that and I'll half kill you."

I read the threat aright, as will be seen; and, turning to follow my uncles, I saw that the man was coming on close behind me, with a look in his countenance wonderfully like that with which he was being followed by Piter, who, unobserved, was close at his heels, sniffing quietly at his legs and looking as if he would like to fix his teeth in one or the other.

Seeing this I stopped back, half expecting that Piter, if left behind, might be kicked by the man's heavy clogs. The others did not notice my absence, but went on out of the grinding-shop, and the engineer came close up to me, stooping down as I waited, and putting his face close to mine.

"Look here, mester," he began in a low threatening tone, "do you know what's meant by keeping thy tongue atween thy teeth?"

"Yes," I cried; and in the same breath, "Mind the dog! Down, Piter! Down!"

The man made a convulsive leap as he caught sight of the dog, and his intention was to alight upon the frame-work of one of the large grindstones close by his side—one that had just been set in motion, but though he jumped high enough he did not allow for the lowness of the ceiling, against which he struck his head, came down in a sitting position on the grindstone, and was instantly hurled off to the floor.

This was Piter's opportunity, and with a low growl and a bound he was upon the man's chest. Another moment and he would have had him by the throat, but I caught him by the collar and dragged him off, amidst the murmur of some, and the laughter of others of the men.

I did not want to look as if I was afraid, but this seemed to be a good excuse for leaving the grinding-shop, and, holding on by Piter's collar, I led him out.

Just before I reached the door, though, I heard one of the men say to his neighbour—heard it plainly over the whirr and churring of the stones:

"I've know'd dawgs poisoned for less than that."

"What shall I do?" I asked myself as soon as I was outside; but the answer did not come. I could only think that my uncles had trouble enough on their hands, and that though it was very evident that the men at work for them were not very well affected, it was not likely that we had any one who would wilfully do us an injury.

After all, too, nobody had threatened to poison the dog; it was only a remark about what had been known to happen.

All this had taken but a very short time, and by the time I had joined my uncles they were just entering the office on the upper floor that looked over the dam.

There were several men at work here at lathes and benches, and their tools made so much noise that they did not notice my entrance, closely followed by the dog; and so it was that I found out that they, too, must have known all about the cowardly attempt of the night, for one said to another:

"Didn't expect to be at work here this morning; did you, mate?"

"No," growled the man addressed; "but why can't they leave un aloan. They pay reg'lar, and they're civil."

"What do you mean?" said the first speaker sharply. "You going to side wi' un! What do we want wi' a set o' inventing corckneys here!"

Just then he caught sight of me, and swung round and continued his work, while I walked straight to the office door and went in, where Uncle Jack was just opening a window that looked out upon the dam.

"Yes," he said, "here we are."

He pointed to a sort of raft formed of a couple of planks placed about five feet apart and across which a dozen short pieces of wood had been nailed, forming a buoyant platform, on which no doubt our enemies had floated themselves down from the head of the dam, where there was a timber yard.

"All plain enough now," said Uncle Jack, grinding his teeth. "Oh, if I could have had hold of those two fellows by the collar when they fell in!"

"Well," said Uncle Bob, "what would you have done—drowned them?"

"Not quite," said Uncle Jack; "but they would have swallowed a great deal more water than would have been good for them."

"Never mind about impossible threats," said Uncle Dick. "Let's examine the powder canister now."

This was taken from its resting-place during the time the men were at breakfast and carried into the office, where the dangerous weapon of our enemies was laid upon the desk and examined.

It was a strong tin canister about ten inches high and six across, and bound round and round, first with strong string and afterwards loosely with some soft black-looking cord, which Uncle Dick said was fuse; and he pointed out where one end was passed through a little hole punched through the bottom of the canister, while the loosely-twisted fuse was held on by thin wire, which allowed the soft connection with the powder to hang out in loops.

"Yes," said Uncle Dick; "if that is good fuse, the very fact of any part touching a spark or smouldering patch of ash would be enough to set it alight, and there is enough, I should say, to burn for a quarter of an hour before it reaches the powder. Yes, a good ten pounds of it," he added, balancing the canister in his hands.

"But it may be a scare," said Uncle Bob: "done to frighten us. We don't know yet that it is powder."

"Oh, we'll soon prove that," cried Uncle Jack, taking out his knife.

"Uncle! Take care!" I cried in agony, for I seemed to see sparks flying from his knife, and the powder exploding and blowing us to atoms.

"If you are afraid, Cob, you had better go back home," he said rather gruffly, as he cut the fuse through and tore it off, to lie in a little heap as soon as he had freed it from the wire.

Then the string followed, and the canister stood upright before us on the desk.

"Looks as harmless as if it were full of arrow-root or mustard," said Uncle Bob coolly. "Perhaps, after all, it is a scare."

I stood there with my teeth closed tightly, determined not to show fear, even if the horrible stuff did blow up. For though there was no light in the room, and the matches were in a cupboard, I could not get out of my head the idea that the stuff *might* explode, and it seemed terrible to me for such a dangerous machine to be handled in what appeared to be so reckless a way.

"Lid fits pretty tight," said Uncle Jack, trying to screw it off.

"Don't do that, old fellow," said Uncle Dick. "It would be grinding some of the dust round, and the friction might fire it."

"Well, yes, it might," replied Uncle Jack. "Not likely though, and I want to examine the powder."

"That's easily done, my boy. Pull that bit of fuse out of the hole, and let some of the powder trickle out."

"Bravo! Man of genius," said Uncle Jack; and he drew out the plug of fuse that went through the bottom of the canister.

As he did this over a sheet of paper a quantity of black grains like very coarse dry sand began to trickle out and run on to the paper, forming quite a heap, and as the powder ran Uncle Jack looked round at his brother and smiled sadly.

"Not done to frighten us, eh, Bob!" he said. "If that stuff had been fired the furnace-house and chimney would have been levelled."

"Why, Cob," said Uncle Dick, laying his hand affectionately upon my shoulder. "You must be a brave fellow to have hauled that away from the furnace."

"I did not feel very brave just now," I said bitterly. "When Uncle Jack began to handle that tin I felt as if I must run away."

"But you didn't," said Uncle Bob, smiling at me.

"Is that gunpowder?" I said hastily, so as to change the conversation.

"No doubt of it, my lad," said Uncle Jack, scooping it up in his hand, so that it might trickle through his fingers. "Strong blasting powder. Shall I fire some and try?"

"If you like," I said sulkily, for it was, I knew, said to tease me.

"Well, what's to be done, boys?" said Uncle Jack. "Are we going to lay this before the police? It is a desperate business!"

"Desperate enough, but we shall do no good, and only give ourselves a great deal of trouble if we go to the law. The police might trace out one of the offenders; but if they did, what then? It would not stop the attempts to harm us. No: I'm of opinion that our safety lies in our own watchfulness. A more terrible attempt than this could not be made."

"What shall we do with the powder, then?" asked Uncle Bob; "save it to hoist some of the scoundrels with their own petard?"

"Oh, of course if you like," said Uncle Jack. "Fancy Bob trying to blow anybody up with gunpowder!"

"When he can't even do it with his breath made into words."

"Ah! Joke away," said Uncle Bob; "but I want to see you get rid of that horrible stuff."

"We don't want to save it then?" said Uncle Jack.

"No, no; get rid of it."

"That's soon done then," said Uncle Jack, tying a piece of the cord round the canister; and, going to the open window, he lowered it down over the deep water in the dam, where it sank like a stone, and drew the cord after it out of sight.

"There," he cried, "that will soon be so soaked with water that it will be spoiled."

"Who's that," I said, "on the other side of the dam? He's watching us."

"Squintum the grinder. What's his name—Griggs. Yes, I shouldn't be a bit surprised if that scoundrel had a hand—"

"Both hands," put in Uncle Bob.

"Well, both hands in this ugly business."

"But couldn't you prove it against him?" I said.

"No, my lad," said Uncle Jack; "and I don't know that we want to. Wretched misguided lumps of ignorance. I don't want to help to transport the villains."

We had drawn back from the window to where there was still a little heap of powder on the desk as well as the fuse.

"Come, Bob," said Uncle Jack; "you may not be quite convinced yet, so I'll show you an experiment."

He took about a teaspoonful of the powder, and placed it in a short piece of iron pipe which he laid on the window-sill, and then taking the rest of the explosive, he gave it a jerk and scattered it over the water.

Then taking about a yard of the black soft cord that he said was fuse, he tucked one end in the pipe so that it should rest upon the powder, laid the rest along the window-sill, and asked me to get the matches.

"Now," he said, "if that's what I think—cleverly made fuse, and good strong powder—we shall soon see on a small scale what it would have done on a large. Strike a match, Cob."

I did as I was told, feeling as if I was going to let off a very interesting firework, and as soon as the splint was well alight I was about to hold the little flame to the end of the fuse, but Uncle Jack stopped me.

"No," he said, "I want to see if a spark would have lit it. I mean I want to see if just drawing the canister over the remains of the furnace-fire would have started the fuse. That's it, now just touch the end quickly with the match."

There was only a little spark on the wood, and no flame, as I touched the side of the fuse.

The effect was instantaneous. The soft black-looking cord burst into scintillations, tiny sparks flew off on all sides, and a dull fire began to burn slowly along the fuse.

"Capitally made," said Uncle Jack. "That would have given the scoundrels plenty of warning that the work was well done, and they would have been able to get to a distance before the explosion took place."

"And now we shall see whether the powder is good," said Uncle Dick.

"But how slowly it burns!" said Uncle Bob.

"But how surely," I had it on my lips to say.

I did not speak though, for I was intently watching the progress of the sparks as they ran along the fuse slowly and steadily; and as I gazed I seemed to see what would have gone on in the great dark building if I had not been awakened by the scraping sound of the canister being hauled over bench and floor.

I shuddered as I watched intently, for the fuse seemed as if it would never burn through, and even when, after what in my excitement seemed a long space of time, it did reach the iron pipe, though a few sparks came from inside, the powder did not explode.

"Uncle Bob's right!" I cried with an intense feeling of relief; "that was not powder, and they only tried to frighten us."

Puff!

There was a sharp flash from each end of the iron tube, and one little ball of white smoke came into the office, while another darted out into the sunny morning air.

"Wrong, Cob," said Uncle Jack. "Splendidly-made fuse and tremendously-strong powder. We have had a very narrow escape. Now, lads, what's to be done?"

"What do you say, Jack?" said Uncle Dick.

"Do our duty—be always on the watch—fight it out."

"That's settled," said Uncle Dick. "Now let's get to work again. Cob, you can come and see us cast some steel ingots if you like."

"Cast!" I said.

"Yes, cast. You know what that is?"

"Yes, of course."

"But you never saw it liquid so that it could be poured out like water."

"No," I said, as I followed him, wondering whether I had not better tell him that I had overheard a strange remark about poisoning a dog, and ask if he thought there was any risk about Piter, who seemed to grow much uglier every day, and yet I liked him better.

The end of it was that I saw the steel lifted out of the furnace in crucibles and poured forth like golden-silver water into charcoal moulds, but I did not speak about the dog.

Chapter Ten.

"'Night, Mate."

As it happened, Mr Tomplin came in that evening, and when he asked how matters were progressing at the works, Uncle Dick looked round and seemed to be asking his brothers whether he should speak.

"Ah! I see," said Mr Tomplin; "they have been up to some tricks with you."

"Tricks is a mild term," said Uncle Jack bitterly.

"They have not tried to blow you up?"

"Indeed but they did!" said Uncle Jack fiercely; "and if it had not been for the coolness and bravery of my nephew there the place would have been destroyed."

"Tut! Tut! Tut!" ejaculated Mr Tomplin; and putting on his spectacles he stared at me in the most provoking way, making me feel as if I should like to knock his glasses off.

"Is it customary for your people here to fire canisters of gunpowder in the workshops of those who are newcomers?"

"Sometimes," said Mr Tomplin coolly.

"But such things would destroy life."

"Well, not always life, my dear sir," said Mr Tomplin, "but very often great bodily injury is done."

"Very often?"

"Well, no, not very often now, but we have had a great many trade outrages in our time."

"But what have we done beyond taking possession of a building for which we have paid a large sum of money?"

"It is not what you have done, my dear sirs; it is what you are about to do. The work-people have got it into their heads that you are going to invent some kind of machinery that will throw them out of work."

"Nothing of the kind, my dear sir. We are trying to perfect an invention that will bring a vast deal of trade to Arrowfield."

"But you will not be able to make them believe that till the business comes."

"And before then, I suppose, we are to be killed?"

Mr Tomplin looked very serious, and stared hard at me, as if it was all my fault.

"My dear sirs," he said at last, "I hardly know how to advise you. It is a most unthankful task to try and invent anything, especially down here. People are so blindly obstinate and wilful that they will not listen to reason. Why not go steadily on with manufacturing in the regular way? What do you say, my young friend?" he added, turning to me.

"Why not ask the world to stand still, sir?" I exclaimed impetuously. "I say it's a shame!"

He looked very hard at me, and then pursed up his lips, while I felt that I had been speaking very rudely to him, and could only apologise to myself by thinking that irritation was allowable, for only last night we had been nearly blown up.

"Would you put the matter in the hands of the police?" said Uncle Dick.

"Well, you might," said Mr Tomplin.

"But you would not," said Uncle Bob.

"No, I don't think I should, if it were my case. I should commence an action for damages if I could find an enemy who had any money, but it is of no use fighting men of straw."

Mr Tomplin soon after went away, and I looked at my uncles, wondering what they would say. But as they did not speak I broke out with:

"Why, he seemed to think nothing of it."

"Custom of the country," said Uncle Bob, laughing. "Come, Dick, it's our turn now."

"Right!" said Uncle Dick; but Uncle Jack laid hold of his shoulder.

"Look here," he said. "I don't like the idea of you two going down there."

"No worse for us than for you," said Uncle Bob.

"Perhaps not, but the risk seems too great."

"Never mind," said Uncle Dick. "I'm not going to be beaten. It's war to the knife, and I'm not going to give up."

"They are not likely to try anything to-night," said Uncle Bob. "There, you two can walk down with us and look round to see if everything is all right and then come back."

"Don't you think you ought to have pistols?" said Uncle Jack.

"No," replied Uncle Dick firmly. "We have our sticks, and the dog, and we'll do our best with them. If a pistol is used it may mean the destruction of a life, and I would rather give up our adventure than have blood upon our hands."

"Yes, you are right," said Uncle Jack. "If bodily injury or destruction is done let them have the disgrace on their side."

We started off directly, and I could not help noticing how people kept staring at my uncles.

It was not the respectably-dressed people so much as the rough workmen, who were hanging about with their pipes, or standing outside the public-house doors. These scowled and talked to one another in a way that I did not like, and more than once I drew Uncle Dick's attention to it, but he only smiled.

"We're strangers," he said. "They'll get used to us by and by."

There was not a soul near the works as we walked up to the gate and were saluted with a furious fit of barking from Piter, who did not know our steps till the key was rattled in the gate. Then he stopped at once and gave himself a shake and whined.

It was growing dusk as we walked round the yard, to find everything quite as it should be. A look upstairs and down showed nothing suspicious; and after a few words regarding keeping a sharp look-out and the like we left the watchers of the night and walked back.

"Cob," said Uncle Jack as we sat over our supper, "I don't like those two poor fellows being left there by themselves."

"Neither do I, uncle," I said. "Why not give up watching the place and let it take its chance?"

"Because we had such an example of the safety of the place and the needlessness of the task?"

"Don't be hard on me, uncle," I said quickly. "I meant that it would be better to suffer serious loss than to have someone badly injured in defending the place."

"You're right, Cob—quite right," cried Uncle Jack, slapping the table.

"Here, you make me feel like a boy. I believe you were born when you were an old man."

"Nonsense!" I said, laughing.

"But you don't talk nonsense, sir. What are you—a fairy changeling? Here, let's go down to the works."

"Go down?" I said.

"To be sure. I couldn't go to bed to-night and sleep. I should be thinking that those two poor fellows were being blown up, or knob-sticked, or turned out. We'll have them back and leave Piter to take care of the works, and give him a rise in his wages."

"Of an extra piece of meat every day, uncle?"

"If you had waited a few minutes longer, sir, I should have said that," he replied, laughing; and taking his hat and stick we went down the town, talking about the curious vibrations and throbbings we could hear; of the heavy rumbling and the flash and glow that came from the different works. Some were so lit up that it seemed as if the windows were fiery eyes staring out of the darkness, and more than once we stopped to gaze in at some cranny where furnaces were kept going night and day and the work never seemed to stop.

As we left the steam-engine part behind, the solitary stillness of our district seemed to be more evident; and though we passed one policeman, I could not help thinking how very little help we should be able to find in a case of great emergency.

Uncle Jack had chatted away freely enough as we went on; but as we drew nearer to the works he became more and more silent, and when we had reached the lane he had not spoken for fully ten minutes.

Eleven o'clock was striking and all seemed very still. Not a light was visible on that side, and the neighbouring works were apparently quite empty as we stood and listened.

"Let's walk along by the side of the dam, Cob," said Uncle Jack. "I don't suppose we shall see anything, but let's have a look how the place seems by night."

I followed close behind him, and we passed under the one gas lamp that showed the danger of the path to anyone going along; for in the darkness there was nothing to prevent a person from walking right into the black dam, which looked quite beautiful and countrified now, spangled all over, as it was, with the reflections of the stars.

I was going to speak, but Uncle Jack raised his hand for me to be silent, and I crept closer to him, wondering what reason he had for stopping me; and then he turned and caught my arm, for we had reached the end of the dam where it communicated with the river.

Just then two men approached, and one said to the other:

"Tell 'ee, they changes every night. Sometimes it's one and the boy, sometimes two on 'em together. The boy was there last night, and— Hullo! 'Night, mate!"

"'Night!" growled Uncle Jack in an assumed voice as he slouched down and gave me a shake. "Coom on, wilt ta!" he said hoarsely; and I followed him without a word.

"I tried it, Cob," he whispered as we listened to the retreating steps of the men. "I don't think they knew us in the dark."

"They were talking about us," I said.

"Yes; that made me attempt to disguise my voice. Here, let's get back. Hark! There's the dog. Quick! Something may be wrong."

We set off at a trot in the direction that the men had taken, but we did not pass them, for they had gone down to their right; but there was no doubt existing that the affairs at the works were well known and that we were surrounded by enemies; and perhaps some of them were busy now, for Jupiter kept on his furious challenge, mingling it with an angry growl, that told of something being wrong.

Chapter Eleven.

Pannell's Pet.

"Who's there?"

"All right—open the door! Cob and I have come down to see how you are getting on," said Uncle Jack.

The gate was unlocked and a stout iron bar that had been added to the defences taken down.

"Why, what brings you two here?" cried Uncle Dick. "What's the matter?"

"That's what we want to know. How long has the dog been uneasy?"

"For the past hour. I had gone to lie down; Bob was watchman. All at once Piter began barking furiously, and I got up directly."

"Let's have another look round," said Uncle Jack.

"Here, Piter!" I cried; "what's the matter, old fellow?"

The dog whined and laid his great jowl in my hand, blinking up at me and trying to make his savage grin seem to be a pleasant smile; but all at once he started away, threw up his head, and barked again angrily.

"What is it, old fellow?" I said. "Here, show us them. What is it?"

Piter looked at me, whined, and then barked again angrily as if there was something very wrong indeed; but he could only smell it in the air. What it was or where it was he did not seem to know.

We had a good look round, searching everywhere, and not without a great deal of trepidation; for after the past night's experience with the powder it was impossible to help feeling nervous.

That's what Uncle Jack called it. I felt in a regular fright.

"Everything seems quite satisfactory," Uncle Jack was fain to say at last. And then, "Look here, boys," he cried, "Cob and I have been talking this matter over, and we say that the works must take care of themselves. You two have to come back with us."

"What! And leave the place to its fate?" said Uncle Dick.

"Yes. Better do that than any mishap should come to you."

"What do you say, Bob?"

"I've a very great objection to being blown up, knocked on the head, or burned," said Uncle Bob quietly. "It's just so with a soldier; he does not want to be shot, bayoneted, or sabred, but he has to take his chance. I'm going to take mine."

"So am I," said Uncle Dick.

"But, my dear boys—"

"There, it's of no use; is it, Bob?" cried Uncle Dick. "If we give way he'll always be bouncing over us about how he kept watch and we daren't."

"Nonsense!" cried Uncle Jack.

"Well, if you didn't," said Uncle Bob, "that cocky consequential small man of a boy, Cob, will be always going about with his nose in the air and sneering. I shall stay."

"Then we will stay with you."

My uncles opposed this plan, but Uncle Jack declared that he could not sleep if he went back; so the others gave in and we stayed, taking two hours turns, and the night passed slowly by.

Every now and then Piter had an uneasy fit, bursting out into a tremendous series of barks and howls, but there seemed to be no reason for the outcry.

He was worst during the watch kept by Uncle Jack and me after we had had a good sleep, and there was something very pathetic in the way the poor dog looked at us, as much as to say, "I wish I could speak and put you on your guard."

But the night passed without any trouble; the men came in to their work, and with the darkness the fear seemed to have passed away. For there in the warm sunshine the water of the dam was dancing and sparkling, the great wheel went round, and inside the works the grindstones were whizzing and the steel being ground was screeching. Bellows puffed, and fires roared, and there was the *clink clank* of hammers sounding musically upon the anvils, as the men forged blades out of the improved steel my uncles were trying to perfect.

Business was increasing, and matters went so smoothly during the next fortnight that our troubles seemed to be at an end. In one week six fresh men were engaged, and after the sluggish times in London, where for a couple of years past business had been gradually dying off, everything seemed to be most encouraging.

Some of the men engaged were queer characters. One was a great swarthy giant with hardly any face visible for black hair, and to look at he seemed fit for a bandit, but to talk to he was one of the most gentle and amiable of men. He was a smith, and when he was at the anvil he used almost to startle me, he handled a heavy hammer so violently.

I often stood at the door watching him seize a piece of steel with the tongs, whisk it out of the forge with a flourish that sent the white-hot scintillations flying through the place, bang it down on the anvil, and then beat it savagely into the required shape.

Then he would thrust it into the fire again, begin blowing the bellows with one hand and stroke a kitten that he kept at the works with his unoccupied hand, talking to it all the time in a little squeaking voice like a boy's.

He was very fond of swinging the sparkling and sputtering steel about my head whenever I went in, but he was always civil, and the less I heeded his queer ways the more civil he became.

There was a grinder, too, taken on at the same time, a short round-looking man, with plump cheeks, and small eyes which were often mere slits in his face. He had a little soft nose, too, that looked like a plump thumb, and moved up and down and to right and left when he was intent upon his work. He was the best-tempered man in the works, and seemed to me as if he was always laughing and showing his two rows of firm white teeth.

I somehow quite struck up an acquaintance with these two men, for while the others looked askant at me and treated me as if I were my uncle's spy, sent into the works to see how the men kept on, Pannell the smith and Gentles the grinder were always ready to be civil.

My friendliness with Pannell began one morning when I had caught a mouse up in the office overlooking the dam, where I spent most of my time making drawings and models with Uncle Bob.

This mouse I took down as a *bonne bouche* for Pannell's kitten, and as soon as he saw the little creature seize it and begin to spit and swear, he rested upon his hammer handle and stopped to watch it.

Next time I went into the smithy he did not flourish the white-hot steel round my head, but gave it a flourish in another direction, banged it down upon the anvil, and in a very short time had turned it into the blade of a small hand-bill.

"You couldn't do that," he said smiling, as he cooled the piece of steel and threw it down on the floor before taking out another.

"Not like that," I said. "I could do it roughly."

"Yah! Not you," he said. "Try."

I was only too eager, and seizing the pincers I took out one of the glowing pieces of steel lying ready, laid it upon the anvil and beat it into shape, forming a rough imitation of the work I had been watching, but with twice as many strokes, taking twice as long, and producing work not half so good.

When I had done he picked up the implement, turned it over and over, looked at me, threw it down, and then went and stroked his kitten, staring straight before him.

"Why, I couldn't ha' done a bit o' forging like that when I'd been at it fower year," he said in his high-pitched voice.

"But my uncles have often shown me how," I said.

"What! Can they forge?" he said, staring very hard at me.

"Oh, yes, as well as you can!"

He blew hard at the kitten and then shook his head in a dissatisfied way, after which it seemed as if I had offended him, for he seized his hammer and pincers and began working away very hard, finishing a couple of the steel bill-hooks before he spoke again.

"Which on 'em 'vented this here contrapshion?" he said, pointing to an iron bar, by touching which he could direct a blast of air into his fire without having the need of a man or boy to blow.

"Uncle John," I said.

"What! Him wi' the biggest head?"

I nodded.

"Yes; he said that with the water-wheel going it was easy to contrive a way to blow the fires."

"Humph! Can he forge a bill-hook or a scythe blade?"

"Oh, yes!"

"Who's 'venting the noo steel?"

"Oh, they are all helping! It was Uncle Richard who first started it."

"Oh, Uncle Richard, was it?" he said thoughtfully. "Well, it won't niver do."

"Why?"

"Snap a two, and never bear no edge."

"Who says so?"

"Traäde," he cried. "Steel was good enough as it weer."

Just then, as luck had it, Uncle Jack came into the smithy, and stood and watched the man as he scowled heavily and flourished out the hot steel as if he resented being watched.

"You are not forging those hand-bills according to pattern, my man," said Uncle Jack, as he saw one finished, Pannell beating the steel with savage vehemence, and seeming as if he wished it were Uncle Jack's head.

"That's way to forge a hand-bill," said the man sourly.

"Your way," said Uncle Jack quietly. "Not mine. I gave you a pattern. These are being made of a new steel."

"Good for nought," said the man; but Uncle Jack paid no heed, assuming not to have heard the remark.

"And I want them to look different to other people's."

"Do it yoursen then," said the great fellow savagely; and he threw down the hammer and pincers.

"Yes, perhaps I had better," said Uncle Jack, rolling up his white shirt-sleeves, after taking off his coat and throwing it to me.

I saw Pannell glower at the pure white skin that covered great muscles as big and hard as his own, while, after unhooking a leather apron from where it hung, the lever was touched, the fire roared, and at last Uncle Jack brought out a piece of white-hot steel, banged it on the anvil, and rapidly beat it into shape.

Every stroke had its object, and not one unnecessary blow fell, while in a short time he held in the water, which hissed angrily, a hand-bill that was beautifully made, and possessed a graceful curve and hook that the others wanted.

"There," said Uncle Jack. "That's how I want them made."

The man's face was set in a savage vindictive look, full of jealous annoyance, at seeing a well-dressed gentleman strip and use the smith's hammer and pincers better than he could have used them himself.

"Make me one now after that pattern," said Uncle Jack.

It seemed to me that the giant was going to tear off his leather apron furiously and stride out of the place; but just then Uncle Jack stretched out his great strong hand and lifted up Pannell's kitten, which had sprung upon the forge and was about to set its little paws on the hot cinders.

"Poor pussy!" he said, standing it in one hand and stroking it with the other. "You mustn't burn those little paws and singe that coat. Is this the one that had the mouse, Cob?"

Just as I answered, "Yes," I saw the great smith change his aspect, pick up the still hot hand-bill that Uncle Jack had forged, stare hard at it on both sides, and then, throwing it down, he seized the pincers in one hand, the forge shovel in the other, turned on the blast and made the fire glow, and at last whisked out a piece of white-hot steel.

This he in turn banged down on the anvil—*stithy* he called it—and beat into shape.

It was not done so skilfully as Uncle Jack had forged his, but the work was good and quick, and when he had done, the man cooled it and held it out with all the rough independence of the north-countryman.

"Suppose that may do, mester," he said, and he stared at where Uncle Jack still stroked the kitten, which made a platform of his broad palm, and purred and rubbed itself against his chest.

"Capitally!" said Uncle Jack, setting down the kitten gently. "Yes; I wouldn't wish to see better work."

"Aw raight!" said Pannell; and he went on with his work, while Uncle Jack and I walked across the yard to the office.

"We shall get all right with the men by degrees, Cob," he said. "That fellow was going to be nasty, but he smoothed himself down. You see now the use of a master being able to show his men how to handle their tools."

"Yes," I said, laughing; "but that was not all. Pannell would have gone if it had not been for one thing."

"What was that?" he said.

"You began petting his kitten, and that made him friends."

I often used to go into the smithy when Pannell was at work after that, and now and then handled his tools, and he showed me how to use them more skilfully, so that we were pretty good friends, and he never treated me as if I were a spy.

The greater part of the other men did, and no matter how civil I was they showed their dislike by having accidents as they called them, and these accidents always happened when I was standing by and at no other time.

For instance a lot of water would be splashed, so that some fell upon me; a jet of sparks from a grindstone would flash out in my face as I went past; the band of a stone would be loosened, so that it flapped against me and knocked off my cap. Then pieces of iron fell, or were thrown, no one knew which, though they knew where, for the place was generally on or close by my unfortunate body.

I was in the habit of frequently going to look down in the wheel chamber or pit, and one day, as I stepped on to the threshold, my feet

89

glided from under me, and, but for my activity in catching at and hanging by the iron bar that crossed the way I should have plunged headlong in.

There seemed to be no reason for such a slip, but the men laughed brutally, and when I looked I found that the sill had been well smeared with fat.

There was the one man in the grinders' shop, though, whom I have mentioned, and who never seemed to side with his fellow workers, but looked half pityingly at me whenever I seemed to be in trouble.

I went into the grinding-shop one morning, where all was noise and din, the wheels spinning and the steel shrieking as it was being ground, when all at once a quantity of water such as might have been thrown from a pint pot came all over me.

I turned round sharply, but every one was at work except the stout grinder, who, with a look of disgust on his face, stood wiping his neck with a blue cotton handkerchief, and then one cheek.

"Any on it come on you, mester?" he said.

"Any come on me!" I cried indignantly—"look."

"It be a shaäm—a reg'lar shaäm," he said slowly; "and I'd like to know who throwed that watter. Here, let me."

He came from his bench, or horse as the grinders call their seat, and kindly enough brushed the water away from my jacket with his handkerchief.

"Don't tak' no notice of it," he said. "They're nobbut a set o' fullish boys as plays they tricks, and if you tell on 'em they'll give it to you worse."

I took his advice, and said nothing then, but naturally enough, spoke to my uncles about it when we were alone at night.

"Never mind," said Uncle Dick. "I daresay we shall get the fellows to understand in time that we are their friends and not their enemies."

"Yes," said Uncle Jack; "they are better. I dare say it will all come right in time."

It was soon after this that I went into the grinding-shop one day while the men were at dinner, and going to the door that opened into the wheel chamber, which always had a fascination for me, I stood gazing down into its depths and listening to the splashing water.

"Iver try to ketch any o' them long eels, Mester Jacob?" said a familiar voice; and, starting and looking back, I saw that Gentles, the fat little grinder, was sitting down close to his wet grindstone eating his dinner, and cutting it with a newly ground knife blade forged out of our new steel.

"Eels, Gentles!" I said. "I didn't know there were any there."

"Oh, but there are," he said; "straänge big 'uns. You set a line with a big bait on, and you'll soon hev one."

"What, down there by the wheel?"

"Ay, or oop i' the dam. Plenty o' eels, lad, theer."

"I'll have a try," I said eagerly, for the idea of catching one or two of the creatures was attractive.

From that I got talking to the man about his work, and he promised to let me have a few turns at grinding.

"On'y, what am I to say if thee coots theesen?" he cried with a chuckle.

"Oh, but you'll show me how to do it without!" I said laughing.

"Nay, but what's good o' thee wanting to grind? Want to tak' work out o' poor men's hands?"

"Nonsense!" I cried angrily. "Why, Gentles, you know better than that. All I want is to understand thoroughly how it is done, so that I can talk to the men about their work, and show them if it isn't right."

"Oh!" he said in a curious tone of voice. "Well, you coom any time when watter-wheel's going, and I'll show thee all that I know. 'Tain't much. Keeps men fro' starving."

"Why, Gentles," I cried; "you drew three pounds five last week, and I saw you paid."

"Three pun' five! Did I?" he said. "Ah, but that was a partic'lar good week. I've got a missus and a lot o' bairns to keep, and times is very bad, mester."

"I'm sorry for it," I said; and I went away and had a look in the books as soon as I reached the office, to find that Master Gentles never drew less than three pounds a-week; but I did not remind him of it, and during the next few days he very civilly showed me how his work was done—that is, the knack of holding and turning the blades, so that I rapidly acquired the way, and was too busy to notice the peculiar looks I received from the other men.

Of course I know how that I was a mere bungler, and clumsy, and slow in the extreme; but at the time I felt as if I must be very clever, and there was something very satisfactory in seeing a blackened hammered blade fresh from the forge turn bright and clean in my hands, while the edge grew sharp and even.

It was playing with edged tools with a vengeance, but I did not understand it then.

Chapter Twelve.

Pannell's Secret.

Every day the works grew more busy, and prosperity seemed to be coming upon us like sunshine. The men worked steadily and well, and the old opposition had apparently died out; but all the same the watching was kept up as regularly as if it was during war time, though, saving an occasional burst of barking from Piter, who used to have these fits apparently without cause, there was nothing to alarm the watchers.

It was my turn at home, and I was up early the next morning, wondering how Uncle Jack and Uncle Bob had got on during the night, when I came down and found Mrs Stephenson and Martha the maid enjoying themselves.

Their way of enjoying themselves was peculiar, but that it afforded them pleasure there could be no doubt. It might have been considered a religious ceremony, but though there was a kind of worship or adoration about it, there was nothing religious in the matter at all.

What they did was this:—To mix up a certain quantity of black-lead in a little pie-dish, and then kneel down before a stove, and work and slave at it till there was a tremendous gloss all over the iron.

In effecting this Mrs Stephenson used to get a little smudgy, but Martha seemed to have an itching nose which always itched most on these occasions, and as you watched her you saw her give six scrubs at the grate with the front of the brush, and then one rub with the back on her face or nose.

This act must have been pleasant, for as she bent down and scrubbed she frowned, as she sat up and rubbed her nose with the back of the brush she smiled.

Now if Martha had confined her rubs to her nose it would not have much mattered, but in rubbing her nose she also rubbed her cheeks, her chin, her forehead, and the consequence was a great waste of black-lead, and her personal appearance was not improved.

I was standing watching the black-leading business, an affection from which most north-country people suffer very badly, when Uncle Jack came hurrying in, looking hot and excited. "Where's Dick?" he cried.

"In his room drawing plans," I cried. "What's the matter? Is Uncle Bob hurt?"

"No, not a bit!"

"Then Piter is?"

"No, no, no. Here, Dick!" he shouted up the stairs. There was a sound on the upper floor as if some one had just woke an elephant, and Uncle Dick came lumbering down.

"What's wrong?" he cried.

Uncle Jack glanced round and saw that Mrs Stephenson was looking up from where she knelt in the front room, with her eyes and mouth wide open as the door, and Martha was slowly rubbing her nose with the black-lead brush and waiting for him to speak.

"Put on your hat and come down to the works," he said.

We moved by one impulse into the passage, and as we reached the door Mrs Stephenson cried:

"Brackfass won't be long;" and then the sound of black-leading went on.

"Now, then," said Uncle Dick as we reached the street, "what is it? Anything very wrong?"

"Terribly," said Uncle Jack.

"Well, what is it? Why don't you speak?"

"Come and see for yourself," said Uncle Jack bitterly. "I thought matters were smoothing down, but they are getting worse, and I feel sometimes that we might as well give up as carry on this unequal war."

"No: don't give up, Uncle Jack," I cried. "Let's fight the cowards."

"Bring them into the yard then so that we can fight them," he cried angrily. "The cowardly back-stabbers; sneaks in the dark. I couldn't have believed that such things could go on in England."

"Well, but we had heard something about what the Arrowfield men could do, and we knew about how in the Lancashire district the work-people used to smash new machinery."

"There, wait till you've seen what has happened," cried Uncle Jack angrily. "You've just risen after a night's rest. I've come to you after a night's watching, and you and I feel differently about the same thing."

Very little more was said before we reached the works, where the first thing I saw was a group of men round the gate, talking together with their hands in their pockets.

Gentles was among them, smoking a short black pipe, and he shut his eyes at me as we passed, which was his way of bestowing upon me a smile.

When we passed through the gate the men followed as if we were a set of doctors about to put something right for them, and as if they had been waiting for us to come.

Uncle Bob was standing by the door as we came across the yard, and as soon as we reached him he turned in and we followed.

There was no occasion for him to speak; he just walked along the great workshop, pointing to right and left, and we saw at once why the men were idling about.

Few people who read this will have any difficulty in understanding what wheel-bands are. They used to be very common in the streets, joining the wheels of the knife-grinders' barrows, and now in almost every house they are seen in the domestic treadle sewing-machine. Similar to these, but varying in size, are the bands in a factory. They may be broad flat leather straps of great weight and size, formed by sewing many lengths together, or they may be string-like cords of twisted catgut. They all come under the same name, and there were scores in our works connecting the shaft wheels of the main shaft turned by the water-power with the grindstones of the lower floor and the lathes and polishers of the upper. By these connections wheel, stone, and chuck were set spinning-round. Without them everything was at a stand-still.

As we walked down between the grindstones it was plain enough to see—every wheel-band had been cut.

It was the same upstairs—broad bands and cords all had been divided with a sharp knife, and Uncle Bob held a piece of whetstone in his hand which had been thrown down by the door, evidently after being used by the miscreant who had done this cowardly trick.

As we went upstairs and saw the mischief there the men followed us like a flock of sheep, waiting to see what we should do, for they were perforce idle. Only the smiths could work, for by accident or oversight the band which connected the shaft with the blowing apparatus had escaped, and as we stood there by the office door we could hear the *clink clink* of the hammers upon the anvils and the pleasant roar of each forge.

"Hallo! What's this?" cried Uncle Jack as he caught sight of something white on the office door, which proved to be a letter stuck on there by a common wooden-handled shoemakers' knife having been driven right through it.

"I did not see that before," said Uncle Bob excitedly.

"No, because it was not there," said Uncle Jack. "I should have seen it if it had been there when I came out of the office first."

"And *I* am sure that I should have seen it," said Uncle Bob.

The letter was opened and read by Uncle Jack, who passed it on to his brothers.

They read it in turn, and it was handed to me, when I read as follows:

"This hear's the nif as coot them weel-bans. Stope makhin noo kine steel, or be strang and bad for wurks."

"Come in the office and let's talk it over," said Uncle Bob. "This must have been placed here by someone in the works."

"Yes," said Uncle Jack bitterly. "It is plain enough: the wheel-bands have been cut by one of the men who get their living by us, and who take our pay."

"And you see the scoundrel who wrote that letter threatens worse treatment if we do not give up making the new silver steel."

"Yes," said Uncle Jack sternly as he turned to Uncle Dick; "what do you mean to do?"

"Begin a fresh batch to-day, and let the men know it is being done. Here, let's show them that we can be as obstinate as they." Then aloud as we approached the men where they had grouped together, talking about the "cooten bands," as they termed it. "You go at once to the machinist's and get a couple of men sent on to repair such of these bands as they can, and put new ones where they are shortened too much by the mending."

Uncle Bob smiled at once.

"Look here," said Uncle Dick sharply, "some of you men can make shift by tying or binding your bands till they are properly done."

"Ay, mester," came in a growl, and shortly after the sound of steel being ground upon the sharply-spinning stones was heard. An hour later a couple of men were fitting bands to some of the wheels, and mending others by lacing them together.

I was standing watching them as they fitted a new band to Gentles' wheel, while he stood with his bared arms folded, very eager to begin work again.

"Ain't it a cruel shaäme?" he whispered. "Here's me, a poor chap paid by the piece, and this morning half gone as you may say. This job's a couple o' loaves out o' my house."

He wiped a tear out of the corner of each half-closed eye as he stared at me in a miserable helpless kind of way, and somehow he made me feel so annoyed with him that I felt as if I should like to slap his fat face and then kick him.

I went away very much exasperated and glad to get out of the reach of temptation, leaving my uncles busily superintending the fitting of the bands, and helping where they could do anything to start a man on again with his work. And all the time they seemed to make very light of the trouble, caring for nothing but getting the men started again.

I went down into the smithy, where Pannell was at work, and as I entered the place he looked for a moment from the glowing steel he was hammering into a shape, to which it yielded as if it had been so much tough wax, and then went on again as if I had not been there.

His kitten was a little more friendly, though, for it ran from the brickwork of the forge, leaped on to a bench behind me, and bounded from that on to my back, and crept to my shoulder, where it could rub its head against my ear.

"Well, Pannell," I said, "you've heard about the cowardly trick done in the shops?"

"Ay, I heered on't," he cried, as he battered away at the steel on his anvil.

"Who did it?"

"Did it!" he cried, nipping the cherry-red steel in a fresh place and thrusting it back in the fire. "Don't they know? Didn't they hear in the night?"

"No," I said; "they heard nothing, not a sound. The dog did not even bark, they say."

"Would he bite a man hard?"

"He'd almost eat a man if he attacked him."

"Ay, he looks it," said Pannell, patting the black coal-dust down over a glowing spot.

"Well, who do you think did it?" I said.

"Someone as come over the wall, I s'pose; but you'd better not talk about it."

"But I like to talk about it," I said. "Oh, I should like to find out who it was! It was someone here."

"Here!" he cried, whisking out the steel.

"Yes, the sneaking, blackguardly, cowardly hound!" I cried.

"Hush!" he whispered sharply; "some one may hear again."

I stared at the great swarthy fellow, for he looked sallow and seared, and it seemed, so strange to me that, while I only felt annoyance, he should be alarmed.

"Why, Pannell," I cried, "what's the matter?"

"Best keep a still tongue," he said in a whisper. "You never know who may hear you."

"I don't care who hears me. It was a coward and a scoundrel who cut our bands, and I should like to tell him so to his face."

"Howd thee tongue, I say," he cried, hammering away at his anvil, to drown my words in noise. "What did I tell thee?"

"That some one might hear me. Well, let him. Why, Pannell, you look as if you had done it yourself. It wasn't you, was it?"

He turned upon me quite fiercely, hammer in hand, making me think about Wat Tyler and the tax-gatherer; but he did not strike me: he brought his hammer down upon the anvil with a loud clang.

"Nay," he said; "I nivver touched no bands. It warn't my wuck."

"Well, I never thought it was," I said. "You don't look the sort of man who would be a coward."

"Oh, that's what you think, is it, lad?"

"Yes," I said, seating myself on the bench and stroking the kitten. "A blacksmith always seems to me to be a bold manly straightforward man, who would fight his enemy fairly face to face, and not go in the dark and stab him."

"Ah!" he said; "but I arn't a blacksmith, I'm a white-smith, and work in steel."

"It's much the same," I said thoughtfully; and then, looking him full in the face: "No, Pannell, I don't think you cut the bands, but I feel pretty sure you know who did."

The man's jaw dropped, and he looked quite paralysed for a moment or two. Then half recovering himself he plunged his tongs into the fire, pulled out a sputtering white piece of glowing steel, gave it his regular whirl through the air like a firework, and, instead of banging it on to the anvil, plunged it with a fierce toss into the iron water-trough, and quenched it.

"Why, Pannell!" I cried, "what made you do that?"

He scratched his head with the hand that held the hammer, and stared at me for a few moments, and then down at the black steel that he had taken dripping from the trough.

"Dunno," he said hoarsely, "dunno, lad."

"I do," I said to myself as I set down the kitten and went back to join my uncles, who were in consultation in the office.

They stopped short as I entered, and Uncle Bob turned to me. "Well, Philosopher Cob," he said, "what do you say? Who did this cowardly act—was it someone in the neighbourhood, or one of our own men?"

"Yes, who was it?" said Uncle Dick.

"We are all divided in our opinions," said Uncle Jack.

"One of our own men," I said; "and Pannell the smith knows who it was."

"And will he tell?"

"No. I think the men are like schoolboys in that. No one would speak for fear of being thought a sneak."

"Yes," said Uncle Dick, "and not only that; in these trades-unions the men are all bound together, as it were, and the one who betrayed the others' secrets would be in peril of his life."

"How are we to find out who is the scoundrel?" I said.

Uncle Dick shook his head, and did what he always found to be the most satisfactory thing in these cases, set to work as hard as he could, and Uncles Jack and Bob followed his example.

Chapter Thirteen.

Only a Glass of Water.

The keeping watch of a night had now grown into a regular business habit, and though we discovered nothing, the feeling was always upon us that if we relaxed our watchfulness for a few hours something would happen.

The paper stuck on the door was not forgotten by my uncles, but the men went on just as usual, and the workshops were as busy as ever, and after a good deal of drawing and experimenting Uncle Dick or Uncle Jack kept producing designs for knives or tools to be worked up out of the new steel.

"But," said I one day, "I don't see that this reaping-hook will be any better than the old-fashioned one."

"The steel is better and will keep sharp longer, my lad, but people would not believe that it was in the slightest degree different, unless they had something to see," said Uncle Dick.

So the men were set to forge and grind the different shaped tools and implements that were designed, and I often heard them laughing and jeering at what they called the "contrapshions."

My turn came round to keep the morning watch about a week after the new bands had been fitted. Uncle Bob had been on guard during the night, and just as I was comfortably dreaming of a pleasant country excursion I was awakened by a cheery, "Tumble up, Tumble up!"

I sat up confused and drowsy, but that soon passed off as Uncle Bob laughingly told me, in sham nautical parlance, that all was well on deck; weather hazy, and no rocks ahead as far as he knew.

"Oh," I said yawning, "I do wish all this watching was over!"

"So do I, Cob," he cried; "but never mind, we shall tire the rascals out yet."

I thought to myself that they would tire us out first, as I went down grumpily and disposed to shiver; and then, to thoroughly waken and warm myself, I had a good trot round the big furnace, where the men had tried to fire the powder.

It was circus-horse sort of work, that running round on the black ashes and iron scales, but it warmed me, and as the miserable shivery feeling went off I felt brighter and more ready for my task.

Piter was with me trotting close behind, as I ran round and round; and when at last I was pretty well out of breath I sat down on a bench, and took the dog's fore-paws on my knees, as I thought about how different my life here seemed from what I had expected. There had been some unpleasant adventures, and a good deal of work, but otherwise my daily career seemed to be very monotonous, and I wondered when our old country trips were to be renewed.

Then I had a good look round the place upstairs and down; and, so sure as I passed an open window, I felt about with my hands for wires, the memory of that powder-tin being too vivid to be forgotten.

I went and listened by the office door, and could hear my uncle breathing heavily.

I went and looked out at the dam, which was always worth looking at for its reflections of the heavens, but it was perfectly still. There was no raft gliding down towards the building.

Down in the grinders' shop all was still, and in the darkness the different shafts and wheels looked very curious and threatening, so much so that it only wanted a little imagination for one to think that this was some terrible torture chamber, the door at the end leading into the place where the water torment was administered, for the curious musical dripping and plashing sounded very thrilling and strange in the solemnity of the night.

That place always attracted me, and though there in the darkness I did not care to open the door and look down at the black water, I went and listened, and as I did so it seemed that there was something going on there. Every now and then, came a splash, and then a hurrying as of something being drawn over wet bars of wood. Then there were a series of soft thuds at irregular intervals, and as I listened all this was magnified by imagination, and I was ready to go and call for Uncle Bob to descend when a faint squeaking noise brought me to my senses and I laughed.

"Why, Piter," I said, "what a dog you are! Don't you hear the rats?"

Piter rubbed his great head against me and whined softly.

"Don't care for rats?" I said. "All right, old fellow. I forgot that you were a bull-dog and did not care for anything smaller than a bull, unless it were a man."

I stood listening for a few minutes longer, wondering whether some of the sounds I could hear down by the stonework were made by eels, and, recalling what Gentles had said, I determined that some evening I would have a try for the slimy fellows either down below the great water-wheel or out of the office-window, where I could drop a line into the deepest part of the dam.

Then I went into the smiths' shops and thought about how sulky Pannell had been ever since I had talked to him about the wheel-bands.

"This won't do, Piter," I said, trying to rouse myself, for I was dreadfully sleepy; and I had another trot with the dog after me in his solid, silent way—for he rarely barked unless it was in anger—but trotted close behind me wherever I might go.

I cannot tell you what a fight I had that night—for it was more like night than morning. I walked fast; I tried all sorts of gymnastic attitudes; I leaped up, caught hold of an iron bar and swung by my arms, and whenever I did these things I grew as lively as a cricket; but as soon as, from utter weariness, I ceased, the horrible drowsiness came on again, and as I walked I actually dreamed that there was a man creeping along the ground towards the building.

This seemed to wake me, and it was so real that I went out to see—nothing.

Then I had another tour of the place; stood leaning against door-posts, and up in corners, ready to drop down with sleep, but fighting it off again.

I went out across the yard and had a look at the dam, lay down on the stone edge, and bathed my face with the fresh cold water, turned my handkerchief into a towel, and walked back in the dim, grey light, seeing that morning was breaking, and beginning to rejoice that I had got rid of my drowsy fit, which seemed unaccountable.

Piter seemed as drowsy as I, holding his head down in a heavy way as if it were more than he could bear.

"Poor old boy! Why, you seem as sleepy as I am, Piter!" I said, as I seated myself on the stairs leading up to the office; and he whined softly and laid his head in my lap.

I thought I heard a noise just then, and looked up, but there was no repetition of the sound, and I sat there at a turn of the stairs, leaning against the wall, and wondering why the dog had not started up instead of letting his heavy head drop lower in my lap.

"Why, you are as drowsy as I am, Piter," I cried again, playing with his ears; "anyone would think you had been taking a sleeping draught or something of that kind."

He answered with a heavy snore, just like a human being, and I sat gazing down and out through the open doorway into the yard, thinking that it would not be long now before it was broad daylight instead of that half darkness that seemed so strange and misty that I could only just see through the doorway and distinguish the stones.

Then I could hardly see them at all, and then they seemed to disappear, and I could see all over the yard, and the dam and the works all at once. It was a wonderful power of sight that I seemed to possess, for I was looking through the walls of the upper shop, and all through the lower shop, and down into the water-pit. Then I was looking round the furnace, and in at the smiths' forges, and at the great chimney-shaft, and at the precipice by Dome Tor.

What a place that seemed! Since my uncle slipped over it the slaty, shaley face appeared to have grown twice as big and high, and over it and down the steep slope a man was crawling right in from the Dome Tor slip to our works. I saw him come along the stone edge of the dam and over the wheel with the water, to bob up and down in the black pit like a cork float when an eel is biting at a bait. There he went—bob—bob—bob—and down out of sight.

It seemed such a splendid bite, that, being fond of fishing, I was about to strike, the absurdity of the idea of fishing with a man for a float never striking me for a moment; but, just as I was going to pull up, the man was crawling over the floor of the grinders' shop, and the water was not there, though the wheel seemed to be going round and uttering a heavy groan at every turn for want of grease.

There he was again, creeping and writhing up the stairs, and higher and higher along the floor among the lathes; then he was in the office, and over the bed where Uncle Bob lay making a snoring noise like the great water-wheel as it turned. What a curiously-long, thin, writhing man he seemed to be as he crawled and wriggled all over the floor and lathes and polishing-wheels. Down, too, into the smiths' shops, and over the half-extinct fires without burning himself, and all the time the wheel went round with its snoring noise, and the man—who was really a big eel—was ringing a loud bell, and—

I jumped up wide-awake, upsetting Piter, and throwing his head out of my lap, when, instead of springing up, he rolled heavily half-way down the stairs as if he were dead.

"Why, I've been to sleep," I said angrily to myself, "and dreaming all sorts of absurd nonsense! That comes of thinking about fishing for eels."

I was cold and stiff, and there was a bell ringing in the distance at some works, where the men began an hour sooner than ours. But I took no notice of that, for I was thinking about Piter, and wondering how he could lie so still.

"Is he dead?" I thought; and I went down and felt him.

He did not move; but it was evident that he was not dead, for he snored heavily, and felt warm enough; but he was too fast asleep to be roused, even when I took hold of his collar and shook him.

I was puzzled, and wondered whether he could have had anything to make him so sleepy.

But if he had had anything to make him sleepy I had not, and yet I must have been soundly asleep for two or three hours.

I remembered, though, that when I last went round the yard Piter had been sniffing about at something, and perhaps he might have eaten what had not agreed with him then.

"Poor old boy! He'll wake up presently," I said to myself as I lifted him up; and heavy enough he seemed as I carried him down to his kennel, just inside the door, where he lay motionless, snoring heavily still.

"Lucky thing that no one has been," I said to myself, as, feeling thoroughly ashamed of my breach of trust, I went down to the dam, taking a towel with me this time from out of my office-drawer, and there, kneeling on the stones, I had a good bathe at my face and forehead, and went back feeling ever so much fresher.

The sounds of toil were rising in the distance, and over the great town the throb and hum and whirr of the busy hive was rising in the sunny morning air, as, with the events of the night fading away, I went in to my office to put away the towel and use the comb and brush I kept there.

That done, I was going to call Uncle Bob and walk back with him to our home, for the men would soon be there.

Just then the water-bottle and glass upon my desk caught my eye, and, like a flash, I remembered that I had filled the glass and drunk a little water, leaving the glass nearly full so as to take some more if I wanted it, for a glass of water was, I found, a capital thing to keep off drowsiness when one was watching.

I was sure I had left that glass nearly full, and standing on the desk; but I had not been and drunk any more, of that I was sure. I don't know why I had not gone back to have some, considering how sleepy I was, but I certainly had not. I was sure of it.

Then the water-bottle! It was a common plain bottle such as is used on a wash-stand, and we had three of them always filled with fresh cold water on the desks. Mine was full when I poured some out in the night, and now it was quite empty; and as I stared at it and then about the room I saw a great patch of wet on the carpet.

I looked farther and there was another patch—a smaller patch or big splash, as if the contents of the glass had been thrown down.

It was very strange, and I could not understand it. I had not thrown the water down. If I had wanted to get rid of it, I should have gone to the sink outside or have opened the window, and thrown it out into the dam.

The matter was of small consequence, and I paid no more attention to it, but went to Uncle Bob, where he was lying, fighting with myself as to whether I should tell him that I had been to sleep.

I did not like to speak, for I felt—well I felt as most boys would under the circumstances; but I mastered my moral cowardice, as I thought, and determined to tell him—after breakfast.

"Ah, Cob, old chap," he cried, jumping up as I laid my hand on his shoulder, "what a delicious sleep! What a morning too—Hah! That's better."

He was dressed, for though whoever lay down, so to speak, went to bed, he never undressed; so that after a plunge of the face and hands in the cool fresh water, and a scrub and brush, Uncle Bob was ready.

"I want my breakfast horribly, Cob," he said; "and we've an hour to wait. Let's have a walk round by the hill as we go home. Have you unlocked the gate?"

"Yes," I said; "before I came up to call you."

"That's right. Ah, here the men come!" for there was the trampling of feet, and the noise of voices crossing the yard. "Fed Piter?"

"No; not yet," I said. "He's asleep."

"Asleep!"

"Yes; he has been asleep these three hours past—asleep and snoring. He's in his kennel now. I couldn't wake him."

"Nice sort of a watch-dog, Cob!"

"Yes," I said, feeling very guilty and shrinking from my confession.

"Do you say you tried to wake him?"

"Yes," I said, "I took him up in my arms, and carried him down to his kennel, and he was snoring all the time."

"Carried him down! Where from?"

"The stairs. He went to sleep there."

"Cob!" he cried, making the blood flush to my face, and then run back to my heart—"why, what's the matter, boy, aren't you well?"

"My head aches a little, and my mouth feels rather hot and dry."

"And you've got dark marks under your eyes, boy. You've not been asleep too, have you?"

I stared at him wildly, and felt far more unwell now.

"Why don't you speak?" he cried angrily. "You haven't been to sleep, have you?"

"I was going to confess it, uncle, if you had given me time," I said. "I never did such a thing before; but I couldn't keep awake, and fell asleep for over two hours."

"Oh, Cob! Cob!"

"I couldn't help it, uncle," I cried passionately. "I did try so hard. I walked and ran about. I stood up, and danced and jumped, and went in the yard, but it was all of no use, and at last I dropped down on the stairs with Piter, and before I knew it I was fast."

"Was the dog asleep too?"

"He went to sleep before I did," I said bitterly.

"Humph!"

"Don't be angry with me, Uncle Bob," I cried. "I did try so hard."

"Did you take anything last night after I left you?"

"No, uncle. You know I was very sleepy when you called me."

"Nothing at all?"

"Only a drop of water out of the bottle."

"Go and fetch what is left," he said. "Or no, I'll come. But Piter; what did he have?"

"I don't know, only that he seemed to pick up something just as we were walking along the yard. That's all."

"There's some fresh mischief afoot, Cob," cried Uncle Bob, "and—ah, here it is! Well, my man, what is it?"

This was to Gentles, whose smooth fat face was full of wrinkles, and his eyes half-closed.

He took off his cap—a soft fur cap, and wrung it gently as if it were full of water. Then he began shaking it out, and brushing it with his cuff, and looked from one to the other, giving me a salute by jerking up one elbow.

"Well, why don't you speak, man; what is it?" cried Uncle Bob. "Is anything wrong?"

"No, mester, there aren't nought wrong, as you may say, though happen you may think it is. Wheel-bands hev been touched again."

Chapter Fourteen.

Uncle Bob's Patient.

Uncle Bob gave me a sharp look that seemed to go through me, and then strode into the workshop, while I followed him trembling with anger and misery, to think that I should have gone to sleep at such a time and let the miscreants annoy us again like this.

"Not cut this time," said Uncle Bob to me, as we went from lathe to lathe, and from to stone. Upstairs and downstairs it was all the same; every band of leather, gutta-percha, catgut, had been taken away, and, of course, the whole of this portion of the works would be brought to a stand.

I felt as if stunned, and as guilty as if I had shared in the plot by which the bands had been taken away.

The men were standing about stolidly watching us. They did not complain about their work being at a stand-still, nor seem to mind that, as they were paid by the amount they did, they would come short at the end of the week: all they seemed interested in was the way in which we were going to bear the loss, or act.

"Does not look like a walk for us, Cob," said Uncle Bob. "What a cruel shame it is!"

"Uncle," I cried passionately, for we were alone now, "I can't tell you how ashamed I am. It's disgraceful. I'm not fit to be trusted. I can never forgive myself, but I did try so very very hard."

"Try, my boy!" he said taking my hand; "why, of course, you did. I haven't blamed you."

"No, but I blame myself," I cried.

"Nonsense, my boy! Let that rest."

"But if I had kept awake I should have detected the scoundrel."

"No, you would not, Cob, because if you had been awake he would not have come; your being asleep was his opportunity."

"But I ought not, being on sentry, to have gone to sleep."

"But, my dear Cob, people who are drugged cannot help going to sleep."

"Drugged!"

"To be sure. Didn't you say that you drank a little water and afterwards grew sleepy?"

"But I did not know it was the water."

"Here, let me look at your bottle and glass."

I took him into the office and showed him the empty receptacles and the two patches on the floor.

"Clumsily done, Cob," he said after looking at and smelling them. "This was done to keep anyone suspicious from examining the water. Yes, Cob, you were drugged."

"Oh, Uncle Bob," I cried excitedly, "I hope I was!"

"I don't see why you need be so hopeful, but it is very evident that you were. There, don't worry yourself about it, my boy. You always do your duty and we've plenty to think of without that. We shall spoil two breakfasts at home."

"But, uncle," I cried, clinging to his arm, "do you really think I may believe that my sleepiness came from being drugged?"

"Yes, yes, yes," he cried half angrily. "Now are you satisfied? Come and let's have a look at the dog."

I felt quite guilty at having forgotten poor Piter so long, and descending with my uncle we were soon kneeling by the kennel.

He had not stirred since I put him in, but lay snoring heavily, and no amount of shaking seemed to have the least effect.

"The poor brute has had a strong dose, Cob," said Uncle Bob, "and if we don't do something he will never wake again."

"Oh, uncle!" I cried, for his words sent a pang through me. I did not know how much I had grown to like the faithful piece of ugliness till my uncle had spoken as he did.

"Yes, the wretches have almost done for him, and I'm glad of it."

"Glad!" I cried as I lifted poor Piter's head in my hand and stroked it.

"Glad it was that which made the poor brute silent. I thought he had turned useless through his not giving the alarm."

"Can't we do something, uncle?" I cried.

"I'm thinking, Cob," he replied, "it's not an easy thing to give dogs antidotes, and besides we don't know what he has taken. Must be some narcotic though. I know what we'll do. Here, carry him down to the dam."

A number of the workmen were looking on stolidly and whispering to one another as if interested in what we were going to do about the dog. Some were in the yard smoking, some on the stairs, and every man's hands were deep in his pockets.

"Say," shouted a voice as I carried the dog out into the yard, following Uncle Bob while the men made room for us, "they're a goin' to drown bull-poop."

I hurried on after my uncle and heard a trampling of feet behind me, but I took no notice, only as I reached the dam there was quite a little crowd closing in.

"Wayert a minute, mester," said one of the grinders. "I'll get 'ee bit o' iron and a bit o' band to tie round poop's neck."

For answer, Uncle Bob took the dog by his collar and hind-legs, and kneeling down on the stone edge of the dam plunged him head-first into the water, drew him out, and plunged him in again twice.

"Yow can't drownd him like that," cried one.

"He's dowsing on him to bring him round," said another; and then, as Uncle Bob laid the dog down and stood up to watch him, there was a burst of laughter in the little crowd, for all our men were collected now.

"Yes, laugh away, you cowardly hounds," said Uncle Bob indignantly, and I looked at him wonderingly, for he had always before seemed to be so quiet and good-tempered a fellow. "It's a pity, I suppose, that you did not kill the dog right out the same as, but for a lucky accident, you might have poisoned this boy here."

"Who poisoned lad?" said a grinder whom I had seen insolent more than once.

"I don't know," cried Uncle Bob; "but I know it was done by the man or men who stole those bands last night; and I know that it was done by someone in these works, and that you nearly all of you know who it was."

There was a low growl here.

"And a nice cowardly contemptible trick it was!" cried Uncle Bob, standing up taller than any man there, and with his eyes flashing. "I always thought Englishmen were plucky, straightforward fellows, above such blackguards' tricks as these. Workmen! Why, the scoundrels who did this are unworthy of the name."

There was another menacing growl here.

"Too cowardly to fight men openly, they come in the night and strike at boys, and dogs, and steal."

"Yow lookye here," said the big grinder, taking off his jacket and baring his strong arms; "yow called me a coward, did you?"

"Yes, and any of you who know who did this coward's trick," cried Uncle Bob angrily.

"Then tek that!" cried the man, striking at him full in the face.

I saw Uncle Bob catch the blow on his right arm, dart out his left and strike the big grinder in the mouth; and then, before he could recover himself, my uncle's right fist flashed through the air like lightning, and the man staggered and then fell with a dull thud, the back of his head striking the stones.

There was a loud yell at this, and a chorus rose:

"In wi' 'em. Throost 'em i' th' dam," shouted a voice, and half a dozen men advanced menacingly; but Uncle Bob stood firm, and just then Fannell the smith strode before them.

"Howd hard theer," he cried in his shrill voice. "Six to one, and him one o' the mesters."

Just then Uncles Jack and Dick strode in through the gates, saw the situation at a glance, and ran to strengthen our side.

"What's this?" roared Uncle Dick furiously, as Uncle Jack clenched his fists and looked round, as it seemed to me, for some one to knock down. "In to your work, every man of you."

"Bands is gone," said a sneering voice.

"Then get off our premises, you dogs!" he roared. "Out of that gate, I say, every man who is against us."

"Oh, we're not agen you, mester," said Gentles smoothly. "I'm ready for wuck, on'y the bands is gone. Yow mean wuck, eh, mates?"

"Then go and wait till we have seen what is to be done. Do you hear? —go."

He advanced on the men so fiercely that they backed from him, leaving Pannell only, and he stooped to help up the big grinder, who rose to his feet shaking his head like a dog does to get the water out of his ears, for there must have been a loud singing noise there.

"Off with you!" said Uncle Dick turning upon these two.

"Aw reight, mester," said Pannell. "I were on'y helping the mate. Mester Robert there did gie him a blob."

Pannell was laughing good-humouredly, and just then Uncle Bob turned upon him.

"Thank you, Pannell," he said quickly. "I'm glad we have one true man in the place."

"Oh, it's aw reight, mester," said the smith. "Here, coom along, thou'st had anew to last thee these two months."

As he spoke he half dragged the big grinder away to the workshop, and Uncle Bob rapidly explained the state of affairs.

"It's enough to make us give up," cried Uncle Dick angrily. "We pay well; we're kind to our men; we never overwork them; and yet they serve us these blackguard tricks. Well, if they want to be out of work they shall be, for I'll agree to no more bands being bought till the scoundrels come to their senses."

"But we will not be beaten," cried Uncle Jack, who looked disappointed at there being no more fighting.

"No," said Uncle Bob, wiping his bleeding knuckles. "I feel as if I had tasted blood, as they say, and I'm ready to fight now to the end."

"And all the time we are talking and letting that poor dog perish! The cowards!" cried Uncle Dick fiercely. "Is he dead?"

"No," I said; "I saw one of his ears quiver a little, but he is not breathing so loudly."

"Give him another plunge," said Uncle Jack.

Uncle Bob took the dog as before and plunged him once more in the cold clean water; and this time, as soon as he was out, he struggled slightly and choked and panted to get his breath.

"We must get him on his legs if we can," said Uncle Bob; and for the next half hour he kept trying to make the dog stand, but without avail, till he had almost given up in despair. Then all at once poor Piter began to whine, struggled to his feet, fell down, struggled up again, and then began rapidly to recover, and at last followed us into the office—where, forgetful of breakfast, we began to discuss the present state of the war.

The first thing that caught my eye as we went in was a letter stuck in the crack of the desk, so that it was impossible for anyone to pass without seeing it.

Uncle Jack took the letter, read it, and passed it round, Uncle Bob reading last.

I asked what it was as I stooped over poor Piter, who seemed stupid and confused and shivered with the wet and cold.

"Shall I tell him?" said Uncle Bob, looking at his brothers.

They looked at one another thoughtfully, nodded, and Uncle Bob handed me the note; and a precious composition it was.

> "*You London Cockneys,*" it began, "*you've had plenty warnings 'bout your gimcracks and contrapshions, and wouldn't take 'em. Now look here, we won't hev 'em in Arrowfield, robbing hard-workin' men of toil of their hard earns and takin' bread out o' wife and childers mouths and starvin' families, so look out. If you three an' that sorcy boy don't pack up your traps and be off, we'll come and pack 'em up for you. So now you know.*"

"What does this mean?" I said, looking from one to the other.

"It means war, my lad," said Uncle Dick fiercely.

"You will not take any notice of this insolent letter?" I said.

"Oh yes, but we will!" said Uncle Jack.

"Not give up and go like cowards?"

"I don't think we shall, Cob," said Uncle Jack laughing. "No; we're in the right and they are in the wrong. We've got a strong tower to fight in and defend ourselves; they've got to attack us here, and I think they'll be rather badly off if they do try anything more serious."

"This has been bad enough," said Uncle Bob. "You did not fully understand how narrow an escape Cob had."

And he related all.

"The scoundrels!" said Uncle Jack, grinding his teeth. "And now this means threatenings of future attacks."

"Well," said Uncle Dick, "if they do come I'm afraid someone will be very much hurt—more so than that man Stevens you knocked down."

"And made a fresh enemy for us," said Uncle Jack, laughing.

"And showed who was a friend," I said, remembering Pannell's action.

"To be sure," said Uncle Jack. "Well, if anyone is hurt it will be the attacking party, for I am beginning to feel vicious."

"Well, what about the wheels?" said Uncle Bob. "Every band has gone, and it will be a heavy expense to restore them."

"Let's go and have breakfast and think it over," said Uncle Dick. "It's bad to decide in haste. Listen! What are the men doing?"

"Going out in the yard, evidently," said Uncle Bob. "Yes, and down to the gate."

So it proved, for five minutes later the place was completely empty.

"Why, they've forsaken us," said Uncle Dick bitterly.

"Never mind," said Uncle Bob. "Let's have our breakfast. We can lock up the place."

And this we did, taking poor old Piter with us, who looked so helpless and miserable that several dogs attacked him on our way home, anticipating an easy victory.

But they did Piter good, rousing him up to give a bite here and another there—one bite being all his enemies cared to receive before rushing off, yelping apologies for the mistake they had made in attacking the sickly-looking heavy-eyed gentleman of their kind.

Piter had jaws like a steel trap, as others beside dogs found before long.

When we went back to the works the gate-keeper left in charge said that several of the men had been back, but had gone again, it having been settled that no more work was to be done till the wheel-bands were restored; so the fires were going out, and the smiths, who could have gone on, had to leave their forges.

"Well," said Uncle Dick, laughing bitterly, as he gave his beard a sharp tug, "I thought that we were masters here."

"Quite a mistake," said Uncle Jack; "the men are the masters; and if we do anything that they in their blind ignorance consider opposed to their interests they punish us."

"Well, you see, sir," said the gate-keeper, "it's like this here, sir—work's quite scarce enough, and the men are afraid, that new steel or new machinery will make it worse."

"Tell them to take the scales off their eyes, then," said Uncle Dick. "Oppose machinery, do they?"

"Yes, sir."

"Then if someone invented a new kind of grindstone to grind tools and blades in a quarter of the time, what would they do?"

"Smash it, sir, or burn the place it was in," said the man with a grin.

"Then why don't they smash up the grindstones they use now? They are machinery."

"What! Grindstones, sir? Oh, no!"

"But they are, man, I tell you," cried Uncle Dick angrily. "The first men who ground knives or shears rubbed, them on a rough piece of stone; then I dare say a cleverer man found it was handier to rub the blade with the stone instead of the stone with the blade; and then someone invented the round grindstone which turned and ground whatever was held against it."

"Come along," said Uncle Jack sharply. "You are wasting breath. They will not believe till they find all this out for themselves."

We went in and had a good look round the place, but there was not a band to be found. There had been no cutting—every one had been carried away, leaving no trace behind; and I wanted a good deal of comforting to make me satisfied that it was not my fault.

But my uncles were very kind to me, and told me at once that I was to say no more, only to be thankful that I had not drunk more heartily of the water, and been made ill as the dog, who, in spite of seeming better, kept having what I may call relapses, and lying down anywhere to have a fresh sleep.

The look round produced no result, and the day was spent in the silent works writing letters, book-keeping, and talking rather despondently about the future.

It seemed so strange to me as I went about. No roaring fires and puffing bellows; no clink of hammer or anvil, and no churr and screech of steel being held against the revolving stones. There was no buzz of voices or shouting from end to end of the workshop, and instead of great volumes of smoke rolling out of the top of the tall chimney-shaft, a little faint grey cloud slowly curled away into the air.

Then there was the great wheel. The dam was full and overflowing, but the wheel was still; and when I looked in, the water trickled and plashed down into the gloomy chamber with its mossy, slimy stone sides, while the light shone in at the opening, and seemed to make bright bands across the darkness before it played upon the slightly agitated waters.

Then a long discussion took place, in which it was asked whether it would be wise to buy new bands, and to ask the men to come back and work; but opinion was against this.

"No," said Uncle Jack. "I'm for being as obstinate as they are. We've had our bands injured once; now let's show them that if they can afford to wait so can we. We can't, neither can they, but there must be a little obstinacy practised, and perhaps it will bring them to their senses."

"And make them bring back our bands?" I ventured to say.

"Ah, I'm not so hopeful about that!" cried Uncle Bob. "I'm afraid thatwe shall have to buy new ones."

"Yes," said Uncle Dick; "but I would not mind that if by so doing we could get the men to behave well to us in the future."

"And we never shall," said Uncle Jack, "till Cob here ceases to be such a tyrant. The men are afraid of him."

"Why, uncle!" I exclaimed; and they all laughed at my look ofinjury.

That night Uncle Jack and Uncle Dick kept watch; next night we took our turn again, and so matters went on for a week. Now and then we saw some of our men idling about, but they looked at us in a heavy stolid way, and then slouched off.

The works seemed to be very melancholy and strange, but we went there regularly enough, and when we had a fire going and stayed in there was no doubt about the matter; we were watched.

Piter grew quite well again, and in his thick head there seemed to be an idea that he had been very badly used, for, as he walked close at my heels, I used to see him give the workmen very ugly looks in aside wise fashion that I used to call measuring legs.

One morning my uncles said that they should not go to the works that day, and as they did not seem to want me I thought I would go back and put a project I had in my mind in force.

I had passed the night at the works in company with Uncle Jack, and all had been perfectly quiet, so, putting some bones in the basket for

Piter, I also thrust in some necessaries for the task I had in hand, and started.

About half-way there I met Gentles, the fat-faced grinder, and he shut his eyes at me and slouched up in his affectionate way.

"Ah! Mester Jacob," he said, "when's this here unhappy strike going to end?"

"When the rascals who stole our bands bring them back," I said, "and return to their work."

"Ah!" he sighed, "I'm afraid they wean't do that, my lad. Hedn't the mesters better give in, and not make no more noofangle stoof?"

"Oh, that's what you think, is it, Gentles?" I said.

"Who? Me, mester? Oh, no: I'm only a pore hardworking chap who wants to get back to his horse. It's what the other men say. For my part I wishes as there was no unions, stopping a man's work and upsetting him; that I do. Think the mesters'll give in, Mester Jacob, sir?"

"I'm sure they will not, Gentles," I said, "and you had better tell the men so."

"Nay, I durstn't tell 'em. Oh, dear, no, Mester Jacob, sir. I'm a quiet peaceable man, I am. I on'y wants to be let alone."

I went on, thinking, and had nearly reached the lane by the works, when I met Pannell, who was smoking a short black pipe.

"Hello!" he cried.

"Hello! Pannell," I said.

"Goin' to open wucks, and let's get on again, lad?"

"Whenever you men like to bring back the bands and apologise, Pannell."

"Nay, I've got nowt to 'pologise for. I did my wuck, and on'y wanted to be let alone."

"But you know who took the bands," I cried. "You know who tried to poison our poor dog and tried to blow up the furnace, now don't you?"

He showed his great teeth as he looked full at me.

"Why, my lad," he said, "yow don't think I'm going to tell, do'ee?"

"You ought to tell," I cried. "I'm sure you know; and it's a cowardly shame."

"Ay, I s'pose that's what you think," he said quietly. "But, say, lad, isn't it time wuck began again?"

"Time! Yes," I said. "Why don't you take our side, Pannell; my uncles are your masters?"

"Ay, I know that, lad," said the big smith quietly; "but man can't do as he likes here i' Arrowfield. Eh, look at that!"

"Well, mate," said a rough voice behind me; and I saw the smith start as Stevens, the fierce grinder, came up, and without taking any notice of me address the smith in a peculiar way, fixing him with his eye and clapping him on the shoulder.

"Here, I want to speak wi' thee," he said sharply. "Coom and drink."

It seemed to me that he regularly took the big smith into custody, and marched him off.

This set me thinking about how they must be all leagued together; but I forgot all about the matter as I opened the gate, and Piter came charging down at me, delighted to have company once more in the great lonely works.

The next minute he was showing his intelligence by smelling the basket as we walked up to the door together.

I gave him some of the contents to amuse him, and then entering the deserted grinding-shop, walked straight to the door at the end opening into the great wheel-pit, and throwing it back stood upon the little platform built out, and looked down at the black water, which received enough from the full dam to keep it in motion and make the surface seem to be covered with a kind of thready film that was always opening and closing, and spreading all over the place to the very walls.

It looked rather black and unpleasant, and seemed to be a place that might contain monsters of eels or other fish, and it was to try and catch some of these that I had taken advantage of the holiday-time and come.

For I had several times called to mind what Gentles had said about the fish in the dam and pit, and meant to have a turn; but now I was here everything was so silent and mysterious and strange, that I rather shrank from my task, and began to wonder what I should do if I hooked some monster too large to draw out.

"What a coward I am!" I said aloud; and taking the stout eel-line I had brought, and baiting the two hooks upon it with big worms, I gathered up the cord quite ready and then made a throw, so that my bait went down right beneath the wheel, making a strange echoing splash that whispered about the slimy walls.

"Looks more horrible than ever," I said to myself, as I shook off my dislike, and sat down on the little platform with my legs dangling over the water.

But I could not quite shake off my dread, for the feeling came over me: suppose some horrible serpentlike water creature were to raise its head out of the black depths, seize me by the foot, and drag me down.

It was an absurd idea, but I could not fight against it, and I found myself drawing my legs up and sitting down tailor fashion with my feet beneath me.

And there I sat with not a sound but the dripping water to be heard, and a curious rustling that I soon after made out to be Piter busy with his bone.

A quarter of an hour, half an hour, passed away, and I did not get a touch, so drawing up my line I restored the baits and threw in again, choosing the far-off corner of the pit close by where the water escaped to the stream below.

The bait had not been down a minute, and I was just wondering whether Gentles was correct about there being any fish there, when I felt the line softly drawn through my fingers, then there was a slight quivering vibration, and a series of tiny jerks, and the line began to run faster, while my heart began to beat with anticipation.

"He was right," I exclaimed, as I tightened the line with a jerk, and then a sharp little struggle began, as the fish I had hooked rushed hither and thither, and fought back, and finally was dragged out of the water, tying itself up in a knot which bobbed and slipped about upon the floor as I dragged it into the grinding-room, and cut the line to set it free, for it was impossible to get the hook out of the writhing creature's jaws.

It was an eel of about a pound weight, and, excited now by the struggle, I fastened on a fresh hook, baited it, and threw in the same place again.

Quite half an hour elapsed before I had another bite, and knowing how nocturnal these creatures are in their habits, I was just thinking that if I liked next time I was on the watch I might throw a line in here, and keep catching an eel every now and then, when—

Check! A regular sharp jerk at the line, and I knew that I had hooked a good one, but instead of the line tightening it suddenly grew quite slack.

For a moment I was afraid that the fish had broken away, but I realised directly that it had rushed over to my side of the wheel-pit, and it had come so swiftly that I began to think that it could not be an eel.

I had not much line to gather in, though, before I felt the check again, and a furious tug given so hard that I let the line run, and several yards were drawn through my fingers before I began to wonder where the eel or other fish I had hooked had gone.

"Perhaps there is a passage or drain under the works," I thought as I dragged at the line, now to feel some answering throbs; but the fish did not run any farther, only remained stationary.

"What a monster!" I cried, as I felt what a tremendous weight there was against me. I drew the line and gained a little, but gave way for fear it should break.

This went on for ten minutes or so. I was in a state of the greatest excitement, for I felt that I had got hold of a monster, and began to despair of dragging it up to where I was. Such a thing seemed impossible, for the line would give way or the hook break from its hold I was sure.

In place of jerking about now, the fish was very still, exercising a kind of inert force against its captor; but I was in momentary expectation of a renewal of the battle, and so powerful did the creature seem, so enormously heavy was it, that I began to regret my success, and to wonder what the consequences would be if I were to get the large eel up there on the floor.

One moment I saw myself flying for my life from a huge writhing open-mouthed creature, and saved by a gallant attack made by Piter, who, hearing the noise, had dashed in open-jawed to seize the fierce monster by the neck; the next I was calling myself a donkey.

"Why, of course!" I cried. "When I hooked it the creature ran in towards me, and has darted in and out of some grating and wound the line tightly there."

That could not be the case, I felt as I pulled, for though it was evident that the fish had entangled the line, it was in something loose which I got nearly to the surface several times, as I gazed down there in the darkness till all at once, just as I was straining my eyes to make out what it was that was entangled with my hook, the cord snapped, there was a dull plash below me, the water rippled and babbled against the side, and all was still once more.

I stood gazing down for a few minutes, and then a flash of intelligence shot through me, and I darted back, rapidly coiling up my wet line and taking it and my basket up into the office, from whence I came hurrying out, and ready to dash down two steps at a time.

"Why, of course," I kept on saying to myself; "what stupids!"

I ran across the yard, unlocked and relocked the gate, leaving Piter disappointed and barking, and hurried back to the house, where my uncles were busy over some correspondence.

"Hurrah!" I cried. "I've found it all out. Come along! Down to the works!"

"You've found out!" cried Uncle Dick starting.

"Found it all out!" I cried excitedly. "Now, then, all of you! Come on and see."

I slipped down to Mrs Stephenson after telling my uncles to go slowly on and that I would overtake them, and that lady smiled in my face as soon as she saw me.

"Don't say a word!" she cried. "I know what you want. Tattsey, get out the pork-pie."

"No, no," I cried; "you mistake. I'm not hungry."

"Nonsense, my dear! And if you're not hungry now, you will be before long. I've a beautiful raised pie of my own making. Have a bit, my dear. Bring it, Tattsey."

It was, I found, one of the peculiarities of these people to imagine everybody was hungry, and their hospitality to their friends was without stint.

Tattsey had not so much black-lead on her face as usual. In fact it was almost clean, while her hands were beautifully white, consequent upon its being peggy day; that is to say, the day in which clothes were washed in the peggy tub, and kept in motion by a four-legged peggy, a curious kind of machine with a cross handle.

So before I could say another word the pork-pie was brought out on the white kitchen-table, and Mrs Stephenson began to cut out a wedge.

"May I take it with me," I said, "and eat it as I go along?"

"Bless the boy; yes, of course," said our homely landlady. "Boys who are growing want plenty to eat. I hate to see people starve."

"But I want you to do me a favour," I said.

"Of course, my dear. What is it?"

"I want you to lend me your clothes-line."

"What, that we are just going to put out in the yard for the clean clothes? I should just think not indeed."

"How tiresome!" I cried. "Well, never mind; I must buy a bit. But will you lend me a couple of meat-hooks?"

"Now, what in the world are you going to do with a clothes-line and two meat-hooks?"

"I'm going fishing," I said impatiently.

"Now don't you talk nonsense, my dear," said our plump landlady, looking rather red. "Do you think I don't know better than that?"

"But I am going fishing," I cried.

"Where?"

"In our wheel-pit."

"Then there's someone drownded, and you are going to fish him out."

"No, no," I cried. "Will you lend me the hooks?"

"Yes, I'll lend you the hooks," she said, getting them out of a drawer.

"We sha'n't want the old clothes-line," said Tattsey slowly.

"No, we sha'n't want the old clothes-line," said Mrs Stephenson, looking at me curiously. "There, you can have that."

"I'll tell you all about it when I come back," I cried as the knot of clean cord was handed to me; and putting an arm through it and the hooks in my pocket I started off at a run, to find myself face to face with Gentles before I overtook my uncles.

"Going a wallucking, Mester Jacob?" he said.

"No; I'm going a-fishing."

"What, wi' that line, Mester?"

"Yes."

"Arn't it a bit too thick, Mester?"

"Not in the least, Gentles," I said; and leaving him rubbing his face as if to smooth it after being shaved, I ran on and overtook my uncles just before we reached the works.

"Thought you weren't coming, Cob," said Uncle Dick. "What are you going to do with the rope?"

"Have patience," I said laughing.

Just then we passed Stevens, who scowled at us as he saw me with the rope, while Pannell, who was with him, stared, and his face slowly lit up with a broad grin.

They turned round to stare after us as we went to the gate, and then walked off quickly.

"What does that mean, oh, boy of mystery?" said Uncle Jack.

"They suspect that I have discovered their plans," I cried joyfully.

"And have you—are you sure?"

"Only wait five minutes, uncle, and you shall see," I cried.

We entered the works, fastened the gate after us, and then, taking the end of my fishing-line as soon as we reached the grinding-shop, I began to bind the two meat-hooks one across the other.

"What, are you going to try for eels that way?" said Uncle Bob laughing, as my uncles seemed to be gradually making out what was to come.

"Well," I said, "they broke my other line."

By this time I had fastened the hooks pretty firmly, and to the cross I now secured the end of the clothes-line.

"Fine eel that, Cob," said Uncle Dick, hunting the one I had caught into a corner, for it had been travelling all over the place.

"Yes," I said; "and now the tackle's ready, throw in and see if you can't get another."

Uncle Dick went straight to the doorway, stepped on to the platform, and threw in the hook, which seemed to catch in something and gave way again.

"Come, I had a bite," he said laughing. "What has been thrown in here —some bundles of wire or steel rods?"

"Try again," I said laughing, and he had another throw, this time getting tight hold of something which hung fast to the hooks, and came up dripping and splashing to the little platform, where it was seized, and Uncle Bob gave a shout of delight.

"Why, I never expected to catch that," cried Uncle Dick.

"I thought it was some stolen rings of wire," said Uncle Jack, as he seized hold, and together they dragged a great tangle of leather and catgut bands over the platform into the grinding-shop, fully half falling back with a tremendous splash.

"Cob, you're a hero," cried Uncle Dick.

"The malicious scoundrels!" cried Uncle Jack.

"Throw in again," said Uncle Bob.

And then Uncle Dick fished and dragged and hauled up tangle after tangle till there was quite a heap of the dripping bands, with rivulets of water streaming away over the stone floor, and right in the middle a monster of an eel, the gentleman I had hooked, and which had wound itself in and out of the catgut bands till it was held tight by the mouth.

"He deserves to have his freedom," said Uncle Dick, as he gave the bands a shake so that the hook came out of the eel's mouth, and it began to writhe and twine about the floor.

"And he shall have it," I cried, taking a walking-stick, and for the next five minutes I was employed trying to guide my prisoner to the doorway leading into the pit.

I suppose you never tried to drive an eel? No? Well, let me assure you that pig-driving is a pleasant pastime in comparison. We have it on good authority that if you want to drive a pig in a particular direction all you have to do is to point his nose straight and then try to pull him back by the tail. Away he goes directly.

Try and drive a big thick eel, two feet six inches long, with a walking-stick, and you'll find it a task that needs an education first. Put his head straight, and he curves to right or left. Pull his tail, and he'll turn round and bite you, and hold fast too. Mine turned round and bit, but it was the walking-stick he seized with his strong jaws, and it wanted a good shake to get it free.

Every way but the right would that eel squirm and wriggle. I chased him round grindstones, in and out of water-troughs, from behind posts and planks, from under benches, but I could not get him to the door; and I firmly believe that night would have fallen with me still hunting the slimy wriggling creature if Uncle Bob had not seized it with his hands after throwing his pocket-handkerchief over its back.

The next instant it was curled up in the silk, writhing itself into a knot, no doubt in an agony of fear, if eels can feel fear. Then it was held over the pit, the handkerchief taken by one corner, and I expected to hear it drop with a splash into the water; but no, it held on, and though the handkerchief was shaken it was some time before it would quit its hold of the silk, a good piece of which was tight in its jaws.

At last: an echoing splash, and we turned back to where my Uncles Jack and Dick were busy with the bands.

"The best day's fishing I ever saw, Cob," cried Uncle Jack. "It was stupid of us not to drag the pit or the dam before."

"I don't know about stupid," said Uncle Bob. "You see we thought the bands were stolen or destroyed. We are learning fast, but we don't understand yet all the pleasant ways of the Arrowfield men."

The rest of the day was spent over the tiresome job of sorting out the different bands and hanging them on their own special wheels to drain or dry ready for use, and when this was done there was a feeling of satisfaction in every breast, for it meant beginning work again, and Uncle Bob said so.

"Yes," said Uncle Jack; "but also means a fresh attempt to stop our work as soon as the scoundrels know."

"Never mind," replied Uncle Dick. "It's a race to see who will tire first: the right side or the wrong, and I think I know."

"What's to be done next?" said Uncle Bob.

"Let the men know that we are ready for them to come back to work if they like to do so," said Uncle Jack.

"Why not get fresh hands altogether?"

"Because they would be just as great children as those we have now. No; let us be manly and straightforward with them in everything. We shall fight for our place, but we will not be petty."

"But they will serve us some other scurvy trick," said Uncle Bob.

"Let them," said Uncle Dick; "never mind. There," he cried, "those bands will be fit to use to-morrow with this clear dry air blowing through. Let's go home now and have a quiet hour or two before we come to watch."

"I wish," said Uncle Jack, "that the works joined our house."

"Go on wishing," said Uncle Bob, "and they won't join. Now, how about telling the men?"

"Let's call and see Dunning and tell him to start the fires," said Uncle Dick; and as we went back the gate-keeper was spoken to, and the old man's face lit up at the idea of the place being busy again.

"And I hope, gentlemen," he whispered from behind his hand, "that you will be let alone now."

"To which," said Uncle Bob as we walked on, "I most devoutly say, Amen."

Chapter Fifteen.

I have an Idea.

The work was started the next morning, and for a fortnight or so everything went on in the smoothest manner possible. The men were quite cheerful and good-tempered, doing their tasks and taking their wages, and though we kept our regular watch nothing disturbed us in the slightest degree.

"An' so you fun 'em in the wheel-pit, did you, Mester Jacob?" said Gentles to me one dinner-hour as he sat by his grindstone eating his bread and meat off a clean napkin spread over his knees.

"Yes," I said, looking at him keenly.

"But how came you to find 'em, mester?"

I told him.

"Did you, now?" he cried, shutting his eyes and grinning. "Think o' that! Why, I put you up to the eels, and so I might say it was me as found the bands, only you see it was not you nor yet me—it was the eel."

He nearly choked himself with laughing, but my next words sobered him, and he sat up looking painfully solemn and troubled of face.

"I'll be bound you know who threw those bands into the water, Gentles," I said.

One of his eyes quivered, and he looked at me as if he were going to speak. He even opened his mouth, and I could see his tongue quivering as if ready to begin, but he shut it with a snap and shook his head.

"Don't tell any stories about it," I said; "but you do know."

"Don't ask me, mester," he cried with a groan. "Don't ask me."

"Then you do know," I cried.

"I don't know nowt," he said in a hoarse whisper. "Why, man alive, it wouldn't be safe for a chap like me to know owt. They'd put a brick round my neck and throw me in the watter."

"But you do know, Gentles," I persisted.

"I don't know nowt, I tell 'ee," he cried angrily. "Such friends as we've been, Mester Jacob, and you to want to get me into a scrarp."

"Why, Gentles!" I cried. "If you know, why don't you speak out like a man?"

"'Cause I'm a man o' peace, Mester Jacob, and don't want to harm nobody, and I don't want nobody to harm me. Nay, I know nowt at all."

"Well, I think you are a contemptible coward, Gentles," I said warmly. "You're taking my uncles' money and working on their premises, and though you know who has been base enough to injure them you are not man enough to speak."

"Now don't—don't—don't, my lad," he cried in a hoarse whisper. "Such friends as we've been too, and you go on like that. I tell 'ee I'm a man of peace, and I don't know nowt at all. On'y give me my grinstone and something to grind—that's all I want."

"And to see our place blown up and the bands destroyed. There, I'm ashamed of you, Gentles," I cried.

"But you'll be friends?" he said; and there were tears in his eyes.

"Friends! How can I be friends," I cried, "with a man like you?"

"Oh dear, oh dear!" I heard him groan as I left the workshop; and going to Piter's kennel I took off his collar and led him down to the dam to give him a swim.

He was a capital dog for the water, and thoroughly enjoyed a splash, so that before the men came back he had had a swim, shaken himself, and was stretched out in the sunshine under the wall drying himself, when, as I stooped to pat him, I noticed something about the wall that made me look higher in a hurried way, and then at the top, and turn off directly.

I had seen enough, and I did not want to be noticed, for some of the men were beginning to come back, so stooping down I patted Piter and went off to the office.

As soon as the men were well at work I went into one of the sheds, where there were two or three holes under the benches where the rats came up from the dam, and where it was the custom to set a trap or two, which very rarely snared one of the busy little animals, though now and then we did have that luck, and Piter had the pleasure of killing the mischievous creature if the trap had not thoroughly done its work.

I soon found what I wanted—an old rusty spring trap with its sharp teeth, and, shaking off the dust, I tucked it under my jacket and strolled off to the smith's shops, where I found Pannell hammering away as hard as ever he could.

He was making reaping-hooks of my uncles' patent steel, and as I stood at the door and watched him I counted the blows he gave, and it was astonishing how regular he was, every implement taking nearly the same number of blows before he threw it down.

"Well, Pannell," I said, "arn't you sorry to have to work so hard again?"

He whisked a piece of hot steel from his forge and just glanced at me as he went on with his work, laying the glowing sparkling steel upon the anvil.

"Sorry!"—*bang*—"no"—*bang*—"not a"—*bing, bang, bang*—"not a"—*bang, bang, bing, bang, bang*—"bit of it."

That was how it sounded to me as he worked away.

"Wife"—*bang*—"bairns"—*bing, bang, bang, bing, chinger, chinger, bing, bang*—"eight"—*bang*—"of 'em. I hate"—*bang*—"to do"—*bang* —"nowt"—*bang*—"but"—*bang*—"smoke all"—*bang*—"day."

"I say, Pannell," I said, after glancing round and seeing that we were quite alone, "how came you to throw our bands in the wheel-pit?"

"What!" he cried, pincers in one hand, hammer in the other; and he looked as if he were going to seize me with one tool and beat me with the other. "Yah! Get out, you young joker! You know it warn't me."

"But you know who did it."

Pannell looked about him, through the window, out of the door, up the forge chimney, and then he gave me a solemn wink.

"Then why don't you speak?"

The big smith took a blade of steel from the fire as if it were a flaming sword, and beat it into the reaping-hook of peace before he said in a hoarse whisper:

"Men's o' one side, lad—unions. Mesters is t'other side. It's a feight."

"But it's so cowardly, Pannell," I said.

"Ay, lad, it is," he cried, banging away. "But I can't help it. Union says strike, and you hev to strike whether you like it or whether you don't like it, and clem till it's over."

"But it's such a cowardly way of making war, to do what you men do."

"What they men do, lad," he whispered.

"What you men do," I repeated.

"Nay, they men," he whispered.

"You are one of them, and on their side, so what they do you do."

"Is that so?" he said, giving a piece of steel such a hard bang that he had to repeat it to get it into shape.

"Of course it is."

"Well, I s'pose you're right, lad," he said, thoughtfully.

"Why don't you tell me, then, who threw the bands in the wheel-pit, so that he could be discharged?"

"Me! Me tell! Nay. Look at that now."

That was a piece of steel spoiled by the vehemence of his blows, and it was thrust back into the fire.

"I will not say who gave me the information," I said.

He shook his head.

"Nobody shall ever know that you told me."

He took a little hook he was forging and made a motion with it as if I were a stalk of wheat and he wanted to draw me to him.

"Lad," he said, "man who tells on his mate aren't a man no longer. I *am* a man."

We stood looking at each other for some time, and then he said in his rough way:

"It aren't no doing o' mine, lad, and I don't like it. It aren't manly. One o' the mesters did owt to me as I didn't like I'd go up to him and ask him to tek off his coat like a man and feight it out, or else I'd go away; but man can't do as he likes i' Arrowfield. He has to do what trade likes."

"And it was the trade who threw our bands away, and tried to blow us up, and half-poisoned me and Piter."

"Hah!" he said with a sigh. "That's it, lad."

"Ah, well, I didn't expect you'd tell me, Pannell," I said, smiling.

"You see I can't, my lad. Now can I?"

"No; it wouldn't be honourable. But I say, Pannell, I mean to do all I can to find out who plays us these dirty tricks."

The big smith looked about him before speaking again.

"Don't, my lad," he whispered. "Yow might get hurt, and I shouldn't like that i'deed."

"Oh, I won't get hurt!" I said. "Look here, Pannell, do you see this?"

"Ay, lad. Trap for the rats. I've sin scores on em."

"We set them to catch the rats," I said, hesitating a moment or two before making my venture. "I say, Pannell," I said, "we're very good friends you and I."

"Course we are, lad; for a Londoner you're quite a decent chap."

"Thank you," I said, smiling. "Well, on the quiet, I want you to do me a favour."

"Long as it aren't to tell on my mates, lad, I'll do owt for you. There!"

That *there* was as emphatic as a blow from his hammer on the anvil.

"I thought you would, Pannell," I said. "Well, look here. My uncles are as good and kind-hearted men as ever lived."

"And as nyste to work for as ever was," said Pannell, giving an emphatic bang on his work as he hammered away.

"Well, I'm very fond of them," I said.

"Nat'rally, lad, nat'rally."

"And as I know they're trying to do their best for everybody who works for them, as well as for themselves, so as to find bread for all—"

I stopped just then, for the big smith's face was very red, and he was making a tremendous clangour with his hammer.

"Well," I said, "it worries me very much to see that every now and then a big rat gets to their sack of wheat and gnaws a hole in it and lets the grain run out."

"Where do they keep their wheat?" said Pannell, leaving off for awhile.

"Here," I said.

"Ah! There's part rats about these here rezzywors," he said, thoughtfully. "Why don't you set that trap?"

"Because it isn't half big enough—not a quarter big enough," I said; "but I wish to catch that rat, and I want you to make me a big trap-like this, only four times as large, and with a very strong spring."

"Eh?"

"I want to set that trap, and I want to catch that, great cowardly rat, and I want you to make me a trap that will hold him."

"Eh?"

"Don't you understand?" I said, looking at him meaningly as he stood wiping the perspiration from his brow with the back of his hand.

"Yow want to set a trap to catch the big rat as comes and makes a hole in the mester's sack."

"Yes," I said. "I want to catch him."

"What! Here about the works?"

"Yes," I said. "Now do you see?"

Poof!

Pannell gave vent to a most curious sound that was like nothing so much as one that might have been emitted if his forge bellows had suddenly burst. To give vent to that sound he opened his mouth wide, clapped his hands on his leather apron, and bent nearly double.

"Why, Pannell!" I exclaimed.

Poof! He stamped first one leg on the black iron dust and ashes, and then the other, going round his anvil and grumbling and rumbling internally in the most extraordinary manner.

Then he looked me in the face and exploded once more, till his mirth and the absurdity of his antics grew infectious, and I laughed too.

"And you're going to set a big trap to catch that there"—*poof*—"that theer very big rat, eh?"

"Yes," I said, "if I can."

"And you want me," he whispered, with his eyes starting with suppressed mirth, "to make you that theer big trap."

"Yes."

"Then I'll do it," he whispered, becoming preternaturally solemn. "Stop! 'Tween man an' man you know."

He held out his great black hard hand, which I grasped.

"On my honour, Pannell, I'll never tell a soul that you made the trap, not for ten years, or twenty, if you like."

"That's enough," he said, giving his leg a slap. "Haw, haw, haw, haw, haw! Here, give us the model. When dyer want it, lad?"

"As soon as ever you can get it made, Pannell."

He looked at me with his face working, and scraping a hole in the ashes he buried the trap, seized hammer and pincers, and worked away again, but stopped every now and then to laugh.

"I say," he said suddenly, "it'll sarve 'em right; but if they knowed as I did it they'd wait for me coming home and give me the knobsticks. Ay, that they would."

"But they will not know, Pannell," I said. "It's our secret, mind."

"Hey, but I'd like to see the rat i' the trap!" he whispered, after exploding with another fit of mirth.

"Let's have the trap first," I said. "I don't know that I shall catch him then."

"What are you going to bait with?" he said between two fierce attacks upon a piece of steel.

"Oh, I have not settled that yet!"

"I'll tell 'ee," he whispered with his face working. "Bait it with a wheel-band."

He roared with laughter again, and if I had had any doubts before of his understanding that I wanted a very strong man-trap, I had none now.

Chapter Sixteen.

Something for me.

Rash—cruel—unwise. Well, I'm afraid it was all those, but I was only a boy, and I was stung by the injustice and cowardly cruelty of the outrages perpetrated on us by the men who earned their bread in our works; and hence it was, that, instead of feeling any compunction in doing what I proposed, I was delighted with the idea, and longed for an opportunity to put it in force.

I was, then, very eager to begin, for the present calm, I felt sure, was only going before the storm, and after what I had found out I was anxious to be ready.

Pannell did not keep me waiting long.

Two days after I had made my plans with him I went into his smithy, and in answer to my inquiring look he said, in a heavy, unmoved way:

"Theer's summut for you hung up i' the forge chimney. She goes hard, but theer's a steel bar 'long wi' her as you can prise down the spring till she's set. On'y mind thysen, lad—mind thysen."

"And will it hold a man, Pannell?" I cried.

"Ay; this here's noo pattern. I haven't got into it yet I've got a rare lot of 'em to do."

"But tell me," I whispered, "will it?"

"Think this here noo steel's better than owd fashion stoof?" he said.

"Bother the steel!" I said, speaking lower still. "I want you to tell me whether—"

"Bull-poop's gettin' too fat, Mester Jacob," said Pannell. "Don't give 'im so much meat. Spoils a dorg. Give un bones as he can break oop and yeat. That's the stoof for dorgs. Gives un such a coat as never was."

"Will you tell me?" I began, angrily.

"Nay, I wean't tell thee nowt," he growled. "I've telled thee enew as it is. Tek it when I'm not here, and good luck to thee!"

I could get no more from him, for he would not say another word about the trap, so I waited impatiently for the night so that I might smuggle it from the forge chimney into my desk.

When the time came it was quite absurd how many hindrances there were to my little task. I did not want to set it that night. I only wanted to get it in safety to my desk; but first there were men hanging about the smithies as if they were watching me; then there were my uncles; and lastly, there was Gentles, who made signs that he wished to speak to me, and I didn't care to say anything to the sleek, oily fellow, who only wanted to what he called make it up.

At last, though, everyone had gone but Uncle Jack, who was busy writing a letter or two, and I was to wait for him, and we were going back together.

I slipped off to the smithy, and just as I was half-way there I turned quickly round, feeling quite cold, and as if I was found out, for I heard a curious yawning noise behind me.

It was only Piter, who looked up in my face and gave his tail a wag, and then butted his great head against my leg, holding it tightly there as if it was so heavy that he was glad to give it a rest.

I went on at once impatiently, and Piter's head sank down, the dog uttering a low, discontented whine on being left. I glanced up at the wall, half expecting to see some one looking over and watching me; then up at the windows, fearing that one of the men might still be left.

But all was perfectly quiet, and though I half anticipated such an accident there was no one seated on the top of either of the great chimney-shafts in the neighbourhood watching me with a telescope.

I had a few more absurdly impossible ideas of this kind as I went along the yard, feeling horribly guilty and ready to give up my undertaking. The very silence and solitariness of the place startled me, but I went on and turned in at the open door of the smithy where Pannell worked, and breathed more freely as I looked round and saw that I was alone.

But to make sure I stepped up on to the work-bench and looked out of the window, but there was nothing but the dam to be seen there, and I leaped down and climbed on to the forge, with the coal-dust crushing under my feet, gave a last glance round, and was about to peer up the funnel-like, sheet-iron chimney, when there was a loud clang, and I bounded down, with my heart beating furiously.

I stamped my foot directly after and bit my lips angrily because I had been such a coward, for I had moved a pair of smiths' tongs when I stepped up, and they had slid off on to the ground.

"I'm doing what I ought not to do," I said to myself as I jumped on to the forge again, "but now I've gone so far I must go on."

I peered up in the dark funnel and could see nothing, but I had come prepared, and striking a match I saw just before me, resting on a sooty ledge, the object of my quest.

I lifted it down, astounded at its size and weight, and found that it was an exact imitation of the rat-trap, but with blunt teeth, and a short steel lever with a point like a crowbar was attached to it by means of a bit of wire.

It was enormous, and I quite trembled at the idea of carrying it to the office; but after a sharp glance out of the doorway I took hold of the trap by the iron chain bound round it, and walked quickly to my own place, hoping that even if I had been seen, the watcher would not have been able to make out what I was carrying.

There was not much room to spare when I had laid the great trap in my desk, the lid of which would only just shut down over it; but once safely there, and with the key in the lock ready for me to turn if I heard steps, I had a good look at my treasure.

I was nervous now, and half repentant, for the instrument looked so formidable that I felt that I should not dare to use it.

I had a good look though, and found that it was very complete with chain and ring, and that the lever had a head to it like a pin, evidently so that after it had been used, it could be placed through the ring at the end of the chain, and driven down to act as a peg in the ground.

I had hardly arrived at all this when I heard Uncle Jack's cough, and hastily closing the desk and locking it, I went to meet him.

"Sorry to keep you waiting so long, my boy," he said; "but I wanted to send word to your father how we are going on."

It was on the second night that I put my plan into practice.

I had thought it all well out, and inspected my ground, which was just below the wall, pretty close to the edge of the dam, where I had seen some marks which had made me suspicious.

So as soon as Uncle Bob had gone to lie down, and I had begun my half of the watch, I fastened up Piter, took out my heavy trap, carried it down to the edge of the dam, and carefully felt the wall for the place I had marked by driving in a little nail.

I soon found it, placed my trap exactly beneath it, and wrenching down the spring by means of the lever, I tried to set it.

I had practised doing this in my own place, and could manage it pretty well, but in the darkness and excitement that troubled me now, it proved to be an exceedingly difficult job. Twice I managed to get it set, and was moving away when it went off with a startling clang that made me jump, and expect to see Uncle Bob come running out, especially as the dog set up a furious bark.

I quieted Piter though each time, and went and tried again till I managed my task, having to take great care that I did not hoist myself with my own petard, for it was a terribly dangerous engine that I was setting, though I did not think so then.

It was now set to my satisfaction, and being quite prepared with a big hammer, my next task was to drive in the lever like a peg right through the ring and up to the head, so that if I did catch my bird, there would be no chance of his getting away.

I felt about in the dark for a suitable place, and the most likely seemed to be just at the extent of the five feet of chain, which reached to the edge of the dam, where, between two of the big stones of the embankment, I fancied I could drive in the lever so that it could not be drawn out.

So taking the steel bar with the sharp edge I ran it through the ring, directed the point between two blocks of stone, and then began to drive.

As I said I was well prepared, having carefully thought out the whole affair, and I had bound several thicknesses of cloth over the head of the hammer like a pad so as to muffle the blows, and thus it was that I was able to drive it home without much noise.

At first it went in so easily that I was about to select a fresh place, but it soon became harder and firmer, and when I had done and felt the head it was quite immovable, and held the ring close down to the stones.

My idea had been to cover the trap with a handful or two of hay, but it was so dark that I thought I would leave it, as it was impossible to see it even from where I looked. I left it, meaning to come the next morning and set it free with a file, for I did not want to take up the peg, and I could get another for lever and join the chain with a strong padlock the next time.

It was about eleven o'clock when I had finished my task, and I did not know whether to be pleased or alarmed. I felt something like a boy might who had set a bait at the end of a line to catch a crocodile, and was then very much alarmed for fear he should have any luck.

I crept away and waited, thinking a great deal about Piter, and what would be the consequences if he walked over the trap, but I argued that the chances were a hundred thousand to one against his going to that particular spot. Besides, if I left him chained up Uncle Bob was not likely to unloose him, so I determined to run the risk, and leave the trap set when I went off guard.

The time went slowly by without any alarm, and though I went now and then cautiously in the direction of my trap it had not been disturbed, and I came away more and more confident that it was in so out of the way a part of the yard that it might be there for weeks unseen.

I felt better after this, and at the appointed time called Uncle Bob, who took his watch, and when he called me in the morning the wheel was turning, and the men were coming up to their work.

"I thought you were tired, Cob, so I let you lie till the last moment."

I was so stupid and confused with sleep that I got up yawning; and we were half-way back home before, like a flash, there came to me the recollection of my trap.

I could not make an excuse and go back, though I tried hard to invent one; but went on by my uncle's side so quiet and thoughtful that he made a remark.

"Bit done up, Cob! You ought to have another nap after dinner."

"Oh, I'm all right, uncle," I said, and I went on home with him to have steel-traps for breakfast and think of nothing else save what they had caught.

For I felt perfectly sure that someone had come over the wall in the night—Stevens I expected it would prove to be—and had put his foot right in the trap, which had sprung, caught him by the leg, and cut it right off, and I felt sure that when I got back I should find him lying there where he had bled to death.

The next thing that struck me was that I was a murderer, and that I should be tried and condemned to death, but respited and sentenced to transportation for life on account of my youth.

With such thoughts as these rushing through my brain it was not likely that I should enjoy the breakfast with the brown and pink ham so nicely fried, and the eggs that were so creamy white, and with such yolks of gold.

I did *not* enjoy that breakfast, and I was feverishly anxious to get back to the works, and though first one and then another advised me to go and lie down, I insisted upon going.

I was all in a tremble as I reached the gate, and saw old Dunning's serious face. I read in it reproach, and he seemed to be saying to me, "Oh, how could you do it?" Seemed, for what he did say was, "Nice pleasant morning, Mester Jacob!"

I told a story, for I said, "Yes, it is," when it was to me the most painful and miserable morning I had ever experienced; but I dared not say a word, and for some time I could not find an opportunity for going down the yard.

Nobody ever did go down there, unless it was to wheel a worn-out grindstone to a resting-place or to carry some broken wood-work of the machinery to throw in a heap. There was the heap of coal and the heap of slack or coal-dust, both in the yard; but those who fetched the coal and slack fetched them from this side, and they never went on the other.

The last time I could recall the men going down there to the dam, was when we threw in Piter to give him a bath.

Piter! Had he been let loose? The thought that had come of him was startling, but easily set right, for there was the bull-dog fast asleep in his kennel.

Then there was Stevens!

The thought was horrible. He ought to be in the grinding-shop, and if he were not—I knew!

It would have been easy to go and look, but I felt that I could not, and I walked back to the gate and spoke to old Dunning.

"All the men come yet?" I said.

"No, Mester Jacob, they hevn't all come yet," he said.

I dare not ask any more. All had not come, and one of those who had not come was, of course, Stevens, and he was lying there dead.

I walked back with Dunning's last words ringing in my ears.

"Ain't you well, Mester Jacob?"

No, I was not well. I felt sick and miserable, and I would have given anything to have gone straight down the yard and seen the extent of the misery I had caused.

Oh! If I could have recalled the past, and undone everything; but that was impossible, and in a state of feverish anxiety I went upstairs to where the men were busy at lathe and dry grindstones, to try and get —a glimpse of my trap, as I hoped I could from one of the windows.

To my horror there were two men looking out, and I stopped dumb-foundered as I listened for their words, which I knew must be about the trapped man lying there.

"Nay, lad," said one, "yow could buy better than they at pit's mouth for eight shillings a chaldron."

Oh, what a relief! It was like life to me, and going to one window I found that they could only see the heap of coals.

From the other windows there was no better view. Even from the room over the water-wheel there was no chance of a glimpse of the trap.

I could not stop up there, for I was all of a fret, and at last, screwing up my nerves to the sticking point, I went down determined to go boldly into the grinder's shop, and see if Stevens was there.

What an effort it was! I have often wondered since whether other boys would have suffered what I did under the circumstances, or whether I was a very great coward.

Well, coward or no, I at last went straight into the grinder's shop, and there was the plashing rumble of the great water-wheel beyond the door, the rattle of the bands and the whirr and whirl and screech of the grindstones as they spun round, and steel in some form or other was held to their edge.

There were half a dozen faces I knew, and there was Gentles ready to smile at me with his great mouth and closed eyes.

But I could only just glance at him and nod, for to my horror Stevens' wheel was not going, and there was no one there.

I felt the cold sweat gather all over my face, and a horrible sensation of dread assailed me; and then I turned and hurried out of the building, so that my ghastly face and its changes should not be seen.

For just then I saw Stevens rise up from behind his grindstone with an oil-can in his hand—he had been busy oiling some part or other of the bearings.

Chapter Seventeen.

My Travelling Companion.

Somehow or another I could not get to that trap all that day, and night came, and still I could not get to it.

I tried, but unless I had wanted to draw people's attention to the fact that I had something there of great interest, I could not go.

Even at leaving time it was as bad, and I found myself in the position that I must either tell one of my uncles what I had done, or leave the trap to take its chance.

I chose the latter plan, and calling myself weak coward, went home, arguing to myself that no one would go in the spot where I had placed the trap, but some miscreant, and that it would serve him right.

To my utter astonishment, directly after tea Uncle Dick turned to me.

"Cob," he said; "we have a special letter to send to Canonbury to your father, and a more particular one to bring back in answer, so we have decided that you shall take it up. You can have three or four days' holiday, and it will be a pleasant change. Your mother and father will be delighted to see you, and, of course, you will be glad to see them."

"But when should I have to go?" I said.

"To-night by the last train. Quarter to eleven—You'll get to London about three in the morning. They expect one of us, so you will find them up."

"But—"

"Don't you want to go?" said Uncle Jack severely.

"Yes," I said; "but—"

"But me no buts, as the man said in the old play. There, get ready, boy, and come back to us as soon as you can. Don't make the worst of our troubles here, Cob."

"No, no," said Uncle Dick, "because we are getting on famously as soon as we can manage the men."

"And that we are going to do," said Uncle Bob. "I say I wish I were coming with you."

"Do, then," I cried.

"Get out, you young tempter! No," said Uncle Bob. "Go and take your pleasure, and have pity upon the three poor fellows who are toiling here."

I was obliged to go, of course, but I must tell them about the trap first.

Tell *them*! No, I could not tell Uncle Dick or Uncle Jack. I was afraid that they would be angry with me, so I resolved to speak to Uncle Bob before I went—to take him fully into my confidence, and ask him to move the trap and put it safely away.

It is so easy to make plans—so hard to carry them out.

All through that evening I could not once get a chance to speak to Uncle Bob alone; and time went so fast that we were on our way to the station, and still I had not spoken. There was only the chance left—on the platform.

"Don't look so solid about it, Cob," said Uncle Jack. "They'll be delighted to see you, boy, and it will be a pleasant trip. But we want you back."

"I should think we do," said Uncle Dick, laying his great hand on my shoulder and giving me an affectionate grip.

"Yes, we couldn't get on without our first lieutenant, Philosopher Cob," said Uncle Bob.

I tried to look bright and cheerful; but that trap had not got me by the leg—it seemed to be round my neck and to choke me from speaking.

What was I to do? I could not get a chance. I dare not go away and leave that trap there without speaking, and already there was the distant rumble of the coming train. In a few minutes I should be on my way to London; and at last in despair I got close to Uncle Bob to speak, but in vain—I was put off.

In came the train, drawing up to the side of the platform, and Uncle Bob ran off to find a comfortable compartment for me, looking after me as kindly as if I had been a woman.

"Oh," I thought, "if he would but have stayed!"

"Good-bye, my lad!" said Uncle Dick. "Take care of yourself, Cob, and of the packet," whispered Uncle Jack.

I was about to slap my breast and say, "All right here!" but he caught my hand and held it down.

"Don't," he said in a low half-angry voice. "Discretion, boy. If you have something valuable about you, don't show people where it is."

I saw the wisdom of the rebuke and shook hands. "I'll try and be wiser," I whispered; "trust me." He nodded, and this made me forget the trap for the moment. But Uncle Bob grasped my hand and brought it back.

"Stand away, please," shouted the guard; but Uncle Bob held on by my hand as the train moved.

"Take care of yourself, lad. Call a cab the moment you reach the platform if your father is not there."

"Yes," I said, reaching over a fellow-passenger to speak. "Uncle Bob," I added quickly, "big trap in the corner of the yard; take it up at once—to-night."

"Yes, yes," he said as he ran along the platform. "I'll see to it. Good-bye!"

We were off and he was waving his hand to me, and I saw him for a few moments, and then all was indistinct beneath the station lamps, and we were gliding on, with the glare and smoke and glow of the busy town lighting up the sky.

It had all come to me so suddenly that I could hardly believe I was speeding away back to London; but once more comfortable in my mind with the promise that Uncle Bob had made to take up the trap, I sat back in the comfortable corner seat thinking of seeing my father and mother again, and of what a series of adventures I should have to relate.

Then I had a look round at my fellow-passengers, of whom there were three—a stout old gentleman and a young lady who seemed to be his daughter, and a dark-eyed keen-looking man who was seated opposite to me, and who held a newspaper in his hand and had a couple of books with him.

"I'd offer to lend you one," he said, touching his books and smiling; "but you couldn't read—I can't. Horrible lights."

Just then a heavy snore from the old gentleman made the young lady lean over to him and touch him, waking him up with a start.

The keen-looking man opposite to me raised his eyebrows and smiled slightly, shading his face from the other occupants with his newspaper.

Three or four times over the old gentleman dropped asleep and had to be roused up, and my fellow-passenger smiled good-humouredly and said:

"Might as well have let him sleep."

This was in a whisper, and he made two or three remarks to me.

He seemed very much disposed to be friendly and pointed out the lights of a distant town or two.

"Got in at Arrowfield, didn't you?" he said at last.

I replied that I did; and it was on the tip of my tongue to say, "So did you," but I did not.

"I'm going on to London," he said. "Nasty time to get in—three in the morning. I hate it. No one about. Night cabs and milk carts, police and market wagons. People at the hotel always sleepy. Ah! Here we are at Westernbow."

For the train was stopping, and when it did draw up at the platform the old gentleman was roused up by the young lady, and they got out and left us alone.

"Ha! Ha!" said my companion, "that's better. Give us room to stretch our legs. Do you bet?"

"No," I said, "never."

"Good, lad! Don't; very bad habit. I do; I've lots of bad habits. But I was going to say, I'll bet you an even half-crown that we don't have another passenger from here to London."

"I hope we shall not," I said as I thought of a nap on the seat.

"So do I, sir—so do I," he said, nodding his head quickly. "I vote we lie down and make the best of it—by and by. Have a cigar first?"

"Thank you; I don't smoke," I said.

"I do. Will you excuse me if I have a cigar? Not a smoking carriage—more comfortable."

I assured him that I should not mind; and he took out a cigar, lit it, and began to smoke.

"Better have one," he said. "Mild as mild. They won't hurt you."

I thanked him again and declined, sitting back and watching him as he smoked on seeming to enjoy his cigar, and made a remark or two about the beautiful night and the stars as the train dashed on.

After a time he took out a flask, slipped off the plated cup at the bottom, and unscrewed the top, pouring out afterward some clear-looking liquid.

"Have a drink?" he said, offering me the flask-cup; but I shook my head.

"No, thank you," I said; and somehow I began thinking of the water I had drunk at the works, and which had made me so terribly sleepy.

I don't know how it was, but I did think about that, and it was in my mind as he said laughingly:

"What! Not drink a little drop of mild stuff like that? Well, you are a fellow! Why it's like milk."

He seemed to toss it off.

"Better have a drop," he said.

I declined.

"Nonsense! Do," he cried. "Do you good. Come, have a drink."

He grew more persistent, but the more persistent he was the more I shrank from the cup he held in his hand; and at last I felt sorry, for he seemed so kind that it was ungracious of me to refuse him so simple a request.

"Oh, very well!" he said, "just as you like. There will be the more for me."

He laughed, nodded, and drank the contents of the cup before putting the screw-top on the flask, thrusting it in his breast-pocket, and then making a cushion of his railway wrapper he lay at full length upon the cushion, and seemed to compose himself to sleep.

It was such a good example that, after a few minutes' silence, I did the same, and lay with my eyes half-closed, listening to the dull rattle of the train, and thinking of the works at Arrowfield, and what a good job it was that I spoke to Uncle Bob about the trap.

Then I hoped he would not be incautious and hurt himself in letting off the spring.

I looked across at my fellow-traveller, who seemed to be sleeping soundly, and the sight of his closed eyes made mine heavy, and no wonder, for every other night I had been on guard at the works, and that seemed to shorten my allowance of sleep to a terrible degree.

I knew there could be no mistake, for I was going as far as the train went, and the guard would be sure to wake me up if I was fast asleep.

And how satisfactory it seemed to be lying there on the soft cushions instead of walking about the works and the yard the previous night. I was growing more and more sleepy, the motion of the train serving to lull me; and then, all at once, I was wide-awake staring at the bubble of glass that formed the lamp in the ceiling, and wondering where I was.

I recollected directly and glanced at my fellow-traveller, to see that he was a little uneasy, one of his legs being off the seat; but he was breathing heavily, and evidently fast asleep.

I lay watching him for a few minutes, and then the sweet restful feeling mastered me again, and I went off fast asleep. One moment there was the compartment with its cushions and lamp with the rush and sway of the carriage that made me think it must be something like this on board ship; the next I was back at the works keeping watch and wondering whether either of the men would come and make any attempt upon the place.

I don't know how long I had been asleep, but all at once, without moving, I was wide-awake with my eyes closed, fully realising that I had a valuable packet of some kind in my breast-pocket, and that my fellow-traveller was softly unbuttoning my overcoat so as to get it out.

I lay perfectly still for a moment or two, and then leaped up and bounded to the other side of the carriage.

"There, it is of no use," said my fellow-traveller; "pull that letter out of your pocket and give it to me quietly or—"

He said no more, but took a pistol out of his breast, while I shrank up against the farther door, the window of which was open, and stared at him aghast.

"Do you hear?" he said fiercely. "Come; no nonsense! I want that letter. There, I don't want to frighten you, boy. Come and sit down; I sha'n't hurt you."

The train was flying along at forty miles an hour at least, and this man knew that the packet I had was valuable. How he knew it I could not tell, but he must have found out at Arrowfield. He was going to take it from me, and if he got it what was he going to do?

I thought it all over as if in a flash.

He was going to steal the packet, and he would know that I should complain at the first station we reached; and he would prevent this, I felt sure. But how?

There was only one way. He had threatened me with a pistol, but I did not think he would use that. No; there was only one way, and it was this—he would rob me and throw me out of the train.

My legs shook under me as I thought this, and the light in the carriage seemed to be dancing up and down, as I put my right arm out of the window and hung to the side to keep myself up.

All this was a matter of moments, and it seemed to be directly after my fellow-passenger had spoken first that he roared out, "Do you hear, sir? Come here!"

I did not move, and he made a dash at me, but, as he did, my right hand rested on the fastening of the door outside, turned the handle, and clinging to it, I swung out into the rushing wind, turning half round as the door banged heavily back, when, by an instinctive motion, my left hand caught at anything to save me from falling, grasped the bar that ran along between door and door, and the next moment, how I know not, I was clinging to this bar with my feet on the foot-board, and my eyes strained back at the open door, out of which my fellow-passenger leaned.

"You young idiot, come back!" he roared; but the effect of his words was to make me shrink farther away, catching at the handle of the next door, and then reaching on to the next bar, so that I was now several feet away.

The wind seemed as if it would tear me from the foot-board, and I was obliged to keep my face away to breathe; but I clung to the bar tightly, and watched the fierce face that was thrust out of the door I had left.

"Am I to come after you?" he roared. "Come back!"

My answer was to creep past another door, to find to my horror that this was the last, and that there was a great gap between me and the next carriage.

What was I to do? Jump, with the train dashing along at such a rate that it seemed as if I must be shaken down or torn off by the wind.

I stared back horror-stricken and then uttered a cry of fear, as the window I had just passed was thrown open and a man leaned out.

"I'll swear I heard someone shout," he said to a travelling companion, and he looked back along the train. "Yes," he continued, "there's someone three compartments back looking out. Oh, he's gone in now.

Wonder what it was!"

Just then he turned his head in my direction, and saw my white face.

I saw him start as I clung there just a little way below him to his right, and within easy reach, and, for I should think a minute, we stared hard at each other.

Then he spoke in a quiet matter-of-fact way.

"Don't be scared, my lad," he said; "it's alright. I can take hold of you tightly. Hold fast till I get you by the arms. That's it; now loose your right hand and take hold of the door; here pass it in. That's the way; edge along. I've got you tight. Come along; now the other hand in. That's the way."

I obeyed him, for he seemed to force me to by his firm way, but the thought came over me, "Suppose he is that man's companion." But even if he had been, I was too much unnerved to do anything but what he bade me, so I passed one hand on to the window-frame of the door, then edged along and stood holding on with the other hand, for he had me as if his grasp was a vice, and then his hands glided down to my waist. He gripped me by my clothes and flesh, and before I could realise it he had dragged me right in through the window and placed me on the seat.

Then dragging up the window he sank back opposite to me and cried to a gentleman standing in the compartment:

"Give me a drop of brandy, Jem, or I shall faint!"

I crouched back there, quivering and unable to speak. I was so unnerved; but I saw the other gentleman hand a flask to the bluff-looking man who had saved me, and I saw him take a hearty draught and draw long breath, after which he turned to me.

"You young scoundrel!" he cried; "how dare you give me such a fright!"

I tried to speak, but the words would not come. I was choking, and I believe for a minute I literally sobbed.

"There, there, my lad," said the other kindly, "You're all right. Don't speak to him like that now, Jordan. The boy's had a horrible scare."

"Scare!" said the big bluff man; "and so have I. Why, my heart was in my mouth. I wouldn't go through it again for a hundred pounds. How did you come there, sir?"

"Let him be for a few minutes," said the other gently. "He'll come round directly, and tell us."

I gave him a grateful look and held out my wet hand, which he took and held in his.

"The boy has had a terrible shock," he said. "He'll tell us soon. Don't hurry, my lad. There, be calm."

I clung to his hand, for he seemed to steady me, my hand jerking and twitching, and a curious sensation of horror that I had never felt before seeming to be upon me; but by degrees this passed off, the more quickly that the two gentlemen went on talking as if I were not there.

"I'm so much obliged," I said at last, and the big bluff man laughed.

"Don't name it," he said, nodding good-humouredly. "Five guineas is my fee."

I shivered.

"And my friend here, Doctor Brown, will have a bigger one for his advice."

"He's joking you, my lad," said the other gentleman smiling. "I see you are not hurt."

"No, sir," I said; "I—"

The trembling came over me again, and I could not speak for a minute or two, but sat gazing helplessly from one to the other.

"Give him a drop of brandy," said the big bluff man.

"No, let him be for a few minutes; he's mastering it," was the reply.

This did me good, and making an effort I said quickly:

"A man in the carriage tried to rob me, and I got on to the foot-board and came along here."

"Then you did what I dare not have done," said the one who dragged me in. "But a pretty state of affairs this. On the railway, and no means of communicating."

"But there are means."

"Tchah! How was the poor lad to make use of them? Well, we shall have the scoundrel, unless he gets out of the train and jumps for it. We must look out when we stop for taking the tickets. We shall not halt before."

By degrees I grew quite composed, and told them all.

"Yes," said my big friend, "it was very brave of you; but I think I should have parted with all I had sooner than have run such a risk."

"If it had been your own," said the other gentleman. "In this case it seems to me the boy would have been robbed, and probably thrown out afterwards upon the line. I think you did quite right, my lad, but I should not recommend the practice to anyone else."

They chatted to me pleasantly enough till the train began at last to slacken speed preparatory to stopping for the tickets to be taken, and at the first symptom of this my two new friends jumped up and let down the windows, each leaning out so as to command a view of the back of the train.

I should have liked to look back as well, but that was impossible, so I had to be content to sit and listen; but I was not kept long in suspense, for all at once the quieter and more gentlemanly of my companions exclaimed:

"I thought as much. He has just jumped off, and run down the embankment. There he goes!"

I ran to the side, and caught a glimpse of a figure melting away into the darkness. Then it was gone.

"There goes all chance of punishing the scoundrel," said the big bluff man, turning to me and smiling good-temperedly. "I should have liked to catch him, but I couldn't afford to risk my neck in your service, young man."

I thanked him as well as I could, and made up my mind that if my father was waiting on the platform he should make a more satisfactory recognition of the services that had been performed.

This did not, however, prove so easy as I had hoped, for in the confusion of trying to bring them together when I found my father waiting, I reached the spot where I had left my travelling-companions just in time to see them drive off in a cab.

Chapter Eighteen.

Against the Law.

The next day, after recounting plenty of my adventures to my mother, but, I am afraid, dressing some of them up so that they should not alarm her, a letter reached me from Uncle Bob.

It was very short. He hoped I had reached town safely, and found all well. The night had passed quite quietly at the works, and he ended by saying:

"I took up the trap. All right!"

That was a great relief to me, and made my stay in town quite pleasant.

I went down to the old works with my father, and it made me smile to see how quiet and orderly everything was, and how different to the new line of business we had taken up. The men here never thought of committing outrages or interfering with those who employed them, and I could not help thinking what a contrast there was between them and the Arrowfield rough independence of mien.

My father questioned me a great deal about matters upon which my uncles had dwelt lightly, but I found that he thoroughly appreciated our position there and its risks.

"Not for another six months, Cob," he said in answer to an inquiry as to when he was coming down.

"You four must pacify the country first," he added laughing, "and have the business in good going order."

My visit was very pleasant, and I could not help feeling proud of the treatment I received at home; but all the same I was glad to start again for Arrowfield and join my uncles in their battle for success.

For there was something very exciting in these struggles with the men, and now I was away all this seemed to be plainer, and the attraction grew so that there was a disposition on my part to make those at home quite at their ease as to the life I was leading down at Arrowfield.

At last the day came for me to start on my return journey, when once more I had a packet to bear.

"I need not tell you that it is of great value, Cob," said my father. "Button it up in your pocket, and then forget all about it. That is the safest way. It takes off all the consciousness."

"I don't suppose I shall meet my friend this time," I said.

My father shuddered slightly.

"It is not likely," he said; "but I should strongly advise you to change carriages if you find yourself being left alone with a stranger."

Word had been sent down as to the train I should travel by, and in due time I found myself on the Arrowfield platform and back at our new home, where Mrs Stephenson and Tattsey were ready with the most friendly of smiles.

"Everything has been going on splendidly," was the report given to me. Piter had been carefully attended to, and the works watched as well as if I had been at Arrowfield.

I felt annoyed, and, I suppose, showed it, for it seemed as if my uncles were bantering me, but the annoyance passed off directly under the influence of the warmth displayed by all three.

"I'm beginning to be hopeful now that work will go on steadily, that this watching can be given up, and that we can take to a few country excursions, some fishing, and the like."

That was Uncle Dick's expressed opinion; and I was glad enough to hear it, for though I did not mind the work I liked some play.

Uncle Jack was just as hopeful; but Uncle Bob evidently was not, for he said very little.

This time I had travelled by a day train, and I was quite ready to take my turn at the watching that night. Uncle Jack, whose turn it was, opposed my going, as I had been travelling so far; but I insisted, saying that I had had my regular night's rest ever since I had left them, and was consequently quite fresh.

I wanted to ask Uncle Bob where he had hidden the trap, but I had no opportunity, and as neither Uncle Dick nor Uncle Jack made any allusion to it I did not start the subject.

Perhaps Uncle Bob had not told them, meaning to have a few words with me first.

It almost seemed like coming home to enter the works again, where Piter was most demonstrative in his affection, and carried it to such an extent that I could hardly get away.

I had a look round the gloomy old place at once, and felt quite a thrill of pride in the faintly glowing furnaces and machinery as I thought of the endless things the place was destined to produce.

"Look here, Cob," said Uncle Jack, "I shall lie down for three hours, mind; and at the end of that time you are to wake me. It is only nine o'clock now, and you can get over that time with a book. There will be no need to walk round the place."

"Would Piter warn us, do you think?" I said.

"Oh, yes! It is getting quite a form our being here. The men are toning down."

He threw himself on the bed, and I took up a book and read for an hour, after which I had a walk through the gloomy workshops, and in and out of the furnace-houses and smithies, where all was quiet as could be.

After this I felt disposed to go and open the big door and look down into the wheel-pit. I don't know why, only that the place attracted me. I did not, however, but walked back to the doorway to look at the glow which overhung the town, with the heavy canopy of ruddy smoke, while away behind me the stars were shining brightly, and all was clear.

I patted Piter, who came to the full length of his chain, and then I had a look about with the lantern to see if I could find where Uncle Bob had put the trap.

I felt that it must be under lock and key somewhere, but the cupboards had nothing to show, and, try how I would, I could think of no likely place for it to be hidden in. So I gave up the task of trying to find it, and walked back to the door, where I found Piter lying down hard at work trying to push his collar over his head.

The patient, persevering way in which he tried, getting both his fore-paws against it, was most amusing, the more so that there was not the slightest possibility of success attending his efforts, for his neck, which the collar fitted pretty closely, was small, and his bullet head enormous by comparison.

"Come," I said, as I bent over him; "shall I undo it for you?"

He looked up at me as I put the dark lantern down, and whined softly. Then he began working at the collar again.

"Look here," I said, as I sat on the bottom step. "Shall I undo it?"

Dogs must have a good deal of reason, for Piter leaped up and laid his head in my lap directly, holding it perfectly still while I unbuckled the strap collar, when he gave a sniff or two at my hands, licked them, and bounded off to have a regular good run all over the place before he came back and settled down close to me in the little office where I was trying to read.

Twelve o'clock at last, and I awoke Uncle Jack, who rose at once, fresh and clear as if he were amply rested, and soon after I was fast asleep, dreaming away and fancying I could hear the rattle and the throb of the train. Then I was talking to that man again, and then swinging out on the carriage-door with the wind rushing by, and the bluff man leaning out over me, and Piter on the carriage with him, barking at my aggressor, who was shrieking for mercy.

Then I was awake, to see that it was Uncle Jack who was leaning over me, and the window was open, admitting a stream of cold air and a curious yelling noise, mingled with the barking of a dog.

"What is the matter?" I cried.

"That's what I want to know," said Uncle Jack. "I went with a candle, but the wind puffed it out. Where did you put the lantern?"

"Lantern—lantern!" I said in a confused way, "did I have it?"

"Yes; you must have had it. Can't you think? Gracious, what a noise! Piter must have got someone by the throat."

"Oh, I know!" I cried as I grew more fully awake. "On the shelf in the entry."

We ran down together, and a faint glow showed its whereabouts, still alight, but with the dark shade turned over the bull's-eye.

"Where does the noise come from?" I said, feeling startled at the alarming nature of the cries, freshly awakened as I was from sleep.

"I can hardly tell," he said, seizing the lantern and taking a sharp hold, of his stick. "Bring a stick with you, my boy, for there may be enemies in the way."

"Why, uncle," I cried, "some poor creature has fallen from the side path into the dam."

"Some wretched drunken workman then," he said, as we hurried in the direction, and there seemed to be no doubt about it now, for there was the splashing of water, and the cry of "Help!" while Piter barked more furiously than ever.

We ran down to the edge of the dam, the light of the bull's-eye flashing and dancing over the ground, so that we were able to avoid the different objects lying about; and directly after the light played on the water, and then threw into full view the figure of the bull-dog as he stood on the stone edge of the dam barking furiously at a man's head that was just above the surface of the water.

"Help! Help!" he cried as we drew near, and then I uttered a prolonged "Oh!" and stood still.

"Quiet, Piter! Down, dog! Can't you see it is a friend!"

But the dog seemed to deny it, and barked more furiously than ever.

"Quiet, sir! Here, Cob, lay hold of the lantern. Will you be quiet, dog! Lay hold of him, Cob, and hold him."

I obeyed in a half stupid way, holding the lantern with one hand, as I went on my knees, putting my arm round Piter's neck to hold him back; and in that way I struggled back from the edge, watching my uncle as I made the light fall upon the head staring wildly at us, a horrible white object just above the black water of the dam.

"Help! Help!" it cried. "Save me! Oh!"

"Catch hold of the stick. That's right; now your hand. Well done! What's holding you down? Have you got your foot entangled? That's better: how did you fall in?"

As my uncle rapidly asked these questions he got hold of the man, and dragged him on to the stone edge of the dam, when there was a horrible clanking noise, the rattle of a chain, the man uttered a hideous yell, and as Piter set up a tremendous barking again I turned off the light.

"Here, don't do that," cried my uncle.

I hardly know what induced me to turn off the light, unless it was a shamefaced feeling on being, as I thought, found out. And yet it did not seem that I was the guilty party. Uncle Bob had said he had taken up the trap, and it was all right. He must have altered his mind and set it again.

"That's better," said my uncle as I turned on the light once more; and then Piter made such a struggle that I could not hold him. There was a bit of a scuffle, and he was free to rush at the man, upon whom he fixed himself as he lay there howling and dripping with water.

The man yelled again horribly, sprang up with Piter holding on to him; there was the same horrible clanking noise on the stones, and down he fell once more groaning.

"Help! Murder! Take away the dorg. Oh, help!" he cried.

"Good gracious! What is the matter?" cried Uncle Jack, telling me what I knew. "The man's leg's in a trap."

He sprang up again, for by main force Uncle Jack had dragged Piter away with his mouth full of trouser leg; but there were only two clanks and a sprawl, for the poor wretch fell headlong again on the stones, praying for mercy.

"Why, his leg's in a great trap, and it's held by a chain," cried Uncle Jack. "Here, how came you in this condition?"

"Eh mester, aw doan know. Deed aw doan know," the fellow groaned. "Hey, but it's biting my leg off, and I'll be a lame man to the end o' my days."

"Why, it's Gentles!" cried Uncle Jack, taking the lantern from me, for I had enough to do to hold the dog.

"Tek off the thing; tek off the thing," groaned the man. "It's a-cootin' my leg i' two, I tell'ee."

"Hold your noise, and don't howl like that," cried Uncle Jack angrily, for he seemed to understand now that the man must have climbed over into the yard and been caught, though he was all the more surprised, for quiet smooth-faced Gentles was the last man anyone would have suspected.

"But I tell'ee its tekkin off my leg," groaned the man, and he made another trial to escape, but was checked by the peg driven tightly into the ground between the stones, and he fell again, hurting himself horribly.

"I shall be a dead man—murdered in a minute," he groaned. "Help! Oh, my poor missus and the bairns! Tek off that thing, and keep away yon dorg."

"Look here," said Uncle Jack, making the light play on the poor wretch's miserable face. "How came you here?"

"Your dorg flew at me, mester, and drove me int'watter."

"Yes, exactly; but how came you in the yard?"

"I d'know, mester, I d'know."

"I suppose not," said Uncle Jack.

"Tek off that thing, mester; tek off that thing. It's most cootin off my leg."

I was ready to add my supplications, for I knew the poor wretch must be in terrible agony; but I felt as if I could not speak.

"I'll take it off by and by, when I know how you came here."

154

"I tell'ee it's 'gen the law to set they montraps," cried the fellow in a sudden burst of anger, "and I'll have the law o' thee."

"I would," said Uncle Jack, still making the light play over the dripping figure, and then examining the trap, and tracing the chain to the peg. "Hullo!" he cried, "what's this?"

He was holding the lantern close to a dark object upon the ground quite close, and Gentles uttered a fresh yell, bounded up, made a clanking noise, and fell again groaning.

"Doan't! Doan't! Thou'lt blow us all to bits."

"Oh, it's powder, then, is it?" cried Uncle Jack.

"Hey, I d'know, mester, I d'know."

"Didn't bring it with you, I suppose?" said Uncle Jack.

"Nay, mester, I didn't bring it wi' me."

"Then how do you know it's powder?"

"Hey, I d'know it's powder," groaned the miserable wretch. "It only looks like it. Tek off this trap thing. Tek away the light. Hey, bud I'm being killed."

"Let me see," said Uncle Jack with cool deliberation. "You climbed over the wall with that can of powder and the fuse."

"Nay, nay, mester, not me."

"And fell into a trap."

"Yes, mester. Tek it off."

"Where did you mean to put that can of powder?"

"Nay, mester, I—"

"Tell me directly," cried Uncle Jack, giving the chain a drag and making Gentles yell out; "tell me directly, or I'll pitch you into the dam."

Uncle Jack's manner was so fierce that the man moaned out feebly:

"If I tell'ee wilt tek off the trap?"

"Perhaps I will. Speak out. Where did you mean to put the powder can?"

"Under big watter-wheel, mester."

"And fire the fuse?"

"Yes, mester."

"How long would it have burned?"

"Twenty minutes, mester."

"Same length as the one that was run in the furnace-house?"

"Yes, mester."

"You cowardly scoundrel! You were in that too, then," cried Uncle Jack, going down on one knee and seizing the man by the throat and shaking him till he realised how horribly he was punishing him, when he loosed his hold.

"Don't kill me, mester. Oh, my wife and bairns!"

"A man with a wife and children, and ready to do such a dastardly act as that! Here, you shall tell me this, who set you on?"

The man set his teeth fast.

"Who set you on, I say?"

"Nay, mester, I canna tell," groaned Gentles.

"But you shall tell," roared Uncle Jack. "You shall stay here till you do."

"I can't tell; I weant tell," groaned the man.

"We'll see about that," cried Uncle Jack. "Pah! What a brute I am! Hold the light, Cob. Piter! You touch him if you dare. Let's see if we can't get this trap open."

He took hold of it gently, and tried to place it flat upon the stones, but the poor trapped wretch groaned dismally till he was placed in a sitting posture with his knee bent, when Piter, having been coerced into a neutral state, Uncle Jack pressed with all his might upon the spring while I worked the ring upon it half an inch at a time till the jaws yawned right open and Gentles' leg was at liberty.

He groaned and was evidently in great pain; but as soon as it was off, his face was convulsed with passion, and he shook his fists at Uncle Jack.

"I'll hev the law of ye for this here. I'll hev the law of ye."

"Do," said Uncle Jack, picking up the can of powder; "and I shall bring this in against you. Let me see. You confessed in the presence of this witness that you came over the wall with this can of powder to blow up our water-wheel so as to stop our works. Mr Gentles, I think we shall get the better of you this time."

The man raised himself to his feet, and stood with great difficulty, moaning with pain.

"Now," said Uncle Jack, "will you go back over the wall or out by the gate."

"I'll pay thee for this. I'll pay thee for this," hissed the man.

Uncle Jack took him again by the throat.

"Look here," he said fiercely. "Have a care what you are doing, my fine fellow. You have had a narrow escape to-night. If we had not been carefully watching you would by now have been hanging by that chain —drowned. Mind you and your cowardly sneaking scoundrels of companions do not meet with some such fate next time they come to molest us. Now go. You can't walk? There's a stick for you. I ought to break your thick skull with it, but I'm going to be weak enough to give it to you to walk home. Go home and tell your wife and children that you are one of the most treacherous, canting, hypocritical scoundrels in Arrowfield, and that you have only got your deserts if you are lamed for life."

He gave Gentles his stick and walked with him to the gate, which he unlocked and held open for him to pass out groaning and suffering horribly.

"Good-night, honest faithful workman!" he said; "friendly man who only wanted to be left alone. Do you want your can of powder? No: I'll keep it as a memento of your visit, and for fear you might have an accident at home."

The man groaned again as he passed out and staggered.

"Poor wretch!" said Uncle Jack, so that I alone heard him. "Ignorance and brutality. Here," he said aloud, "take my arm. I'll help you on to your house. One good turn deserves another."

Uncle Jack went to him and took his stick in his hand, when, fancying I heard something, I turned on the light just in time to show Uncle Jack his danger, for half a dozen men armed with sticks came out of the shadow of the wall and rushed at him.

It was fortunate for him that he had taken back the stout oak walking-stick that he made his companion on watching nights, or he would have been beaten down.

As it was he received several heavy blows, but he parried others, and laid about him so earnestly that two men went down, and another fell over Gentles.

By that time my uncle had retreated to the gate, darted through, and banged and locked it in his enemies' face.

"Rather cowardly to retreat, Cob," he panted; "but six to one are long odds. Where's the powder can?"

"I have it, uncle," I said.

"Ah, well, suppose you give it to me, or else the light! The two don't go well together. They always quarrel, and it ends in what Mr O'Gallagher in *Perceval Keene* called a blow up."

I gave him the can, and then listened to the muttering of voices outside, half expecting that an attempt might be made to scale the wall.

"No," said Uncle Jack; "they will not do that. They don't make open attacks."

"Did you see who the others were?"

"No, it was too dark. There, let's get inside. But about that trap. I won't leave it there."

I walked with him in silence, and lighted him while he dragged the iron peg out of the ground, and carried all back to the office, where he examined the trap, turning it over and over, and then throwing it heavily on the floor.

He looked hard at me then, and I suppose my face told tales.

"I thought so," he said; "that was your game, Master Cob."

"Yes," I said; "but I thought it was taken up. I told Uncle Bob to take it up when I went to London."

"He thought you meant the trap of the drain," cried Uncle Jack, roaring with laughter. "He had the bricklayer to it, and said there was a bad smell, and it was well cleaned out."

"Oh!" I exclaimed; "and I made sure that it was all right again."

"How came you to set the trap there?"

"I had seen marks on the wall," I said, "where someone came over, but I never thought it could be Gentles."

"No, my lad, one don't know whom to trust here; but how came you to think of that?"

"It was the rat-trap set me thinking of it, and when I made up my mind to do it I never thought it would be so serious as it was. Are you very angry with me?"

Uncle Jack looked at me with his forehead all in wrinkles, and sat down on a high stool and tapped the desk.

I felt a curious flinching as he looked so hard at me, for Uncle Jack was always the most stern and uncompromising of my uncles. Faults that Uncle Dick would shake his head at, and Uncle Bob say, "I say, come, this won't do, you know," Uncle Jack would think over, and talk about perhaps for two or three days.

"I ought to be very angry with you, Cob," he said. "This was a very rash thing to do. These men are leading us a horrible life, and they deserve any punishment; but there is the law of the land to punish evildoers, and we are not allowed to take that law in our own hands. You might have broken that fellow's leg with the trap."

"Yes, I see now," I said.

"As it is I expect you have done his leg serious injury, and made him a worse enemy than he was before. But that is not the worst part of it. What we want here is co-operation—that's a long word, Cob, but you know what it means."

"Working together," I said.

"Of course. You are only a boy, but you are joined with us three to mutually protect each other, and our strength lies in mutual dependence, each knowing exactly what the other has done."

"Yes, I see that, Uncle," I said humbly.

"How are we to get on then if one of the legs on which we stand—you, sir, gives way? It lets the whole machine down; it's ruin to us, Cob."

"I'm very sorry, uncle."

"We are four. Well, suppose one of us gets springing a mine unknown to the others, what a position the other three are in!"

"Yes," I said again. "I see it all now."

"You didn't spring a mine upon us, Cob, but you sprang a trap."

I nodded.

"It was a mistake, lad, though it has turned out all right as it happened, and we have been saved from a terrible danger; but look here, don't do anything of the kind again."

"Shall you go to the police about this?" I said.

"No, and I'm sure the others will agree with me. We must be our own police, Cob, and take care of ourselves; but I'm afraid we have rough times coming."

Chapter Nineteen.

Pannell says Nothing.

"Better and better!" cried Uncle Dick, waving a letter over his head one morning after the post had come in. "All we have to do is to work away. Our steel is winning its way more and more in London, and there is already a greater demand than we can supply."

"It seems funny too," I said. "I went through Norton's works yesterday with Mr Tomplin, and saw them making steel, and it seemed almost exactly your way."

"Yes, Cob," said Uncle Dick, "*almost*. It's that trifling little difference that does it. It is so small that it is almost imperceptible; but still it is enough to make our steel worth half as much again as theirs."

"You didn't show them the difference, did you, Cob?" said Uncle Jack, laughing.

"Why, how could I?"

"Ah! I forgot; you don't know. But never mind, you'll arrive at years of discretion some day, Cob, and then you will be trusted with the secret."

"I consider that he could be trusted now," cried Uncle Dick. "I am quite willing to show him whenever he likes. We make a fresh batch to-morrow."

"No," I said; "I don't want to be shown yet. I can wait."

"Is that meant sulkily, or is it manly frankness?" said Uncle Jack sharply.

"Oh, I'll answer that," replied Uncle Dick—"certainly not sulkily."

"I endorse that," said Uncle Bob; and I gave them both a grateful look.

"He shall learn everything we know," said Dick. "It is his right as his father's son. If we have not shown him sooner it is on account of his father's interests, and because we felt that a secret that means property or nothing is rather a weighty one for a lad of his years to bear. Well, once more, Cob, you will not mind being left?"

"No," I said, "you will not be away many hours. The men will hardly know that you have gone, and if they were to turn disagreeable I'm sure Pannell would help me."

"Oh, there's no fear of any open annoyance," said Uncle Jack; "the men have been remarkably quiet since we caught Master Gentles. By the way, anyone know how he is?"

"I know," I said. "I've seen Mrs Gentles every day, and he leaves the infirmary to-morrow."

"Cured?"

"Yes; only he will walk a little lame, that's all, and only for a month or two."

"Well, take care of the place, Cob," said Uncle Jack. "I don't suppose the men will interfere with you, but if they do you can retreat."

"If you thought they would interfere with me," I said, "you would not go."

They all laughed, and, as we had arranged, they left the works one by one, and I went on just as usual, looking in at one place, and then another, to see how the men were going on, before returning to the office and copying some letters left for me to do.

It was a month since the adventure with the trap, and to see the men no one could have imagined that there was the slightest discontent among them.

Pannell had said very little, though I had expected he would; in fact he seemed to have turned rather surly and distant to me. As for the other men, they did their work in their regular independent style, and I had come to the conclusion that my best way was to treat all alike, and not make special friends, especially after the melancholy mistake I had made in putting most faith in one who was the greatest scoundrel in the place.

My uncles had gone to the next town to meet a firm of manufacturers who had been making overtures that seemed likely to be profitable, and this day had been appointed for the meeting.

After a time I went into Pannell's smithy, to find him hammering away as earnestly as ever, with his forehead covered with dew, his throat open, and his shirt-sleeves rolled up, so as to give his great muscles full play.

"Well," he said all at once, "want another trap?"

"No," I said, smiling. "I say, Pannell, what did the men think about it?"

He opened his lips to speak, but closed them directly.

"No," he said shortly; "won't do. I'm on t'other side, you see."

"But you might tell me that," I cried. "I say, I should as soon have thought of catching you as old Gentles."

"Hush! Say rat," he whispered. "Don't name names. And say, lad, don't talk about it. You don't want to get me knocked on the head?"

"No, Pannell," I said; "indeed I don't. You're too good a fellow."

"Nay, I'm not," he said, shaking his head. "I'm a downright bad un."

"Not you."

"Ay, but I am—reg'lar down bad un."

"What have you been doing?"

"Nowt," he said; and he brought down his hammer with a tremendous bang as if he meant to make a full stop at the end of his sentence.

"Then why are you a bad one?"

He looked at me, then out of the window, then front the door, and then back at me.

"I'm going to Lunnon to get work," he said.

"No, don't; we like you—you're such a good steady workman. Why are you going?"

"Don't like it," he said. "Man can't do as he pleases."

"Uncle John says he can't anywhere, and the masters are the men's servants here."

"Nay, lad," he whispered as he hammered away. "Men's worse off than the masters. Wuckman here hev to do what the trade tells him, or he'd soon find out what was what. Man daren't speak."

"For fear of getting into trouble with his mates?"

"Nay, his mates wouldn't speak. It's the trade; hish!"

He hammered away for some time, and his skill with his hammer fascinated me so that I stopped on watching him. A hammer to me had always seemed to be a tool to strike straightforward blows; but Pannell's hammer moulded and shaped, and always seemed to fall exactly right, so that a piece of steel grew into form. And I believe he could have turned out of the glowing metal anything of which a model had been put before his eyes.

"Well," I said, "I must go to my writing."

"Nay, stop a bit. We two ain't said much lately. They all gone to Kedham?"

"Yes; how did you know?"

"Oh, we knows a deal. There aren't much goes on as we don't know. Look ye here; I want to say summat, lad, and I can't—yes, I can."

"Well, say it, then," I said, smiling at his eagerness.

"Going to—look here, there was a rat once as got his leg caught in a trap."

"Yes, I know there was," I replied with a laugh.

"Nay, it's nowt to laugh at, lad. Rats has sharp teeth; and that there rat —a fat smooth rat he were—he said he'd bite him as set that trap."

"Pannell!" I cried, as a curious feeling of dread came over me for a moment and then passed away.

"Ay, lad."

"You don't mean to say that?"

"Me!—I mean to say! Nay, lad, not me. I never said nothing. 'Tain't likely!"

I looked at him searchingly, but his face seemed to turn as hard as the steel he hammered; and finding that he would not say any more, I left him, to go thoughtfully back to my desk and try to write.

But who could write situated as I was—left alone with about thirty workmen in the place, any one of whom might be set to do the biting in revenge for the trap-setting? For there was no misunderstanding Pannell's words; they were meant as a sort of warning for me. And now what was I to do?

I wished my uncles had not gone or that they had taken me, and I nearly made up my mind to go for a walk or run back home.

But it seemed so cowardly. It was not likely that anyone would touch me there, though the knowledge the men evidently had of their masters' movements was rather startling; and I grew minute by minute more nervous.

"What a coward I am!" I said to myself as I began writing, but stopped to listen directly, for I heard an unusual humming down in the grinders' shop; but it ceased directly, and I heard the wheel-pit door close.

"Something loose in the gear of the great wheel, perhaps," I thought; and I went on writing.

All at once the idea came upon me. Suppose they were to try and blow me up!

I slipped off my stool and examined all the papers beneath my desk and in the waste-paper basket, and then I felt so utterly ashamed that I forced myself back into my seat and tried to go on writing.

But it was impossible. The day was bright and sunny and the water in the dam was dancing and glittering, for the wind was off the hills and blew the smoke in the other direction—over the town. There was a great patch of dancing light on the ceiling reflected from the dam, and some flowers in the window looked bright and sent out a sweet perfume; but I could see nothing but men crawling in the dark with powder-cans and fuses; and to make myself worse, I must go to Uncle Jack's cupboard and look at the can that we had found by Gentles that night, just as it had been picked up, with a long fuse hanging out of the neck and twisted round and round.

I went back after locking it up and taking out the key, and after opening the window I stood looking out to calm myself, wishing the while that I was right away among the hills far from the noise of whirring stones and shrieking metal. I knew the sun was shining there, and the grass was green, and the view was spread out for miles; while from where I stood there were the great black buildings, the tall shafts, and close beneath me the dam which, in spite of the sunshine, suggested nothing but men coming down from the head on rafts of wood to work some mischief.

The situation became intolerable; I could not write; I could not get calm by walking up and down; and every time there was a louder noise than usual from the upper or lower workshop I started, and the perspiration came out upon my face.

What a coward! You will say.

Perhaps so; but a boy cannot go through such adventures as fell to my lot and not have some trace left behind.

I stood at last in the middle of the little office, and thought of what would be the best thing to do.

Should I run away?

No; that would be too cowardly.

I came to the right conclusion, I am sure, for I decided to go and face the danger, if there was any; for I said to myself, "Better to see it coming than to be taken unawares."

Now, please, don't think me conceited. In place of being conceited, I want to set down modestly and truthfully the adventures that befell me while my lot was cast among a number of misguided men who, bound together in what they considered a war against their masters, were forced by their leaders into the performance of deeds quite opposed to their ordinary nature. It was a mad and foolish combination as then conducted, and injured instead of benefiting their class.

Urged by my nervous dread of coming danger, I, as I have said, determined to see it if I could, and so be prepared; and in this spirit I put as bold a face on the matter as possible, and went down the long workshop where the men were grinding and working over the polishing-wheels, which flew round and put such a wonderful gloss upon a piece of metal.

Then I went down and into the furnace-house, where the fires were glowing, and through the chinks the blinding glare of the blast-fed flame seemed to flash and cut the gloom.

The men there gave me a civil nod, and so did the two smiths who were forging knives, while, when I went next into Pannell's smithy, feeling all the more confident for having made up my mind to action, the big fellow stared at me.

"Yow here agen?" he said.

"Yes."

"Well, don't stay, lad; and if I was you I should keep out of wet grinders' shop."

"Why?" I said.

He banged a piece of steel upon his anvil, and the only answers I could get from him were raps of the hammer upon the metal; so I soon left him, feeling highly indignant with his treatment, and walked straight to his window, stepped up on the bench, and looked down, wondering whether it would be any good to fish from there.

The water after some hours' working was much lower, so that a ledge about nine inches wide was laid bare and offered itself as a convenient resting-place; but I thought I would not fish while my uncles were away, especially since they had left me in charge.

166

So I walked right to the very place I had been warned to avoid, and found the men as busy as usual, and ready enough to say a few civil words.

And so the afternoon wore away, and telling myself that I had been scared at shadows, I felt a great deal more confident by tea-time when the men were leaving.

I sat in the office then as important as if I were the master, and listened to their leaving and crossing the yard. I could hear them talking to the gate-keeper, and then I fancied I heard a rustling noise outside the building, but it was not repeated, and I began listening to the last men going, and soon after, according to his custom, old Dunning the gate-keeper came to bring his key.

I heard the old fellow's halting step on the stairs, and trying to look very firm I answered his tap with a loud and important "Come in!"

"All gone, Mester Jacob, sir," he said. "I s'pose you'll tek a look round?"

"Yes; I'll do that, Dunning," I replied.

"Then, good-night, sir!"

"One moment, Dunning," I cried, as he turned to go. "I know you don't mix with the quarrels between masters and men."

"Not I, Mester Jacob. I just do my bit o' work here, which just suits me, being a worn-out sort o' man, and then goes back home to my tea and my garden. You've nivver seen my bit o' garden, Mester Jacob, sir. You must come."

"To be sure I will, Dunning; but tell me, how do the men seem now?"

"Bit tired, sir. End o' the day's wuck."

"No, no; I mean as to temper. Do you think they are settling down?"

"O ay; yes, sir. They'd be quiet enew if the trade would let 'em alone."

"No threats or anything of that sort?"

"Well, you see, sir, I've no right to say a word," he replied, sinking his voice. "If they thought I was a talker, mebbe they'd be falling upon me wi' sticks; but you've always been a kind and civil young gentleman to me, so I will tell you as Gentles says he means to pay you when he gets a chance."

"Then I must keep out of Mr Gentles's way," I said, laughing outside, for I felt very serious in.

"Ay, but that arn't it, Mester Jacob, sir," said old Dunning, to make me more comfortable. "You see, sir, you nivver know where to hev a man like that. He might hit at you wi' his own fisty, but it's more'n likely as he'll do it wi' some one else's, or wi' a clog or a knobstick. You can nivver tell. Good-night, Mester Jacob, sir. Keep a sharp look-out, sir, and so will I, for I shouldn't like to see a nice well-spoken young gentleman like you spoiled."

I followed Dunning down to the gate, and turned the key after him, feeling horribly alarmed.

Spoiled—not like to see a boy like me spoiled. What did spoiling mean? I shuddered at the thought, and though for a moment I thought of rushing out and getting home as quickly as I could, there was a sort of fear upon me that a party of men might be waiting at one of the corners ready to shoot me.

"I must wait a bit, and get cool," I said; and then looking about me, I shivered, for the great works looked strange and deserted, there was a horrible stillness in the place, and I had never felt so lonely and unpleasantly impressed even when watching in the middle of the night.

Just then there was a whine and a bark, and Piter gave his chain a jerk.

There was society for me at all events, and, going to the kennel, I unhooked the spring swivel and set the dog free, when, as usual, he showed his pleasure by butting his great head at me and trying to force it between my legs.

I was used to it and knew how to act, but with a stranger it would have been awkward and meant sitting down heavily upon the dog unless he leaped out of the way.

Of course I did not sit down on Piter, but lifted a leg over him, and as soon as he had become steady made a sort of inspection of the place to see that nothing was wrong, feeling that it was a sort of duty to do, as I was left alone.

Piter kept close to me, rubbing my leg with one ear as we went all over the place, and as I found no powder-cans and fuses, no bottles full of fulminating silver, or any other deadly implement, my spirits rose and I began to laugh at myself for my folly.

There was only the lower workshop with its grindstones to look through, and lit up as it was by the evening sun there did not seem to be anything very terrible there. The floor was wet, and the stones and their frames and bands cast broad shadows across the place and on the opposite wall, but nothing seemed to be wrong, only I could hear the hollow echoing plash of the water falling from the wheel sluice down into the stone-walled pit.

There was nothing new in this, only that it seemed a little plainer than usual, and as I looked I saw that the door had been left open.

That was nothing particular, but I went on to close it, not being able to see the bottom, the view being cut off by a great solid bench in the middle of the floor. On passing round this, though, I saw that there was something wrong; two or three bands had gone from as many grindstones, and had evidently been hastily thrown into the wheel-pit, whoever had done this having left one on the floor, half in and half out, and keeping the door from shutting close.

"That couldn't be Gentles," I said aloud as I threw back the door, and my words echoed in the great black place, where the sunlight was cutting the shadow in a series of nearly horizontal rays as it came in past the wheel.

I could see at a glance the amount of the mischief done: one band was evidently down in the water, and hung hitched in some way on to the band upon the floor. It had been intended to be dragged in as well, but it had caught against the iron of the rail that surrounded the bracket-like platform the width of the door and projecting over the water, which was ten feet below.

I recalled standing upon it to catch eels, when I contrived to catch the lost bands as well, and thinking that perhaps after all there were several of the straps sunken below me, I stooped down, took hold of the band, and pulled.

It would not come, being caught somehow at the edge of the platform; so gathering it closely in my hands rather unwillingly, for it was a wet oily affair, I stepped on to the platform, uttered a shriek, and fell with a tremendous splash into the water below. I felt the platform give way, dropping at once from beneath my feet, and though I snatched at it my hands glided over the boards in an instant and I was down amidst a tangle of bands in the deep black water.

Chapter Twenty.

A Companion in Trouble.

I can't tell you the horrors of those moments as they appeared to me. No description could paint it all exactly; but one moment I was down in darkness with the current thundering in my ears, the next I was up at the surface beating and splashing, listening to the echoing of the water, which sounded hollow and strange, looking up at the sunshine that streamed in past the wheel, and then I went under.

It is a strange admission to make, but in those first few moments of surprise and horror I forgot that I knew how to swim, and all my movements were instinctive and only wearied and sent me down again after I had risen.

Then reason came to my help, and I began to strike out slowly and swam to the side of the great stone chamber, passing one hand along the slimy wall trying to get some hold, but finding none; and then swimming straight across to the other side and trying there, for I dared not approach the wheel, which looked horrible and dangerous, and I felt that if I touched it the great circle would begin to revolve, and perhaps take me down under the water, carry me up on the other side, and throw me over again.

It looked too horrible, all wet, slimy, and dripping as it was, or possibly I might have climbed up it and reached the edge of the dam, so I swam right beyond it and felt along the other side, but without avail. There was nothing but the slimy stonework, try where I would, and the chill of horror began to have a numbing effect on my arms.

I swam on to and fro beneath the doorway, with the little platform hanging by one end far above my had, and once as I swam my foot seemed to touch something, which might have been a piece of the sunken wood or iron work, but which made me shrink as if some horrible monster had made a snatch at me.

I shouted, but there was only the hollow echoing of the stone chamber and the lapping and whispering of the water; and, knowing that I was alone locked in the works, the terrible idea began to dance before me that I was going to die, for unless I could save myself I need not expect help.

The thought unnerved me more and more and made me swim more rapidly in the useless fashion I was pursuing, and once more I stared in a shrinking way at the great wheel, which, innocent enough in itself, seemed a more terrible engine than ever. I knew it would move if I swam across and clung to it, and I really dared not go near.

There was always something repellent and strange even in a big water cistern in a house, and as a mere boy I have often started back in terror at the noise made by the pipes when the water was coming driving the air before it with a snorting gurgle, and then pouring in, while to climb up a ladder or set of steps and look down into the black watery place always gave me a shudder and made me glad to get away.

It is easy to imagine, then, what my feelings were, suddenly cast into that great stone-walled place, with I did not know what depth of water beneath me, and inhabited as I knew by large twining eels.

I daresay the eels were as much afraid of me as I was of them; but that made no difference to my feelings as I swam here and there trying in vain for something to which to cling; but in the darkest parts as well as the lightest it was always the same, my hand glided over the stones and splashed down again into the water.

I was too much confused to think much, and moment by moment I was growing more helpless. I can remember making a sort of bound to try and get a hold of the broken platform above my head, but the effect of that effort was only to send me below the surface. I can recall, too, thinking that if I let my feet down I might find bottom, but this I dared not do for fear of what might be below; and so, each moment growing more feeble, I stared at the opened doorway through which I had come, at the iron-barred grating through which the water escaped, and which was the entrance to a tunnel or drain that ran beneath the works. Then I turned my eyes up at the sunlit opening through which seemed to come hope surrounding the black tooth-like engine that was hung there ready to turn and grind me down.

My energy was nearly exhausted, the water was above my lips, and after a wild glare round at the slimy walls the whispering lapping echoes were changed for the thunderous roar and confusion felt by one plunged beneath the surface; and in my blind horror I began beating the water frantically in my last struggle for life.

Natural instinct seems to have no hesitation in seizing upon the first help that comes. It was so here. I might have swum to the wheel at first and clung to it, but I was afraid; but now, after going under once or twice—I'm sure I don't know which—I came up in close proximity to the great mass of slimy wood-work, one of my hands touched it, the other joined it directly, and I clung panting there, blind, confused, helpless, but able to breathe.

Almost at the same moment, and before I knew what I was holding on by, there came a sound which sent hope and joy into my heart. It was the whimpering whine of Piter, who directly after set up a short yapping kind of bark, and I had a kind of idea that he must be somewhere on the wood-work inside the wheel.

I did not know that he had fallen in at the same time as I; and though once or twice I had heard him whining, I did not realise that he was also in danger; in fact the horrible overwhelming selfishness of the desire for self-preservation had swept away everything but the thought of how I was to get out of my trouble.

Every moment now gave me a little confidence, though it was nearly driven away when, able to see clearly again, I found myself holding on by one of the wooden pocket-like places formed with boards on the outer circumference of the engine—the places in fact into which, when the sluice was opened, the water rushed, and by its weight bore the wheel round.

After a few minutes' clinging there, beginning to feel numbed and chilled by the cold, I realised that the sun was setting, that the patches of light were higher, and that in a very few minutes the horrors of this place would be increased tenfold by my being plunged in profound darkness.

I dreaded moving, but I knew that the water could not come down upon me unless the sluice was opened, and that was turned off when the men left work, so that the water was saved for the next day, and the wheel ceased to turn. I determined then to try and climb up from pocket to pocket of the wheel and so reach the stone-race at the opening, along which the water poured.

My courage revived at this, and drawing my legs under me I got them upon one of the edges of the pocket beneath the water, raised myself up and caught hold of one higher than I had hold of before, and was about to take a step higher when, to my horror, the huge wheel began to feel the effect of my weight, and gradually the part I held descended.

At the same moment there was a loud splash, a beating of the water, a whining barking noise, and I knew I had shaken Piter off the bar or spoke to which he had been clinging inside.

"Here, Piter; here dog," I shouted; and he swam round to me, whining piteously and seeming to ask me for help.

This I was able to give him, for, holding tightly with one hand, I got my right arm round him and helped him to scramble up into one of the pockets, though the effort had weighed down the wheel and I sank deeper in the water.

I made another trial to climb up, but though the resistance of the great wheel was sufficient to support me partly it soon began to revolve, and I knew that it would go faster if I tried to struggle up.

I heaved a despairing sigh, and for the first time began to think of Gentles.

"This must be his doing," I said to myself. He had set some one to take out the support of the little platform, and I was obliged to own that after all he had only set a trap for me just as I had set one for him.

Still there was a great difference: he was on his way to do harm when he was caught—I was engaged in my lawful pursuits and trying to do good.

I had another trial, and another, but found it would, in my exhausted state, be impossible to climb up, and as I clung there, up to my chest in the water, and with the dog close to me, he whined piteously and licked my face.

The next minute he began to bark, stood up with his hind feet on the edge of one bar, his fore-paws on the one above, and made a bound.

To my surprise he reached his aim, and his weight having no effect on the wheel, he scrambled up and up till I knew he must have reached the top.

There was no doubt about it.

The next minute I heard the rattling shaking noise made by a dog when getting rid of the water in its coat. Then a loud and joyous barking. Then only the dripping, plashing sound of the water that escaped through the sluice and came running in and falling about the wheel.

What time was it? About half-past six, and the men would not come to work till the next morning. Could I hang there till then?

I knew it was impossible—that in perhaps less than half an hour I should be compelled to loose my hold and fall back into the black water without strength to stir a paralysed arm.

I shouted again and again, but the walls echoed back my cry, and I knew it was of no use, for it was impossible for any one to hear me outside the place. It was only wasting strength, and that was wanted to sustain me as long as possible.

There was one hope for me, though: my uncles would be returning from Redham at ten or eleven o'clock, and, not finding me at home, they would come in search of me.

When it is too late!

I must have said that aloud, for the word *late* came echoing back from the wall, and for a time I hung there, feeling numbed, as it were, in my head, and as slow at thinking or trying to imagine some way of escape as I was at movement.

But I made one more effort.

It seemed to be so pitiful that a wretched, brainless dog, when placed in a position like this, should be able to scramble out, while I, with the power of thinking given to me, with reason and some invention, was perfectly helpless.

This thought seemed to send a current like electricity through me, nerving me to make another effort, and loosening one hand I caught at the bar above me as before, changed the position of my feet, and began to climb.

I gave up with a groan, for I was only taking the place of the water and turning the wheel just as a turnspit dog would work, or a squirrel in its cage, only that I was outside the wheel and they would have been in.

I came down with a splash; and as I clung there I could hear the water go softly lapping against the wall and whispering in the corners as if it were talking to itself about how soon I should have to loose my hold, sink down, and be drowned.

I was weakened by this last effort as well as by the strain upon my nerves, and as the water ceased to lap and whisper a horrible silence crept down into the place in company with the darkness. Only a few minutes before all was bright where the sun rays flashed in; now there was only a soft glow to be seen, and all about me blackgloom.

I grew more and more numbed and helpless, and but for the fact that I hung there by my hands being crooked over the edge of the board across the wheel, I believe I must have fallen back, but my fingers stiffened into position and helped me to retain my hold, till at last they began to give way.

I had been thinking of home and of my uncles, and wondering how soon they would find me, and all in a dull nerveless way, for I suppose

I was too much exhausted to feel much mental or bodily pain, when all at once I began to recall stories I had read about the Saint Bernard dogs and the travellers in the snow; and then about the shepherds' collies in the north and the intelligence they displayed.

Several such tales came to my memory, and I was just thinking to myself that they were all nonsense, for if dogs had so much intelligence, why had not Piter, who had a head big enough for a double share of dogs' brains, gone and fetched somebody to help me, instead of making his own escape, and then going and curling himself up by one of the furnaces to get dry—a favourite place of his if he had the chance.

Just then, as I seemed to be half asleep, I heard a sharp bark at a distance, then another nearer, and directly after Piter was on the top of the wheel, where he had stepped from the sluice trough, barking with all his might.

"Wheer is he then, boy? Wheer is he then?" said a gruff hoarse voice.

Piter barked more furiously than ever, and the glow seemed to give way to darkness overhead, as the voice muttered:

"Dear, dear! Hey! Think o' that now. Mester Jacob, are you theer?"

"Help!" I said, so faintly that I was afraid I should not be heard.

"Wheerabouts? In the watter?"

"I'm—on—the wheel," I cried weakly, and then, as I heard the sound of someone drawing in his breath, I strove to speak once more and called out:

"Turn the wheel."

It began to move directly, but taking me down into the water, and I uttered a cry, when the wheel turned in the other direction, drawing me out and up. My arms straightened out; I was drawn closer to the woodwork. I felt that I should slip off, when my toes rested upon one of the bars, while, as I rose higher, the tension on my arms grew less, and then less, and at last, instead of hanging, I was lying upon my chest. Then a pair of great hands laid hold of me, and Piter was licking my face.

Pannell told me afterwards that he had to carry me all along the narrow stone ledge to the window of his smithy, and thrust me through there before climbing in after me, for it was impossible to get into the yard the other way without a boat.

175

I must have fainted, I suppose, for when I opened my eyes again, though it was in darkness, the icy water was not round me, but I was lying on the warm ashes down in one of the stoke-holes; and the faint glow of the half-extinct fire was shining upon the shiny brown forehead of the big smith.

"Pannell!" I exclaimed, "where am I?"

"Get out!" he growled. "Just as if yow didn' know."

"Did you save me?"

"'Sh, will yo'!" he whispered. "How do we know who's a-watching an' listening? Yow want to get me knob-sticked, that's what yow want."

"No, no," I said, shivering.

"Yow know where we are, o' course. Down in the big stokul; but be quiet. Don't shout."

"How did you know I was in there?"

"What, in yonder?"

"Yes, of course; oh how my arms ache and throb!"

"Let me give 'em a roob, my lad," he said; and strongly, but not unkindly, he rubbed and seemed to knead my arms, especially the muscles above my elbows, talking softly in a gruff murmur all the while.

"I did give you a wink, lad," he said, "for I know'd that some'at was on the way. I didn' know what, nor that it was so bad as that theer. Lor' how can chaps do it! Yow might hev been drowned."

"Yes," I said with a shiver. "The cowards!"

"Eh! Don't speak aloud, lad. How did you get in? Some un push thee?"

"Push me! No; the platform was broken loose, and a trap set for me, baited with a wheel-band," I added angrily.

Pannell burst into a laugh, and then checked himself.

"I weer not laughing at yow, lad," he whispered, "but at owd Gentles. So yow got in trap too?"

"Trapped! Yes; the cowardly wretches!"

"Ay, 'twere cowardly. Lucky I came. Couldn't feel bottom, eh?"

"No."

"Nay, yow wouldn't; there's seven foot o' watter there, wi'out mood."

"How did you know I was there?"

"What! Didn' I tell ye?"

"No."

"I were hanging about like, as nigh as I could for chaps, a waitin' to see yow go home; but yow didn't coom, and yow didn't coom; and I got crooked like wi' waiting, and wondering whether yow'd gone another way, when all at once oop comes the bull-poop fierce like, and lays holt o' me by the leg, and shakes it hard. I was going to kick un, but he'd on'y got holt of my trowsis, and he kep on' shacking. Then he lets go and barks and looks at me, and takes holt o' my trowsis agin, and hangs away, pulling like, till I seemed to see as he wanted me to coom, and I followed him."

"Good old Piter!" I said; and there was a whine. I did not know it, but Piter was curled up on the warm ashes close by me, and as soon as he heard his name he put up his head, whined, and rapped the ashes with his stumpy tail.

"He went to the wucks fast as he could, and slipped in under the gate; but I couldn't do that, you see, Mester, and the gate was locked, so I was just thinking what I'd best do, and wondering where you might be, when I see Stivens come along, looking as if he'd like to howd my nose down again his grindstone, and that made me feel as if I'd like to get one of his ears in my tongs, and his head on my stithy. He looked at me, and I looked at him, and then I come away and waited till he'd gone."

"It seemed as if help would never come," I said.

"Ay, it weer long time," said Pannell; "but I found no one about at last, and I slipped over the wall."

"Yes, and I know where," I said.

"And there was Piter waiting and wanting me to follow him. But there was no getting in—the doors were locked. I seemed to know, though, that the dog wanted to get me to the wheel-pit, and when I tried to think how to get to you I found there was no way 'cept through my forge. So I got out o' my window, and put the dorg down, and—well, I came. Arn't much of a fire here, but if I blow it up Stivens or some on 'em will hear it, or see it, or something; and I s'pose I shall have it for to-night's work."

I did feel warmer and better able to move, and at last I rose to make the best of my way back.

"Nobody will notice my wet things," I said, "now it's dark. I don't know what to say to thank you, Pannell."

"Say I was a big boompkin for meddling ower what didn't consarn me. If I don't come to wuck to-morrow you'll know why."

"No; I shall not," I cried wonderingly.

"Ah, then, you'll have time to find out," he muttered. "Good-night, lad!"

"Stop a moment and I'll open the gate," I cried.

"Nay, I shall go out as I come in. Mayn't be seen then. Mebbe the lads'll be watching by the gate."

He stalked out, and as I followed him I saw his tall gaunt figure going to the corner of the yard where the trap was set, and then there was a scuffling noise, and he had gone.

I left the place soon after, and as I fastened the gate I fancied I saw Stevens and a man who limped in his walk; but I could not be sure, for the gas lamp cast but a very feeble light, and I was too eager to get home and change my things to stop and watch.

The run did me good, and by the time I had on a dry suit I was very little the worse for my immersion, being able to smile as I told my uncles at their return.

They looked serious enough, though, and Uncle Jack said it was all owing to the trap.

The question of putting the matter in the hands of the police was again well debated, but not carried out—my uncles concluding that it would do no good even if the right man were caught, for in punishing him we should only have the rest who were banded together more bitter against us.

"Better carry on the war alone," said Uncle Dick; "we must win in the end."

"If we are not first worn-out," said the others.

"Which we shall not be," cried Uncle Dick, laughing. "There are three of us to wear out, and as one gets tired it will enrage the others; while when all three of us are worn-out we can depute Cob to carry on the war, and he is as obstinate as all three of us put together."

They looked at me and laughed, but I felt too much stirred to follow their example.

"It is too serious," I said, "to treat like that; for I am obstinate now much more than I was, and I should like to show these cowards that we are not going to be frightened out of the town."

"Cob don't know what fear is," said Uncle Jack with a bit of a sneer.

"Indeed but I do," I replied. "I was horribly frightened when I fell into that place; but the more they frighten me, the more I want for us to make them feel that we are not to be beaten by fear."

"Bravo!" cried Uncle Bob, clapping his hands.

"There! Let's go on with our work," said Uncle Dick; "we must win in the end."

To have seen the works during the next few days, anyone would have supposed that there had never been the slightest trouble there. After due consideration the little platform had been replaced and the bands taken from the grindstone gear duly put in position, the men taking not the slightest notice, but working away most industriously.

Pannell, however, did not come back, and his forge was cold, very much to my uncles' annoyance. On inquiry being made we were told that his mother was dying, and that he had been summoned to see her.

I felt a little suspicious, but could hardly believe that anything was wrong, till one evening Uncle Jack proposed that we two should have a walk out in the country for a change.

I was only too glad, for the thought of getting away from the smoke and dirt and noise was delightful.

So as to get out sooner we took a short cut and were going down one of the long desolate-looking streets of rows of houses all alike, and built so as to be as ugly as possible, when we saw on the opposite side a man seated upon a door-step in his shirt-sleeves, and with his head a good deal strapped and bandaged.

"That's one of the evils of a manufacturing trade where machinery is employed," said Uncle Jack. "I'm afraid that, generally speaking, the accidents are occasioned by the men's carelessness or bravado; but even then it is a painful thing to know that it is your machinery that has mutilated a poor fellow. That poor fellow has been terribly knocked about, seemingly."

"Yes," I said, looking curiously across the road.

"So far we have been wonderfully fortunate, but—here, this way! Where are you going?"

"Over here," I said, already half across the road; for the brawny arms and long doubled-up legs of the man seemed familiar.

"Why?" cried Uncle Jack; but he followed me directly.

"Pannell!" I exclaimed.

"What, Mester Jacob!" he cried, lifting up his head with his face in my direction, but a broad bandage was over his eyes.

"Why, what's all this?" I cried; "have you had some accident?"

"Yes, met wi' acciden' done o' purpose."

"But they said your mother was dying," I cried as I held the great hard hand, which was now quite clean.

"Ay, so I heard say," replied the great fellow.

"Is she better?"

"Better! Well, she ain't beenbadly."

"Not dying?" said Uncle Jack.

"What's that yow, Mester?" said Pannell. "Sarvice to you, sir. My mother!—dying! Well, I suppose she be, slowly, like the rest of us."

"But what have you been doing?" I cried. "What a state you are in!"

"State I'm in! Yow should have seen me a fortnit ago, my lad. I'm splendid now—coming round fast."

"But how was it?" cried Uncle Jack, while I turned white as I seemed to see it all.

"How was it, Mester!" said Pannell laughing. "Well, you see, I weer heving bit of a walluck, wi' my pipe in my mooth, and it being bit dusk like that night I didn't see which way I were going, and run my head again some bits o' wood."

"Sticks!" I said excitedly.

He turned his head towards me smiling.

"Couldn't see rightly as to that, Mester Jacob," he said; "I dessay they weer."

"And a set of cowards had hold of them!" I cried.

"Nay, I can't say," replied the great fellow. "Yow see, Mester, when owt hits you on the head it wuzzles you like, and you feel maäzed."

Uncle Jack stood frowning.

"You know very well, Pannell," I cried angrily, "that you have been set upon by some of these treacherous cowards for helping me that evening. Oh, Uncle Jack!" I cried, passionately turning to him, "why don't you go to the police?"

"Howd thee tongue, lad!" cried Pannell fiercely. "Yow don't know nowt about it. Don't yow do nowt o' t' sort, Mester. Let well alone, I say."

"But I cannot stand still and see these outrages committed," said Uncle Jack in a low angry voice.

"Hey, but thou'lt hev to, 'less you give up maäkin' 'ventions. Trade don't like 'em, and trade will hev its say."

"But that you should have been so brutally used for doing a manly action for this boy," began Uncle Jack.

"Theer, theer, theer," said Pannell; "I don't kick agen it. I s'pected they'd do some'at. I know'd it must coom. Chap as breaks the laws has to tek his bit o' punishment. Chaps don't bear no malice. I'm comin' back to work next week."

"Look here," said Uncle Jack, who was a good deal moved by the man's calm patience, "what are we to do to come to terms with the workmen, and have an end to these outrages?"

"Oh, that's soon done," replied Pannell, rubbing one great muscular arm with his hand, "yow've just got to give up all contrapshions, and use reg'lar old-fashioned steel, and it'll be all right."

"And would you do this, my man?" said Uncle Jack, looking down at the great muscular fellow before him.

"Ay, I'd do it for sake o' peace and quiet. I should nivver go agen trade."

"And you would advise me to give up at the command of a set of ignorant roughs, and make myself their slave instead of master."

"Mester Jacob," said Pannell, "I can't see a bit wi' this towel round my head; look uppards and downards; any o' the chaps coming?"

"No," I said.

"Then look here, Mester, I will speak if I nivver do again. No, I wouldn't give up if I was you, not if they did a hundred worse things than they've done yet. Theer!"

Uncle Jack looked down on the man, and then said quickly:

"And you, what will you do?"

"Get to wuck again, Mester, as soon as I can."

"And the men who beat you like that?"

"Eh, what about 'em?"

"Shall you try and punish them?"

"Punish 'em, Mester! Why, how can I? They punished me."

"But you will turn upon them for this, Pannell, will you not?"

"Nay, Mester; I went again 'em, and they knob-sticked me for it, and it's all done and over. I shall soon be back at my stithy, if you'll hev me again."

"Have you! Yes, my man, of course," said Uncle Jack. "I wish we could have more like you."

"Cob," said Uncle Jack as we strode on and got well out into the country, "we've got a very strong confederation to fight, and I do not feel at all hopeful of succeeding; but, there: we've put our hands to the plough, and we can't look back. Now never mind business, let's listen to the birds and enjoy the fresh country air for a time."

We were going up the valley, passing every now and then "a wheel" as it was called, that is a water-wheel, turning a number of grindstones, the places being remarkably like ours, only that as we got farther out the people who ground and forged did their work under the shade of trees, while the birds piped their songs, and air and water were wonderfully different from what they were about our place on the edge of the great town.

"Let's get back, Cob," said Uncle Jack despondently. "It makes me miserable to hear the birds, and see the beauty of the hills and vales, and the sparkling water, and know that men toiling together in towns can be such ruffians and so full of cruelty to their fellow creatures."

"And so strong and true and brave and ready to help one another."

"As who are, Cob?" said my uncle.

"Well, for want of thinking of anyone else just now," I said, "there's poor Pannell; he saved me, and he has just shown us that he is too faithful to his fellow-workmen to betray them."

Uncle Jack laid his hand upon my shoulder and gave it a hearty grip.

"You're right, my lad," he said. "You're the better philosopher after all. There's good and bad, and like so many more I think of the bad and overlook the good. But all the same, Cob, I'm very uneasy. These men have a spiteful feeling against you, and we shall not be doing right if we trust you out of our sight again."

Chapter Twenty One.

What I caught and heard.

"I should say you will very likely have some sport," said Uncle Dick. "Try by all means."

"I hardly like to, uncle," I said.

"Nonsense, my lad! All work and no play makes Jack—I mean Jacob —a dull boy."

"But it will seem as if I am neglecting my work."

"By no means. Besides, we shall not be busy for a day or two. Have a few hours' fishing, and I daresay one of us will come and see how you are getting on."

The opportunity was too tempting to be lost, so I got a cheap rod and a dear line—a thoroughly good one, asked a gardener just outside to dig up some small red worms for me, and, furnishing myself with some paste and boiled rice, I one morning took my place up at the head of the dam where the stream came in, chose a place where the current whirled round in a deep hole and began fitting my tackle together prior to throwing in.

I had been longing for this trial, for I felt sure that there must be some big fish in the dam. It was quite amongst the houses and factories, but all the same it was deep, there was a constant run of fresh water through it, and I had more than once seen pieces of bread sucked down in a curiously quiet way, as if taken by a great slow moving fish, a carp or tench, an old inhabitant of the place.

Certainly it was not the sort of spot I should have selected for a day's fishing had I been offered my choice, but it was the best I could obtain then, and I was going to make the most of it.

I laughed to myself as I thought of the eels, and the great haul I had made down in the wheel-pit, and then I shuddered as I thought of the horrors I had suffered down there, and wondered whether our troubles with the men were pretty well over.

I hoped so, for from what I heard the business was succeeding beyond the hopes of the most sanguine of my uncles, and if we were left alone success on the whole was assured.

Of course it was this brilliant prospect that induced them to stay on and dare the perils that lurked around, though, during the past few weeks, everything had been so quiet that once more we were indulging in the hope that the war was at an end.

In spite of Dr Johnson's harsh saying about a fisherman, I know of no more satisfactory amusement than is to be found in company with a rod and line. The sport may be bad, but there is the country, the bright sky, the waving trees, the dancing waters, and that delicious feeling of expectation of the finest bite and the biggest fish that never comes but always may.

I was in this state of expectancy that day. The sport was not good certainly, for the fish I caught were small, but I argued that where there were small fish there must be large, and sooner or later some of the monsters of the dam would see and take my bait.

I fished till dinner-time, varying my position, and when the bell rang some of the men came and sat on the edge and watched me, chatting civilly enough as they smoked their pipes.

As luck had it I caught a couple of good-sized silvery roach, and Stevens gave his leg a regular slap as he exclaimed:

"Well if they'd towd me there was fish like that i' th' dam I wouldn't hev believed it."

The bell rang for work to be resumed, and the men slowly moved along the dam edge, Stevens being left, and he stopped to fill and light his pipe—so it seemed to me; but as he stooped over it, puffing away large clouds of smoke, I heard him say:

"Don't look. Soon as men's gone in, yow go and stand on ledge close under grinding-shop windows, and see what you catch."

"It's such an awkward place to get to," I said. "I suppose it's deep, but —"

"You do what I tell'ee, and don't talk," growled Stevens, and he strolled off with his hands in his pockets after his mates.

"I sha'n't go," I said. "It's a very awkward place to get to; the ledge is not above nine inches wide, and if I got hold of a big fish, how am I to land him!"

The very idea of getting hold of a fish that would be too hard to land was too much for me, and I should have gone to the ledge if it had only been four and a half inches wide. So, waiting to have a few more throws, which were without result, I picked up my basket, walked right round the end of the dam, and then along the top of a narrow wall till I reached the end of the works at the far side, and from there lowered myself gently down on the ledge, along which Pannell had brought me when he rescued me from the wheel-pit, right at the other end, and towards which I was slowly making my way.

It was slow travelling, and my feet were not above a couple of inches above the water, while the windows of the grinding-shop were about four feet above my head.

I made no special selection, but stopped right in the middle, just where I imagined that the dam head would be deepest, and softly dropped in my line after setting down my basket and leaning my back against the stone building.

As I did so I wished that there had been a place to sit down, but there was of course only just room to stand, and there I was with the water gliding on and over the great wheel a few yards to my left; to my right the windows, out of which poured the black smoke of the forges, and from which came the *clink chink* of hammer upon anvil, while above me came throbbing and vibrating, screeching and churring, the many varied sounds made by the grinders as they pressed some piece of steel against the swiftly revolving stone, while, in spite of dripping drenching water, the least contact drew from the stone a shower of sparks.

I fished on, after making a few alterations in the depth of my bait, finding the water far deeper than I expected. I renewed that bait, too, but no monstrous fish came to take it, to hook itself, and to make a rush and drag me off my ledge. The sounds buzzed and rattled overhead; there was the echoing plash of the water over the wheel, and the whispering echoes which did not sound at all terrible now, and above all from the windows overhead, in intervals of the grinding, I could hear the men talking very earnestly at times.

I paid very little heed, for I was interested in my fishing and the water across which the spiders were skating. I wanted a big bite—that big bite—but still it did not come, and I began to wonder whether there were any fish of size in the place.

"There's every reason why there should be," I thought. Deep clear water fed by the great dam up in the hills, and of course that dam was fed by the mountain streams. This place was all amongst buildings, and plenty of smuts fell on the surface; in fact the wind used to send a regular black scum floating along to the sides.

Plop!

My heart gave a throb of excitement, for there was a rise evidently made by a big fish over to my right close inshore.

"Now if I had been there," I thought, "I should have most likely been able to catch that fish and then—"

Bah! Who wanted to catch a great water-rat that had plumped off the bank into the water? I could see the sleek-coated fellow paddling about close inshore. Then he dived down, and there were a lot of tiny bubbles to show his course before he went right in under the bank, which was full of holes.

I could almost fancy I was in the country, for there were a few rushes and some sedgy growth close to where the rat had been busy. Farther off, too, there was the sound that I had heard down in a marshy part of Essex with my uncles, during one of our excursions. "*Quack, quack, quack! Wuck, wuck, wuck!*"—a duck and a drake just coming down to the water to drink and bathe and feed on the water-weed and snails.

Yes; it quite put me in mind of the country to have wild ducks coming down to the pool, and—there were the two wild ducks! One, as the cry had told me, was a drake, and he had once been white, but old age and Arrowfield soot and the dirty little black yard where he generally lived had changed his tint most terribly, and though he plunged in, and bobbed and jerked the water all over his back, and rubbed the sides of his head and his beak all among his feathers, they were past cleaning.

As to his wife, who expressed herself with a loud quack, instead of saying *wuck, wuck* in more smothered tones, she was possibly quite as dirty as her lord, but being brown the dirt did not show. Her rags did, for a more disreputable bird I never saw, though she, too, washed and napped her wings, and dived and drenched herself before getting out on the bank to preen and beak over her feathers.

Alas! As people say in books, it was not the country, but dingy, smoke-bewithered Arrowfield, and I wondered to myself why a couple of birds with wings should consent to stay amongst factories and works.

I knew the top of my float by heart; so must that skating spider which had skimmed up to it, running over the top of the water as easily as if it were so much ice. I was growing drowsy and tired. Certainly I leaned my back up against the wall, but it was quite upright, and there was no recompense. Whatever is the use of watching a float that will not bob?

It may be one of the best to be got in a tackle-shop, with a lovely subdivision of the paint—blue at the bottom and white at the top, or green and white, or blue and red, but if it obstinately persists in sitting jauntily cocked up on the top of the water immovable, fishing no longer becomes a sport.

But I did not fish all that time for nothing.

As I said, I was becoming drowsy with looking so long at the black cap at the top of my float. Perhaps it was the whirr and hum of the machinery, and the faint sound of plashing water; even the buzz and churr and shriek of the steel upon the fast spinning stones may have had something to do with it. At any rate I was feeling sleepy and stupid, when all at once I was wide-awake and listening excitedly, for the shrieking of blade held upon grindstone ceased, and I heard a voice that was perfectly familiar to me say:

"Tell 'ee what. Do it at once if you like; but if I had my wayer I'd tie lump o' iron fast on to that theer dorg's collar and drop 'im in dam."

"What good ud that do?" said another voice.

"Good! Why we'd be shut on him."

"Ay, but they'd get another."

"Well, they wouldn't get another boy if we got shut o' this one," said the first voice.

"But yow wouldn't go so far as to—"

The man stopped short, and seemed to give his stone a slap with the blade that he was grinding.

"I d'know. He's a bad un, and allus at the bottom of it if owt is found out."

"Ay, but yow mustn't."

"Well, p'r'aps I wouldn't then, but I'd do something as would mak him think it were time to go home to his mother."

My face grew red, then white, I'm sure, for one moment it seemed to burn, the next it felt wet and cold. I did not feel sleepy any longer, but in an intense state of excitement, for those words came from the window just above my head, so that I could hear them plainly.

"It's all nonsense," I said to myself directly after. "They know I'm here, and it's done to scare me."

188

Just then the churring and screeching of the grinding steel burst out louder than ever, and I determined to go away and treat all I had heard with silent contempt. Pulling up my line just as a fisher will, I threw in again for one final try, and hardly had the bait reached the bottom before the float bobbed.

I could not believe it at first. It seemed that I must have jerked the line —but no, there it was again, another bob, and another, and then a series of little bobs, and the float moved slowly off over the surface, carrying with it a dozen or so of blacks.

I was about to strike, but I thought I would give the fish a little more time and make sure of him, and, forgetting all about the voices overhead, I was watching the float slowly gliding away, bobbing no longer, but with the steady motion that follows if a good fish has taken the bait.

And what a delight that was! What a reward to my patience! That it was a big one I had no doubt. If it had been a little fish it would have jigged and bobbed the float about in the most absurd way, just as if the little fish were thoughtless, and in a hurry to be off to play on the surface, whereas a big fish made it a regular business, and was calm and deliberate in every way.

"Now for it," I thought, and raising the point of the rod slowly I was just going to strike when the grinding above my head ceased, and one of the voices I had before heard said:

"Well, we two have got to go up to the *Pointed Star* to-night to get our orders, and then we shall know what's what."

I forgot all about the fish and listened intently.

"Nay, they can't hear," said the voice again, as if in answer to a warning; "wheels makes too much noise. I don't care if they did. They've had warnings enew. What did they want to coom here for?"

"Ay," said another, "trade's beginning to feel it a'ready. If we let 'em go on our wives and bairns 'll be starving next winter."

"That's a true word, lad; that's a true word. When d'yow think it'll be?"

"Ah, that's kept quiet. We shall know soon enew."

"Ay, when it's done."

"Think this 'll sattle 'em?"

"Sattle! Ay, that it will, and pretty well time. They'll go back to Lonnon wi' their tails twix' their legs like the curs they are. Say, think they've got pistols?"

"Dunno. Sure to hev, ah sud say."

"Oh!"

"Well, s'pose they hev? You aren't the man to be scarred of a pop-gun, are yo'?"

"I d'know. Mebbe I should be if I hev the wuck to do. I'm scarred o' no man."

"But you're scarred of a pistol, eh lad? Well, I wunner at yo'."

"Well, see what a pistol is."

"Ay, I know what a pistol is, lad. Man's got a pistol, and yo' hit 'im a tap on the knuckles, and he lets it fall. Then he stoops to pick it up, and knobstick comes down on his head. Nowt like a knobstick, lad, whether it be a man or a bit o' wood. Wants no loading, and is allus safe."

"Well, all I've got to say is, if I have the wuck to do I shall—"

Churr, churry, screech, and grind. The noise drowned the words I was eager to hear, and I stood bathed with perspiration, and hot and cold in turn.

That some abominable plot was in hatching I was sure, and in another minute I might have heard something that would have enabled us to be upon our guard; but the opportunity had passed, for the men were working harder than ever.

I was evidently in very bad odour with them, and I thought bitterly of the old proverb about listeners never hearing any good of themselves.

What should I do—stop and try to hear more?

Jig, jig, tug, tug at the top of my rod, and I looked down to see that the float was out of sight and the rod nearly touching the water.

My fisherman's instinct made me strike at once, and in spite of the agitation produced by the words I had heard I was ready for the exciting struggle I expected to follow. I had certainly hooked a fish which struggled and tugged to get away; but it was not the great carp or tench I expected to capture, only a miserable little eel which I drew through the water as I walked slowly along the ledge towards the end of the works farthest from the wheel, where I climbed on the wall, and, still dragging my prize, I went right on to the far end, where the water came in from the stream. There I crossed the wooden plank that did duty for a bridge, and glanced furtively back at the windows of the works looking out upon the dam.

As far as I could make out I had not been seen, and I had obtained some very valuable information that might be useful for our protection.

When I had reached the spot where I had begun fishing I drew in my capture; but it was not a long eel, but a mass of twined-up, snake-like fish which had wreathed itself into a knot with my line.

To get it free seemed to be impossible, so I cut off the piece of line just above the knot and let it fall into the water to extricate itself, while I went back to the office to have a few words with my uncles about what I had heard.

"I think we are in duty bound to send you home, Cob," said Uncle Jack, and the others murmured their acquiescence.

"Send me home!" I cried. "What! Just when all the fun is going to begin!"

"Fun!" said Uncle Dick, "Fun that the frogs suffered when the boys stoned them, eh?"

"Oh, but you know what I mean, uncle. I don't want to go."

"But we have run you into terrible risks already," cried Uncle Bob, "and if you were hurt I should feel as if I could never face your father and mother again."

"Oh, but I sha'n't be hurt," I cried. "There, I'm ready for anything, and shall always try to get on the safe side."

"As you always do," said Uncle Jack grimly. "No, my boy, you must not stay. It is evident from what you overheard that the men have some design against us on hand. Above all, they have taken a great dislike to you, and in their blind belief that you are one of the causes of their trouble they evidently feel spiteful and will not shrink from doing you harm. And that's rather a long-winded speech," he added, smiling.

"Can't we make them see that we are working for them instead of against them?" said Uncle Dick.

"No," said Uncle Bob. "No one can teach prejudiced workmen. The light comes to them some day, but it takes a long time to get through their dense brains. I think Cob must go."

"Oh! Uncle Bob," I exclaimed.

"I can't help it," my lad. "There seems to be no help for it. I shall regret it horribly, for your uncles are very poor company."

"Thankye," said Uncle Dick.

"Nice remark from the most stupid of three brothers," grumbled Uncle Jack.

"But you ought not to be exposed to these risks," continued Uncle Bob, "and now that by your own showing there is something worse on the way."

"Oh, it can't be worse than it has been; and besides, the men said I was always the first to find anything out. You see I have this time—again."

"Yes, with a vengeance," said Uncle Jack.

"And I'm sure you can't spare me."

"No, we can ill spare you, Cob," said Uncle Dick, "but we should not be doing our duty if we kept you here."

"Now, uncle," I cried, "I believe if I went home—though, of course, they would be very glad to see me—my father would say I ought to be ashamed of myself for leaving you three in the lurch."

"Look here! Look here! Look here!" cried Uncle Bob. "We can't sit here and be dictated to by this boy. He has run risks enough, and he had better go back to them at once."

"Oh, you see if I would have said a word if I had known that you would have served me like this!" I cried angrily. "Anyone would think I was a schoolgirl."

"Instead of a man of sixteen," said Uncle Bob.

"Never mind," I cried, "you were sixteen once, Uncle Bob."

"Quite right, my boy, so I was, and a conceited young rascal I was, almost as cocky as you are."

"Thank you, uncle."

"Only I had not been so spoiled by three easy-going, good-natured uncles, who have made you think that you are quite a man."

"Thank you, uncle," I said again, meaning to be very sarcastic.

"Instead of a soft stripling full of sap."

"And not fit to stand against the blows of oak cudgels and the injured

Arrowfield workmen," said Uncle Dick.

"Oh, all right! Banter away," I said. "I don't mind. I shall grow older and stronger and more manly, I hope."

"Exactly," said Uncle Jack; "and that's what we are aiming at for you, my lad. We don't want to see you scorched by an explosion, or hurt by blows, or made nervous by some horrible shock."

"I don't want to be hurt, of course," I said, "and I'm not at all brave. I was terribly frightened when I found the powder canister, and when I fell in the wheel-pit. I believe I was alarmed when I heard the men talking about what they were going to do; but I should be ashamed of myself, after going through so much, if I ran away, as they said you three would do."

"How was that?" cried Uncle Bob.

"With your tails between your legs, regularly frightened away like curs."

"They may carry us to the hospital without a leg to stand upon, or take us somewhere else without heads to think, but they will not see us running away in such a fashion as that," quoth Uncle Dick.

"Boy," said Uncle Jack, in his sternest way, "I would give anything to keep you with us, but I feel as if it has been a lapse of duty towards you to let you run these risks."

"But suppose I had been made a midshipman, uncle," I argued, "I should have always been running the risks of the sea, and the foreign climate where I was sent, and of being killed or wounded by the enemy."

"If there was war," suggested Uncle Bob.

"Yes, uncle, if there was war."

"Cob, my lad," said Uncle Dick, "that's a strong argument, but it does not convince us. Your Uncle Jack speaks my feelings exactly. I would give anything to keep you with us, for your young elastic nature seems to send off or radiate something brightening on to ours; and, now that you are going away, I tell you frankly that your courage has often encouraged us."

"Has it, uncle?" I cried.

"Often, my lad."

"Ay that it has," said Uncle Jack. "I've often felt down-hearted and ready to throw up our adventure; but I've seen you so fresh and eager, and so ready to fight it out, that I've said to myself—If a boy like that is ready to go on it would be a shame for a man to shrink."

"Yes," said Uncle Bob, "I confess to the same feeling."

"Well, that is shabby," I cried.

"What is, boy?" said Uncle Jack.

"To send me off like this. Why, you'll all break down without me."

"No, no; that does not follow," said Uncle Bob.

"Ah, won't it! You'll see," I said.

"Look here, Cob, be reasonable," exclaimed Uncle Jack, walking up and down the room in a very excited way. "You see, ever since you were born we've made a sort of playmate of you, and since you grew older, and have been down here with us, you know we have not treated you as if you were a boy."

"Well, no, uncle, I suppose you have not."

"We have talked with you, consulted with you, and generally behaved towards you as if you were a young man."

"And now all at once you turn round and punish me by treating me as if I were a little boy."

"No, no, my lad; be reasonable. We have been consulting together."

"Without me."

"Yes, without you; because we felt that we were not doing you justice —that we were not behaving as good brothers to your mother, in letting you go on sharing these risks."

"But there may be no more, uncle."

"But there will be a great many more, my boy," said Uncle Jack solemnly; "and what would our feelings be if some serious accident were to happen to you?"

"Just the same, Uncle Jack," I cried, "as mine would be, and my father's and mother's, if some accident were to happen to you."

Uncle Jack wrinkled up his broad forehead, stared hard at me, and then, in a half-angry, half amused way, he went to the table, took up an imaginary piece of soap and began to rub it in his palms.

"I wash my hands of this fellow, boys," he said. "Dick, you are the oldest; take him in hand, dress him down, give him sixpence to buy hardbake and lollipops, and send him about his business."

"Make it half-a-crown, uncle," I cried, with my cheeks burning with anger; "and then you might buy me a toy-horse too—one with red wafers all over it, and a rabbit-skin tail."

"My dear Cob," said Uncle Jack, "why will you be so wilfully blind to what is good for you?"

My cheeks grew hotter, and if I had been alone I should have burst into a passion of tears, but I could not do such a thing then, when I wanted to prove to these three that I was fit to be trusted and too old to be sent home.

"We do not come to this conclusion without having carefully thought it out, boy," cried Uncle Bob.

"Very well, then!" I cried, almost beside myself with passion.

"Confess now," said Uncle Bob; "haven't you often felt very much alarmed at having to keep watch of a night in that lonely factory?"

"Of course I have."

"And wished yourself at home?" said Uncle Dick.

"Scores of times, uncle."

"Well, then, now we wish you to go, feeling that it is best for you, and you turn restive as that jackass we hired for you to ride down in Essex."

"Haven't you three fellows been teaching me ever since I was a little tot, to try and be a man?"

"Yes," said Uncle Dick.

"When I've tumbled down and knocked the skin off my knees haven't you said 'don't cry: be a man!'"

"Oh yes! Guilty!" said Uncle Dick.

"If I fell out of the swing didn't you hold your cool hand to the great lump on my head and tell me that I must try to bear it without howling: like a man?"

"Yes, boy, yes."

"And when I broke my arm, after getting up the rock after the gulls' eggs, didn't you tell me about the Spartan boys?"

"I did, Cob, I did."

"Yes, of course you did," I cried indignantly. "You were all three alike: always teaching me to bear pain and be courageous, and master my natural cowardice and be a man. Now didn't you?"

"Ay, ay, ay! Captain Cob," they chorused.

"And here," I cried passionately, "after fighting all these years and making myself miserable so as to do exactly what you all taught me, now that there is a chance of showing that I know my lesson and have done well, you all treat me like a mollycoddle, and say to me by your looks: 'you're a poor cowardly little cub; go home to your mother and be nursed.'"

"Have you done with the soap?" said Uncle Dick, turning to Uncle Jack, as I stood there, feeling angry, passionate, excited, and carried out of myself.

"Eh?" said Uncle Jack staring.

"I say, have you done with the metaphorical soap? I want to wash my hands of him too."

"It's too bad, uncle," I cried.

"Here, Bob," said Uncle Dick in his grim way, "you take him in hand."

"No, thank you," said Uncle Bob. "I'll trouble you for the soap when you've done."

"And now," I cried, speaking to them as I had never done before, "you make worse of it by laughing at me."

"No, no," cried Uncle Dick; "we were not laughing at you, but we do now;" and starting with a tremendous "Ha-ha-ha!" the others joined in, and I stalked out of the parlour and went up to my room, where I set to work, and in about ten minutes had all my belongings carefully packed in my little carpet-bag—the new one that had been bought for me—and the little brass padlock on and locked.

Just then the parlour door opened as I was looking out of my bed-room window at the smoke and glow over the town, and thinking that after all I liked the noise and dirt and busy toil always going on, knowing, as I did, how much it had to do with the greatness of our land.

"Cob!" came up Uncle Dick's big voice.

"Yes, uncle," I said quietly.

"Tea's ready."

"I don't want any tea," I said.

"Yes, you do, lad. Fried ham and eggs."

"Come," I said to myself, "I'll let them see that I can behave like a man. Perhaps I shall have to go home by the last train to-night or the first in the morning. Poor old Piter," I thought, "I should like to have taken you!"

So I went down quite coolly and walked into the parlour, where my uncles were waiting for me before seating themselves at the table.

That touched me; it was so full of consideration and respect for the boy they were going to send away.

Plump, comfortable Mrs Stephenson was just ready to take off the bright tin dish-cover, and as she did so there was a perfect pile of fried ham and eggs, looking brown and white and pink and orange, and emitting a most appetising odour.

"Is Mr Jacob a bit sadly, gentlemen?" said Mrs Stephenson, looking at me with interest.

"Oh no," I said quickly; and a bit touched too by Mrs Stephenson's respectful way and the *Mr* "Only tired. I shall be all right when I've had my tea."

"That's bonnie," she cried nodding. "I'd better butter a couple more cakes, hadn't I, gentlemen?"

"That you had," said Uncle Bob. "Let's eat well, or we shall never be able to fight it out with your fellow-townsmen."

"Ah, deary me, gentlemen," she cried; "it's sore work, that it is! I'm sure if they only knew what I do they'd behave better to you. Them trades is doing more harm than good."

She bustled out of the room, and as soon as the door was closed Uncle Dick turned to me.

"Shake hands, Cob, my boy," he said.

I held mine out frankly, for I had had my say, and I was determined to show them that I could act like a man.

"Now with me," said Uncle Jack in his hard stern way.

"And with me," said Uncle Bob.

I shook hands all round; but in spite of every effort my lip would quiver, and I had to bite it hard to keep down the emotion I felt.

"Shall I speak?" said Uncle Jack.

Uncle Dick nodded.

"Why not wait till after tea?" said Uncle Bob.

"No, I shall tell him now," said Uncle Jack grimly. "I'm hungry, and we may as well spoil his tea and get his share, for he will not be able to eat after what I've said. Cob, my lad, we've been talking this over again very seriously."

"All right, uncle!" I said quietly. "I'm quite ready to go. I've packed up, but I'd rather go to-morrow morning. I want to go and shake hands with Pannell and bid Piter 'good-bye.'"

"You have packed up?" he said rather sternly.

"Yes, uncle."

"Did you do that in a fit of passion or sulks?"

"No," I said sharply; "but because I wanted to show you to the very last that I had not forgotten what you taught me about self-denial and all that."

"God bless you, my lad!" he cried, hurting me horribly as he shook hands exceedingly hard. "I'm glad to hear you say that, for we've been saying that if we want to win in this fight we can't afford to part with one quarter of the Company. Cob, my lad, we want you to stay."

"Uncle!" I cried.

"Yes, my lad, you are older in some things than your years, and though I'd do anything rather than run risks for you, I do feel that with right on our side, please God, we shall win yet, and that it would be cowardly for us even to let you turn tail."

I don't know what I should have said and done then, as Uncle Jack exclaimed:

"Have I said right, Dick, Bob?"

"Yes, quite," said Uncle Dick warmly; "and for my part—"

"Hush! Sit down," cried Uncle Bob, hastily setting the example so as to end the scene. "Yes, two eggs, please. Quick, here's Mrs Stephenson coming with the cakes."

Chapter Twenty Two.

Stevens has a Word with me.

Next morning I went down to the works, feeling as if I had grown in one night a year older, and after giving Piter the bones I always took him down, and receiving the ram-like butt he always favoured me with to show his gratitude, I was going round the place, when I heard a familiar clinking and saw a glow out of the little smithy that had for some time been cold.

I ran in, and there, looking rather pale and with a bit or two of sticking-plaster about his temples, was Pannell hammering away as if he were trying to make up for lost time.

"Why, Pannell, old man," I cried, running in with outstretched hand, "back again at work! I am glad to see you."

He looked up at me with a scowl, and wiped his brow with the arm that was terminated by a fist and hammer—a way, I have observed, much affected by smiths.

His was not a pleasant face, and it was made more repulsive by the scars and sticking-plaster. As our eyes met it almost seemed as if he were going to strike me with his hammer; but he threw it down, gave his great hand a rub back and front upon his apron, probably to make it a little blacker, and then gripped mine as badly as Uncle Jack had on the previous night. In fact, you see, I suffered for people liking me.

"Are you glad, mun?" he said at last hoarsely; "are you glad? Well that's cheering anyhow, and thank ye."

He nodded and went on with his work again while I went to mine about the books, but with a suspicious feeling of impending trouble on my mind, as I passed two of the men who saw me come out of the smithy, and who must have seen me shaking hands with Pannell.

I don't know why they should have minded, for I should have done the same with either of them had we been on as friendly terms.

As I entered my little office my eyes lit on the common fishing-rod I had used, and that set me thinking about the conversation I had heard as I stood on the ledge.

I recalled what had been said overnight in a long discussion with my uncles, and the advice they had given.

"Don't show suspicion," Uncle Dick had said, "but meet every man with a frank fearless look in the eye, as if you asked no favour of him, were not afraid of him, and as if you wanted to meet him in a straightforward way."

I thought a good deal about it all, and how my uncles said they meant to be just and kind and stern at the same time; and it certainly did seem as if this was the most likely way to win the men's respect.

"For now that we have concluded to keep you with us, Cob, I must warn that we mean business, and that we have made up our minds that we shall win."

That morning went off quietly enough, and though we all kept a quiet searching look-out, there was nothing to excite suspicion. Then evening came, and the watching, in which again that night I had no share, but it was an understood thing that I was to be at the works at the same time as the men next day.

It was a lovely autumn morning with the wind from the country side, and as I hurried up and off to the works there was a feeling in the air that seemed to tempt me away to the hills and vales, and made me long for a change.

"I'll see if one of them won't go for a day," I said to myself; and hopeful of getting the holiday, and perhaps a run up to the great dam, I reached the works before the men.

"Well done, industrious!" cried Uncle Bob, who opened the gate to me. "You are first."

"That's right," I said. "No, it isn't. Where's Uncle Dick? Why, you look pale."

"Uncle Dick isn't awake," he said quickly. "Fact is, Cob, I've had a scare. As you say, I found that they'd been at Piter again. The poor dog has been drugged, and that must mean something wrong."

Sure enough, poor Piter lay fast asleep and breathing heavily; but after our last experience we did not feel so despondent about bringing him to again, so, leaving him in his kennel where he had crept, we roused Uncle Dick and told him.

"We can't look round now," he said. "The men are coming in to their work, but we shall soon hear if there is anything wrong. The bands again, I expect."

Just then we heard the noise made by the drawing of the sluice, the wheel went plashing round, the shaft rumbled, connections were being made, and in a very few minutes the first grindstone was sending forth its loud churring noise.

Then there was more and more, and at last the works were in full swing.

"There's nothing wrong, then, with the bands," said Uncle Dick; and then we waited, wondering what trick had been played, till about an hour had passed, during which the same remedies as were tried before were put into force with poor old Piter, and he recovered sufficiently to wag his tail.

Just about that time Uncle Jack arrived, and was put in possession of our fresh trouble.

"And you can find nothing wrong?" he said.

"Nothing."

"Have you looked under the desks, and in the cupboards?"

"We've quietly searched everywhere," replied Uncle Bob earnestly.

"Then we must go on as usual," said Uncle Jack. "There, you two go home: Cob and I will chance the risks."

"It may have been an attempt to get rid of the dog," I said, "and nothing more."

"That's what I've been thinking," said Uncle Jack; and soon after we were left alone.

Towards mid-day I went down to have a chat with Pannell, and to ask him how he had got on during his long illness.

"Tidy," he said sourly. "There was the club helped me, but the mesters did most."

"What! My uncles?"

"Ay, didn't you know?" he cried, busying himself about lighting a smaller forge at the back of the first.

I shook my head.

"Paid me pound a-week all the time I was badly, my lad."

"And very kind of them too," I said warmly.

"Ay, 'twas. Felt at times, lad, as if I warn't worth the money, that I did."

Just then Stevens made his appearance, crossing from the grinders' shop to one of the smithies at the end; and as he went along at some distance I saw him look curiously over at where I was standing talking to Pannell.

"Theer it is again," said the latter. "You mean well, lad, and it's very kind on you; but I shall hev it 'fore long on account o' talking to thee."

"Oh, surely not!" I cried angrily. "The men will never be such cowards as to attack you for that."

"Men weant, but trade will," said Pannell. "Mates can't do as they like about it. Look ye yonder; what did I say?"

He nodded in the direction of Stevens, who had returned directly, stopped opposite the smithy, but at some distance, and as soon as I looked up he began to signal to me to go to him.

I never liked the man, for he always seemed to dislike me, and I gave him the credit of being one of the active parties in the outrages that had been committed upon us. But I remembered what our plans were to be—frank, straightforward, and fearless—and I walked right up to Stevens, whose brow was lowering and full of menace.

"Here, I want a word with you," he said fiercely.

"All right, Stevens!" I said. "What is it?"

"Come over here," he replied, "and I'll tell ye."

He led the way along the yard to the other side of the great coal heap, which lay there massive and square, through its sides being carefully built up with big blocks of coal.

We were quite out of sight there, and, as I thought, how easy it would be for him to knock me down with one of the lumps.

I was perfectly cool though, till he suddenly seized me by the jacket.

I struck up at his hand, but he held on tightly, and there was a curious smile on his face as he said:

"Nay, you don't, lad; I'm stronger than thou."

"What do you want?" I cried, making a virtue of necessity and standing firm.

"What do I want, eh?" he said slowly. "Oh, just a word or two wi' thee, my lad. There, you needn't call thee uncle."

"I was not going to call him," I retorted. "Why should I?"

"Because you're scarred about what I'm going to do to thee."

"No, I'm not," I replied boldly; "because you daren't do anything unless it's in the dark, when you can attack a man behind his back."

He winced at this and scowled, but turned it off with a laugh.

"'Tack a what?" he said.

"A boy, then," I cried. "I know I'm a boy; but I meant people generally."

"Nivver you mind that," he said. "You don't understand trade. But joost you look there. Yow've been saying I did some'at to the dog."

"That I have not," I cried.

"Ay, but you did say it," he repeated fiercely.

"I did not say so," I cried almost as angrily; "but if I had said it, I don't suppose I should have been far wrong."

"Nay, lad, I did nowt to the dog. I did nowt—I—"

He let his hand fall, and a feeling of relief from some expectation came over his face. He had been talking to me, but it was in a curious way, and all the time he talked he seemed to be looking over my shoulder more than in my face.

But now he drew a long breath and seemed satisfied with the explanation; and just then I uttered a cry of horror, for there was a loud report, and the yard seemed to be filled with flying cinders and smoke.

Stevens gave me a grim look and laid his hand on my shoulder.

"Lucky yow weern't theer," he said. "Might have been hurt. Come and see."

We joined the men who were hurrying in the direction of the smoke that obscured one end of the yard.

"What is it, Uncle Jack?" I cried, as I ran to his side.

"I don't know yet," he said.

"It was somewhere by the smithies."

"Yes; that's plain enough," said my uncle, and we pressed on in front of the men, to come upon Pannell, tending down and rubbing his eyes.

"Pannell!" I cried; "you are not hurt?"

"Nay, not much," he said sourly. "Got the cinder and stuff in my eyes, but they missed me this time."

"What! Was it not an accident?"

"Oh, ay!" he replied, "reg'lar accident. Powder got into my little forge, and when I started her wi' some hot coal from t'other one she blew up."

"But you are not hurt?"

"Nay, lad, I weer stooping down, and were half behind the forge, so I didn't ketch it that time."

The smoke was by this time pretty well cleared away, and we walked into the smithy to see what mischief had befallen us.

Fortunately no harm had been done to the structure of the building, and there being no glass in the windows there was of course none to blow out. The coal ashes and cinders had been scattered far and wide, and the iron funnel-shaped chimney knocked out of place, while some of the smiths' tools, and the rods of steel upon which Pannell had been working, were thrown upon the floor.

The walls, forge, and pieces of iron about told tales for themselves without the odour of the explosive, for everything had been covered with a film of a greyish-white, such as gunpowder gives to iron or brickwork when it is fired.

"Where was the powder?" cried Uncle Jack, after satisfying himself that Pannell had not the slightest burn even upon his beard.

"In little forge all ready for me when I fired up," growled Pannell sourly, as he scowled round at the little crowd of men; "but they missed me that time."

Uncle Jack had a good look round the place, and the workmen stared at us as if in full expectation of being taken to task as the cause of the explosion.

I watched their faces cautiously in search of a look of regret, but the only peculiar expression I could see was on the countenance of Stevens, who stood softly rolling up his shirt-sleeves closer and closer to his shoulders, and there was such a curious smile in his eyes that he inspired me with a thought.

"Oh, if I have been deceived in him!"

That was my thought. For I seemed to see at a glance that he had known the explosion would take place, and that the talk about the dog was an excuse to get me away and save me from the consequences.

Just then Uncle Jack turned round to me and laid his hand on my shoulder.

"Look here," he said quietly, as if he were showing me a curiosity, but loud enough for all the men to hear—"down in the south of England, my boy, when a workman is disliked it generally comes to a settlement with fists, and there is a fair, honest, stand-up fight. Down here in Arrowfield, Jacob, when another workman does something to offend his fellows—"

"Traäde," shouted a voice.

"To offend his fellow-workmen," repeated Uncle Jack.

"Traäde," shouted the voice again, and there was a murmur of assent.

"Well, have it your own way," said Uncle Jack. "To offend the trade, they try to blind him for life by filling his forge with powder, so that it may explode in his face. Jacob, my lad, next time I go anywhere, and hear people talk about what brave strong manly fellows the Englishmen are, I shall recommend them to come down and stay in Arrowfield for a month and see what is done."

There was a low murmur among the men; but we did not stop to listen, and they all returned to their work except Pannell, who went down to the dam and bathed his eyes, after which he went as coolly as could be back to his smithy, took a shovel and borrowed some glowing fire from the next forge, lit up his own, and was soon after hammering his funnel chimney back in its place, and working up rods of steel as if nothing whatever had been amiss.

About the middle of the afternoon, though, he came up through the workshop straight to the office, with his hammer in his hand, and gave a loud thump at the door.

I opened it and admitted him; for I was in the big office with my uncles, who were talking about this last trouble.

"Well, my man, what is it?" said Uncle Jack.

Pannell began to lift up his hammer-head slowly and let it fall back again into his left hand, staring straight before him with his dark eyes, which were surrounded with the black marks of the gunpowder which clung still to the skin.

"What do you want, Pannell?" I said, giving him a touch on the arm; but the hammer rose and fell still by the contraction of his right hand, and went on tap—tap—falling into his left.

"Why don't you speak?" I said again, quite impatiently.

"I know," he growled. "I want to speak."

"We are listening," said Uncle Dick. "What have you to say?"

"Look here," cried Pannell, giving his hammer a flourish round his head as if he were about to attack us. "I'm a man—I am."

"And a good big one, Pannell," said Uncle Bob smiling.

"Wish I were twyste as big, mester! Theer!" cried Pannell.

"I wish you were if it would be any comfort to you," said Uncle Bob to himself.

"I've been a-thinking o' this out while I've been hammering yonder, and I want to speak."

"Yes," said Uncle Jack. "Go on."

"Look ye here, then," cried Pannell, flourishing his hammer round as if he were a modern edition or an angry Thor; "does anyone say I telled on 'em? Did I tell on 'em, mesters? Answer me that."

"What! About the outrages?" said Uncle Dick firmly.

"Outrages, mester!"

"Well, the attempts to blow us up."

"Ay!—the trade business. Did I ivver come and say word to anny of you?"

"Never."

"Or to yow, youngster?"

"Never, Pannell. You always went against us," I said, "when a word from you would—"

"Theer, that'll do. Tell me this—Did I ivver tell on anny on 'em?"

"No; you have always been true to your party, Pannell—if that is what you mean."

"And that is what I mean," said the great fellow, throwing his head about and jerking out his words, each with a menacing flourish of the hammer or a mock blow, as if they were steel words that he wanted to strike into shape.

"Nobody accused you of tale-bearing to us," said Uncle Dick.

"Didn't they, mester?" he roared. "What's this, then, and this, and this?"

He touched the scars upon his head and brow, and the sticking-plaster left on.

"Don't you call that saying I telled on 'em, wi'out the poother in my forge this morning?"

"A cowardly brutal thing to have done, my man."

"Ay, so 'twas. I'd done nowt but be civil to young mester here. Say," he cried fiercely, "yow telled 'em I forged that trap!" and he turned on me.

"Oh, Pannell!" I cried, flushing indignantly.

That was all I said, but it was enough.

"Beg pardon, young gentleman!—yow didn't, I can see that. Nay, it was the altogetherishness o' the whole thing. They set me down—me, a mate in the union—as hevvin' telled on 'em and gone agen 'em, and being friends wi' the mesters; and yow see what they've done."

"Indeed we do, Pannell—"

"Howd hard, mester," said the big smith, flourishing about his hammer. "I hevn't had my spell yet. I want to speak."

Uncle Dick nodded, as much as to say, "Go on."

"Look here, then, mesters—I've thowt this out. It's cowards' business, ivvery bit on it, 'cept Matt Stivvins this morning coming and fetching young mester out of the way."

"Yes," I said, "he did."

"And they'll knobstick 'im for it if they know—see if they don't!"

"Then they mustn't know," I cried eagerly. "I don't like Stevens, but he did save me this morning."

"Ay, he did, 'cause he said once yow weer a trump, my lad; but he didn't give me a word. I sha'n't tell on him, but I sha'n't hev nought more to do wi' anny on 'em. I've been union man all these years and paid, and here's what I've got for it. I says to mysen, I says: If this here's what comes o' sticking to union through all their games I've done wi' 'em, and I'm a master's man—that's all."

He turned short round to go, but Uncle Dick stopped him.

"I don't quite understand what you mean, Pannell."

"What I mean! Why, what I said—that's what I mean."

"That you have done with the trades-union, Pannell," I cried, "and mean to be on our side?"

"That's so, mester. Now I mun go or my fire'll be out."

He strode out of the place and banged the door after him; and as he went along the shop I could see him in imagination staring defiantly from side to side, in answer to the savage murmur that greeted him from the men whom he had made up his mind to defy.

"What do you think of that?" said Uncle Dick, as soon as we heard the farther door close with a crash.

"It's the beginning of the end," said Uncle Jack with an eager look in his eyes. "Keep firm, boys, and we shall have them all honestly on our side, and we can laugh at all trades-unions in Arrowfield that fight with cowardly weapons. The men do not do what their own feelings prompt, but obey the law of a secret society which forces them to do these cruel wrongs."

It must have been intentional on his part, for as I went down into the furnace house about half an hour after, at my usual time, to take down an account of work done, I met Stevens coming towards me.

We were in the big empty building, the furnace being cold, and no work going on that day, and he slouched towards me as if he were going by, but I stopped him and held out my hand.

"Thank you, Stevens," I said. "I didn't understand it then, but you saved me from something terrible to-day."

He gave a quick glance or two about, and then regularly snatched my hand, gave it a squeeze, and threw it away.

"All right, my lad!" he said in a hoarse whisper. "You're on'y one o' the mesters, but I couldn't abear to see thee in for it too."

He went on his away and I went mine, feeling that Uncle Jack was right, and that though it might be a long journey first, it was the beginning of the end.

Chapter Twenty Three.

I start for a Walk.

"Who's for a walk?" said Uncle Dick one morning. "I'm going up the hills to the millstone-grit quarry."

I started, and my heart gave a throb, but I did not look up.

"I can't go," said Uncle Jack.

"And I'm busy," said Uncle Bob.

"Then I shall have to put up with Cob," said Uncle Dick gloomily. "Will you come, my lad?"

"Will I come!" I cried, jumping and feeling as if I should like to shout for joy, so delightful seemed the idea of getting away into the hills, and having one of our old walks.

"Well, it must be at mid-day, and you will have to meet me out at Ranflitt."

"Two miles on the road?" I said.

"Yes; you be there, and if I'm not waiting I sha'n't be long, and we'll go on together."

"What time shall I start?" I asked.

"When the men go to their dinner will do. I have some business at the far end of the town, and it will not be worth while for me to come back. I'll take the other road."

So it was settled, and I took my big stick down to the office, and a net satchel that was handy for anything when slung from the right shoulder and under my left arm. Before now it had carried fish, partridges, fruits, herbs, roots of plants, and oftener than anything else, lunch.

That seemed to be a long morning, although I wrote hard all the time so as to get a good day's work over first; but at last the dinner-bell rang, and, saying good-bye to the others, I slipped the satchel into my pocket, took my stick, and started.

We had not thought of those who would be loitering about during their dinner-hour, but I soon found that they were thinking of me, for not only were our own men about the streets, but the men of the many other works around; and to my dismay I soon found that they all knew me by sight, and that they were ready to take notice of me in a very unpleasant way.

I was walking steadily on when a stone hit me in the leg, and instead of making haste and getting out of range, I stopped short and looked round angrily for my assailant.

I could see a dozen grinning faces, but it was of course impossible to tell who threw, and before I turned back an oyster-shell struck me in the back.

I turned round angrily and found myself the object of a tremendous shout of laughter.

Almost at the same moment I was struck by an old cabbage-stump and by a potato, while stones in plenty flew by my head.

"The cowards!" I said to myself as I strode on, looking to right and left, and seeing that on both sides of the way a number of rough boys were collecting, encouraged by the laughter and cheers of their elders.

We had not a single boy at our works, but I could see several of our men were joining in the sport, to them, of having me hunted.

To have a good hunt, though, it is necessary to have a good quarry, that is to say, the object hunted must be something that will run.

Now, in imagination I saw myself rushing away pursued by a mob of lads, hooting, yelling, and pelting me; but I felt not the slightest inclination to be hunted in this fashion, and hence it was that I walked steadily and watchfully on, stick in hand, and prepared to use it too, if the necessity arose.

Unfortunately I was in a road where missiles were plentiful, and these came flying about me, one every now and then giving me such a stinging blow that I winced with pain. The boys danced round me, too, coming nearer as they grew bolder from my non-resistance, and before long they began to make rushes, hooting and yelling to startle me, no doubt, into running away.

But so far they did not succeed; and as I continued my walking they changed their tactics, keeping out of reach of my stout stick, and taking to stones and anything that came to hand.

I could do nothing. To have turned round would only have been to receive the objects thrown in my face; and when at last, stung into action by a harder blow than usual, I did turn and make a rush at the boy I believed to have thrown, he gave way and the others opened out to let me pass, and then closed up and followed.

It was a foolish movement on my part, and I found I had lost ground, for to get on my way again I had to pass through a body of about a dozen lads, and the only way to do this as they gathered themselves ready to receive me, was by making a bold rush through them.

They were already whispering together, and one of them cried "Now!" when I made a rush at them, stick in hand, running as fast as I could.

They made a show of stopping me, but opened out directly, and as soon as I had passed yelled to their companions to come on, with the result that I found I could not stop unless I stood at bay, and that I was doing the very thing I had determined not to do—racing away from my pursuers, who, in a pack of about forty, were yelling, crying, and in full chase.

To stop now was impossible: all that was open to me was to run hard and get into the more open suburb, leaving them behind, while I had the satisfaction of knowing that before long the bells at the different works would be ringing, and the young vagabonds obliged to hurry back to their places, leaving me free to maintain my course.

So that, now I was involuntarily started, I determined to leave my pursuers behind, and I ran.

I don't think I ever ran so fast before, but fast as I ran I soon found that several of the lightly clothed old-looking lads were more than my equals, and they kept so close that some half a dozen were ready to rush in on me at any moment and seize me and drag me back.

I was determined, though, that they should not do that, and, grasping my stick, I ran on, more blindly, though, each moment. 'Tis true, I thought of making for the outskirts and tiring the boys out; but to my dismay I found that fresh lads kept joining in the chase, all eager and delighted to have something to run down and buffet, while my breath was coming thickly, my heart beat faster and faster, and there was a terrible burning sensation in my chest.

I looked to right for some means of escape, but there was none; to left was the same; behind me the tolling pack; while before me stretched the lanes, and mill after mill with great dams beyond them similar to ours.

I should have stopped at bay, hoping by facing the lads to keep them off; but I was streaming with perspiration, and so weak that I knew, in spite of my excitement, that I should hardly be able to lift my arm.

On and on, more and more blindly, feeling moment by moment as if my aching legs would give way beneath me. I gazed wildly at my pursuers to ask for a little mercy, but unfortunately for me they, excited and hot with their chase, were as cruel as boys can be, and men too at such a time.

There was nothing for it but to rush on at a pace that was fast degenerating into a staggering trot, and in imagination, as the boys pushed me and buffeted me with their caps, I saw myself tripped up, thrown down, kicked, and rolled in the dust, and so much exhausted that I could not help myself.

One chance gave me a little more energy. It must be nearly time for the bells to ring, and then they would be bound to give up the pursuit; but as I struggled I caught sight of a clock, and saw that it wanted a quarter of an hour yet.

There were some men lounging against a wall, and I cried out to them, but they hardly turned their heads, and as I was hurried and driven by I saw that they only laughed as if this were excellent sport.

Next we passed a couple of well-dressed ladies, but they fled into a gateway to avoid my pursuers, and the next minute I was hustled round a corner, the centre of the whooping, laughing crowd, and, to my horror, I found that we were in a narrow path with a row of stone cottages on one side, the wall of a dam like our own, and only a few inches above the water on the other.

I had felt dazed and confused before. Now I saw my danger clearly enough and the object of the lads.

I was streaming with perspiration, and so weak that I could hardly stand, but, to avoid being thrust in, and perhaps held under water and ducked and buffeted over and over again, I felt that I must make a plunge and try and swim to the other side.

But I dared not attempt it, even if I could have got clear; and blindly struggling on I had about reached the middle of the dam path when a foot was thrust out, and I fell.

Sobbing for my breath, beaten with fists, buffeted and blinded with the blows of the young savages' caps, I struggled to my feet once more, but only to be tripped and to fall again on the rough stony path.

I could do no more. I had no strength to move, but I could think acutely, and feel, as I longed for the strength of Uncle Jack, and to hold in my hand a good stout but limber cane.

Yes, I could feel plainly enough the young ruffians dragging at me, and in their eagerness and number fighting one against the other.

"In wi' him!"

"Dook him, lads!"

"Now, then, all together!"

I heard all these cries mingled together, and mixed up with the busy hands and faces, I seemed to see the row of houses, the clear sky, the waters of the dam, and Gentles the grinder leaning against a door and looking on.

I was being lifted amidst shouts and laughter, and I knew that the next moment I should be in the dam, when there was a tremendous splash, and some drops of water sprinkled my face.

Then there was the rattle of the handle of a bucket, and another splash heard above all the yelling and shouting of the boys. There was the hollow sound of a pail banged against something hard, and mingled with cries, shouts, laughter, and ejaculations of pain I felt myself fall upon the path, to be kicked and trampled on by someone contending, for there were slaps, and thuds, and blows, the panting and hissing of breath; and then the clanging of bells near and bells far, buzzing in ears, the rush and scuffling of feet, with shouts of derision, defiance, and laughter, and then, last of all, a curious cloud of mist seemed to close me in like the fog on the Dome Tor, and out of this a shrill angry voice cried:

"Ah, ye may shout, but some on ye got it. Go and dry yourselves at the furnace, you cowardly young shacks. Hey, bud I wish I'd hed holt o' yon stick!"

"Yon stick!" I felt must be mine; but my head was aching, and I seemed to go to sleep.

"I wish you'd be quiet," I remember saying. "Let me be."

"Fetch some more watter, mester," said a pleasant voice, and a rough hand was laid upon my forehead, but only to be taken away again, and that which had vexed and irritated we went on again, and in a dreamy way I knew it was a sponge that was being passed over my face.

"I fetched Mester Tom one wi' bottom o' the boocket, and I got one kick at Tom, and when the two boys come home to-night they'll get such a leathering as they never hed before."

"Nay, let 'em be," said a familiar voice.

"Let 'em be! D'ye think I'm going to hev my bairns grow up such shacks? Nay, that I wean't, so yo' may like it or no. I'd be shamed o' my sen to stand by and let that pack o' boys half kill the young gentleman like that."

"I warn't going to stop 'em."

"Not you, mester. Yow'd sooner set 'em on, like you do your mates, and nice things come on it wi' your strikes and powder, and your wife and bairns wi' empty cupboard. Yow on'y let me know o' next meeting, and if I don't come and give the men a bit o' my mind, my name arn't Jane Gentles."

"Yow'd best keep thy tongue still."

"Mebbe you think so, my man, but I don't."

My senses had come back, and I was staring about at the clean kitchen I was in, with carefully blackleaded grate and red-brick floor. Against the open door, looking out upon the dam, and smoking his pipe, stood—there was no mistaking him—our late man, Gentles; while over me with a sponge in her hand, and a basin of water by her on a chair, was a big broad-shouldered woman with great bare arms and a pleasant homely face, whose dark hair was neatly kept and streaked with grey.

She saw that I was coming to, and smiled down at me, showing a set of very white teeth, and her plump face looked motherly and pleasant as she bent down and laid her hand upon my forehead.

"That's bonny," she said, nodding her head at me. "You lie still a bit and I'll mak you a cup o' tea, and yo'll be aw reight again. I'm glad I caught 'em at it. Some on 'em's going to hev sore bones for that job, and so I tell 'em."

I took her hand and held it in mine, feeling very weak and dreamy still, and I saw Gentles shift round and give me a hasty glance, and then twist himself more round with his back to me.

"Howd up a minute," she said, passing one strong arm under me and lifting me as if I had been a baby; and almost before I had realised it she slipped off my jacket and placed a cushion beneath my head.

"There, now, lie still," she said, dabbing my wet hair with a towel. "Go to sleep if you can."

By this time she was at the other end of the common print-covered couch on which I lay and unlacing my boots, which she drew off.

"There, now thou'lt be easy, my lad. What would thy poor moother say if she saw thee this how?"

I wanted to thank her, but I was too dreamy and exhausted to speak; but I had a strange feeling of dread, and that was, that if I were left alone with Gentles he would, out of revenge, lay hold of me and throw me into the dam, and to strengthen my fancy I saw him keep turning his head in a furtive way to glance at me.

"Here," exclaimed the woman sharply, "take these here boots out to the back, mester, and clean 'em while I brush his coat."

"Eh?" said Gentles.

"Tak them boots out and brush 'em. Are yo' deaf?"

"Nay, I'm not going to clean his boots," growled Gentles.

"Not going to clean the bairn's boots!" said the woman sharply; "but I think thou art."

She left me, went to the door, took Gentles' pipe from his mouth, and then thrust the boots under his arm, laying a great hand upon his shoulder directly after, and seeming to lead him to a door behind me, through which she pushed him, with an order to make haste.

"Yes," she said, tightening her lips, and smiling, as she nodded to me, "I'm mester here, and they hev to mind. Was it thou as set the big trap ketched my mester by the leg?"

I never felt more taken aback in my life; but I spoke out boldly, and said that it was I.

"And sarve him right. Be a lesson to him. Mixing himself up wi' such business. I towd him if he crep into people's places o' neets, when he owt to hev been fast asleep i' bed wi' his wife and bairns, he must reckon on being ketched like a rat. I'd like to knock some o' their heads together, I would. They're allus feitin' agen the mesters, and generally for nowt, and it's ooz as has to suffer."

Mrs Gentles had told me to try and sleep, and she meant well; but there were two things which, had I been so disposed, would thoroughly have prevented it, and they were the dread of Gentles doing something to be revenged upon me, and his wife's tongue.

For she went on chattering away to me in the most confidential manner, busying herself all the time in brushing my dusty jacket on a very white three-legged table, after giving the cloth a preliminary beating outside.

"There," she said, hanging it on a chair; "by and by you shall get up and brush your hair, and I'll give you a brush down, and then with clean boots you will not be so very much the worse."

She then sat down to some needlework, stitching away busily, and giving me all sorts of information about her family—how she had two boys out at work at Bandy's, taking it for granted that I knew who Bandy's were; that she had her eldest girl in service, and the next helping her aunt Betsey, and the other four were at school.

All of which was, no doubt, very interesting to her; but the only part that took my attention was about her two boys, who had, I knew, from what I overheard, been in the pack that had so cruelly hunted me down.

And all this while I could hear the slow *brush, brush* at my boots, evidently outside the back-door, and I half expected to have them brought back ripped, or with something sharp inside to injure me when I put them on.

At last, after Mrs Gentles had made several allusions to how long "the mester" was "wi' they boots," he came in, limping slightly, and after closing the door dropped them on the brick floor.

"Why, Sam!" exclaimed Mrs Gentles, "I'd be ashamed o' mysen—that I would!"

But Gentles did not seem to be in the slightest degree ashamed of himself, but took his pipe from the shelf, where his wife had laid it, struck a match, relit it, and went off with his hands in his pockets.

Mrs Gentles rose and followed him to the door, and then returned, with her lips tightened and an angry look in her face.

"Now he's gone off to booblic," she said angrily, "to hatch up and mess about and contrive all sorts o' mischief wi' them as leads him on. Oh the times I've telled him as they might make up all the differ by spending the time in work that they do in striking again' a sixpence took off or to get one putt on! Ay, but we missuses have but a sorry time!"

The absence of Gentles' furtive look sent back at me from the door seemed to change the effect of his wife's voice, which by degrees grew soothing and soft, and soon after I dropped off asleep, and dreamed of a curious clinking going on, from which dream I awoke, with my head cooler, and Mrs Gentles bending over me and fanning my face with what looked like an old copy-book.

I looked at her wonderingly.

"That's better," she said. "Now set up and I'll help thee dress; and here's a nice cup of tea ready."

"Oh, thank you!" I said. "What time is it?"

"Close upon five, and I thowt you'd be better now after some tea."

She helped me on with my jacket, and I winced with pain, I was so stiff and sore. After this she insisted upon putting on my boots.

"Just as if I heven't done such things hundreds of times," she said cheerfully. "Why, I used to put on the mester's and tak 'em off all the time his leg was bad."

"I'm sorry I set that trap," I said, looking up at her rough, pleasant face, and wondering how such a sneaking, malignant fellow could have won so good a wife.

"I'm not," she said laughing. "It sarved him right, so say no more about it."

That tea was like nectar, and seemed to clear my head, so that I felt nearly recovered save when I tried to rise, and then I was in a good deal of pain. But I deemed myself equal to going, and was about to start when I missed my cap.

"Hey, but that'll be gone," she said. "Oh, they boys! Well, yow must hev Dick's."

Before I could protest she went upstairs, and returned with a decent-looking cap, which I promised to return, and then, bidding my Samaritan-like hostess good-bye, I walked firmly out of her sight, and then literally began to hobble, and was glad as soon as I could get into the main road to hail one of the town cabs and be driven home, not feeling strong enough to go to the works and tell of my mishap.

Mr Tomplin came in that evening after Uncle Dick had heard all my narrative and Uncle Bob had walked up and down the room, driving his fist into his hand every now and then with a loud *pat*.

We had had a long conversation, in which I had taken part with a terribly aching head, and I should have gone to bed only I would not show the white feather.

For they all three made this a reason why I should give up to them,

217

and after all go back.

"You see the men are dead against us, Cob, and the boys follow suit, and are against you." So said Uncle Dick.

"All the men are not against you," I said. "Look at Pannell! He has come round, and," I added, with a laugh that hurt me horribly, "I shall have some of the boys come round and help me."

"The young scoundrels!" cried Uncle Bob. *Pat*—that was his fist coming down into his hand. "The young scoundrels!"

"Well, you've said that twenty times at least, Bob," said Uncle Jack.

"Enough to make me!" said Uncle Bob sharply. "The young scoundrels!" *Pat*.

"I only wish I'd been there with a good handy riding-whip," said Uncle Jack. "There would have been some wailing among them."

"Yes; and summonses for assault, and all that bother," said Uncle Dick. "We don't want to come to blows, Jack, if we can help it."

"They are beyond bearing," cried Uncle Bob, keeping up his walk; "the young scoundrels!" *Pat*.

"My dear Bob," cried Uncle Dick, who was very much out of temper; "if you would be kind enough to leave off that trot up and down."

"Like a hungry lion," said Uncle Jack.

"In the Zoo," cried Uncle Dick, "you would very much oblige me."

"I can't sit down," said Uncle Bob, thumping his hand. "I feel too much excited."

"Then bottle it up for future use," said Uncle Dick. "You really must."

"To attack and hurt the boy in that way! It's scandalous. The young ruffians—the young savages!"

Just then Mr Templin came in, looked sharply round, and saw there was something wrong.

"I beg your pardon," he said quickly; "I'll look in another time."

"No, no," said Uncle Bob. "Pray sit down. We want your advice. A cruel assault upon our nephew here"—and he related the whole affair.

"Humph!" ejaculated Mr Templin, looking hard at me.

"What should you advise—warrants against the ringleaders?"

"Summonses, Mr Robert, I presume," said Mr Tomplin. "But you don't know who they were?"

"Yes; oh, yes!" cried Uncle Bob eagerly. "Two young Gentles."

"But you said the mother saved our young friend here from the lads, dowsed them and trounced them with a pail, and made her husband clean his boots, while she nursed him and made him tea."

"Ye–es," said Uncle Bob.

"Well, my dear sir, when you get summonses out against boys—a practice to which I have a very great objection—it is the parents who suffer more than their offspring."

"And serve them right, sir, for bringing their boys up so badly."

"Yes, I suppose so; but boys will be boys," said Mr Tomplin.

"I don't mind their being boys," said Uncle Bob angrily; "what I do object to is their being young savages. Why, sir, they half-killed my nephew."

"But he has escaped, my dear sir, and, as I understand it, the mother has threatened to—er—er—leather the boys well, that was, I think, her term—"

"Yes," I said, rather gleefully, "leather them."

"And judging from the description I have heard of this Amazon-like lady, who makes her husband obey her like a sheep, the young gentlemen's skins will undergo rather a severe tanning process. Now, don't you think you had better let the matter stand as it is? And, speaking on the *lex talionis* principle, our young friend Jacob here ought to be able to handle his fists, and on the first occasion when he met one of his enemies he might perhaps give him a thrashing. I don't advise it, for it is illegal, but he might perhaps by accident. It would have a good effect."

"But you are always for letting things drop, Mr Tomplin," said Uncle Bob peevishly.

"Yes; I don't like my friends to go to law—or appeal to the law, as one may say. I am a lawyer, and I lose by giving such advice, I know."

"Mr Tomplin's right, Bob," said Uncle Jack. "You think of that boy as if he were sugar. I'm sure he does not want to take any steps; do you, Cob?"

"No," I said; "if I may—"

I stopped short.

"May what?"

"Have a few lessons in boxing. I hate fighting; but I should like to thrash that big boy who kept hitting me most."

Chapter Twenty Four.

Uncle Jack and I have a Run.

I did not have any lessons in boxing, in spite of my earnest desire.

"We do not want to be aggressors, Cob," said my Uncle Dick.

"But we want to defend ourselves, uncle."

"To be sure we do, my lad," he said; "and we'll be ready as we can when we are attacked; but I don't see the necessity for training ourselves to fight."

So I did not meet and thrash my enemy, but went steadily on with my duties at the works.

In fact I was very little the worse for my adventure, thanks to Mrs Gentles, to whom I returned the cap she had lent me and thanked her warmly for her goodness.

She seemed very pleased to see me, and told me that her "mester" was quite well, only his leg was a little stiff, and that he was at work now with her boys.

The matters seemed now to have taken a sudden turn, as Mr Tomplin said they would: the men were evidently getting over their dislike to us and the new steel, making it up and grinding it in an ill-used, half contemptuous sort of way, and at last the necessity for watching by night seemed so slight that we gave it up.

But it was felt that it would not be wise to give up the air of keeping the place looked after by night, so old Dunning the gate-keeper was consulted, and he knew of the very man—one who had been a night watchman all his life and was now out of work through the failure of the firm by whom he had been employed.

In due time the man came—a tall, very stout fellow, of about sixty, with a fierce look and a presence that was enough to keep away mischief by the fact of its being known that he was there.

He came twice, and was engaged to be on duty every night at nine; and in the conversation that ensued in the office he took rather a gruff, independent tone, which was mingled with contempt as he was told of the attempts that had been made.

"Yes," he said coolly; "it's a way the hands have wherever new folk come and don't hev a reg'lar watchman. There wouldn't hev been none of that sort o' thing if I had been here."

"Then you don't expect any more troubles of this kind?"

"More! Not likely, mester. We've ways of our own down here; and as soon as the lads know that Tom Searby's on as watchman there'll be no more trouble."

"I hope there will not," said Uncle Dick as soon as the man had gone. "It will be worth all his wages to be able to sleep in peace."

About this time there had been some talk of my father and mother coming down to Arrowfield, but once more difficulties arose in town which necessitated my father's stay, and as my mother was rather delicate, it was decided that she should not be brought up into the cold north till the springtime came again.

"All work and no play makes—you know the rest," said Uncle Jack one morning at breakfast. "I won't say it, because it sounds egotistic. Cob, what do you say? Let's ask for a holiday."

"Why not all four go?" I said eagerly; for though the works were very interesting and I enjoyed seeing the work go oil, I was ready enough to get away, and so sure as the sun shone brightly I felt a great longing to be off from the soot and noise to where the great hills were a-bloom with heather and gorse, and tramp where I pleased.

Uncle Dick shook his head.

"No," he said; "two of us stay—two go. You fellows have a run to-day, and we'll take our turn another time."

We were too busy to waste time, and in high glee away we went, with no special aim in view, only to get out of the town as soon as possible, and off to the hills.

Uncle Jack was a stern, hard man in the works, but as soon as he went out for a holiday he used to take off twenty years, as he said, and leave them at home, so that I seemed to have a big lad of my own age for companion.

It was a glorious morning, and our way lay by the works and then on past a series of "wheels" up the valley, in fact the same route I had taken that day when I was hunted by the boys.

But I had Uncle Jack by my side, and in addition it was past breakfast time, and the boys were at work.

We had nearly reached the dam into which I had so narrowly escaped a ducking, and I was wondering whether Uncle Jack would mind my just running to speak to the big honest woman in the row of houses we were about to pass, when he stood still.

"What is it?" I said.

"Cob, my lad," he cried, "I want a new head or a new set of brains, or something. I've totally forgotten to ask your Uncle Dick to write to the engineer about the boiler."

"Let me run back," I said.

"Won't do, my boy; must see him myself. There, you keep steadily on along the road as if we were bound for Leadshire, and I'll overtake you in less than half an hour."

"But," I said, "I was going this way to meet Uncle Dick that day when he went to buy the stones, and what a holiday that turned out!"

"I don't think history will repeat itself this time, Cob," he replied.

"But will you be able to find me again?"

"I can't help it if you keep to the road. If you jump over the first hedge you come to, and go rambling over the hills, of course I shall not find you."

"Then there is no fear," I said; and he walked sharply back, while I strode on slowly and stopped by the open window of one factory, where a couple of men were spinning teapots.

"Spinning teapots!" I fancy I hear some one say; "how's that done?"

Well, it has always struck me as being so ingenious and such an example of what can be done by working on metal whirled round at a great speed, that I may interest some one in telling all I saw.

The works opposite which I stopped found their motive power in a great wheel just as ours did, but instead of steel being the metal used, the firm worked in what is called Britannia metal, which is an alloy of tin, antimony, zinc, and copper, which being mixed in certain proportions form a metal having the whiteness of tin, but a solidity and firmness given by the three latter metals, that make it very durable, which tin is not.

"Oh, but," says somebody, "tin is hard enough! Look at the tin saucepans and kettles in every kitchen."

I beg pardon; those are all made of plates of iron rolled out very thin and then dipped in a bath of tin, to come out white and silvery and clean and ready to keep off rust from attacking the iron. What people call tin plates are really *tinned* plates. Tin itself is a soft metal that melts and runs like lead.

As I looked through into these works, one man was busy with sheets of rolled-out Britannia metal, thrusting them beneath a stamping press, and at every clang with which this came down a piece of metal like a perfectly flat spoon was cut out and fell aside, while at a corresponding press another man was holding a sheet, and as close as possible out of this he was stamping out flat forks, which, like the spoons, were borne to other presses with dies, and as the flat spoon or fork was thrust in it received a tremendous blow, which shaped the bowl and curved the handle, while men at vices and benches finished them off with files.

I had seen all this before, and how out of a flat sheet of metal what seemed like beautiful silver spoons were made; but I had never yet seen a man spin a teapot, so being holiday-time, and having to wait for Uncle Jack, I stood looking on.

I presume that most boys know a lathe when they see it, and how, out of a block of wood, ivory, or metal, a beautifully round handle, chess-man, or even a perfect ball can be turned.

Well, it is just such a lathe as this that the teapot spinner stands before at his work, which is to make a handsome tea or coffee-pot service.

But he uses no sharp tools, and he does not turn his teapot out of a solid block of metal. His tool is a hard piece of wood, something like a child's hoop-stick, and fixed to the spinning-round part of the lathe, the "chuck," as a workman would call it, is a solid block of smooth wood shaped like a deep slop-basin.

Up against the bottom of this wooden sugar-basin the workman places a flat round disc or plate of Britannia metal—plate is a good term, for it is about the size or a little larger than an ordinary dinner plate. A part of the lathe is screwed up against this so as to hold the plate flat up against the bottom of the wooden sugar-basin; the lathe is set in motion and the glistening white disc of metal spins round at an inconceivable rate, and becomes nearly invisible.

Then the man begins to press his wooden stick up against the centre of the plate as near as he can go, and gradually draws the wooden tool from the centre towards the edge, pressing it over the wooden block of basin shape.

This he does again and again, and in spite of the metal being cold, the heat of the friction, the speed at which it goes, and the ductility of the metal make it behave as if it were so much clay or putty, and in a very short time the wooden tool has moulded it from a flat disc into a metal bowl which covers the wooden block.

Then the lathe is stopped, the mechanism unscrewed, and the metal bowl taken off the moulding block, which is dispensed with now, for if the spinner were to attempt to contract the edges of his bowl, as a potter does when making a jug, the wooden mould could not be taken out.

So without the wooden block the metal bowl is again fixed in the lathe, sent spinning-round, the stick applied, and in a very short time the bowl, instead of being large-mouthed, is made to contract in a beautiful curve, growing smaller and smaller, till it is about one-third of its original diameter, and the metal has seemed to be plastic, and yielded to the moulding tool till a gracefully formed tall vessel is the result, with quite a narrow mouth where the lid is to be.

Here the spinner's task is at an end. He has turned a flat plate of metal into a large-bodied narrow-mouthed metal pot as easily as if the hard cold metal had been clay, and all with the lathe and a piece of wood. There are no chips, no scrapings. All the metal is in the pot, and that is now passed on to have four legs soldered on, a hole cut for the spout to be fitted; a handle placed where the handle should be, and finally hinges and a lid and polish to make it perfect and ready for someone's tray.

I stopped and saw the workman spin a couple of pots, and then thinking I should like to have a try at one of our lathes, I went on past this dam and on to the next, where I meant to have a friendly word with Mrs Gentles if her lord and master were not smoking by the door.

I did not expect to see him after hearing that he was away at work; but as it happened he was there.

For as I reached the path along by the side of the dam I found myself in the midst of a crowd of women and crying children, all in a state of great excitement concerning something in the dam.

I hurried on to see what was the matter, and to my astonishment there was Gentles on the edge of the dam, armed with an ordinary long broom, with which he was trying to hook something out of the water—what, I could not see, for there was nothing visible.

"Farther in—farther in," a shrill voice cried, making itself heard over the gabble of fifty others. "My Jenny says he went in theer."

I was still some distance off, but I could see Gentles the unmistakable splash the broom in again, and then over and over again, while women were wringing their hands, and giving bits of advice which seemed to have no effect upon Gentles, who kept splashing away with the broom.

Just then a tall figure in bonnet and shawl came hurrying from the other end of the path, and joined the group about the same time as I did.

There was no mistaking Mrs Gentles without her voice, which she soon made heard.

"Whose bairn is it?" she cried loudly, and throwing off her bonnet and shawl as she spoke.

"Thine—it's thy little Esau—playing on the edge—got shoved in," was babbled out by a dozen women; while Gentles did not speak, but went on pushing in the broom, giving it a mow round like a scythe, and pulling it out.

"Wheer? Oh, my gracious!" panted Mrs Gentles, "wheer did he go in?"

Poor woman! A dozen hands pointed to different parts of the bank many yards apart, and I saw her turn quite white as she rushed at her husband and tore the broom from his hands.

"What's the good o' that, thou Maulkin," (scarecrow) she cried, giving him a push that sent him staggering away; and without a moment's hesitation she stooped, tightened her garments round her, and jumped right into the dam, which was deeper than she thought, for she went under in the great splash she made, losing her footing, and a dread fell upon all till they saw the great stalwart woman rise and shake the water from her face, and stand chest deep, and then shoulder deep, as, sobbing hysterically, she reached out in all directions with the broom, trying to find the child.

"Was it anywheers about here—anywheers about here?" she cried, as she waded to and fro in a state of frantic excitement, and a storm of affirmations responded, while her husband, who seemed quite out of place among so many women, stood rubbing his head in a stolid way.

"Quiet, bairns!" shrieked one of the women, stamping her foot fiercely at the group of children who had been playing about after childhood's fashion in the most dangerous place they could find.

Her voice was magical, for it quelled a perfect babel of sobs and cries. And all the while poor Mrs Gentles was reaching out, so reckless of herself that she was where the water reached her chin, and could hardly keep her footing.

"Call thysen a man!" shouted the woman who had silenced the children. "Go in or thou'llt lose thy wife and bairn too."

But Gentles paid no heed to the admonition. He stood rubbing his ear softly, though he gave a satisfied grunt as he saw the fierce virago of a woman who had spoken, leap in after Mrs Gentles, and wade out so as to hold her left hand.

Where had the child tumbled in? No one knew, for the frightened little ones who had spread the news, running away home as soon as their playmate had toppled in with a splash, were too scared to remember the exact spot.

I had not been idle all this time, but as the above scene was in progress I had taken off jacket, vest, and cap, handing them to a woman to hold, and had just finished kicking off my boots and socks, carefully watching the surface of the water the while, under the impression that the poor child would rise to the surface.

All at once I caught sight of something far to the right of us, and evidently being taken by the current towards the sluice where the big wheel was in motion.

It might be the child, or it might only be a piece of paper floating there, but I had no time to investigate that, and, running along the path till I was opposite the place, I plunged head-first in, rose, shook the water from my eyes, and swam as rapidly as my clothes would allow towards the spot.

The women set up a cry and the children shrieked, and as I swam steadily on I could hear away to my left the two women come splashing and wading through the water till they were opposite to where I was swimming.

"Oh, quick! Quick, my lad!" cried Mrs Gentles; and her agonised voice sent a thrill through me far more than did the shrieking chorus of the women as they shouted words of encouragement to me to proceed.

I did not need the encouragement, for I was swimming my best, not making rapid strokes, but, as Uncle Jack had often shown me in river and sea, taking a long, slow, vigorous stroke, well to the end, one that is more effective, and which can be long sustained.

But though I tried my best, I was still some feet from the spot where I had seen the floating object, when it seemed to fade away, and there was nothing visible when I reached the place.

"There! There!" shrieked Mrs Gentles; "can't you see him—there?"

She could not see any more than I could, as I raised myself as high as possible, treading water, and then paddling round like a dog in search of something thrown in which has sunk.

The little fellow had gone, and there was nothing for it but to dive, and as I had often done before, I turned over and went down into the black water to try and find the drowning child.

I stayed down as long as I could, came up, and looked round amidst a tremendous chorus of cries, and then dived again like a duck.

Pray, don't think I was doing anything brave or heroic, for it seemed to me nothing of the kind. I had been so drilled by my uncles in leaping off banks, and out of a boat, and in diving after eggs thrown down in the clear water, that, save the being dressed, it was a very ordinary task to me; in fact, I believe I could have swum steadily on for an hour if there had been any need, and gone on diving as often as I liked.

So I went under again and again, with the current always taking me on toward the sluice, and giving way to it; for, of course, the child would, I felt, be carried that way too.

Every time I rose there was the shrieking and crying of the women and the prayerful words of the mother bidding me try; and had not her woman friend clung to her arm, I believe she would have struggled into deep water and been drowned.

I caught glimpses of her, and of Gentles standing on the bank rubbing his ear as I dived down again in quite a hopeless way now, and, stopping down a much shorter time, I had given a kick or two, and was rising, when my hands touched something which glided away.

This encouraged me, and I just took my breath above water, heard the cries, and dived again, to have the water thundering in my ears.

For a few moments I could feel nothing; then my left hand touched a bundle of clothes, and in another moment I was at the surface with the child's head above water, and swimming with all my might for the side.

There was a wild shriek of excitement to greet me, and then there was very nearly a terrible catastrophe for finale to the scene, for, as soon as she saw that I had hold of her child, the frantic mother shook off her companion, and with a mingling of the tragic and ludicrous reached out with the broom to drag us both in.

Her excitement was too much for her; she took a step forward to reach us, slipped into deep water, went under, and the next minute she had risen, snatched at me, and we were struggling together.

I was quite paralysed, while the poor woman had lost her head completely, and was blind by trying to save herself—holding on to me with all her might.

Under the circumstances it is no wonder that I became helpless and confused, and that we sank together in the deep water close now to the dam head, and then all was black confusion, for my sensations were very different to what they were when I made my voluntary dives.

It was matter of moments, though, and then a strong hand gripped me by the arm, we were dragged to the side, and a dozen hands were ready to help us out on to the bank.

"Give me the child," said a strange voice. "Which is the house? Here— the mother and one woman, come. Keep the crowd away."

In a confused way I saw a tall man in black take the child in his arms, and I thought how wet he would make himself; while Mrs Gentles, panting and gasping for breath, seized me by the hand; and then they passed on in the middle of the crowd, augmented by a number of workmen, and disappeared into the cottage I knew so well.

"What! Was it you, Uncle Jack?" I said, looking up in his grave big eyes.

"Yes, my boy; and I only just came in time. How are you?"

"Horribly wet," I said grimly and with a shiver. Then forcing a laugh as he held my hands tightly in his. "Why, you're just as bad."

"Yes, but you—are you all right?"

"Oh, yes, uncle! There's nothing the matter with me."

"Then come along and let's run home. Never mind appearances; let's get into some dry clothes. But I should like to hear about the child."

It was an easy thing to say, but not to do. We wanted to go to Gentles' house, but we were surrounded by a dense crowd; and the next minute a lot of rough men were shaking both Uncle Jack's hands and fighting one with the other to get hold of them, while I—

Just fancy being in the middle of a crowd of women, and all of them wanting to throw their arms round me and kiss me at once.

That was my fate then; and regardless of my resistance one motherly body after another seized me, kissing my cheeks roundly, straining me to her bosom, and calling me her "brave lad!" or her "bonny bairn!" or "my mahn!"

I had to be kissed and hand-shaken till I would gladly have escaped for very shame; and at last Uncle Jack rescued me, coming to my side smiling and looking round.

"If he's thy bairn, mester," cried the virago-like woman who had helped Mrs Gentles, "thou ought to be proud of him."

"And so I am," cried Uncle Jack, laying his hand upon my shoulder.

Here there was a loud "hurrah!" set up by the men, and the women joined in shrilly, while a couple of men with big mugs elbowed their way towards us.

"Here, lay holt, mester," said one to Uncle Jack; "drink that—it'll keep out the cold."

At the same moment a mug was forced into my hand, and in response to a nod from Uncle Jack I took a hearty draught of some strong mixture which I believe was gin and beer.

"How is the child?" said Uncle Jack.

"Doctor says he can't tell yet, but hopes he'll pull bairn through."

"Now, my lads," said Uncle Jack, "you don't want us to catch cold?"

"No.—Hurray!"

"Nor you neither, my good women?"

"Nay, God bless thee, no!" was chorused.

"Then good-bye! And if one of you will run down to our place and tell us how the little child is by and by, I'll be glad."

"Nay, thou'llt shake han's wi' me first," said the big virago-like woman, whose drenched clothes clung to her from top to toe.

"That I will," cried Uncle Jack, suiting the action to the word by holding out his; but to his surprise the woman laid her hands upon his shoulders, the tears streaming down her cheeks, and kissed him in simple north-country fashion.

"God bless thee, my mahn!" she said with a sob. "Thou may'st be a Lunnoner, but thou'rt a true un, and thou'st saved to-day as good a wife and mother as ever stepped."

Here there was another tremendous cheer; and to avoid fresh demonstrations I snatched my clothes from the woman who held them, and we hurried off to get back to Mrs Stephenson's as quickly and quietly as we could.

Quickly! Quietly! We were mad to expect it; for we had to go home in the midst of a rapidly-increasing crowd, who kept up volley after volley of cheers, and pressed to our sides to shake hands.

That latter display of friendliness we escaped during the finish of our journey; for in spite of all Uncle Jack could do to prevent it, big as he was, they hoisted him on the shoulders of a couple of great furnacemen, a couple more carrying me, and so we were taken home.

I never felt so much ashamed in my life, but there was nothing for it but to be patient; and, like most of such scenes, it came to an end by our reaching Mrs Stephenson's and nearly frightening her to death.

"Bless my heart!" she cried, "I thought there'd been some accident, and you was both brought home half-killed. Just hark at 'em! The street's full, and the carts can hardly get by."

And so it was; for whenever, as I towelled myself into a glow, I peeped round the blind, there was the great crowd shouting and hurrahing with all their might.

For the greater part they were workmen and boys, all in their shirt-sleeves and without caps; but there was a large sprinkling of big motherly women there; and the more I looked the more abashed I felt, for first one and then another seemed to be telling the story to a listening knot, as I could see by the motion of her hands imitating swimming.

Two hours after we were cheered by the news that my efforts had not been in vain, for after a long fight the doctor had brought the child to; and that night, when we thought all the fuss was over, there came six great booms from a big drum, and a powerful brass band struck up, "See, the Conquering Hero comes!" Then the mob that had gathered cheered and shouted till we went to the window and thanked them; and then they cheered again, growing quite mad with excitement as a big strapping woman, in a black silk bonnet and a scarlet shawl, came up to the door and was admitted and brought into the parlour.

I was horrified, for it was big Mrs Gentles, and I had a dread of another scene.

I need not have been alarmed, for there was a sweet natural quietness in the woman that surprised us all, as she said with the tears running down her cheeks:

"I'm only a poor common sort of woman, gentlemen, but I think a deal o' my bairns, and I've come to say I'll never forget a prayer for the bonny boy who saved my little laddie, nor for the true brave gentleman who saved me to keep them still."

Uncle Jack shook hands with her, insisting upon her having a glass of wine, but she would not sit down, and after she had drunk her wine she turned to me.

I put out my hand, but she threw her arms round my neck, kissed me quickly on each cheek, and ran sobbing out of the room, and nearly oversetting Mr Tomplin, who was coming up.

"Hallo, my hero!" he cried, shaking hands with me.

"Please, please don't, Mr Tomplin," I cried. "I feel as if I'd never do such a thing again as long as I live."

"Don't say that, my boy," he cried. "Say it if you like, though. You don't mean it. I say, though, you folks have done it now."

We had done more than we thought, for the next morning when we walked down to the office and Uncle Jack was saying that we must not be done out of our holiday, who should be waiting at the gate but Gentles.

"Ugh!" said Uncle Jack; "there's that scoundrel. I hate that man. I wish it had been someone else's child you had saved, Cob. Well, my man," he cried roughly, "what is it?"

Gentles had taken off his cap, a piece of politeness very rare among his set, and he looked down on the ground for a minute or two, and then ended a painful silence by saying:

"I've been a reg'lar bad un to you and yours, mester; but it was the traäde as made me do it."

"Well, that's all over now, Gentles, and you've come to apologise?"

"Yes, mester, that's it. I'm down sorry, I am, and if you'll tek me on again I'll sarve you like a man—ay, and I'll feight for thee like a man agen the traäde."

"Are you out of work?"

"Nay, mester, I can always get plenty if I like to wuck."

"Do you mean what you say, Gentles?"

"Why, mester, wouldn't I hev been going to club to-day for money to bury a bairn and best wife a man ivver hed if it hadn't been for you two. Mester, I'd do owt for you now."

"I believe you, Gentles," said Uncle Jack in his firm way. "Go back to your stone."

Gentles smiled all over his face, and ran in before us whistling loudly with his fingers, and the men all turned out and cheered us over and over again, looking as delighted as so many boys.

"Mr Tomplin's right," said Uncle Dick; "we've done it at last."

"No, not yet," said Uncle Jack; "we've won the men to our side and all who know us will take our part, but there is that ugly demon to exorcise yet that they call the traäde."

That night I was going back alone when my heart gave a sort of leap, for just before me, and apparently waylaying me, were two of the boys who had been foremost in hunting me that day. My temper rose and my cheeks flushed; but they had come upon no inimical errand, for they both laughed in a tone that bespoke them the sons of Gentles, and the bigger one spoke in a bashful sort of way.

"Moother said we was to come and ax your pardon, mester. It were on'y meant for a game, and she leathered us both for it."

"And will you hev this?" said the other, holding out something in a piece of brown-paper.

"I sha'n't take any more notice of it," I said quietly; "but I don't want any present."

"There, moother said he'd be over proud to tak it," said the younger lad resentfully to his brother.

"No, I am not too proud," I said; "give it to me. What is it?"

"Best knife they maks at our wucks," said the boy eagerly. "It's rare stoof. I say, we're going to learn to swim like thou."

They both nodded and went away, leaving me thinking that I was after this to be friends with the Arrowfield boys as well as the men.

They need not have put it in the newspaper, but there it was, a long account headed "Gallant rescue by a boy." It was dressed up in a way that made my cheeks tingle, and a few days later the tears came into my eyes as I read a letter from my mother telling me she had read in the newspaper what I had done, and—

There, I will not set that down. It was what my mother said, and every British boy knows what his mother would say of an accident like that.

It was wonderful how the works progressed after this, and how differently the men met us. It was not only our own, but the men at all the works about us. Instead of a scowl or a stare there was a nod, and a gruff "good morning." In fact, we seemed to have lived down the prejudice against the "chaps fro' Lunnon, and their contrapshions;" but my uncles knew only too well that they had not mastered the invisible enemy called the trade.

Chapter Twenty Five.

A Terrible Risk.

"What are you staring at, Cob?"

It was Uncle Jack who spoke, and Uncle Dick had just come up with him, to find me in the yard, looking up at the building.

It was dinner-hour, and all the men had gone but Pannell, who was sitting on a piece of iron out in the yard calmly cutting his bread and meat into squares and then masticating them as if it were so much tilt-hammer work that he had to do by the piece.

"I was thinking, Uncle, suppose they were to set fire to us some night, what should we do?"

"Hah! Yes: not a bad thought," said Uncle Dick sharply. "Pannell!"

"Hillo!" said that gentleman, rising slowly.

"Finish eating your bread and meat as you go, will you, and buy us twenty-four buckets."

"Fower-and-twenty boockets," said Pannell, speaking with his mouth full. "What do yow want wi fower-and-twenty boockets?"

"I'll show you this evening," replied my uncle; and, handing the man a couple of sovereigns, Pannell went off, and both Uncle Jack and I laughed at the quick way in which Uncle Dick had determined to be provided for an emergency.

The buckets came, and were run by their handles upon a pole which was supported upon two great hooks in one of the outhouses against the wall of the yard, and some of the men noticed them, but the greater part seemed to pay not the slightest heed to this addition to our defences.

But at leaving time, after a few words from Uncle Dick to Uncle Jack, the latter stood in the yard as the men came out, and said sharply:

"Four-and-twenty men for a window wash. Who'll help?"

A few months before, such a demand would have been met with a scowl; but quite a little crowd of the men now stopped, and Pannell said with a grin:

"Wonder whether there'll be a boocket o' beer efter?"

"Why, of course there will, my lad," cried Uncle Jack, who ranged the men in order.

"Why, 'tis like being drilled for milishy, mester," said one man, and there was a roar of laughter as the buckets were passed out of the shed, and the men were placed in two rows, with Uncle Jack at one end, Uncle Dick at the other; the two ends resting, as a soldier would say, on the dam, and on the works.

It was wonderful how a little management and discipline made easy such a business as this, and I could not help smiling as I saw how my idea had been acted upon.

There were a few sharp words of command given, and then Uncle Jack dipped his bucket into the dam from the stone edge where we had bathed poor Piter, filled it, passed it on to Number 1 of the first row, and took a bucket from the last man of the second row, to fill. Meanwhile the first bucket was being passed on from hand to hand through a dozen pairs when it reached Uncle Dick, who seized it, hurled it up against the grimy windows of the works, and then passed it to the first man of the second row.

In a minute or two the men were working like a great machine, the pails being dipped and running, or rather being swung, from hand to hand till they reached Uncle Dick, who dashed the water over the windows, and here and there, while the empty buckets ran back to Uncle Jack.

The men thoroughly enjoyed it, and Pannell shouted that this would be the way to put out a fire. But my uncles did not take up the idea, working steadily on, and shifting the line till the whole of the glazed windows had been sluiced, and a lot of the grit and rubbish washed away from the sills and places, after which the buckets were again slung in a row and the men had their beer, said "Good-night!" quite cheerily, and went away.

"There," said Uncle Dick, "I call that business. How well the lads worked!"

"Yes," said Uncle Jack with a sigh of content as he wiped his streaming brow; "we could not have got on with them like that three months ago."

"No," said Uncle Bob, who had been looking on with me, and keeping dry; "the medicine is working faster and faster; they are beginning to find us out."

"Yes," said Uncle Dick. "I think we may say it is peace now."

"Don't be in too great a hurry, my boys," said Uncle Jack. "There is a good deal more to do yet."

It is one of the terrible misfortunes of a town like Arrowfield that accidents among the work-people are so common. There was an excellent hospital there, and it was too often called into use by some horror or another.

It would be a terrible tale to tell of the mishaps that we heard of from week to week: men burned by hot twining rods; by the falling of masses of iron or steel that were being forged; by blows of hammers; and above all in the casting-shops, when glowing fluid metal was poured into some mould which had not been examined to see whether it was free from water.

Do you know what happens then? Some perhaps do not. The fluid metal runs into the mould, and in an instant the water is turned into steam, by whose mighty power the metal is sent flying like a shower, the mould rent to pieces, and all who are within range are horribly burned.

That steam is a wonderful slave, but what a master! It is kept bound in strong fetters by those who force its obedience; but woe to those who give it the opportunity to escape by some neglect of the proper precautions.

One accident occurred at Arrowfield during the winter which seemed to give the final touch to my uncles' increasing popularity with the work-people, and we should have had peace, if it had not been for the act of a few malicious wretches that took place a month or too later.

It was one evening when we had left the works early with the intention of having a good long fireside evening, and perhaps a walk out in the frosty winter night after supper, that as we were going down one of the busy lanes with its works on either side, we were suddenly arrested by a deafening report followed by the noise of falling beams and brickwork.

As far as we could judge it was not many hundred yards away, and it seemed to be succeeded by a terrible silence.

Then there was the rushing of feet, the shouting of men, and a peculiar odour smote upon our nostrils.

"Gunpowder!" I exclaimed as I thought of our escapes.

"No," said Uncle Dick. "Steam."

"Yes," said Uncle Jack. "Some great boiler has burst. Heaven help the poor men!"

Following the stream of people we were not long in reaching the gateway of one of the greatest works in Arrowfield. Everything was in such a state of confusion that our entrance was not opposed; and in a few minutes we saw by the light of flaring gas-jets, and of a fire that had begun to blaze, one of the most terrible scenes of disaster I had ever witnessed.

The explosion had taken place in the huge boiler-house of the great iron-works, a wall had been hurled down, part of the iron-beamed roof was hanging, one great barrel-shaped boiler had been blown yards away as if it had been a straw, and its fellow, about twenty feet long, was ripped open and torn at the rivets, just as if the huge plates of iron of which it was composed were so many postage-stamps torn off and roughly crumpled in the hand.

There was a great crowd collecting, and voices shouted warning to beware of the falling roof and walls that were in a crumbling condition. But these shouts were very little heeded in the presence of the cries and moans that could be heard amongst the piled-up brickwork. Injured men were there, and my uncles were among the first to rush in and begin bearing them out—poor creatures horribly scalded and crushed.

Then there was a cry for picks and shovels—some one was buried; and on these being brought the men plied them bravely till there was a warning shout, and the rescue party had only just time to save themselves from a falling wall which toppled over with a tremendous crash, and sent up a cloud of dust.

The men rushed in again, though, and in an incredibly short space of time they had dug and torn away a heap of broken rubbish, beneath which moans could be heard.

I stood close beside my uncles, as, blackened and covered with dust and sweat, they toiled away, Uncle Jack being the first to chase away the horrible feeling of fear that was upon me lest they should be too late.

"Here he is," he cried; and in a few minutes more, standing right down in a hole, he lifted the poor maimed creature who had been crying for our help.

There was a tremendous cheer raised here, and the poor fellow was carried out, while Uncle Dick, who, somehow, seemed to be taking the lead, held up his hand.

"Hark!" he said.

But there was no sound.

"If there is no living creature here," he said, "we must get out. It is not safe to work till the roof has been blown down or fallen. If there is anyone alive, my lads, we must have him out at all risks."

There was a cheer at this, and then, as soon as he could get silence, Uncle Jack shouted:

"Is anyone here?"

There was a low wailing cry for help far back beyond the ripped-up boiler, and in what, with tottering wall and hanging roof, was a place too dangerous to approach.

"Come, lads, we must have him out," cried Uncle Dick; but a gentleman, who was evidently one of the managers, exclaimed:

"No, it is too dangerous."

"Volunteers!" cried Uncle Dick.

Uncle Jack, Uncle Bob, Pannell, Stevens, and four more men went to his side, and in the midst of a deathly silence we saw them go softly in and disappear in the gloom of the great wrecked boiler-house.

Then there was utter silence, out of which Uncle Dick's voice came loud and clear, but ominously followed by the rattling down of some fragments of brick.

"Where are you? Try and speak."

A low piteous moan was the reply.

"All right, my lads, down here!" we heard Uncle Jack cry. "No picks— hands, hands."

"And work gently," cried Uncle Dick.

Then, in the midst of the gloom we could hear the rattling of bricks and stones, and though we could see nothing we could realise that these brave men were digging down with their hands to try and get out the buried stoker.

The flames burned up brightly, casting curious shadows, and though we could see nothing, lighting the men over their gallant task, while I, as I gazed in, trying to penetrate the gloom, felt as if I ought to be there by my uncles' side.

This feeling grew so strong that at last I took a few steps forward, but only to be seized by a pair of strong arms and brought back.

"Nay, nay, lad," said a voice that I started to hear, for it was Gentles'; "there's plenty risking their lives theer. Yow stay."

Just then there was a hoarse shriek of terror, a wild yell from the crowd, for a curious rushing rumble was heard, a dull thud, and another cloud of dust came rolling out, looking like smoke as it mingled with the fire.

In the midst of this the men who had been digging in the ruins came rushing out.

"Part of the roof," cried Uncle Dick, panting, "and the rest's falling. Are you all here, lads?"

"Ay, all," was answered as they looked from one to the other in the flickering light.

"Nay, not all," shouted Stevens. "Owd lad Pannell's buried alive. I see 'un fall."

There was a murmur of horror and a burst of wailing, for now a number of women had joined the throng.

"Are you hurt?" I cried anxiously.

"Only a few cuts and bruises, Cob," said Uncle Dick. "Now, my lads, quick. We must have them out."

The men stopped short, and there was a low angry murmur like the muttering of a coming storm.

"Quick, my lads, quick!"

There was a hoarse cry for help from out of the ruins, and I knew it must be our poor smith.

"No, sir, stop," cried the gentleman who had before spoken. "I'd dare anything, but we have sacrificed one life in trying to save others. I have just been round, and I say that at the least movement of the ruins the left wall must come down."

There was a loud cry of assent to this, and amongst shouts and a confused murmur of voices there came out of the gloom that fearful cry again:

"Help!"

"The wall must fall, men," cried Uncle Dick loudly. "I can't stand and hear that cry and not go. Once more volunteers."

Half a dozen men started out of the crowd; but the peril was too great. They shrank back, and I saw my three uncles standing together in the bright light of the burning building, blackened, bleeding, and in rags.

Then Uncle Dick put out his two hands, and Uncle Jack and Uncle Bob took them. They stood together for a short minute, and then went towards the tottering wall.

"Stop!" cried the gentleman. "You must not risk your lives."

For answer Uncle Jack turned his great manly face towards us and waved his hand.

Then they disappeared in the gloom, and a curious murmur ran along the great crowd. It was neither sigh, groan, nor cry, but a low hushed murmur of all these; and once more, as a dead silence fell, we heard that piteous cry, followed by a hoarse cheer, as if the sufferer had seen help come.

Then, as we listened in dead silence, the rattling of brickwork came again, mingled with the fluttering of the flames and the crackle and roar of burning as the fire leaped up higher and higher from what had been one of the furnace-holes, and across which a number of rafters and beams had fallen, and were blazing brightly, to light up the horrible scene of ruin.

Battle and crash of bricks and beams, and we all knew that my uncles must be working like giants.

"I daren't go, Mester Jacob," whispered Gentles. "I'd do owt for the brave lads, but it's death to go. It's death, and I daren't."

All at once, as everyone was listening for the fall of the tottering wall, some one caught sight of the moving figures, and a deafening cheer rose up as Uncle Dick appeared carrying the legs and Uncles Jack and Bob the arms of a man.

They came towards where I was standing, so that I was by when poor Pannell was laid down, and I went on one knee by his side.

"Much hurt?" I panted.

"Nay, more scared than hurt, lad," he said. "I was buried up to my neck, and feeling's gone out of my legs."

"Stop now, gentlemen, for heaven's sake!" cried the manager.

"What! And leave a poor fellow we have promised to come back and help!" cried Uncle Dick with a laugh.

"But it is certain death to go in, gentlemen," cried the manager passionately. "At the least vibration the roof will fall. I should feel answerable for your lives. I tell you it is death to go."

"It is moral death to stay away," cried Uncle Dick. "What would you do, Cob?"

"Go!" I cried proudly, and then I started up panting, almost sobbing, to try and stop them. "No, no," I cried; "the danger is too great."

I saw them wave their hands in answer to the cheer that rose, and I saw Pannell wave his with a hoarse "Hooroar!" and then the gloom had swallowed them up again.

"I lay close to the poor lad," whispered Pannell. "Reg'lar buried alive. Asked me to kill him out of his misery, he did, as I lay there; but I said, 'howd on, my lad. Them three mesters 'll fetch us out,' and so they will."

"If the roof don't fall," said a low voice close by me, and the same voice said, "Lift this poor fellow up and take him to the infirmary."

"Nay, I weant go," cried Pannell, "aw want to stay here and see them mesters come out."

"Let him rest," said the manager, and upon his asking me I raised Pannell's head, and let him rest against my chest.

Then amidst the painful silence, and the fluttering and crackling of the fire, we heard again the rattling of bricks and stones; but it was mingled with the falling of pieces from the roof. Then there was a crash and a shriek from the women as a cloud of dust rose, and my heart seemed to stand still, for I felt that my uncles must have been buried; but no, the sound of the bricks and stones being dragged out still went on, and the men gave another cheer.

The manager went round again to the back of the place, and came tearing back with three or four men shouting loudly:

"Come out! Come out! She's going!"

Then there was a horrible cry, for with a noise like thunder the left side and part of the roof of the building fell.

The dust was tremendous, and it was some minutes before the crowd could rush in armed with shovels and picks to dig out the bodies of the brave men buried.

The murmur was like that of the sea, for every man seemed to be talking excitedly, and as I knelt there by Pannell I held the poor fellow's hand, clinging to him now, and too much shocked and unnerved to speak.

"They're killed—they're killed," I groaned.

But as I spoke the words the people seemed to have gone mad; they burst into such a tremendous cheer, backing away from the ruins, and dividing as they reached us to make way for my uncles to bear to the side of Pannell the insensible figure of the man they had saved.

That brave act performed for an utter stranger made the Arrowfield men talk of my uncles afterwards as being of what they called real grit; and all through the winter and during the cold spring months everything prospered wonderfully at the works. We could have had any number of men, and for some time it was dangerous for my uncles —and let me modestly say I seemed to share their glory—to go anywhere near a gathering of the workmen, they were so cheered and hero-worshipped.

But in spite of this good feeling there was no concealing the fact that a kind of ill-will was fostered against our works on account of the new inventions and contrivances we had. From whence this ill-will originated it was impossible to say, but there it was like a smouldering fire, ready to break forth when the time should come.

"Another threatening letter," Uncle Jack would say, for he generally attended to post matters.

"Give it to me," said Uncle Bob. "Those letters make the best pipe-lights, they are so incendiary."

"Shall we take any notice—appeal to the men—advertise a reward for the sender?"

"No," said Uncle Dick. "With patience we have got the majority of the workmen with us. We'll show them we trust to them for our defence. Give me that letter."

Uncle Jack passed the insulting threat, and Uncle Dick gummed it and stuck it on a sheet of foolscap, and taking four wafers, moistened them and stuck the foolscap on the office door with, written above it to order by me in a bold text hand:

"Cowards' Work."

and beneath it:

"To be Treated with the Contempt it Deserves."

But as time went on the threats received about what would be done if such and such processes were not given up grew so serious that when Mr Tomplin was told he said that we ought to put ourselves under the care of the police.

"No," said Uncle Dick firmly; "we began on the principle of being just to our workmen, and of showing them that we studied their interests as well as our own, that we are their friends as well as masters, and that we want them to be our friends."

"But they will not be," said Mr Tomplin, shaking his head.

"But they are," said Uncle Dick. "What took place when I stuck that last threat on the door?"

"The men hooted and yelled and spat upon it."

"But was that an honest demonstration?"

"I believe it was."

"Well," said Mr Tomplin, "we shall see. You gentlemen quite upset my calculations, but I must congratulate you upon the manner in which you have made your way with the men."

"I wish we could get hold of the scoundrels who send these letters."

"Yes," said Mr Tomplin; "the wire-pullers who make use of the men for their own ends, and will not let the poor fellows be frank and honest when they would. They're a fine race of fellows if they are led right, but too often they are led wrong."

The days glided on, and as there were no results from these threats we began to laugh at them when they came, especially as Tom Searby the watchman also said they were good for pipe-lights, and that was all.

But one night Uncle Dick took it into his head to go down to the works and see that all was right.

Nothing of the kind had been done before since the watchman came, for everything went on all right; the place was as it should be, no bands were touched, and there seemed to be no reason for showing any doubt of the man; and so Uncle Jack said when Uncle Dick talked of going.

"No, there is no reason," said Uncle Dick; "but I cannot help feeling that we have been lulling ourselves too much into a feeling of security about the place. I shall wait till about one o'clock, and then walk down."

"No, no," said Uncle Jack; "I'm tired. Had a very heavy day, and of course you cannot go alone."

"Why not?"

"Because we should not let you. Even Cob would insist upon going."

"Of course!" I said. "I had made up my mind to go."

"It's quite right," said Uncle Bob. "We've been remiss. When sentries are set the superior officers always make a point of going their rounds to see if they are all right. Go, Dick, and we'll come with you."

Uncle Dick protested, but we had our own way, and about a quarter to one on a bitter March night we let ourselves out and walked down to the works.

For my part I would far rather have gone to bed, but after a few minutes the excitement of the proceeding began to assert itself, and I was bright and wakeful enough.

We walked quickly and briskly on till we came to the lane by the factory wall; but instead of turning down we all walked on along the edge of the dam, which gleamed coldly beneath the frosty stars. It was very full, for there had been a good deal of rain; and though the air was frosty there was a suggestion of change and more rain before long.

When we reached the top of the dam we turned and looked back.

Everything was as quiet as could be, and here and there the glow from the lowered furnace-fires made a faint halo about the dark building, so quiet and still after the hurry and buzz of the day.

As we went back along the dam the wavelets lapped the stone edge, and down below on the other side, as well as by the waste sluice, we could hear the water rushing along towards the lower part of the town, and onward to the big river that would finally carry it to the sea.

We were very silent, for every one was watching the works, till, as Uncle Dick and I reached the lane, we stopped short, for I caught his arm.

I had certainly heard whispering.

There were half a dozen persons down near the gate, but whoever they were they came towards us, said "good-night!" roughly, turned the corner, and went away.

It looked suspicious for half a dozen men to be down there in the middle of the night, but their manner was inoffensive and civil, and we could see nothing wrong.

Uncle Dick slipped his key into the lock, and as he opened the little door in the gate there was a low growl and the rush of feet.

"Piter's on the watch," I said quietly, and the growl turned to a whine of welcome.

"Be on the look-out," said Uncle Dick; "we must speak or Searby may attack us."

"Right," said Uncle Jack; "but he had better not."

The dog did not bark, but trotted on before us, and we could just see him as we took a look round the yard before going into the buildings.

Everything was quite right as far as we could tell. Nothing unusual to be seen anywhere, and we went at last to the main entrance.

"Nothing could be better," said Uncle Dick. "Only there is no watchman. I say, was I right in coming?"

"Right enough," replied Uncle Jack; "but look out now for squalls. Men in the dark have a suspicious look."

We entered, peered in at the great grinding-shop, and then began to ascend the stairs to the upper works.

"All right!" said Uncle Dick. "I wish we had a light. Can you hear him?"

He had stopped short on the landing, and we could hear a low, muttering noise, like a bass saw cutting hard leather.

Score! Score! Score! Slowly and regularly; the heavy breathing of a deep sleeper.

"I'm glad we've got a good watcher," said Uncle Jack drily. "Here, Piter, dog, fetch him out. Wake him then."

The dog understood him, for he burst into a furious fit of barking and charged up into the big workshop, and then there was a worrying noise as if he were dragging at the watchman's jacket.

"Get out! Be off! Do you hear!"

"Hi, Searby!" roared Uncle Jack.

There was a plunge, and a rush to the door, and Searby's big voice cried:

"Stand back, lads, or I'll blow out thee brains."

"What with?" said Uncle Bob; "the forge blast? There, come down."

Searby came down quickly.

"Lucky for yow that one of yo' spoke," he said. "I heard you coming, and was lying wait for you. Don't do it agen, mesters. I might hev half-killed yo'."

"Next time you lie in wait," said Uncle Dick, "don't breathe so loudly, my man, or you will never trap the visitors. They may think you are asleep."

"Give him another chance," said Uncle Jack as we went home.

"Yes," said Uncle Bob; "it is partly our fault. If we had visited him once or twice he would have been always on the watch."

"Well," said Uncle Dick, "I don't want to be unmerciful, and it will be a lesson. He'll work hard to regain our confidence."

Next morning there were two letters in strange hands, which Uncle Jack read and then handed round.

One was a threat such as had often been received before; but the other was of a very different class. It was as follows:

"*Mesters,—There's somewhat up. We don't kno wat, but game o' some kind's going to be played. Owd Tommy Searby gos sleep ivvery night, and he's no good. Some on us gives a look now an' then o' nights but yowd beter wetch im place yoursens.—Some frends.*"

"That's genuine," said Uncle Dick emphatically. "What's to be done?"

"Go and do as they advise," said Uncle Jack. "You see we have won the fellows over, and they actually act as a sort of police for us."

The consequence of this letter was that sometimes all four, sometimes only two of us went and kept watch there of a night, very much to old Searby's disgust, but we could not afford to heed him, and night after night we lost our rest for nothing.

"Are we being laughed at?" said Uncle Bob wearily one night; "I'm getting very tired of this."

"So we all are, my dear fellow," said Uncle Jack: "but I can't help thinking that it is serious."

Uncle Jack was right, for serious it proved.

Chapter Twenty Six.

Fire and Water.

One dark night at the end of March we went down to the works all four, meaning to watch two and two through the dark hours. The wind blew hard and the rain fell, and as we reached the lane we could hear the water lapping and beating against the sluice and the stones that formed the head of the dam, while the waste rushed away with a hollow roar.

"Pity to lose so much good power," said Uncle Jack.

"Sun and wind will bring it back to the hills," said Uncle Dick gravely. "There is no waste in nature."

I half expected to see a group of men, friends or enemies, waiting about; but not a soul was in sight, and as we reached the gates I shivered involuntarily and thought that people must have very serious spite against us if they left their snug firesides to attack us on a night like that.

Uncle Dick opened the little door in the gate and we stepped in, but to our surprise there was no low growl and then whine of recognition from Piter.

"That's strange," said Uncle Jack suspiciously, and he walked on quickly to the door of the building and listened.

There was no dog there, and his chain and collar did not hang over the kennel as if they had been taken from the dog's neck. They were gone.

This seemed very strange, and what was more strange still, though we went from grinding-shop to smithy after smithy, furnace house and shed, there was no sign of the dog, and everything seemed to point to the fact that he had been led away by his chain, and was a prisoner somewhere.

"Looks like mischief," whispered Uncle Bob. "Where's that scoundrel lying asleep?"

We went upstairs to see, and expected to find our careful watchman carefully curled up somewhere, but there was no snoring this time, and Uncle Bob's threat of a bucket of water to wake him did not assume substance and action.

For though we searched everywhere it soon became evident that Searby was not present, and that we had come to find the works deserted.

"Then there is going to be some attack made," said Uncle Dick. "I'm glad we came."

"Shall you warn the police?" I whispered.

"No," said Uncle Jack sharply. "If we warn the police the scoundrels will get to know, and no attack will be made."

"So much the better," I said. "Isn't it?"

"No, my lad. If they did not come to-night they would be here some other time when we had not been warned. We are prepared now, so let them come and we may give them such a lesson as shall induce them to leave us in peace for the future."

"Do you mean to fight, then?" I asked.

"Most decidedly, boy. For our rights, for our place where we win our livelihood. We should be cowards if we did not. You must play the dog's part for us with your sharp eyes and ears. Recollect we have right on our side and they have wrong."

"Let's put the fort in a state of defence," said Uncle Dick merrily. "Perhaps it will turn out to be all nonsense, but we must be prepared. What do you say—divide in two watches as we proposed, and take turn and turn?"

"No: we'll all watch together to-night in case anything serious should be meant."

It did seem so vexatious that a small party of men should be able to keep up this system of warfare in the great manufacturing town. Here had my uncles brought a certain amount of prosperity to the place by establishing these works; the men had found out their worth and respected them, and everything was going on in the most prosperous way, and yet we were being assailed with threats, and it was quite possible that at any moment some cruel blow might be struck.

I felt very nervous that night, but I drew courage from my uncles, who seemed to take everything in the coolest and most matter-of-fact way. They went round to the buildings where the fires were banked up and glowing or smouldering, ready to be brought under the influence of the blast next day and fanned to white heat. Here every precaution was taken to guard against danger by fire, one of the most probable ways of attack, either by ordinary combustion or the swift explosion of gunpowder.

"There," said Uncle Jack after a careful inspection, "we can do no more. If the ruffians come and blow us up it will be pretty well ruin."

"While if they burn us we are handsomely insured," said Uncle Dick.

"By all means then let us be burned," said Uncle Bob laughing. "There, don't let's make mountains of molehills. We shall not be hurt."

"Well," said Uncle Dick, "I feel as if we ought to take every possible precaution; but, that done, I do not feel much fear of anything taking place. If the scoundrels had really meant mischief they would have done something before now."

"Don't halloa till you are out of the wood," said Uncle Jack. "I smell danger."

"Where, uncle?" I cried.

"In the air, boy. How the wind blows! Quite a gale. Brings the smell of naphtha from those works half a mile away. Shows how a scent like that will travel."

"I say, boys," said Uncle Bob, "what a trade that would be to carry on— that or powder-mills. The scoundrels would regularly hold one at their mercy."

"Wind's rising, and the water seems pretty lively," said Uncle Dick as we sat together in the office, listening to the noises of the night.

We were quite in the dark, and from time to time we had a look round about the yard and wall and that side of the building, the broad dam on the other side being our protection.

"What a curious gurgling the water makes!" said Uncle Bob as we sat listening; "anyone might think that half a dozen bottles were being poured out at once."

"The water plays in and out of the crevices amongst the stones, driving the air forth. I've often listened to it and thought it was someone

249

whispering out there beneath the windows," said Uncle Dick.

Then came a loud gust of wind that shook the windows, and directly after there was the strong sour scent of naphtha.

"They must have had an accident—upset a tank or something of the kind," said Uncle Jack. "How strong it is!"

"Yes; quite stinging. It comes each time with the puffs of wind. I suppose," continued Uncle Dick, "you would consider that which we smell to be a gas."

"Certainly," said Uncle Bob, who was, we considered, a pretty good chemist. "It is the evaporation of the spirit; it is so volatile that it turns of itself into vapour or gas and it makes itself evident to our nostrils as it is borne upon the air."

"There must be great loss in the manufacture of such a spirit as that."

"Oh, they charge accordingly!" said Uncle Bob; "but a great deal does undoubtedly pass off into—"

He stopped short, for Uncle Jack laid his hand upon his knee and we all listened.

"Nothing," said the latter; but I felt sure I heard a noise below.

"I heard the gurgling sound very plainly," said Uncle Dick. "There it is again. One might almost think there was water trickling into the building."

"Or naphtha, judging by the smell," said Uncle Bob. "It's very curious. I have it!" he cried.

"What do you mean?" said Uncle Jack sharply.

"There has been an accident, as we supposed, at the naphtha works, and a quantity of it has floated down the stream and into our dam."

"It has been very clever then," said Uncle Jack gruffly, "for it has floated up stream a hundred yards to get into our dam, and— Good heavens!"

He sprang to the window and threw it open, for at that moment a heavy dull explosion shook the room where we were, and in place of the darkness we could see each other distinctly, for the place seemed to have been filled with reflected light, which went out and then blazed up again.

"Ah!" ejaculated Uncle Jack, "the cowards! If I had a gun!"

I ran to his side, and in the middle of the dam, paddling towards the outer side, there was a sort of raft with three men upon it, and now they were distinctly seen, for the black water of the dam seemed to have suddenly become tawny gold, lit by a building burning furiously on our right. That building was our furnace-house and the set of smithies and sheds that connected it with the grinding-shops and offices.

Uncle Jack banged to the window and took the command.

"Cob," he cried, "run to the big bell and keep it going. Our lads will come. Dick, throw open the gate; Bob, follow me. Fire drill. We may nip the blaze in the bud."

The fire-bell was not rung, the gate was not thrown open; for as we ran out of the office and down the stairs it was to step into a pool of naphtha, and in a few instants we found that a quantity had been poured in at the lower windows—to what extent we could not tell—but it was evident that this had been done all along the basement by the scoundrels on the raft, and that they had contrived that some should reach one of the furnaces, with the result that in an instant the furnace-house had leaped into a mass of roaring flame, which the brisk gale was fanning and making the fire run along the naphtha-soaked buildings like a wave.

"Stop, stop!" roared Uncle Jack; "we can do nothing to stay this. Back to the offices and secure all books and papers."

So swiftly was the fire borne along by the gale that we had hardly time to reach the staircase before it came running along, licking up the naphtha, of which a large quantity had been spilled, and as it caught there were dozens of little explosions.

I do not think either of us gave a thought to how we were to get away again, for the valuable books and plans had to be saved at all hazards; so following Uncle Jack we rushed into the big office, the safe was opened, and as rapidly as possible a couple of tin boxes were filled with account-books, and a number of papers were bound round with string.

"You must look sharp," said Uncle Bob.

"But we must take my books, and odds and ends, and fishing-tackle," I cried.

"Better try and save our lives," said Uncle Bob. "Are you ready?"

"No; there are some plans we must take," said Uncle Dick.

"You must leave them," shouted Uncle Bob. "There, you are too late!" he cried, banging to the door at the end of the workshop; "the flame's coming up the stairs."

"We can get out of the windows," said Uncle Jack coolly.

"The place beneath is all on fire," cried Uncle Bob, flinging himself on his knees. "The floor's quite hot."

We should have been suffocated only that there was a perfect rush of cold air through the place, but moment by moment this was becoming hot and poisonous with the gases of combustion. The flames were rushing out of the grinding-shop windows beneath us, and the yard on one side, the dam on the other, were light as day.

In one glance over the fire and smoke I saw our wall covered with workmen and boys, some watching, some dropping over into the yard. While in a similar rapid glance on the other side I saw through the flame and smoke that on one side the dam bank was covered with spectators, on the other there were three men just climbing off a rough raft and descending towards the stream just below.

"Now," said Uncle Jack, seizing one box, "I can do no more. Each of you take your lot and let's go."

"But where?—how?" I panted.

"Phew!"

Uncle Jack gave vent to a long whistle that was heard above the crackling wood, the roar of flames carried along by the wind, and the shouts and cries of the excited crowd in the yard.

"It's worse than I thought," said Uncle Jack. "We can't get down. Keep cool, boys. We must save our papers. Here, there is less fire at that window than at either of the others—let's throw the boxes out there. They'll take care of them."

We ran to the far corner window, but as we reached it a puff of flame and smoke curved in and drove us back.

It was so with every window towards the yard, and escape was entirely cut off.

The men were trying to do something to save us, for there was a tremendous noise and excitement below; but they could do absolutely nothing, so rapidly had the grinding-shop beneath us been turned into a fiery furnace.

And now the flames had mastered the end door, which fell inward, and flame and black and gold clouds of smoke rolled in.

"Quick, Cob!—into the office!" roared Uncle Dick; and I darted in with some of the papers, followed by the rest, Uncle Jack banging to the door.

"Keep cool, all of you," he cried. "I must save these books and papers."

"But we must save our lives, Jack," said Uncle Dick. "The floor's smoking. Our only chance is to jump into the dam."

"Through that blaze of flame!" said Uncle Bob gloomily.

"It is our only chance," said Uncle Jack; "but let's try to save our boxes as well. They will float if we take care."

"Now, then, who's first?"

The window was open, the tin boxes and the packets on the table, the dam beneath but invisible; for the flame and smoke that rose from the window below came like a fiery curtain between us and the water; and it was through this curtain that we should have to plunge.

Certainly it would be a momentary affair, and then we should be in the clear cold water; but the idea of taking such a leap made even my stout uncles shrink and vainly look round for some other means of escape.

But there were none that we could see. Above the roar and crackling of the flames we could hear the shouting of the mob and voices shrieking out more than crying, "Jump! Jump!" Everything, though, was one whirl of confusion; and I felt half-stifled with the terrible heat and the choking fumes that came up between the boards and beneath the door.

It was rapidly blinding as well as confusing us; and in those exciting moments leadership seemed to have gone, and if even I had made a bold start the others would have followed.

At last after what seemed to have been a long space of time, though it was doubtless only moments, Uncle Jack cried fiercely:

"Look: the floor's beginning to burn. You, Dick, out first, Cob shall follow; and we'll drop the two tin boxes to you. You must save them. Now! Are you ready?"

"Yes," cried Uncle Dick, climbing on a chair, and thrusting his arm out of the window.

As he did so, there was a puff like some gigantic firework, and a large cloud of fiery smoke rose up full of tiny sparks; and he shrank back with an ejaculation of pain.

"Hot, Dick?" cried Uncle Jack almost savagely. "Go on, lad; it will be hotter here. In five minutes the floor will be burned through."

"Follow quickly, Cob," cried Uncle Dick; and then he paused, for there was a curious rushing noise, the people yelled, and there were shrieks and cries, and above all, a great trampling of feet.

We could see nothing for the flame and smoke that rose before the window; and just then the roar of the flames seemed to increase, and our position became unendurable.

But still that was a curious rushing noise in the air, a roar as of thunder and pouring, hissing rain, and a railway train rushing by and coming nearer and nearer every moment; and then, as Uncle Dick was about to step forth into the blaze and leap into the dam, Uncle Jack caught him and held him back.

Almost at the same moment the rush and roar increased a hundred-fold, confusing and startling us, and then, as if by magic, there was a tremendous thud against the walls that shook the foundations; a fierce hissing noise, and one moment we were standing in the midst of glowing light, the next moment we were to our waists in water dashed against the opposite wall, and all was black darkness.

As we struggled to our feet the water was sinking, but the horrible crashing, rushing noise was still going on—water, a huge river of water was rushing right through our factory threatening to sweep it away, and then the flood seemed to sink as quickly as it had come, and we stood holding hands, listening to the gurgling rush that was rapidly dying away.

"What is it?" panted Uncle Bob.

"Life. Thank heaven, we are saved!" said Uncle Dick fervently.

"Amen!" exclaimed Uncle Jack. "Why, Dick," he cried, "that great dam up in the hills must have burst and come sweeping down the vale!"

Uncle Jack was right, for almost as he spoke we could hear voices shouting "rezzyvoyer;" and for the moment we forgot our own troubles in the thought of the horrors that must have taken place up the vale.

But we could not stay where we were, half suffocated by the steam that rose, and, opening the door, which broke away half-burned through, we stood once more in the long workshop, which seemed little changed, save that here and there a black chasm yawned in the floor, among which we had to thread our way to where the stout door had been.

That and the staircase were gone, so that our only chance was to descend by lowering ourselves and dropping to the ground.

Just then we heard the splashing of feet in the yard, and a voice we recognised as Pannell cried:

"Mebbe they've got away. Ahoy there, mesters! Mester Jacob!"

"Ahoy!" I shouted; and a ringing cheer went up from twenty throats.

"We're all right," I cried, only nearly smothered. "Can you get a short ladder?"

"Ay, lad," cried another familiar voice; and another shouted, "Owd Jones has got one;" and I was sure it was Gentles who spoke.

"How's the place, Pannell?" cried Uncle Dick, leaning out of one of the windows.

"So dark, mester, I can hardly see, but fire's put right out, and these here buildings be aw reight, but wheer the smithies and furnace was is nobbut ground."

"Swept away?"

"Pretty well burned through first, mester, and then the watter came and washed it all clear. Hey but theer's a sight of mischief done, I fear."

A short ladder was soon brought, and the boxes and papers were placed in safety in a neighbouring house, after which in the darkness we tramped through the yard, to find that it was inches deep in mud, and that the flood had found our mill stout enough to resist its force; but the half-burned furnace-house, the smithies, and about sixty feet of tall stone wall had been taken so cleanly away that even the stones were gone, while the mill next to ours was cut right in two.

There was not a vestige of fire left, so, leaving our further inspection to be continued in daylight, we left a couple of men as watchers, and were going to join the hurrying crowd, when I caught Uncle Dick's arm.

"Well?" he exclaimed.

"Did you see where those men went as they got off the raft?"

"They seemed to be climbing down into the hollow beside the river," he said:

"Yes," I whispered with a curious catching of the breath, "and then the flood came."

He gripped my hand, and stood thinking for a few moments.

"It is impossible to say," he cried at last. "But come along, we may be of some service to those in trouble."

In that spirit we went on down to the lower part of the town, following the course of the flood, and finding fresh horrors at every turn.

Chapter Twenty Seven.

Eight Years Later.

Fancy the horrors of that night! The great dam about which one of my uncles had expressed his doubts when we visited it the previous year, and of which he had spoken as our engine, had given way in the centre of the vast earthen wall like a railway embankment. A little crack had grown and grown—the trickling water that came through had run into a stream, then into a river, and then a vast breach in the embankment was made, and a wall of water had rushed down the valley swiftly as a fast train, carrying destruction before it.

The ruin of that night is historical, and when after a few hours we made our way up the valley, it was to see at every turn the devastation that had been caused. Mills and houses had been swept away as if they had been corks, strongly-built works with massive stone walls had crumbled away like cardboard, and their machinery had been carried down by the great wave of water, stones, gravel, and mud.

Trees had been lifted up by their roots; rows of cottages cut in half; banks of the valley carved out, and for miles and miles, down in the bottom by the course of the little river, the face of the country was changed. Here where a beautiful garden had stretched down to the stream was a bed of gravel and sand; there where verdant meadows had lain were sheets of mud; and in hundreds of places trees, plants, and the very earth had been swept clear away down to where there was only solid rock.

When we reached the great embankment the main part of the water was gone, and in the middle there was the huge gap through which it had escaped.

"Too much water for so frail a dam," said Uncle Jack sententiously. "Boys, we must not bemoan our loss in the face of such a catastrophe as this."

We had no right, for to us the flood, exhausted and spread by its eight-mile race, had been our saving, the greater part of our destruction being by fire, for which we should have recompense; while for the poor creatures who had been in an instant robbed of home and in many cases of relatives, what recompense could there be!

The loss of life was frightful, and the scenes witnessed as first one poor creature and then another was discovered buried in sand and mud after being borne miles by the flood, are too painful to record.

Suffice it that the flood had swept down those eight miles of valley, doing incalculable damage, and leaving traces that remained for years. The whole of the loss was never known, and till then people were to a great extent in ignorance of the power that water could exercise. In many cases we stood appalled at the changes made high up the valley, and the manner in which masses of stonework had been swept along. Stone was plentiful in the neighbourhood and much used in building, and wherever the flood had come in contact with a building it was taken away bodily, to crumble up as it was borne along, and augment the power of the water, which became a wave charged with stones, masses of rock, and beams of wood, ready to batter into nothingness every obstacle that stood in its way.

"It seems impossible that all this could be done in a few minutes," said Uncle Dick.

"No, not when you think of the power of water," said Uncle Jack quietly. "Think of how helpless one is when bathing, against an ordinary wave. Then think of that wave a million times the size, and tearing along a valley charged with *débris*, and racing at you as fast as a horse could gallop."

We came back from the scene of desolation ready to make light of our own trouble, and the way in which my uncles worked to help the sufferers down in the lower part of the town gave the finishing touches to the work of many months.

There was so much trouble in the town and away up the valley, so much suffering to allay, that the firing of our works by the despicable scoundrels who worked in secret over these misdeeds became a very secondary matter, and seemed to cause no excitement at all.

"But you must make a stir about this," said Mr Tomplin. "The villains who did that deed must be brought to justice. The whole affair will have to be investigated, and I'm afraid we shall have to begin by arresting that man of yours—the watcher Searby."

But all this was not done. Searby came and gave a good account of himself—how he had been deluded away, and then so beaten with sticks that he was glad to crawl home; and he needed no words to prove that he had suffered severely in our service.

"Let's set the prosecution aside for the present," said Uncle Jack, "and repair damages. We can talk about that when the work is going again."

This advice was followed out, and the insurance company proving very liberal, as soon as they were satisfied of the place having been destroyed by fire, better and more available buildings soon occupied the position of the old, the machinery was repaired, and in two months the works were in full swing once more.

It might almost have been thought that the flood swept away the foul element that originated the outrages which had disgraced the place. Be that as it may, the burning of our works was almost the last of these mad attempts to stop progress and intimidate those who wished to improve upon the old style of doing things.

I talked to Pannell and Stevens about the fire afterwards and about having caught sight of three men landing from a raft and going down towards the river just before the flood came.

But they both tightened their lips and shook their heads. They would say nothing to the point.

Pannell was the more communicative of the two, but his remarks were rather enigmatical.

"Men jynes in things sometimes as they don't like, my lad. Look here," he said, holding a glowing piece of steel upon his anvil and giving it a tremendous thump. "See that? I give that bit o' steel a crack, and it was a bad un, but I can't take that back, can I?"

"No, of course not, but you can hammer the steel into shape again."

"That's what some on us is trying to do, my lad, and best thing towards doing it is holding one's tongue."

That spring my father and mother came down, and that autumn I left Arrowfield and went to an engineering school for four years, after which I went out with a celebrated engineer who was going to build some iron railway bridges over one of the great Indian rivers.

I was out there four years more, and it was with no little pleasure that I returned to the old country, and went down home, to find things very little changed.

Of course my uncles were eight years older, but it was singular how slightly they were altered. The alteration was somewhere else.

"By the way, Cob," said Uncle Dick, "I thought we wouldn't write about it at the time, and then it was forgotten; but just now, seeing you again, all the old struggles came back. You remember the night of the fire?"

"Is it likely I could forget it?" I said.

"No, not very. But you remember going down to the works and finding no watchman—no dog."

"What! Did you find out what became of poor old Jupiter?"

"Yes, poor fellow! The scoundrels drowned him."

"Oh!"

"Yes. We had to drain the dam and have the mud cleaned out three—four years ago, and we found his chain twisted round a great piece of iron and the collar still round some bones."

"The cowardly ruffians!" I exclaimed.

"Yes," said Uncle Jack; "but that breed of workman seems to be dying out now."

"And all those troubles," said Uncle Bob, "are over."

That afternoon I went down to the works, which seemed to have grown smaller in my absence; but they were in full activity; and turning off to the new range of smithies I entered one where a great bald-headed man with a grisly beard was hammering away at a piece of steel.

He did not look up as I entered, but growled out:

"I shall want noo model for them blades, Mester John, and sooner the better."

"Why, Pannell, old fellow!" I said.

He raised his head and stared at me.

"Why, what hev yow been doing to theeself, Mester John?" he said. "Thou looks—thou looks—"

He stopped short, and the thought suddenly came to me that last time he saw me I was a big boy, and that in eight years I had grown into a broad-shouldered man, six feet one high, and had a face bronzed by the Indian sun, and a great thick beard.

"Why, Pannell, don't you know me?"

He threw down the piece of steel he had been hammering, struck the anvil a clanging blow with all his might, shouted "I'm blest!" and ran out of the smithy shouting:

"Hey! Hi, lads! Stivins—Gentles! The hull lot on yo'! Turn out here!

Hey! Hi! Here's Mester Jacob come back."

The men who had known me came running out, and those who had not known me came to see what it all meant, and it meant really that the rough honest fellows were heartily glad to see me.

But first they grouped about me and stared; then their lips spread, and they laughed at me, staring the while as if I had been some great wild beast or a curiosity.

"On'y to think o' this being him!" cried Pannell; and he stamped about, slapping first one knee and then the other, making his leather apron sound again.

"Yow'll let a mon shek hans wi' thee, lad?" cried Pannell. "Hey, that's hearty! On'y black steel," he cried in apology for the state of his hand.

Then I had to shake hands all round, and listen to the remarks made, while Gentles evidently looked on, but with his eyes screwed tight.

"Say a—look at his arms, lads," cried Stevens, who was as excited as everybody. "He hev growed a big un. Why, he bets the three mesters 'cross the showthers."

Then Pannell started a cheer, and so much fuss was made over me that I was glad to take refuge in the office, feeling quite ashamed.

"Why, Cob, you had quite an ovation," said Uncle Bob.

"Yes, just because I have grown as big as my big uncles," I said in a half-vexed way.

"No," said Uncle Dick, "not for that, my lad. The men remember you as being a stout-hearted plucky boy who was always ready to crush down his weakness, and fight in the cause of right."

"And who always treated them in a straightforward manly way," said Uncle Jack.

"What! Do you mean to say those men remember what I used to do?"

"Remember!" cried Uncle Bob; "why it is one of their staple talks about how you stood against the night birds who used to play us such cowards' tricks. Why, Gentles remains *Trappy* Gentles to this day."

"And bears no malice?" I said.

"Malice! Not a bit. He's one of our most trusty men."

"Don't say that, Bob," said Uncle Jack. "We haven't a man who

261

wouldn't fight for us to the end."

"Not one," said Uncle Dick. "You worked wonders with them, Cob, when you were here."

"Let's see, uncles," I said; "I've been away eight years."

"Yes," they said.

"Well, I haven't learned yet what it is not to be modest, and I hope I never shall."

"What do you mean?" said Uncle Dick.

"What do I mean!" I said. "Why, what did I do but what you three dear old fellows taught me? Eh?"

There was a silence in the office for a few minutes. No; only a pause as to words, for wheels were turning, blades shrieking, water splashing, huge hammers thudding, and there was the hiss and whirr of steam-sped machines, added since I went away, for "Russell's," as the men called our works, was fast becoming one of the most prosperous of the small businesses in our town.

Then Uncle Dick spoke gravely, and said: "Cob, there are boys who will be taught, and boys whom people try to teach and never seem to move. Now you—"

No, I cannot set down what he said, for I profess to be modest still. I must leave off sometime, so it shall be here.

The End.